UBUNTU

UBUNTU

SIOBHAN LOFTUS

Quartet Books

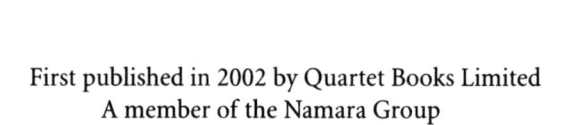

First published in 2002 by Quartet Books Limited
A member of the Namara Group
27 Goodge Street, London W1P 2LD

Copyright © Siobhan Loftus 2002

All rights reserved. No part of this book may be reproduced in any form or by any means without the prior written permission of the publisher

Siobhan Loftus has asserted her right to be identified as the author of this work

A catalogue entry for this book is available from the British Library

ISBN 07043 81664

Typeset by Antony Gray
Printed and bound in Finland
by WS Bookwell

Author's Note

The San people of Southern Africa consisted of a large number of different clans. The name 'Bushman' has evolved as an internationally recognised collective grouping for these peoples and their descendants. If the name 'San' were more widely recognised, I would have chosen it in preference to 'Bushman', a name which in some societies has become derogatory. Wherever possible I have tried to use a clan name to identify a particular group.

The Karoo, 2001

Sophie Makela sat by the fire under the thorn tree in the middle of the yard. Everyone else had gone to bed, but she still sat. I am getting old, she thought. I need less sleep now. Her solitude, the sounds of the night, the life of the fire and the warmth of her blanket were pleasures. Perhaps, she smiled, I am finally learning about living life, not just surviving it. She breathed in the cold night air. She liked this, knowing that outside the fire the land stretched endlessly around her. Our land. Our country.

Timothy had explained once that the earth moves steadily through the universe – which itself is so big that we never seem to move at all. That is why the stars are always in the same place every year. He had drawn earth's galaxy in the dust for his mother, who remembered more about the curve of his arms, the sheen on his skin and the light that shone from inside him as he pointed to the circles in the sand than she did about the names of the planets. Looking up into the depths of the sky she could feel herself perched on this planet that her son described as moving on its endless journey through infinity. She put another branch on the fire and folded her blanket around her. Her thoughts were expanding and sharpening like the soft spreading light of the Milky Way.

As he had talked she had listened to his maturity – to his care not to let her feel the lack of her education, to his teasing, his occasional touch upon her arm, the reassurance of his presence. Yes, that night as they sat not far from here and he explained the universe to her, she had breathed out and eased her mind. Her son was a man. Compassion is the signature of a man. Despots, bullies, torturers, the power hungry, these are forever trapped in the selfishness of childhood.

She patted the envelope in her apron pocket. Michael's letter. She had read some of it to the group around the fire. They shared news like they shared everything else. At first she had been surprised at Michael's innate youth. He looked like a man, had the sophistication of a European. He was nearly as old as Timothy. But had no sense of being white, or any colour. And there was something in Michael that she had liked from the first. Perhaps it was his honesty. Perhaps it was that he was so very obviously lost. Not all boys become men. Yet they control our world. She smiled again to herself. It is no wonder we on the outside are confused.

Michael and Timothy had found their common ground in the world of ideas. Timothy had said, 'Great men live for others. They are easily followed because their concerns are greater than their own well-being, greater even than their own ambition. But if a man pretends concern to hide a massive ambition, he will be despised when the truth is revealed. Then he must rule by force and fear, but ruling is what he truly desired. There have been few great men. But if, after all these hundreds of years, we come to produce many good men, then there is hope for the future. Perhaps not the future that the world demands of us – but a future that is humane. One that makes more sense than the world we see around us.'

Sophie let the memory wash over her. She had only vaguely remembered the words. In his letter Michael had recalled the conversation, repeated it for her. She remembered their faces – Timothy throwing back his head, laughing . . . She smiled. Joy is permanent. You can visit it always. It is with joyful moments that you should strive to fill your life. And quiet moments like these. When you can wrap the land around you and know that your ancestors are proud, that you are free.

1

The Western Cape, 1812

The flat mountain sat like an armchair, its back to the Cedarberg and its arms reaching towards the invisible ocean. High up, Tsatsi leant against an outcrop of rock and looked out across the plains, where shadows from shrubs and rocks gave the small night animals some protection from the cold moonlight.

He was an old man, with the weathered erosion in his face of thousands upon thousands of daybreaks. His knees were drawn up and the whole of him was wrapped inside an animal skin, the faded terracotta of the eland invisible in the night. Only his head, covered in a white dusting of small puffs of hair, his small feet and gnarled toes with their jagged nails and his delicate fingers touched the night air. He sat very still, waiting to blend with the night and lose his consciousness of himself. He knew his ears would still hear the faintest clink of a far-off horse's reins or the rustling of his predators. He would smell them too, if they came from downwind. He was on watch tonight.

How strange it was that when he should be readying himself for his death he should still be so needed. Perhaps he was destined to live a very long time. But his body told him, in the ache in his hip and the loosening of his teeth and in the way it always took a little longer to obey him, that it was not true. The truth was that the natural order had been overturned. There would be no quiet contemplation of death. It would probably come like the lion's kill, a violent dragging down and the merciful, fatal stroke. He would not have the luxury of undertaking the final reckoning of self before he prepared to meet the others who had gone before.

He knew he was letting his mind wander, that he would not be able to blend into the calming nothingness of the deep sky with these random thoughts in his brain. He didn't fight it. His spirit was still in shock from the previous trance. It had been six whole moons ago and he had not yet accepted it.

The mysterious beings that came from the water where the sun slept were constantly increasing in number. He had seen the first one when he was a child, a strange pale man of great height. This man had been gentle and interested, a deceiver for those who were to follow.

When he was just a grown man he had seen his first theft. The family had been camped, as was usual, a couple of miles away from one of their water-holes. The wildebeest were due to pass through and a hunt had been planned for the next day, some miles away from the water. The women had gone with the ostrich shells in their nets to collect water before the evening. They had seen the man with his wagon a hundred yards from the water, helping himself as if it didn't belong to anyone, and on the ground next to him were the carcasses of six springbok; six for just one man and his woman! The wildebeest would smell death near the water and they would not come. Having destroyed the harmony of the watering-hole and stolen the game that belonged to the Bushmen, the man went on his way.

The young men had tracked him and wondered whether they should kill him for it. But Tsatsi remembered how they had thought that perhaps he just did not know he should ask first; that a traveller would never be denied water or food. But to take so much . . . and yet he was a harbinger of what was to follow. Sometimes Tsatsi thought that they should have killed each one as they arrived. Because they got worse and worse and now they didn't stop coming at all.

They had absorbed into their world the land of many of the KhoiKhoi, who acted as their trackers and spies. The old man spat in anger. The KhoiKhoi are now the servants of these strange pale creatures with their fire sticks they call guns and the animals they ride upon. They may be grateful that it is we !Xam and not they that are being hunted. But they and their descendants are damned. They are cursed for many generations by their cowardice. If these pale and senseless creatures can hunt us like animals, then what are they not capable of doing? These creatures I cannot call men collect our heads. They have boiled the bodies of the dead and sent the bones over the sea. They are happy to kill women and children for no reason. Where will it end if this is how they begin? What limit is there to what they can do? They wish us not to be. Even the sun agrees.

Then his vision came to him again. He had sought guidance from his ancestors. The family were being pushed ever north and west towards the red lands that could barely sustain life. The pale ones were killing machines, a pestilence on the land. They killed game for sport, leaving the carcasses to rot on the ground. They took possession of watering-holes that had been shared among the people since the beginning of memory. They put up fences to keep their cattle safe and these fences stopped the movement of the animals. The cattle and the sheep were being kept in numbers that the land could not sustain. All natural creatures were being pushed off the land. The quagga was no more. He himself had not seen the great eland for many moons. The animals, like the people, were being pushed north.

He had beseeched his ancestors, 'We have been fighting them for most of my life, our children have grown to manhood in the time of the fighting and now have children themselves. But the families that have been killed, that are with you now, these families are many.' He had recited the list of names of those he knew who had been killed. It took the form of a chant that lasted for hours. To give proper respect he would mention every name, and ask forgiveness from those who had not been brought to his attention, that they may not be forgotten either. He wanted to know whether they should continue north to the land of seasonal waters, whether the pale ones would follow them there; or if they should continue to fight here in their own lands for their own water as they had done for so very long. 'We are tired, my fathers. We are filled with anger and this keeps us strong, but we are tired. The world is being destroyed, there are demons with white faces devouring our lands.' And there had been no rain. For six summers the rain had come and looked upon the land and withheld its bounty. The game was thinning with the drought and the invasion of the white man. No rain magic worked.

It was then that he had seen in his trance how the moon was devoured altogether by the sun. Every month, since our time began, he thought, we have watched the moon cut down by the sun until its backbone only pleads for life for its children. And we took comfort that in the times when our own bones were showing there would be a fattening again. The moon governs our passage into the afterlife. For our foolishness it denies us a return to this world. If it is devoured, then there is no longer any hope for us. We will cease to be. But still tonight it sits fat and sullen in the sky. Instinctively he made an act of worship. But doubt followed immediately afterwards. I cannot doubt, he thought, I must keep strong and my beliefs whole. What is a man if he has no beliefs? Just an empty vessel to be filled by others. I am frightened, he thought. I am an old, tired, man and I am frightened. I have no magic strong enough to defeat these terrible creatures. We are abandoned. All we have left is the courage of our deaths. And an old tired man has less courage than most. I would turn myself to the fire they send and let it take me, if I would not be shamed forever by that act.

He sighed heavily and looked out over the plain beneath him. They tended to come in the early hours of the morning. Maybe no one would come tonight. His family had been moving constantly to avoid the trackers. Any camp that lasted more than a day or two would be found and then there would be the killing. He shook his head. He used to know, even when they were far away, when the killings were happening. At first it had been like a hot spear plunged into his heart and brain, a rending of his own psyche like the unbearable screams of the women who were disturbed in their sleep and saw their children run through before the long knives designed for killing people, not animals, turned mercifully on themselves. He had thought the world was ending the first time. But now, many many seasons later, he could no longer tell. He had become dulled; the volume of pain was so loud that he was deaf to it. Tonight his family slept like a pride of lions, interlaced and warm in absolute quiet in the small cave behind him.

If they came, he knew what he had to do. A fight was certain, if they were found. There was no escape across the open plain. The creatures followed on animals that could outrun them. //Kabbo, his eldest son, would lead the defence. The family would fight, if necessary to the end. Their defence here was strong. The creatures would be exposed on the plain. If the men failed, then with good fortune the women and children would escape or be taken as servants. There was no guarantee.

Last week in passing and for no reason the creatures had shot an elderly !Xam woman sleeping under a tree. They seemed to act on random impulses that he could not fathom.

Every adult man would fight to the death if needs be. Except himself. He would take into hiding the two brightest children. The thought of being without his community frightened him more than death. But he knew it was inevitable. It was simply a question of when. The interminable waiting was wearing everybody's nerves.

Dawid Rooider was a lanky man in his late twenties with blue eyes and very fair hair. He had travelled for six months from the polderlands of Holland to reach this small house: a shack made of mud with a grass roof in the middle of an empty plain. Now he raised his mug to his host, Jan Freek. The black-haired Boer farmer leant across the roughly made table towards him. They had reached that stage of the witblitz, a potent homebrew derived from fruit, herbs, maroela-tree fruit – anything, where solidarity could be confirmed and a certain amount of manly exaggeration was expected.

'You know I lived just like you, always scratching for life in the bitter cold and damp. That damp of Europe. But in Africa, I am a king. There is enough game walking past my front door for me never to worry about hunger. There is water under the ground, enough to live on. The winter is mild and the summers are hotter than hell. When they come, the rains in the summer are like God's blessing on us. In Africa you can live free. The land itself can sustain you. And there is no overlord to rule you. You do not need to bow your head to anyone. The only bugger – and there is always a bugger, hey? God's joke on us, there's always a bugger, hey? – is the Kaffir.

Not the good Kaffirs, like you see on my farm. No . . . ' the big man swayed a little over his homebrew.

They had been drinking steadily to celebrate the arrival of this young man from his home town, bringing with him messages and old local gossip. Perhaps the stories from his long-ago village were pushing the big man to reinforce his decision to come to this enormous empty land. Or perhaps it was that his wife, who had buried two children out here, had covered her head with her apron and wailed her despair on hearing of her sisters' own children and the death of her mother so far away. Or perhaps it was the presence of the adolescent son, with his eyes that worshipped the black-bearded, balding man. Now as the candle flickered his silhouette huge and hunched against the wall, the Boer unleashed his hatred.

'They are vicious animals. The little Bushman bastards just kill our cattle or else they cut the tendons to cripple a whole herd in the dark of the night. They will not accept that this land is ours, given to us by God. They are heathens. They don't even have proper language. You cannot look upon them as people. They aren't human. It's like hunting baboon. Of course you have to kill them. They don't know the meaning of the word surrender. We must kill a hundred of the dirty little savages in a month and still they won't stop. It wears you down, I swear it does.'

'You hunt people?' Dawid hadn't meant the shock to sound so in his voice.

'I just told you,' the Boer growled, 'they aren't people. You'll see. We're going out early tomorrow. A local commando. Just the neighbours. We've been following a family of them. I've got a reason to want this lot. They killed two of my sheep last month.' He was enjoying expressing his extreme sentiments, seeing their effect.

*

Dawid Rooider had endured a four-month journey by sea and a further two months' travelling into the interior, the last two weeks on horseback following directions from the Boer who had brought him this far. He was not unaware of the fact that his family had scraped together the money to get him to this place because in the long run it would probably be the cheapest alternative. It wasn't, Dawid reflected, that he was actually lazy. It was just that he would rather sit here and drink this vicious brew with this old Boer than till his fields for him. And if, as the old man said, there was free labour here to do the work for him, then maybe he had ended up in the right place after all.

'Can't you use them on the farm?'

Freek roared with laughter. Then slammed his fist hard down on the table.

'Use them? Bushmen? Never. The only Kaffir worth having is a slave Kaffir. Then you have respect. Respect and obedience. You'll never get a white man's day of work out of them. But you'll get enough to raise your sheep or cattle. But you tell me now they want to get rid of slavery. What will the poor bastard slaves do, hey? You tell me what they'll do. They've got everything they need right now. The Rooineks [literally Rednecks, a derogatory term used to describe the English], with their bleeding hearts and their Parliament thousands of miles away, they think they know what's what here. Well, they don't! They should just leave us alone. We know this country and how things should be done here.'

Dawid was unconcerned by the ranting of the man. He was a relic, he thought, something from another time. The enlightenment of Europe had not shed its rays this far. But Freek's face! It was creased like an old piece of leather. The wife's clothes had obviously been patched and turned inside out and upside down so many times that the only thing that gave her outfit a sense of unity was the big apron that looked like it was made of sacking and covered the immense front of her. She had a few strategic teeth missing. She was obviously strong and the sharp downward crescent of her mouth showed a certain stoicism. It was in the determined set of that mouth that he could see the girl that her relatives remembered as the shrew who had been sent out here to Jan Freek as his wife because her family knew that no man in their village would have her. She was supposed to have been attractive, a fact often repeated to indicate how much of a shrew she must have been. Or to relieve their guilt, he thought now. Well, he wouldn't be going back in a hurry to tell how coarse and weathered she had become. She could cook and that was the main thing. He wondered idly how much Freek had had to do with the missing teeth. You could do almost anything out here and no one would know. Or care much, he thought with some satisfaction.

While they were outside, 'watering the land' before bedtime, Freek gave his instructions for the morning. His wife would make them coffee well before daybreak and they would leave almost immediately. He was to bring his gun and as much gunpowder and shot as he had with him. Freek would see to his supplies, but he must fill his water-bottle himself from the well in the yard. They could expect to be away for three or four days. But he mustn't bring anything except his greatcoat. They would be riding hard and fast.

It seemed that no sooner had he settled down to sleep than the son, Jong Jan, was nudging him awake. His horse had been saddled for him by one of the black men who now stood impassive with his hands cupped for him to mount. Out of habit and a need to assert himself he checked the girth and found it good. He stepped into the man's hands and swung himself up.

The two men and the boy rode across Jan Freek's

borderless land in the moonlight, the older man in the front, the boy to the rear and their guest in the middle. Since he arrived Dawid had found the African night very loud, a constant rustling and high-pitched keening, the sound of a billion insects and their fellow creatures making silence in the land equal to emptiness. But the pre-dawn was still, a different sound altogether from the night. It had a church-like feel to it, he thought. Then the dusty smell of the old church and the thundering voice of the preacher, the uncomfortable fit of his Sunday best revisited him.

He smiled to himself as he revised his opinion. It was very fresh, very clean. It would be easier to believe in God in the presence of this land mass, he thought. Freek believed in God. They had said a prayer in the kitchen before leaving, invoking the protection of the Lord for their expedition. Freek had explained to the Almighty the difference in status between himself and those with whom he was about to engage in combat. He had reminded Him of His own Bible in which He said that the black man was the child of Ham, ordained to be the hewer of wood and the drawer of water. In doing what God required of him, Freek hoped that God would bless and protect him as he, Freek, glorified His holy name. Dawid saw no irony of note in the prayers. His own religious tradition told him that he was one of the saved, even when his behaviour created doubt. And these black creatures were undoubtedly heathens. He had seen in the mixed-blood women and men in Cape Town licentiousness and a liking for alcohol that had instantly appealed to him, but he of course had the advantage of being Christian.

It had been a sin for him to spend a few hours in that hovel with the pretty little brown maid. His body stirred at the memory. She had been more comfortable naked than clothed, he was sure of it. Her previous customers must have been a rum lot, he thought, considering the options she laid out before him. She had moved her body this way and that, highlighting with her hands and stroking movements the areas of obvious interest and some that even he had not considered. He supposed she was about fifteen. She was a good actress too. It was only when he caught her watching him in the looking-glass placed next to the stretcher that pretended to be a bed that he saw how impassive her face was. He caught her eye in the glass and for a split second, had he been capable of the insight, he would have seen the dullness that coated her soul, the fear that drove the immediate giggle and wiggling of the buttocks. Instead he saw a flagging of her efforts and rewarded her with a smack on her plump rump. A whore's a whore after all, he thought. He'd secretly hoped she'd been enjoying it.

Still, it was a sin. There was no question about it. He would have to repent at some point. The slight lightening of the still night around him gave him confidence. I could repent, he mused. Freek had said that it was very lonely for a man to be out here without God. And in his two weeks alone he had felt that loneliness. Besides, it was inappropriate for him to be a non-believer in this land where belief brought such obvious advantages. Perhaps he could repent here, before the sun rose, then he could greet the new day cleansed, a new man. And if anything happened to him today, then he would be ready to meet his Maker. He bowed his head and mouthed his prayers.

The six other men were waiting next to a water-hole. The three newcomers dismounted and led their horses to drink. The sun had not yet appeared, but the sky was lightening fast enough for them to see the great empty plain around them. Introductions were brief. A mood that had its seed in the first cup of coffee taken in the cold morning air had blossomed now into a deep manliness that made their voices a little more gruff, their actions deliberately relaxed, their chests broader and their stomachs flatter. They were soon to face danger together. Freek had explained that the rebellious little people had arrows, poisonous ones. If they entered your skin they would almost certainly kill you. There was a rumour that the little people used to cut out the flesh around a wound caused by a poison arrow and so save the person, but this was just a rumour. The area of removed flesh was supposed to be very large. By the time most people shot by one of the arrows were sick enough to contemplate such a large-scale excavation of their flesh, it was too late. The trick, supposedly, was to do it as soon as it happened, even if one had to do it oneself. But as no one ever did this and most died from the poison, it was consigned to the ranks of Bushman mischief, along the lines of their annoying habit of wearing their sandals backwards to confuse one as to the direction a man may have taken.

Dawid felt intoxicated by the clean air, the danger that awaited them and the smell of the horses' sweat and the damp leather. The leader of this expedition was a very large man, bigger even than Freek. He was introduced as Hans, the kommandant. He had a magnificent reddish-brown beard and arms that looked as though they could each lift a calf, one on either side. They were discussing, together with the big man's two black servants, in the basic language that he was thankful to find he could understand, the direction they would take. The robber band they were after had holed up on a mountain ridge. The mountain itself was in the middle of this plain, visible in the far distance as a grey hump. The robbers had obviously been intending to move farther north and had made themselves vulnerable on this mountain top at a precarious stage of their journey. No one would be able to leave the mountain and not be seen from its summit. The danger would be that the little bastards would have cover from which to launch their arrows. They would have to split up, attack from two fronts and guard the action from the rear. As he was the newest, Dawid would be given the task of guarding the rear. Anyone he saw he was to kill. That was his instruction. The kommandant looked carefully at him, weighing his calibre. Did he properly understand? He was to kill whoever came off the mountain. There were to be no exceptions. They needed no servants. Dawid's mouth felt dry but his heartbeat quickened and he felt a rush of power in his body as he kept his jaw as steady as he could and gruffly repeated his instructions. The big man relaxed the intensity of his gaze and smiled. He put his arm around Dawid's shoulder and welcomed him. Jan Freek gave Dawid a look of approval. Jong Jan was assigned to him as his deputy.

They mounted and rode nine abreast, the reins in their left hands, a strange array of guns ready in their right, shot and powder in bags slung across their shoulders. Dawid's guns had excited much interest. He had an elegantly finished Dutch flintlock lightweight musket and a duck's-foot pistol. The duck's-foot's four splayed barrels and appetite for shot had been carefully examined, its accuracy questioned. The kommandant carried a pistol and an early blunderbuss. Jan Freek and most of the others carried flintlocks, the most basic of models with no decoration, a simple mechanism and a long barrel. Jong Jan had a crossbow slung over his back. All the men had swords, varying in size and elegance. The two trackers in their worn jackets and sackcloth trousers trotted barefoot alongside their master. It was Dawid's first real experience of inclusion and acceptance. His back straightened and he thanked his God, humbly, as befitted his newly repentant state, for this opportunity. Jong Jan was riding next to him, and Dawid could see pride in the line of the boy's body and the way he held his reins. He knew better than to smile at the boy.

The mountain became more recognisable as the light improved. The kommandant pointed to what looked like a brown sand pan some distance to the left. A reddish brown, it seemed to shift with his gaze. 'Veldbok,' said Jong Jan. They rode towards the terracotta mass, which stretched in a wide band as far as Dawid could see. As they neared the outskirts of this living sea the delicate creatures took off, leaping into the air, moving like a wave away from the men until a way through was clear. It was like Moses parting the Red Sea, Dawid thought. The sheer abundance of their numbers created exhilaration. Even Jong Jan was grinning.

'This is a small herd,' he said, trying for nonchalance. 'Once, when I was small, we saw a herd twice this size. We shot all day that day. It was my first time. That was a herd.'

Buoyed by camaraderie and the scale and splendour of the canvas they inhabited, they moved steadily towards the mountain.

Tsatsi had seen the moving dots on the landscape at first light. By the time the first ray of sun glinted off a halter buckle, the family had dispersed. As agreed he took the two youngest, !Katchu and Ka, deep into the cave. There was no time for formal goodbyes. The three took one ostrich shell of water with them. His sons disguised the opening with an old branch and stones collected the previous evening for the purpose. He had lifted each one to be sure that he could manage them. Now the family gathered themselves and the women and children set off, as fast as was sustainable, to descend to the other side of the mountain. They would head north towards the Great Noise while the men held back the pale creatures. There were no tears. All agreed to meet at the Great Noise.

By the time the mountain loomed over the horizon ahead of the nine hunters, the six !Xam men were in position, blocking the routes to the summit. Each one had a quiverful of arrows and a heart that had greatly slowed as it did in the deadly calm of the hunt. Tsatsi pictured them at their posts. //Kabbo, who brought us laughter and three children, he would be in the last line of defence. So would Zzorri, who was the most successful of hunters, protected by the eland and father of !Katchu. /A!kunta, who was blessed by the ancestors and father to six children, four of whom were even now running with their mother across the plain, would be crouched behind the rock of surprise; the most deadly with the bow, he would be the most protected. In the front line would be the three cousins, all of whom had become men together; they had hunted their first elands in the same season, produced children in the same year. These three, tied together by family and shared history were !Gubbu, Kushi and /Kan.

Tsatsi, who had guided them from youth to manhood, knew their characters well. They would be making little jokes even now, but they would have said their serious goodbyes in their hearts and in the clasping of each other before they took their posts. If one died, all would die to avenge his death. They were like three trunks of the same tree. He gave the children a treat that he had been saving, a sweet root to chew. As they chewed it he saw them grow sleepy. In minutes they were sound asleep, and would remain so for hours.

The horsemen approached the mountain cautiously. Staying well out of arrow's reach, the kommandant surveyed the routes to the top. There was only one that looked passable. If the Bushmen were there then they would be waiting for them. Either that or they had already left. The trackers were confident that they were still there. He sent Jong Jan to circle the mountain to the east and Dawid to circle it from the west. They were to remain in position at the rear unless one of them was injured, in which case they would both return to this point. If all the Bushmen, and the trackers estimated that there may be as many as twenty altogether, were on the far side of the mountain, then they were to return so that they could reverse the plan.

They needed, the kommandant said, to draw the little bastards' fire. Then they could see where they were. In the meantime, they would split up, to make it more difficult to follow their actions. If necessary they would pretend to go past and then attack under cover of darkness. They would not ride into their fire.

Dawid had the shorter distance to go round the mountain. He rode well out of arrow's range, carefully scanning the mountain beside him. The sun had risen and the mountain was casting a morning shadow to the west. He was grateful for its coolness. He paused at the edge of the shadow and looked up at the inhospitable crag. There was no way up from here. But a little farther on there was what looked to be a path winding down between rocks. Careful to stay back, he saw the route ran down to the plain. His eyes followed it north and in the distance he saw what looked like a small armadillo shifting across the veldt. At the same time he saw the approach of Jong Jan at the farthest end. He whistled and pointed and the two men set off for the moving brown lump. They met up at the point where they could see that their quarry was indeed Bushmen. 'But it's only the womenfolk and the brats,' Jong Jan shouted. He was excited, the canter had raised his colour.

'Shall we turn back? Go for the men?' Dawid was shouting too.

'We have our orders!' Jong Jan was shocked. 'They won't be armed.'

Dawid was stung by the contempt in the boy's voice. Hearing the horses the little band had stopped. There was nowhere to hide. The women had placed their children behind them and were standing, waiting, for the two riders.

Grouped together they made a perfect target. Dawid wrapped the reins around his saddle pommel and took aim with the duck's-foot. Jong Jan primed his crossbow. They looked at each other, and at a nod from the boy, they both fired. Three of the women fell to the ground. Dawid took his musket and they fired again. Now there was screaming, the noise was pleading, there was no need for language. The little band scattered, the children running in all directions across the plain. The two men spurred their horses and used their swords like scythes. They chased the tiny creatures, running them through from the back, slowing to release the sword before turning to the next. When it was over Jong Jan rescued his arrows from the bodies of the women. There were five adult women corpses and eleven dead children. They slowly rode around the bodies to inspect the damage. One of the women had been shot in the shoulder, another in the stomach. These two were not yet dead. Dawid finished them quickly with his sword, hoping Jong Jan had not noticed the trembling in his hands. There was no question that these were people. Savages, certainly. But human. Each of the women had a bag and each bag was fashioned in skin and beads, finely and with skill. He wanted to get away from this place. One of the boy children was trying to crawl away, holding its seeping stomach. Jong Jan suggested that they take it back with them. 'We can taunt them out,' he grinned, exhilarated. Dawid grinned back, the bile heavy in his throat as the boy swung the child over his saddle. On the ride back a camaraderie struck up between the two men.

In the cave Tsatsi knew by the fall in temperature that it was night. The children slept on. He needed much less sleep now that he was so much older. //Kabbo had not come to fetch him. Even though he knew he would not come he still hoped. Tsatsi closed his eyes and felt the pain of the battle as a leaden weight within him. His throat was closed and aching and his eyes felt as if they had been staring into a dust storm. He knew his children and his children's children were dead. He felt cursed to outlive them. But he had promised he would ensure the continuation of their family. This he must do. But I am a river of pain, he thought. I am deadened, numbed and not alive. How can I nurture these children?

He tried to plan ahead for the journey. He knew the route, it had been unchanged for centuries. He knew where they could get water. He would be able to hunt for what they needed and Ka was already proficient with her digging stick. !Katchu was too young to hunt. He would pass into manhood alone, there would be no brothers to accompany him into that stage of his life. Ka would become a woman alone. If his sister was still alive, she could instruct the girl. Otherwise he would have to rely upon his sister's family. Their traditions would be different. Much will be lost, he thought to himself. And if I am unable to survive for long enough, then even more will go. It was unnatural. To try to keep oneself alive past the time when it made sense. He had outlived everyone and his anger rose inside him like a bitter fruit. There would be no one to say the formal goodbyes when it was his time to stay alone in the bush and meet his death. There would be no place marked out as sacred because he had died there. Anyone in this new unnatural world could settle in his death place. He was not in his place on the other side to greet his children and their children. It was they who would greet him. And yet he should have gone first. It was my work to prepare the way for them. To be there to welcome them. To introduce my children to their great-great-grandparents. That was my honour and the evil ones have taken it from me.

He didn't want to leave the cave. He wanted to lie there with the children and slip into some netherworld of quiet and peace. He knew he would have to face whatever was left. But as agreed with //Kabbo, for the sake of the children's safety he would wait for three nights in the cave. If they had killed any of the enemy, then he and the children would be hunted if there was any rumour they had escaped. He looked at the two innocents. Their legacy was hard. They were not blood relatives, they would have children. They would also have to learn everything he could teach them of the history, the stories and healing ways of their people. He would take them north to the land that was dry until the river came, and there he would seek shelter. His sister had married into a family there and they would share whatever they had with the three of them. That was the way it had always been. And then his own frailty mocked him. You are the link between the past and the future. An old man whose legs cannot carry him as far as he would like, who can only hunt the smallest of creatures, a man who has lost many teeth now. Why didn't we choose a stronger link? He would gladly have died. But none of the men would have let the others die without them. The old ones and the children were always together. He could not fight. It made sense.

Freek was pleased with his countryman. Dawid had not disgraced himself. According to Jong Jan, there had been a moment when he had seemed to falter, but in the end he had come through. Africa needed men, white men hard enough to push the frontiers back and to protect each other. He was accepted now, land would be found and his need would be the need of all the men in this commando. They were bound together.

If he survived. The arrow had entered his chest just above the heart. The poison was already coursing through his body. The men had made camp some miles from the fight and

Dawid lay now with a fever. If he lasted the night then he would be all right. He was instructed not to move too much, not to help the poison. He had a terrible thirst for which there did not seem to be enough water. The men left him to his mumblings as they sat around the fire. He would make it by the morning or he would be dead. They had done everything they could for him, now it was in the hands of God. Their blood was still coursing with the rush of the battle.

Jong Jan was glowing with the compliments he had received for his foresight in bringing the child. The kommandant admitted that he had been dreading a long encampment as they tried to draw the little devils out of their cover. But the child had done the trick. One of the little bastards had stood up and aimed straight at Dawid. The poor bugger didn't stand a chance. But the kommandant and the others had been ready. As the figures appeared, they had been shot. It hadn't lasted very long. Their aim was good and the little bastards were closer than they had thought they'd be. If they hadn't had the child to taunt them with, they might have had more casualties. One of the servants of the kommandant had also received an arrow. He had set off with another of the servants in a different direction from the group of men. He would die alone. But the survivor would return. Still, it was easier to enjoy the victory without them around.

The African night drew its cloak over the sky. It was soon the deep blue-black of the wilderness, ghost lit by the still swollen moon. With the cool night air, the smell of their fire and the coffee they had brewed, they were content in God's country. Each was pledged to this land. And for a while now each had been pledged to the other. They thrived in the fear of their common enemies.

Dawid lay outside the circle and listened to the murmur of the men. He didn't want to die. He couldn't believe that he would die. It was ridiculous. Death didn't feature in any normal course of events. He was far too young to die. But he might die. He stared into the depths of the sky above him and felt alone and insignificant. No one would know where he was buried. No one would care. He would be in a shallow grave in this wild land. His life had been meaningless and his death would be the same. He left nothing. Perhaps it wasn't time then. Perhaps God would realise that he had not yet done anything with this life, perhaps he could make a deal. He prayed for another chance to do something, to build a church or to be a positive member of this community he had found. In his eagerness, he built a picture of himself that God could surely not refuse. As the poison left him weaker it slowed his thoughts. He knew he was incapable of keeping his bargain. Well, he would do something then. If God spared him, he would do whatever God showed him needed doing. His thoughts slowed again and he knew that his chances had all been laid out before him. At every step of his life there had been a chance and a choice and he had taken the choice of not choosing, not committing to anything of worth or value. He was flotsam. God was not within his reach. The piety of the morning was missing. There was no linkage. There was no God. There was only this cold universe above him and fear, a cold fear that began to seep into his body, paralysing him and shutting him down. He was unable to move or speak, but he could feel himself being slowly closed down. The only pain was in that knowledge and his fear, everything else was numb. He summoned his strength to ask for help and gave a final grunt. The men continued with their stories, their coffee, Jong Jan with his examination of Dawid's duck's-foot.

2

As first light revealed the branches concealing the cave on the morning of the fourth day, Tsatsi began talking and moving about to wake the children. It took a while before they surfaced gently from their deep sleep. It was dangerous to rouse people abruptly. They were groggy from the days and nights of sleep he had imposed on them. All three were hungry. As simply as he could he explained what had happened. They may see some terrible sights when they left the cave. They should look and remember, not with fear, but with pride. Their family had gone with courage and honour to meet the ancestors and now they would be guiding their children's paths. The bodies were empty husks, like seed pods after bursting, they were not to be saddened by them. Their parents and friends were no longer on this earth. They were rejoicing together in the afterlife with their ancestors. He had kept some dried meat and roots for their first breakfast and they ate these in silence. The children were sombre, and it was fitting. Then they left the cave. The clear sky was a relief.

With the advantage of height Tsatsi could see the remains of the crumpled small body on the ground at the foot of the mountain. So that was how they had lured his family. Anger shook him. Women and children were never killed in warfare.

It was known. He turned the children to the route that led behind the mountain. At least he could spare them their cousin and their fathers, already half-eaten by the vultures and hyenas, what remained of their faces covered in ants and flies.

They crept slowly down the mountain, for, as Tsatsi had told them, they did not know if the white ones were still with them. Tsatsi went ahead, !Katchu behind, with Ka protected between them. The path curved tightly at the end. As they neared the bend Tsatsi saw a brown foot extended across the path. It was not a foot of his people. The three stopped, barely breathing, to listen. There was no wind to betray them. The foot moved slightly. Tsatsi motioned to the children to move as quietly as they could back up the path. Then he drew his bow and aimed. It was close enough to be a good hit. The owner of the foot yelled and stood up. A KhoiKhoi, he was not armed. Tsatsi kept his bow and arrow ready nevertheless.

'Ai! Grandfather! What are you doing?' The man was looking in horror at the arrow sticking out of his foot. 'There is poison on this arrow!'

'You bring the white ones to our hiding place. You betray us, you with whom we have lived together for so long. You are one of them. You cannot also be one of us.' The old man was edging round to see if the man was alone.

'Grandfather, please . . . I do not want to die.' He could not stop staring at his foot.

'I do not want to kill you. But the poison is strong because I am old and weak. You will die.' He looked with some interest at the foot too. 'Why are you here?' he asked.

'My cousin died from the !Xam poisoned arrow. I came to be with him while he died and to bury him.' The man sat down again, unable to take his eyes from his foot which had now gone completely numb.

'And where are you from?'

'I was born near the flat mountain but my home is no longer my home. I live now at the farm of Baas Hans, the kommandant.'

'Why do you have him as patron?' The anger was beginning to resurface.

'I have been there since I was a child. The white ones brought a spotted sickness on the boats that took all my family. They took our family lands and our cattle and our people's children. Our elders tell us that the KhoiKhoi fought hard and bravely for five seasons but that the sickness won in the end. I belong to Baas Hans and he says he will have me broken on the wheel like the slaves if I do not obey him. He is a man who is quick to pick up his sjambok. But if I am dying now then I wish I had known I would die and I would have killed him in his sleep before meeting my death today.'

The old man nodded soberly. He could understand the sentiment. He had not lied, the poison was very strong. Too old to track his injured prey for long, his poison was stronger than most. The youth in front of him would be dead within a few hours. He wanted him dead to know that their secret was safe. He would have to bury him, or the evidence of the arrow would lead to the children. He sighed deeply. And now a burial. Where was he to find the strength for all this?

'They will come looking for you.'

'Baas Hans always finds his runaway slaves. He beats them nearly to death in front of us all. I am not a slave but he would beat me nevertheless. He will come looking for me.'

The old man considered the problem silently.

'But of course I will be dead when he finds me.'

The old man wasn't listening. The young KhoiKhoi realised he was just an obstacle in this man's journey.

'Perhaps,' the young man suggested, 'when I am dead you could bury just my leg, and it could look as though a leopard had dragged me.'

'Hmmm. It is a problem for these old bones,' the old man began. Then he paused. 'I am sorry to be insensitive to your death . . . I wish you happiness with your ancestors. If there are rights you need me to perform, then please instruct me . . . It is just that I have a great responsibility . . . '

Then !Katchu appeared. He held a tiny scorpion by its tail. 'Grandfather, look! It was under the rock.'

The old man beamed. 'You have disobeyed me, but to good purpose.' He presented his grandson to the dying young man. !Katchu went to fetch Ka. The young man offered his clothes as some penance for bringing the white ones to the mountain. The old man declined. Anything that could identify any of them with his death would be dangerous. And they did not wear clothes in the style of the white man. Then he felt sorry for the young man. He had grown up without family, without community. In what was the normal way of things he, Tsatsi, may have traded skins for milk with this man's own grandfather before the invasion.

He shook his head. 'It is evil, to break the way of the people. They have powerful magic, the white ones.'

The young man shook his head too. 'Forgive me, grandfather, for disagreeing with you. But they have no magic. That is their magic. They have no spirits which frighten them, they need no Ngaki to protect them, they are as the wild beasts. But unlike the wild beasts they have a hunger for things. They want the land. You !Xam are the protectors of the land and the people see that you are dying too. They will have everything because they believe they can own the land. And they have powerful weapons. But they have no magic.'

Sitting quietly the old man tried to understand how such power could be achieved without magic of any kind. The young man was slowing in his speech and the old man was saddened to see him slipping away.

'They have put tribe against tribe,' he said. 'You have

helped them to kill all my family and I have killed you. And yet we have no quarrel, you and I.'

Tsatsi and !Katchu drew the sting from the scorpion into the leg of the dead man. They removed the arrow and watched the poison further distort the leg. Then they left the husk of the scorpion next to the body, tucked under the sackcloth trousers to protect it from birds. They were careful in leaving to cover their own tracks with a branch each carried, stepping backwards, leaving the tracks of the man and his cousin clear. They walked this way, backwards and clearing their traces, until they reached the carnage of the plain. They did not speak to each other as they faced the scattered remains, not much was left by scavengers in these days of drought. Tsatsi counted the bodies to see if any had been spared. Not one. Even the baby that would have been tied within young //Dhu-//hu's kaross, close to her breast for travelling, was now just a small cracked skull.

The little girl ran, suddenly violent, at the vulture pecking at what little remained of the corpse of her mother. She collected her mother's bag and slung it with some defiance across her small shoulder where it flapped against her legs until she tied the thongs short.

They stopped a little distance away and looked for one last time. Tsatsi wondered about the thoughts that were running through his silent grandson's head. Tsatsi sighed. There was no good to be found. The boy would never forget. And in this foul memory lay the future. They turned and headed north. !Katchu's head was bowed, his shoulders curved forward. Ka's chin jutted forward, her shoulders were pushed back. She looks like a warrior, Tsatsi thought. He revised some of his teaching priorities. The strength of women fermented and soured if it was not used.

That night the horror of the morning lay like a thick broth in the air between the three of them, sitting close to !Katchu's small fire. Tsatsi had kept them moving quickly for most of the day. They were vulnerable on the plain and there was little food. In the late afternoon they had seen a large herd of springbok, downwind and calm. Tsatsi had crept forward until he was within bow range. He shot a small doe, which raced into the middle of the herd, sending the small creatures leaping away from him and the two children. They had followed the tracks of the poisoned one for an hour, until as the sun began to sink towards the horizon they found her lying on her side, alive but immobile. Tsatsi had killed her swiftly. There was no time to take the skin or use the horns. He had taken meat and removed the waterproof stomach from the carcass, then left it to the vultures and hyenas.

They had cooked the meat over the fire that the young boy had built while the girl searched for twigs and small sticks to feed the fire. He had tried to keep them busy with small tasks that would not tax them. He did not expect them to be capable of thought. They were under a small overhang of rock. The little girl had swept the ground with a fallen branch. Tsatsi had checked the area for large predator tracks, and found none. The fire would afford some protection. They sat very quiet. The little girl tracing the pattern of the beads on her mother's bag, over and over, the young boy feeding bits of grass to the fire. Tsatsi didn't know how to unlock the horror he saw resting in their chests. They were too few for the cleansing dances. He cleared his throat.

'The ancestors smiled on our meal tonight, to keep the wind in the right place and the herd so close to us. I wonder if it was your father, Zzorri, who kept the wind straight for us? Surely we are lucky to have the most skilled of hunters to guide us on our journey.' The boy stopped burning grasses and looked at the old man.

'Where is my father, Tsatsi?'

'He is with all the others, with Ka's mother, with his own mother whom he hasn't seen for many, many moons . . . they are in the world of the afterlife. But while we are on our journey they will guide us. All of them, all of our family.'

'My mother is coming back. When we finish our journey, she will be there.' The little girl was speaking to the bag, not looking at Tsatsi.

'Ka . . .' He didn't know what to say. 'Ka . . . The little buck we were given for our meal . . . will she come back?' The girl stilled. Then she looked at him. And he felt his own losses magnified in her despair. He didn't try to hide it. The tears rolled down his face, and still they looked at each other. Then she slowly shook her head again and again. 'No,' she said. 'No. No.' His eyes could give her no comfort from the truth. She turned to the rock-face behind her and began to beat it rhythmically with her fists, grunting, 'No. No. No. No.' The boy looked a question and Tsatsi shook his head. They sat and waited for the storm to pass through her. The boy concentrated all his attention on feeding the little fire. Soon this fire will be as big and useless as those of the white ones, Tsatsi thought.

Ka was sobbing gently now, her head drooped against the rock behind them. Gently he prised her away from the rock and wrapped her in her kaross, then he tucked her close to him, wrapped his own cloak around her and whispered to the boy to join them. The three of them rested against each other inside his cloak and watched the flames of the fire. He had kept some of the sleeping root and now gave a piece to each of them. Sleep and daybreak. That was as far as he could think ahead tonight.

The rain clouds that denied the Great Karoo swept through the night into the plains of Namaqualand and a day's walk ahead of the three travellers it let fall its burden, splashing dust into small whorls in the barren ground that lay red between the outcrops of granite rock. Seeds that had lain dormant for the past seven years had ignored the rainfall of a week ago, but this additional gift was enough for them to take note.

The route for Tsatsi and the children was a zigzag determined by water. So it wasn't until four days had passed that they climbed a rise and came to the land that had been blessed with water. Instead of the reddened earth and rocks, a thick carpet of white and yellow flowers stretched as far as the eye could see on all sides.

The three walked through the plains of flowers, heartened by the fertility of the earth and the miles they were putting behind them.

After many weeks, and as they moved farther inland, they found the tracks of their own tribe. They counted about eight adults and three children. As they had played tracking games all day every day, Tsatsi was pleased to see how quickly the children found the tracks and immediately counted them out. They knew there were three women, too. They were learning to scout the ground all the time, as if by second nature. Soon it would be automatic, a habit. But now it was still a game.

All three were excited. Company was an unexpected gift in prospect. They followed the tracks and were pleased to stand on the edge of the small settlement of grass huts and wait for their owners to return. They came all together; there was fruit near by and they had spent the afternoon picking and eating. Greetings were exchanged and Tsatsi was pleased to see one of the daughters of one of his sons and pleased too that the people were fat. It was an occasion for everybody.

!Katchu and Ka stood together and greeted the other children. An awkward silence fell among the five of them.

They separated and two of the children began to play the game of mimicry, one pretending to be an animal and the other copying every move. They enacted a baboon-mating for the benefit of their guests and !Katchu and Ka watched gravely. The daughter of the son of Tsatsi watched her cousins. She looked a question at Tsatsi. He nodded and tears began to flow down his cheeks. The family sat in a circle and let the old man cry silently while they plied him with water and fruit and a special pipe was readied. He told the story of their journey. Only now, in the blessed relief of being among his own and able to tell it did he seem to be coming out of the state of numbness that had held him in one piece.

!Katchu and Ka were still watching the two children, but they knew what was being told. The family sat and listened and a silence fell upon them all. The playing children looked at the grave faces of their two distant cousins. Then the youngest girl took Ka by the hand and led her to the group to sit against her own mother, and the boy, !Dikwain, went to a tree and took a small bow and a sheath of arrows that hung from it and handed them to !Katchu. They smiled shyly at each other and then went off to practise.

That night the family prevailed upon Tsatsi to tell the story of the chameleon, for one had been seen that very day, so surely it would rain soon and this was something that the children had never yet experienced. It was a long tale, and as it was his duty to tell it exactly as it had been told to him – and he had received the story, as he told the children, from his father's father, who in turn had heard it from his father's father's father as far back as it could be remembered – it was a story that repeated itself somewhat. But if they would be patient with him, then he would tell them what had been told to him by his father's father's father's father's father, as far back as it could be remembered. The children all nodded importantly, for this was the prelude to a real story of the people and it wasn't one they had heard before. The adults passed around another of the special pipes and got ready to contribute noises and exclamations and tut-tuts and tsk-tsks in all the right places.

Tsatsi explained how the children had been walking with the old woman, the old woman that was their mother, when they came upon a chameleon on a bush and how the old woman had asked the chameleon if it would rain because the children were thirsty and there was no water. And the chameleon had looked up at the sky and at the ground and when it had come down from its bush it had turned white like a rain cloud and the woman had been assured that it would rain.

And then the two children had found a gambro creeper in a driedoorn tree, and had told the mother, who had broken the root on the ground to see if the water would fall on the earth so that she could be sure it would rain. And the children had eaten of the gambro root and the boy, who had smelled the coming rain in the wind on the small hill, had given his sister the springbok bush to smell and she had bled from the nose by smelling that bush but they had hidden that from the mother. And the children had found a tortoise which the little boy put on the fire to cook and when it was cooked he broke it in half and gave half to his sister and they ate the tortoise and the rain came finally in a first raindrop which landed on the boy's arm and he went to look at it in the firelight and he and his sister looked at the lightning and then went inside for the raindrops were very many and they woke their mother who heard the rain and sent them to get the shell of the great female tortoise that they might collect the water outside while they slept in the hut and listened to the rain.

They sat afterwards, smelling the air and discussing whether it would rain the next day or the day after, and all the children smelled the air knowledgeably but had to admit, under Tsatsi's leadership, that it did not yet smell like rain. When it did, he assured them, they would know.

Long after the children were asleep, Tstasi sat with the men. He explained his plan to take the children to his daughter who lived with the !Kung in the red Thirstlands on the other side of the Orange River. It was, he thought, the only place where the white man would not go.

It was a hard place to live, the men agreed.

But freedom too was important, and their own freedom, even this far north, was under threat. There were no farms as yet, but they could see in the east and in the southern territories that the white ones were moving ever up and out. And they were determined to kill all the !Xam people. Tsatsi told of his vision and the men were silent. It was incomprehensible to them. Even with the knowledge of the mass murders taking place in the south, they found it hard to accept. The men spoke one after the other.

'If what you say is true, grandfather, and I have no reason to doubt you, then all our lives are to change. We are to go from the land that has been ours for these generations upon generations and ask to live in the lands that can barely sustain the peoples who are already there. We cannot all go. We would all die, our brothers in the north as well.'

There were nods of agreement.

'I hear that in the south, where they have been taken as servants, the children wear rags and broken shoes and are given no instruction in the ways of the land or the animals. They are servants of servants and only their eyesight is valued. The boys do not become men and the girls do not become women.'

All looked to Tsatsi for confirmation. He nodded. 'It is even worse to see the adults that have gone willingly into service, they are so proud of their patched greatcoats and stupid hats and things that they have scavenged. They want to be like the white ones, they admire them in their hearts. They think that we are the ones who are foolish to give our lives so readily. They will survive, but I do not know what will really become of them. And yet I cannot blame them. They have no land. How else are they to live? And you are right. We cannot all go to the Thirstlands. The land is too fragile. There are not enough melons for us all.'

'And yet,' said another, 'we do not win the war. We kill a few, but we ourselves are dying in our thousands. We do not have a way to defeat them.'

'Whatever happens, we are doomed. I would rather die than be the servant of these savages.'

'I too,' they choroused.

'Grandfather,' said the father of !Dikwain, 'since we are all doomed, we must admire your son for saving the two children.'

Indeed it was wise, all agreed.

'Grandfather, perhaps we can send our children with you to the Thirstlands? They at least will have ancestors and we will know that we have children on the earth.'

Tsatsi sighed. 'My sons, I am an old man. I cannot take five children alone and feed them and give them water. The two I have are stretching my old bones.'

'We could give you a woman to look after the children and to find food. You have much knowledge, grandfather. You have survived thousands of nights of the lion's roar. You can teach the children. And if they do not eat much meat, then they will not complain.'

'I can still hunt!' Tsatsi was stung. The apologies were long and fulsome. He agreed to sleep on the proposition.

The following day he watched the children carefully. They

were sharing the hut of !Dikwain and his mother. They had already established a sleeping pattern, with !Katchu pressing his back against the front of the old man who wrapped his arm around him and then the little girl with her back against !Katchu, who clasped her to him, and then the bag of her mother held against her tummy. Last night !Katchu had sat up sharply, unable to breathe, needing to walk under the stars. The three of them had slipped from the hut and made a little fire. The boy had calmed quickly. Still, Tsatsi was relieved to see that the poison of the killings was coming out. In soft whispers he painted the canvas of the stars, singing the song to Sirius that all !Xam must sing, teaching them the words that they too might sing. 'Sirius, Sirius! Wink like Canopus. Sirius! Sirius! Wink like Canopus.' Every star had a story and a purpose and a place in the seasons. Ka loved the luminous fog of the Milky Way, the ashes of a fire thrown into the sky by an early !Xam girl to light the way home for the hunters.

Now he watched Ka and the littlest of the girls engrossed in playing together. Ka's bag was temporarily ignored in the dust behind her.

He went to sit with the men. Then there was a disturbance.
 'Baboon! Baboon!' The littlest girl was pointing at Ka.
 Ka held her mother's bag close to her and shook her head again and again. Then she took her kaross and laid it at the feet of the little girl. Then her beads from her wrist. There was nothing else. The little girl stopped yelling. She went to fetch her own kaross and her own beads were taken from her wrist and placed in front of Ka. Then she held out her hand for the bag. Ka shook her head. The little girl's mother intervened.
 'And what can be causing such trouble between two friends, //Du-//hu my daughter?'

The girl pointed at Ka. 'She says the bag is hers. Only the baboons chase things and yell, "It is mine, it is mine!" She will not let me see it or play with it.'

The woman considered while Ka clung tightly to the bag and stared up at her. 'Ah,' she said, 'I think I understand the confusion. This bag,' she said, 'this bag is not for playing with. This is a sacred bag. Sacred to the spirit of Ka's mother. She must look after it and protect it until she has found the right place to bury it. Then we will have a burial and say goodbye. She cannot give it to you, my daughter. It is not hers to give you.'

The little girl considered the matter. 'And if I could help her find a place for the burial?'

'That may be. But it is a matter for Ka. Perhaps she will ask for your help in some way.'

Ka nodded emphatically. The little girl picked up her own beads and put them on Ka's wrist and then took Ka's and put them on her own wrist. They beamed at each other, as the mother wandered back to where the women were sitting piercing pieces of ostrich-egg shell.

That night the conversation around the fire was lengthy. Tsatsi had a new proposition.

'I have thought long and watched the children playing together. I have seen both !Katchu and Ka smile, the first time since . . . And I have thought to myself that these children will be well served by having companions.'

The men nodded.

'And the mother of little //Du-//hu, she has shown me the wisdom of having a woman to care for them.'

The men nodded again.

'So, to have a woman's help and to have the children together is a good thing.' He paused. The men were listening intently, as were the women, who were seated slightly to one side. The wise experience of a man who had survived so many thousand daybreaks was indisputable.

'But,' he continued, 'I am old. When we reach the Thirstlands I may not live long enough to protect the children and the woman until the children are grown. We do not know how long it will be before the white ones come into these lands. We cannot go east, as the great chief Mizelikazi would have us as his dogs. There is nowhere but the Thirstlands after all. But we have a little time. Let us all stay together and I will teach all the children and we will all enjoy the benefit of each other's company. If the white ones come, then perhaps some of you will go with the children to the Thirstlands. If the white ones do not come, then the journey is unnecessary except for the two children who must go for their ancestors' sake. But they can go when they are grown and my death will not threaten them.'

There was a very long pause. Then the next oldest man cleared his throat.

'Grandfather,' he said, 'as was expected you have spoken with great wisdom. I am sure you have considered how we will teach the children and ourselves, if it becomes necessary, to cope with the Thirstlands. Here we have animals; even with the lack of rain and the dry pans we still have two waterholes we can use. The dry river-beds still run with water underground. In the Thirstlands there is no water at all for many seasons. There is little game. It is a way of life to which we are not accustomed. We will need to decide how we are going to acquire these skills for the children.'

Tsatsi nodded his agreement. 'When it was first discussed with my son, the great hunter Zzorri, he voiced your concern. His suggestion was that we cross the Great River and move to the edge of the Thirstlands. That we move in and out of these lands knowing that the Great River will be there to sustain us through our learning. Also we would seek out my daughter, who married into a family of the Thirstlands. They would surely help us.'

They paused again. And then everyone, in descending order of age, put forward opinions and made suggestions. When all had had their turn – even the youngest man who wanted to start attacking the white ones right away – it was left to the eldest to welcome Tsatsi and his grandchildren.

'And,' he said, 'the women have seen the tracks of the oryx to the east of the water-hole. Grandfather, would you bring your headband and accompany us tomorrow?'

Tsatsi beamed. 'My brothers, I will smooth the cut groove between my thumb and forefinger with this fire's charcoal in readiness.'

That night, !Katchu awoke again with a start. This time they did not leave the hut. Instead, at Ka's request, Tsatsi told them the story of the child who went with his father to collect sticks to throw at the baboons. While his father was gone, and being an honest and good child, he had answered each enquiry of the baboons as to his purpose with the truth, until he was surrounded by baboons, who killed him and took his eye for a ball and threw it amongst themselves. 'Mine! It is mine!' each of them yelled, as they fought over the eye of the child they had killed. But eventually the Mantis came as an old man and took the eye from the baboons, killing them where necessary, and threw the eye into the water-hole and the child's eye sang out for sorrow to the Great Mantis and to his father and the Mantis made him whole once more, but the baboons did not change their nature.

'The baboons,' whispered Ka, 'are like the white ones. They must be tricked or they will kill you.'

In the little shack on the Great Karoo, Gerda Freek stroked the nearly new linen of the dead man's shirts. She would alter only one for Jong Jan, the rest she would put by for when he was older. The same with the trousers. The shoes fitted him already. She had sifted through the dead man's few things. There were pictures of his family, none of her own. She vaguely recognised one or two of the women, but time had changed them and she couldn't be sure. The house was quiet. The men were out with the sheep and the slowed afternoon time was comforting.

She was glad he had died. There. Take that, she threw at the God with whom she was at war. She had seen the way the man's eyes had made an inventory of her life, storing away details for later use. She could imagine exactly what he would have said and how it would have been phrased. Oh, she understood her countryman too well. But now her life was still her own, her beauty intact. She smiled at the linen. And Jong Jan had some decent clothes for when he went courting. And she herself had the small sewing-kit that must have been given to him by his mother. The thimble was silver, too.

The light in the small room was changing and she went to the window. Purple clouds were massing on the horizon, heading towards the north. She went outside to feel the slight chill in the air and to see the changed light. Perspectives that had been flattened by the white midday sun were returned now, and the earth colours of the land stood clear against the green and brown scrub. The bleached whites of the dried grasses were luminous against the darkening sky. She did not expect rain. The sky had threatened and withheld so often over the past years. She decided on a chicken for the meal tonight.

The soft, round daughter of one the servants was playing in the yard. Pretty, with a ready smile, she was, Gerda had observed, a very happy child. She and one of the others were engaged in some complicated ritual with sticks and stones that caused them to concentrate and then laugh. The clarity of the girl's laughter, the light in her eyes, affronted the woman. She set the girl to catch one of the hens. With her small companion they made a game of it, chasing the hen around and around, laughing at it and each other. Gerda felt a swell of anger. She grabbed the child's arm and took her into the kitchen. Together they filled the burning stove with wood and then she sat the child on the plate and held her down for two long seconds while she heard the screams and then she lifted her off and looked to see if the light had left her eyes.

3

The Northern Cape, April 1840

Jong Jan and his father stood shoulder to shoulder at the foot of the mountain. The wagons would have to be taken apart and the convoy carried in pieces. There was no other way. They had scaled the ridge ahead of them on foot, leading their horses. The oxen had managed the foothills, standing fast when they could not go forward, straining against the yoke until the horses and men were brought to bear on the heavily laden wagons. But they had nearly lost a wagon and they could not afford further risk. The women and children were unloading. It was late afternoon and they would make camp for the night here, dismantle the wagons at first light.

Jong Jan looked back at Hester. Heavily pregnant, she was sitting on a rock. It would be her fourth child. The other three were unloading their wagon under her direction. She was in her eighth month, thirty-one years old but looking much older. The daughter of Kommandant Hans, Hester Marais had been a softly rounded girl of seventeen when he married her. Everyone was pleased with the match. At twenty-three, Jong Jan had been a tall, strong young man. His mother had urged him to find a strong girl, not one who would burden him, preferably one who was used to the ways of the land, not one of the new settlers' girls, smoother, maybe, and more beautiful, but not hardy. At twenty, Jong Jan had been enchanted by the daughter of the new judge of the district court, a Miss Judith Carlisle, but she had laughed at him one too many times, and tired of feeling clumsy and rough, he had taken his mother's advice. He smiled to himself now to imagine Miss Judith sitting on Hester's rock with all her possessions piling up around her ready for a three-day walk over the mountain. He left his father's side and went to give his water-bottle to his wife.

The British, with their interfering ways, had finally become more than any real man could bear. The hanging of four of the Dutch settlers at Slagtersnek in 1816 had been just the beginning. Jong Jan and his father had been there, to see the ropes break and to hear the cries of the crowd as they rejoiced at the finger of God pointing at the British who would not understand that a white man could not be killed by a Hottentot, whether in British army employ or not, without his brothers rising against them. And then the stubborn English mule of an officer had ordered them to be hung again. Twice! The men died, and every man there had learned that the new masters were intending to be just that. Then the slaves. Hang the Boer and free the slaves. With reimbursement payable in England! The trip would have eaten up all the money. Sly bastards. And then their damned Ordnance 50. As if a KhoiKhoi could ever really have the same rights as a Christian white man. Jong Jan dropped the kist he had unloaded with more force than was strictly necessary, winning him a sour look from his wife.

So now, like thousands of their kinsmen, they were moving out of reach, away from taxes and district courts into an empty land where a man did not have to see the smoke from another man's chimney. Many had gone east and north-east, but the small band from the North-Western Cape had decided to go directly north.

Hannes Kruger, the hunter, had spent many nights on his way down to Cape Town in the Freek shack, describing the land which was proving much as he had said. Once they had climbed the mountains, they would have an arid land ahead until they reached the waters of the Orange River. It was there that Jong Jan and his extended family intended to settle. They were accompanied by five other families and their servants, enough to protect each other, not so many as to create discord. Hannes had advised them against going too far east. The land was in disarray. Dingane had inherited from his half-brother Shaka the powerful Zulu nation, which dominated the land beyond the eastern border. And even though the victory at Blood River had demonstrated completely that the hand of God was guiding the Trekboers, the Zulus were far from conquered. The battle was lost, but there was still a war pending. Shaka's Zulu conquests had caused a chain reaction that had pushed all the smaller tribes to overrun each other. With Mizelikazi's Matabele dominating the north-east, Jong Jan and his family were left to contend with the remnants of the Bushmen in the north of the Cape, and there they were confident.

They had been travelling for a month, hoping to reach the mountains at the end of the rains. This year the heavens had been benign and they had spent many afternoons digging the wagons out of mud. Rain was precious and nobody minded too much. His mother, Gerda, could be heard muttering about the vegetables she had left behind, but they had seeds to begin again. And Gerda, like Hester, would never make a real fuss. That night they read from the Bible and prayed for God's guidance over the mountain, thanking Him for bringing them this far. Afterwards, in the firelight, they sat quietly, all lost in their own thoughts. Crickets and beetles filled the silence around them. It had been a hard day. Even the children were quiet. It took a real effort to relax aching muscles and stiffened limbs for sleep.

Hester Freek lay under the canvas canopy, pushed against the side by the bulk of her husband, snoring with a little 'fft-fft' beside her. She had prayed for sleep, but it eluded her. The baby inside her was quiet. It had been unsettled as she lay in the jolting wagon, sharing with her every stone and rut in the unchartered ground. She knew she would have the baby on the journey. Where there was no choice there was less opportunity for fear. Her legs suffered from cramps. She would have liked to get up, feed the fire a little and walk around, but she did not want to disturb Jan. On balance, she was satisfied with her husband. He was an able man and not lazy. Shrewd in the ways of the world. What he lacked in tenderness he made up for in the security he provided. He was touchy, easily roused to anger, but she could not envisage survival without him. Keeping him well and strong was her primary task.

Her mother-in-law had been kindness itself on this journey. Suffering elicited the best from Gerda. It was when she and Jan, newly married, had arrived at the Freek farm that Gerda had been difficult. To distract herself from the pain and edginess in her legs, she began once more to count her blessings. Each time she tried to add a new one. Tonight she gave thanks for the miles they had covered that day without serious incident.

But still there was that part of her that brooded for her daughters. It was a vice, but she allowed herself a dream of a long white farmhouse, filled with good solid furniture and fabrics, how she dreamed of fabrics! Some of the materials that the new English settler women had brought with them had rendered her almost speechless with desire. Her mind filled now with rich red brocades, burgundy tassels, finest

Irish lace. She wanted more than this endless struggle for her daughters.

She wanted them to have ribbons and trinkets and a few beautiful pieces of glass and china. And proper shoes, not the veldskoen that they made themselves from animal skins. Little boots with buttons and hooks and a small heel. And more than one bonnet of a colour other than serviceable. Her mind filled with a picture of little Sannie, her sweet face framed with a bonnet trimmed with broderie anglaise, a pale blue sash around her waist and a dress of creamy stuff, her hands all soft and white, her hair glossy and carefully arranged. And next to her Jong Gerda, a plain child, but even plainness could be helped by pretty things. And her serious nature might turn into an attractive poise, a composed calm. Yes, she could see Gertjie in something a little more severe, but perhaps more striking in colour than the frills she had selected for Sannie.

And the child to come . . . much could be achieved before this child was grown. If it was a boy – and how she longed for it to be a boy, a younger brother for Klein Jan – then perhaps by the time he was grown and going courting he would have his own leather boots and an English saddle for his horse. Soft gloves and a white linen shirt. It wouldn't happen for Klein Jan. Twelve years old and he was a young man already, toughened by his father; before too long he would be looking for his own wife. And he would have to choose someone like herself. There was no place yet for lightheartedness. All was work. She could feel the flickers of discontent and turned again to her fabrics. Before she died she would have these fabrics. She would go all the way to Graaf Reniet or Cape Town even and visit the stores and stroke the rolls of material and haggle over the prices and order a wagonload. Then she could sew with a light heart into her old age. She had thought about promising God she would give up her frivolous vice if he would ease the birth, but she knew she couldn't let it go. God would have to help her anyway.

In the moonlight, !Katchu and his son Zzorri looked down on the small laager. The five wagons were arranged in an irregular square, lashed together. Thorn branches were stuffed underneath them to deter predators, and the oxen, horses and sheep were tethered in a living belt around them. The unloaded possessions sat in the middle, to the side of the fire. The Boers and their families slept in the wagons, their servants on the ground inside the laager. The !Xam hunters had been tracking and watching the Trekboers for days. Their routine was predictable. They rose early and struck camp. Then they would set off, the children herding the sheep, the men taking turns to ride out ahead to find the best route. As the heat of the day gathered momentum, they would stop and let the animals graze, make food, rest. In the afternoon they would continue. Each night they built their fortress. To !Katchu and Zzorri their progress seemed incredibly slow. But it was relentless. They envied them their hunting sticks, instruments with a range that made hunting unbearably easy. These mountains were the last obstacle before the Great River.

The family had discussed endlessly the best way to repel these invaders. The options were few. They could launch an attack, trying to pick off the outriders first. An ambush would be easy to construct, their movements were fairly predictable and the Bushmen had the advantage of the terrain.

Yet the Boers had done nothing as yet. If they were simply travelling through the land, then to kill them would be wrong. And killing them would surely bring hundreds more to avenge their deaths. None of the family had seen a white before. They had expected something monstrous, but apart from their size (even the women were taller than the average !Xam man), they seemed very normal. Dull, even. They obviously had no knowledge of the land as they would walk straight past edible roots and fruits without even noticing them. Their tracking skills were pitiful. But those shooting sticks! And the animals that they rode! What was needed, it was decided, was a means of turning them back. Perhaps they could divert the travellers into another territory.

Watching the sleeping laager, !Katchu felt a tightness in his chest. Since the Boer arrival he had suffered from an excess of adrenalin. It made his legs kick in the night and his heart beat overfast. Even his hands, to his horror, he saw occasionally shaking. His mouth was always drawn tight, his jaw set. Tsatsi would have known what to do, he thought. It was ten years since the old man had finally said his goodbyes. !Katchu and Ka had received his blessings upon them and their children. The white ones had stayed away for those ten years and another eighteen. !Katchu and Ka still went every winter to the Great Noise to meet with their ancestors and to remember. And now in the present they found that future of which they had always spoken.

It seemed impossible, watching as they had done earlier in the day the little children playing and the women cooking together, that these were the same people who would kill women and children. !Katchu had said as much, and reasoned whether one family could be punished for the evil of another. It was Ka who had said there was no difference between them. That no !Xam in the entire history of the people had ever done what these white ones were capable of doing. They were governed by spirits that made them seem innocent until they unleashed their evil. They must be stopped and the !Xam must use cunning, because when those evil spirits were aroused, then the killing taste would come into their mouths and the !Xam would be doomed.

We are doomed anyway, !Katchu thought. Tsatsi saw it. And we are so few. We no longer meet our people in the bush.

He felt stung by Ka's words. But she was right. Where was there for these strange people to go? They had made no sign of going east.

All the !Xam men were positioned around the laager. When they were sure that all were asleep and as soon as the moon slipped behind a cloud, !Katchu raised his arm. Each armed with a razor-sharp knife, their bows and arrows slung over their shoulders, they stealthily approached the oxen. It took more than half an hour for them all to be in position, sixteen men around fifty still quiet oxen. Then, at a signal, in one lightning-fast stroke, each severed the tendons of the two oxen nearest him. By the time the animals realised their pain and could no longer stand on their back legs and began to bellow, the men were running up their prearranged routes away from the camp, leaving sixteen different sets of tracks.

Lion! was the first thought. The Boer men grabbed their rifles and from the backs of the wagons tried to see what had upset the oxen. Many were now seated, bellowing; the ones able to stand were trying to break away from the leather that held them, rocking the wagons.

'Do you see anything?' the men called to each other. In their underclothes, they examined the animals and found the blood on the backs of their legs and saw that they had been rendered useless. Only the vermin Bushmen would stoop to this.

Ka raised her daughters and her granddaughters to be brave women. They would always have to serve the men, there was never any question about that. And the sight of the men bringing home an oryx after a time of no meat made serving them a pleasure. The women knew when the kill was made and what it was because they just did. They did not know that it was unusual to know these things over great distances, or that others did not have this knowing. Ka had grown into a strong woman, a good breeder, with seven children of her own and now three grandchildren, two boys and a girl. The girl, Little Ka, named after her as was the tradition, was her heart's favourite. In the stance of the child and her strength of will, Ka saw herself, and she loved the little girl. As was expected of a grandmother, she spent endless hours telling her stories and teaching her skills. She was determined to make her nimble, equipped to deal with a world of change. As well as survival, she taught her cunning, encouraged her to take risks. In her secret heart she wished the child could learn to hunt, then she would be entirely self-sufficient, but this was never going to be possible. The little girl found her grandmother demanding, not understanding why she should be subjected to extra tasks, harder, it seemed, than her peers. It was a great love they had for each other, but for now, it was visible only to Ka.

That afternoon, Little Ka and her brother had gone, as they did every afternoon at this time of year, to look for the nest of the great she-tortoise that ambled in a radius around the area. It was the season when they could hope to find the succulent baby tortoises that they would roast, using their shells to carry precious herbs or to drink from, always leaving enough behind for when they returned the following year. But the she-tortoise was becoming cannier every year and the two children were growing tired of being teased by the family for failing in their search. They wandered farther than they had meant to. But somehow the knowledge that the first challenge had been hurled at the white giants was intoxicating to the entire family. The men's audacity thrilled them, while fear of reprisal worked its way into the stomachs of the women. The children felt bound to succeed on this wave of triumph.

The camp was well hidden on the far side of the mountain

and the multitude of tracks they had left, crossing and recrossing each other's paths in the early hours of the morning, would confuse even the most expert of trackers. Each track led to rock and it was a matter of guessing where the tracks might start again after the rock ended. This Klein Jan found to be a challenge. He had seen his father shoot Wanderlust, his oxen, the one he had raised from a calf and that answered to its name so readily. He had loved that animal without reserve. It would come to his voice from the herd and it had never shown anything but loyalty to him. The only thing that was truly his the bastard vermin Bushmen had rendered a carcass, and Klein Jan was alternately sick with hatred and gripped with pain. It was his first experience of real loss and he was unnerved by the physicality of the emotion.

Little Ka and her brother had found more than they bargained for. Looking for the nest near the water-hole they had disturbed a Cape cobra and now both children had their eyes covered as they walked slowly backwards. The cobra, with its great head swaying back and forth, could kill a lion if it spat its poison in its eyes. They looked at the ground as they backed more and more rapidly before turning and running, laughing at their escape. So it was that Klein Jan, relying on water rather than the tracks, saw them with the binoculars from the rock on which he lay.

His heart leapt. He would fetch his father and they would track these children back to their camp. But first he watched them a little. They were digging up some root or other and he could hear the click-click of their speech and their giggling. He was surprised at the carefree giggling. He had not experienced much laughter in his twelve years. He focused on the little girl, the noisier of the two, and was surprised to find her pretty. He felt he wanted to own her rather than kill her. That giggling! He would fetch his father but he would ask for the little girl as his servant.

In the middle of their game Little Ka's brother suddenly collapsed, a hole oozing blood on his chest, surprise in his eyes. They stared, speechless at each other. Instinct made her break that gaze and look around her – but she saw no one. She did not know if she should run for help or if she should stay with her brother. But the choice was made for her when the spirit of her brother left her to join the ancestors. She did not know how she knew but she knew that the small body next to her was suddenly no longer alive. Then she stood and saw that the giants on their animals were advancing upon her. Faced with the monsters of her deepest fears and every childhood game, Little Ka was unable to move. She stared at the massive creatures on horseback, her mind blank. They made unintelligible noises to each other, and then one of the men dismounted and began to walk towards her, leading his horse. Her bodily control disappeared then, and as she stood rooted to the earth, urine spilled down her shaking legs. The very young man softened his voice and placed his hand on her shoulder. It was surprisingly warm. She'd expected it to feel like the scales of a fish. Then he tied her hands together in front of her and taking a long leather rein he attached her hands to one end and the other to the stirrup of his saddle. She did not know if she was more terrified of the horse or the rider. Somehow she felt safer when the rider was with the horse, but that presumed a kindness in the rider. With the little Bush girl trotting alongside his horse, Klein Jan and the other men followed her tracks to the Bushman camp.

The wanton destruction of their hard reared cattle was a violation the Boers could neither understand nor accept. They shot the animals one by one and dragged the carcasses to one side. They would skin them and dry as much of the meat as they could. The women would melt the fat and use it for candles, grease, anything that needed lubricating. Jan Freek felt his hatred burning inside his belly as he realised that there were only enough oxen left to draw one and a half wagons. Well, they would have to get some more. Steal them, if necessary. The vermin Bushmen didn't keep cattle. Savages. They would have to trade with the Kaffirs to the east. Some would have to go and find new oxen, while others would have to protect the women and children and their belongings. The Kaffirs wanted to trade with rifles now. Bugger that. They could have an old musket or two and with a bit of luck do themselves some damage with the things. Anyway they were too bloody stupid some of them to realise that you needed ammunition. He kept an eye on his daughter-in-law. She was due soon, his wife said. Well, she would have to wait until they were over the mountain. She was sitting, as she had been instructed to do. Hester was no longer allowed to do anything that might encourage the arrival of the baby. Not until the carcasses of the oxen were buried and they had moved away. The flies that surrounded the camp and settled in a thick blanket on each animal and in the pools of blood were like a plague. Jan Freek ignored them as they crawled across his face, blinking them out of his eyes. The sickly sweet fatty smell of the dead animals bothered him more than the flies.

In the end, Zzorri reflected, perhaps it had been his father's fear of fear that made him brave. Violence was not the way of the people. But since the arrival of the white ones on the other side of the mountain, !Katchu had made himself drink deep of its cup. He had a need to avenge his family. Zzorri understood this now. It was accepted that a man never forgot an insult or an injury and always remembered acts of kindness. A man is entirely responsible for the results of his actions, now and in the life after life. But the white ones were terrifying to contemplate, with their horses and their firearms. And his father had carried the added burden of history. He knew at first hand what they were capable of doing. Now Zzorri knew too. He could understand.

Zzorri stood on the crest of a brick-red sand-dune. They had been coming to the Thirstlands every year since he was a child and now his chest eased a little as he accepted into his spirit the vast sea of sand that stretched seemingly endlessly ahead of him. No other people could live here. No white, no Bantu. Just the !Xam people and the animals. Zzorri and his initiation brothers, away on the hunt, had returned to find the camp destroyed, the family dead. Only Little Ka was missing. He assumed she was captive. He would try to find her, one day.

Looking at the tracks around the camp, still visible even with the battling of the hyenas and the vultures over the corpses, he had been able to piece together a scenario. It seemed that the horses had been standing still just outside the camp. The people had been seated and then had stood, then his father's tracks had appeared to one side. His bow and arrows had fallen beside him. Then there had been a scattering and the killing. He would never know exactly how it had happened, but there was no escaping what had happened. It was too quick. Too final. He and his three brothers couldn't accept it. They, !Xam men, the last of their kind, would have to find !Kung or G/wi brides from the families deep in the interior. Other than Little Ka, they knew of no !Xam women left. Like a persistent tongue of flame in the darkness, the urge to find wives was immediate and immensely strong. New life, they needed new life.

Hester laid out the leather mat and the sheets that she needed for the birth. The pains were very regular now, her waters had broken in the early hours of the morning. She had kept moving, stopping to rest on a wagon wheel or to crouch in the dust as necessary. But now it was time. The men spread out, guns ready, in a wide circle of protection. Gerda and the other women readied knives and cloths and took the children out of sight. Little Ka was ignored where she sat under the wagon. She watched impassively as Hester squatted, still in her dress for decency, on the mat. The Boer woman was biting on a piece of rawhide, the veins standing out on her neck and face. She did not give in to the pain, she seemed to fight against it. The strong cross spirits these women carried inside them! They never seemed to have peace. Little Ka scouted the underside of the wagon. It would not do as protection. Tonight she knew that she needed to be away from the tracks that she had crossed three times now, four lionesses and one lion were circling the Trekboer party. And the smell of the new birth would carry for miles. She had no intention of telling her new employers. She was torn between the safety of the laager and its confinement. The thorns that would go under the wagons and encircle the sheep were not adequate protection. The sheep would be the easiest targets, then the oxen. The lions would probably wait until nightfall. She would stay alert.

After a seemingly endless day, Hester gave birth to her longed-for son. Jong Jan, relieved from his watch by his mother, went to greet the infant wrapped in a cloth and ready for his inspection. The baby was taken to each of the men and women for inspection and congratulations. The atmosphere lightened. New life was so close to death that the party had been holding its breath for the past few weeks. Hester lay calm, the child finally tucked in beside her as the adults prepared to celebrate the birth of their latest member.

Gerda sent Little Ka for firewood, an elaborate charade of instructions that involved lifting pieces of wood and bringing them to Gerda. The child pretended not to understand until she saw the light in Gerda's eyes darkening, then she went off, picking up a stick on the way to show she had got the message. Out of sight, she took her time, checking the ground for tracks. She returned with a small bundle of twigs and one medium-sized log. Gerda sighed. She pointed at the medium log and indicated that the child should get more like this. The child was either deliberately obtuse or truly did not understand why more firewood was needed. Gerda was less and less sure that what she saw was what she got with this tiny apricot-coloured creature. She cuffed her ears just in case. And Little Ka went to search for more wood. Her ears rang and smarted. Somehow this small affront enraged her more than the other, more shocking tragedy which was still too big to comprehend. But the smarting ears were real enough.

That night the Trekboers gave thanks to God from inside their laager and Jong Jan christened his newest son Paul, entering his name in the family Bible. In the excitement of the ceremony nobody noticed Little Ka, shifting forward on her stomach and moving the thorns under the wagons to one side. She had excelled at the game of proximity, where the children sneaked up on surricates and dassies in imitation of their hunting fathers, flattening themselves on the ground and staying downwind. The lions would be put off by the fire and the alien sounds the Boers made, but they would be driven to distraction by the smell of the birth. She had a little time. Sensing the cats in a wide circle around the camp, she called on the spirit of her great-grandmother, //Dhu-//hu, who had survived the attack of a lion, and shielding herself amongst the oxen, she looked deep into the night for their eyes. She saw two sets, far off still, lying flat in the grass, on this side of the laager. There was little she could do to satisfy her desire that Gerda be eaten up by one of these great animals except return to the safety of the fire. But it comforted her that she alone knew they were there.

The laager was not sealed until everyone had performed their ablutions. The child's hope rose as each one went past the spot of the birth to relieve themselves, but the great cats kept their distance, disappointing her mightily.

In the morning, the trekkers exclaimed over two missing sheep while they were loading the oxen, horses and people with their belongings. Sannie and Jong Gerda carried the kist between them. Inside were the precious vegetable seeds, the few medicines they had, the family Bible, some sheets of paper and envelopes, ink, clean cloths for the baby, the silver-plated knives and forks that had been Hester's dowry and the family's only set of good clothing. The brass handles on either side, a source of pride, soon cut into their hands. They wrapped their aprons around the handles and put the box down every five minutes or so to shift position. It was barely off the ground as the two girls, almost level in height, were only ten and thirteen. Neither would have thought to complain.

Little Ka watched the kist swaying between the two girls ahead of her. She was astounded that they were allowed to carry it. In the few weeks she had been captive here she realised that a fierce household god lived in each kist, as it was the most preciously guarded of all the Boer items. She had sat upon it once and found herself sprawled in the dirt with a thick numbness on the left side of her head that was just beginning to sting. Gerda towered over her and the tone of her voice was clear. It was through Gerda's voice that she learned her name was 'bleddy boesman'. Little Ka was increasingly surprised how little she needed words to understand things. She knew that she was a disappointment to Klein Jan, that he desperately wanted her to laugh and play, and she drew satisfaction from treating him and his overtures with indifference. So busy was Little Ka deciphering all the messages and clues in this alarming world, that she did not have time to contemplate her fate. It was a minute-to-minute survival strategy, trying to understand what was required of her but not trying too hard – deliberately understanding just enough at the point where punishment could be avoided by a hair's breadth – she was a reluctant worker at best and most soon found her to be too much bother. There were others more willing, less difficult.

She hated the dress she was made to wear. It reached to her feet and had armholes that were too large for her. It encumbered her unmercifully and she felt ashamed to wear the uniform of the enemy. It also got very dirty and she was supposed to wear it all the time. It stank, she felt, and she hated the scratchiness of the coarse fabric. The dress was the poorest of all the dresses in this strange world and she could see that by wearing it she was put in her rightful place in the pecking order. She vowed to remove it and escape one day. Many, many vows Little Ka made in those first few weeks.

She broke a big one quite early on. They had finally descended the mountain and Klein Jan, encouraged by his mother and grandmother, had taken her off to a small clearing, her hands tied again. She had a wild thought that he would set her free, that she was going home. But he took off her dress and tied her to a tree and then spoke at her for some time. Listening behind the words, she knew he didn't want to hurt her, but that he was going to. Her legs began to tremble. She couldn't understand him saying how it was important that she respected him and did his bidding, that his grandmother and his mother had told him that he was becoming a laughing stock with his passion for the little Bush girl, that it was a test of his manliness, that he had to beat her into submission. That it would be for her own good, in the end. But her legs trembled and he saw fear in her eyes. She began to shake her head and plead, even desperately making a kind of giggling noise at him, but he had tied her arms around the tree so he would not see her eyes and she could not break free. He forced himself to hear the baiting of his womenfolk and he thrashed, with his sjambok, tentatively at first but then with a cold relentlessness until he could see the welts through the dark apricot skin and spattered blood made whorls of redness on the whole back of her body. The act of thrashing her calmed him.

The other servants saw the blood sticking the child's dress to her small body, the numbness in her eyes. She accepted their little kindnesses. But inside her spirit was a white space, empty. That this could happen, that there was no question of fighting back, that the boy considered it acceptable, necessary even, to tie her and beat her, that this was the true nature of their relationship, that he did not consider himself unmanned by this cowardly act – this unlocked her reality. All were dead. All. She had seen it herself. Dead. She was alone, surrounded by evil. There was no Mantis, there was no Moon God, there was no power on earth or above to stop these creatures. She sat rocking slowly, looking inward, with no tears, no feeling. Now she was Ka, because her grandmother was dead.

After the mountain the land was flat, scattered with shrub and red-coloured earth. It wasn't saucer flat with distinguishable mountains, like the expansive Karoo they had left behind, but rather it was a series of hilly undulations that gave an impression of flatness. They refused to be disheartened by the solidity of the ground on which they rode. It felt iron hard, a perfect mate for the endless rocks that littered the ground around them, making the horses step carefully, slowing their pace. It was the river they were after. Hannes Kruger had told them that it ran all year every year. With water anything was possible.

The Great River revealed itself slowly. The men felt a quickening of their hearts as they saw the landscape subtly change, become a little greener. There were trees, more birds; in the presence of birdsong, they realised the land they had crossed had been near silent. And finally there were bulrushes and great towering pampas grasses, as tall as a mounted rider, thickly packed together, guarding the river-bank. They rode slowly until they found a way through. Leaving the horses, they walked to the edge of the river-bank. Water! And, praise the Blessed Lord above, it was running blue and clear and full, with a sound of gentle rushing and a width that made crossing a complicated matter, and, praise God, this was the beginning of the dry season and look at how full it was! The mighty river unfolded as it had done for thousands of years. The three men, father, son and grandson, watched the rays of the setting sun turn the azure blue water golden, and fell to their knees and thanked the Good Lord for leading them to the promised land.

4

Northern Botswana, 1958

In a slow turning, the great herd of wildebeest started the long journey to the waters that would come from the flood of the delta. Was it a change in the air? Perhaps the temperature? The number of flies or of new insects in the grass? Maybe it was the morning dew that gave the sign. It began as a lumbering walk. But after days, as the land around them, stripped by cattle, became a testing ground, the herd gathered momentum. Some ancient pattern directed the route. There was no question of getting lost, just of getting through the ever more arid land to the floodwaters that came every year.

The !Kung family had chosen their camp carefully and now began to experience the high spirits that come before a storm, heightened always before the coming of the great flood. The water would seep through the land slowly, gently even, waterways would form where there had been none the year before. Last year's pool may be this year's dry pan. But with the waters would come vegetation and game. Thousands of wildebeest, impala, kudu, water-buck and giraffe and great herds of buffalo would soon throng the area. The family had been surviving on the spring hares that had fringed the delta for weeks now. They were grateful for the hare, but missed the hunt. Now there was excitement. The smallest thing was funny. The children were greatly affected and demanded endless stories about the waters. Enough water to stand in! But you would have to brave the crocodile's teeth. Everyone was waiting, and the waiting was delicious.

The great flood came, seeping across the Kalahari sands, bringing birds and beauty. The !Kung waited for the game. For centuries the game had passed along the old routes to the water. They went out in small parties, four at a time, to see what had changed. At night they sat around the fire, filled with foreboding. They knew the animals. They did not change their patterns overnight. Some terrible thing must have happened. After much discussion it was decided that a small hunting party would walk the route back, to the source of the animals if necessary, to see what might have happened there. Perhaps there had been a sickness. Perhaps the land had opened up and swallowed them all. But would they not have felt its rumblings? The great flood had arrived, but it had come alone.

The small band walked on intrepidly for seven days before they came upon it. They had never seen a fence before. They tried to push it over but succeeded only in making dents in it. It gave so far and then no further. And it stretched as far as they could see on either side of the corner in a straight line. It bordered the arid land, enclosing the water. On top it had sharp thorns which made climbing over it near impossible. Given time, they could have dismantled it in some way, climbed it. But now they were only concerned to see how far it went. They headed north, walking alongside the fence. Perhaps, they thought, it only goes a little way. Then the herds could have gone round it.

After three days of walking they started to find the bones and horns of wildebeest on the other side of the fence, picked clean so quickly it was hard to tell how long they had been there. This thing that stood between the animals and the water was evil. They stayed as far away from it as they could, for fear of contamination.

The district veterinary surgeon for the Northern Territory was pleased with the progress that had been made in treating the cattle under his care. Foot-and-mouth had spread like wildfire in this free-grazing environment. Now his territory at least would be sealed off from other, infected herds. Effective quarantine, he mused. It'll do the job. He was a dedicated man.

The four !Kung men watched a dehydrated, skeletal wildebeest charge weakly at the fence. Its horns caught in the iron mesh, it buckled at the knees. They had seen enough.

South Africa, 1960

The thick afternoon heat melted time. In the yard, the mongrel dogs lay panting in the shade. Even the chickens were subdued. Melanie's legs were draped over the arm of an old leather armchair in a corner of the wide veranda. There was nothing to do. Oom Karel was reading the scriptures and Tannie Esther was having a lie down. Bessie was visiting with her girlfriend Sara after church. Piet was somewhere, she didn't know where. There was no noise other than the dogs' slow panting and the hum of the crickets and Christmas beetles that never stopped. A thin column of ants was making its way across the polished red floor. She had read everything she had to read and even if she hadn't she didn't want to read anyway.

Because it was Sunday she would only be allowed to listen to religious programmes on the radio. Oom would object if she played anything but hymns on the piano. It was too hot to go for a walk. She sighed deeply. So what if it was hot. She had a hat. She couldn't stand the stillness. It was claustrophobic, somehow, being attached to the house in this quiet heat. The stillness of the air felt like something you could stir with your foot.

She felt a little guilty. Sunday was a day of reflection, a day to come close to the Lord and examine the soul. The sermon this morning had been about examining one's own conscience and finding the Good Lord inside one's own actions. Doing unto others as you would have them do unto you. She stifled a raucous laugh that lurched out of nowhere to answer the phrase.

Oom was very devout. On Sunday evenings he would listen to the service on the radio. He would sit with his eyes shut and his hand over his forehead and murmur responses. If members of the family were in the house he would make them kneel down with him. Oom was very strict. He didn't allow make-up or perfume, and all Melanie and Bessie's clothes had to conform to his concept of modesty. Whenever she was home from college, she had to wear her hair scraped off her forehead into a pony-tail or plait, as did Bessie. Oom was a deity in his own home. Melanie was deeply frightened of him but didn't quite recognise the emotion as fear. When she was small, he had administered punishment with a leather strap on her hands or bottom. Talking back or disobedience were clear evidence of the devil in her. She was obliged to honour him and Tannie and do their bidding. It wasn't unnatural in the community. He was, she had always supposed, a good man. She certainly respected his authority.

He controlled his anger and was generally calm when he administered his punishments. Since she was a teenager, he had forbidden her to appear in any state of undress in the house. She knew that if he saw her sitting with her legs over the side of the chair he would be very displeased. Especially on a Sunday.

But difficult thoughts kept slipping into her consciousness. She had prayed they would go away, but never having a devout belief in God's care of her, she wasn't having much luck. And when time stood still on a Sunday afternoon it was hard to distract herself. It was hard not to feel a tinge of revulsion at Oom's extreme Sunday piety. Hard not to think about what she had seen last Thursday night when she couldn't sleep. Ja. Last Thursday night. It had been unbearably hot. She had woken in the early hours with stomach cramps and gone quickly to the bathroom.

That night she didn't bother with the light because the moon was so bright. She was at her bedroom window, watching the moon, when she saw Oom leaving the house with a torch. He was in his white undershorts, a vest and his veldskoen. He must have closed the front door very quietly. He stood at the edge of the yard and flashed his torch on and off three times. And then he just stood there. There was a soft sound, a woman's voice, and then a figure joined him. They walked off together into the darkness. Melanie thought she recognised the daughter of one of the farm-workers. What was Oom doing going out into the darkness with her? Perhaps someone was sick. Perhaps there were thieves about. But he had no gun, no medicines. She waited to see him come back. After about an hour he walked quietly, quickly, back into the yard, alone. You always knew when Oom was up and about because he made the clanging racket of the selfish. But not tonight. Tonight he had been deliberately quiet, furtive. She wished she had dreamt it, she really did.

She took her hat and set off for the ridge behind the house. It was out of the question to ride today. Trousers were forbidden on the Sabbath.

From a distance the ridge looked as though it rose straight up out of the flat Karoo scrub that stretched relentlessly in front of it, an oatmeal-flecked brown carpet that eventually melted in a violet haze into the white blue of the sky. It was a round view from the ridge, the horizon seemed to curve, but so distant that you couldn't take it all in with one glance. The climb to the ridge actually started half a mile from the house, the ground rising gradually; when the sun set it would set behind the ridge, leaving this side in shadow. Melanie and Bessie used to beg Oom to take them up to the top of the ridge when they were small to watch the huge red beachball of a winter sun slip under the edge of the earth. They would walk back home by the light of a paraffin lamp, with Oom telling the stars apart, telling how, even before the Great Trek, his great-great-great-grandfather had followed his special bright star from the Cape to where it sat now, right above them, marking his land. And how they had moved on, towards the Orange River, and then after the Boer War, when the cursed English had scorched the land, the families had returned, their farms destroyed, and all convened here, where his great-great-great-grandfather had begun.

Oom told a lot of stories, most of them ending with the need to protect the heritage that cost his forefathers so much. He had been married to Ida, Melanie's real aunt and guardian, an Englishwoman, who died giving birth to Oom's son Piet. He had, she now reminded herself sternly, no blood tie with her. Neither he nor Tannie Esther, his second wife, had been obliged to keep her for all these years, treating her as one of their own. There had never been different rules for her cousins. They had lived and been treated like siblings.

Well, maybe Piet was allowed more freedom. But that was to be expected.

Still, with Aunt Ida dead, there was no one to tell her stories about her mother and father, or to fill her in on their relatives, on her own heritage. Long ago she adopted the history of her uncle.

The concentration camps of the Boer War were a particular embarrassment. The Boer commandos would have ridden under cover of night to a farm just like this one. She could picture the men in their greatcoats, the panting breath of the horses, the soft clanking of stirrups, halters. A brave yellow light shining out from the open door into the great openness of the Karoo and the men clustered around it as the loyal Boer woman gave them all the biltong, coffee and sugar she could, because who knows, her own men would be at someone else's door, and please God they would find loyalty there too.

'It was the strong Boer women that they had to get off the land, because the men could have lasted for years, slowly killing off the ridiculous British. No, they took the war to the women and children. My great-uncle told me that, for him, it took the heart out of the fight. The men were sick with worry. And they burned the farms. There is no limit to what the English will do. They took Kimberley into the Cape when they found diamonds and they took the Transvaal and the Free State when they found gold. And we Boers lived in poverty for years. Absolute poverty. Boer families living in the veldt like Kaffirs, while Englishmen dined at the Rand Club. The damned English. They are arrogant and Godless. It is only through the Broederbond and with God's help that we will manage to rise above them.'

She squirmed at the stories told over and over at school and at home. She wondered how Oom had managed to marry an Englishwoman. She almost never spoke English.

After three miles she stopped and looked back. She had

climbed sufficiently high for the farm buildings to be laid out in front of her. The green tin roof spread out in a neat square, overhanging the wide red veranda that surrounded the house. It was quite still. The house and all that surrounded it was covered in a shimmering heat haze, making it difficult to see the exact outlines of the buildings. The trees next to the house and the patches of shrubbery stood out in their green; the windmill next to the round concrete watertank glinted in the sun. It was quite still. The farm-workers' quarters were even farther away but Melanie could just see the outline of the low flat building, situated about a quarter of a mile from the house. It was up here that she first realised that behind the building was where the farm-workers spent most of their free time. She avoided the area studiously, both because she was instructed to do so and because she knew she wasn't welcome.

It had been after the Sophie thing. She turned her mind away from it. It had all happened a long time ago. It is one of my greatest strengths, she thought. I can completely blot out anything that I need to forget. But the Oom thing was proving difficult. He stood as the foundation of her world, the rationale behind its contradictions. If he were to fall, drop like a sinkhole into the ground, then Melanie's structure of life would go with him. She knew this, somehow, and avoided the logical lines of thought that ran out from last Thursday. Thick and clear among them was Oom's devout religious beliefs. The black people were descended from Ham. His ancestors had brought this belief with them from Holland. There was nothing, nothing whatsoever, wrong in treating them differently from the Afrikaner, who was one of God's chosen people. Had God not proved it at Blood River? And in the Great Trek?

For years he had instructed Melanie and his children in how to treat the Kaffirs. Firm, but fair. Like they are children.

He might laugh at his great-great-great-grandmother, who sat a picannin firmly on her prized black coal stove to teach her not to go near it, but he himself felt her to have been a little harsh, felt that physical punishment should only be meted out in extreme cases, for example if a black man frightened a white woman. Or if there was theft, something really tangible. Then a thrashing was essential for respect. But otherwise he tried to be fair. He was a great supporter of Prime Minister Verwoerd.

Well . . . The thought of Oom having sex was almost impossible. Sex with one of the black women was incomprehensible. For Oom. Melanie didn't share her cousins' revulsion towards the blacks. She didn't know why, possibly it was a failing in her, but some part of her cringed and curled in upon itself when Bessie would shout abuse at the housemaids for forgetting something, or breaking something. Melanie would look down in embarrassment as the shouting led to a blow or something being thrown, to a tearful response from the maid.

'Ag Bessie, isn't it enough now?'

'Enough? How many times have I told the stupid girl, hey? How many times have I told you, you stupid monkey? You can't learn, can you? Or is it just that you won't learn? Well, I'll make you learn whether you want to or not!' Then another slap and more tears. For some reason Melanie's intervention always made it worse. Bessie despised her softness. And she was right, the maids didn't respect her. Perhaps they could sense her guilt. She didn't have the God-given right to rule that belonged so unashamedly to the rest of her family. She just didn't. Her responses to the maids were a mixture of awkward friendliness and stern command. It didn't help that she knew she was being creepy, false, that she knew she ended up being neither one thing nor another, a typical English, as Bessie would say, dangling between wanting the maid to do what she wanted and not wanting to take responsibility for her own authority. Because it isn't fair, she thought. It isn't fair. Even if it is in the Bible, it isn't fair. They don't have a choice.

Maybe Oom thinks . . . who knows what he thinks? A rush of guilt overcame her. You don't know what he was doing, or why he was out there. You don't know. You'll have to ask him. Then you'll know. You can't judge him on coming and going like that. It isn't fair. You'll just have to ask him. Ask him if something is wrong, if anybody is sick. Casual. Just drop it in. Then you'll know. And won't you feel stupid if you're wrong, hey? The tide within her calmed a little at the thought of being wrong. The foundations steadied. She looked about her and saw how the edges of the sky were tinted pink. There were no clouds to catch the setting sun and reflect it back down to her. The sky itself did its best, the edges on the horizons turning from shimmering white to lightest pink. It was time to go home.

At the dinner-table Melanie sat, as always, on her uncle's left, opposite Piet and next to Bessie. Tannie Esther sat next to Piet. Oom bowed his head and clasped his hands in front of him to say grace. It was generally a bit longer on a Sunday. Melanie found herself looking out the corner of her eye at the triangle she could see of his hair, his temple and his left hand. For the first time she really saw his skin. He became a physical being to her during grace. He was a man with a funny black mole on his temple, ragged cuticles and brown marks and thick veins on the backs of quite slender hands, almost delicately shaped, but rough from the work of the farm. Dirt was semi-permanently etched into the grooves of skin on his fingers, but on a Sunday the lines were light, barely noticeable. She found herself examining the strands of his hair. Dark, and thick. It looked as though it would be quite heavy, certainly a little greasy from the stuff he put on it on a Sunday to keep it in place. You could see the comb markings laying out the hair in neat lines, the heavier lines threatening to flop down on to the lesser lines below. He wasn't, she realised, a particularly attractive man.

Afterwards, Melanie was convinced that events happened within a chain. Everything could stay exactly the same for a very long time until you did one thing, one fundamental thing to change the way things were. Then that one thing led to another one thing until you found yourself in a completely different place doing completely different things. And when you looked back you couldn't quite believe it.

One thing that happened was the sound of her uncle going out again in the early hours of the morning. She was especially attuned to the light click of the opening of the front door, the slight swish of the wood as it went over the rough mat that Tannie put in front of it for people to wipe their feet.

She was waiting on the veranda for him when he came back. She must have looked like a ghost or an avenging angel, sitting in her white nightdress in the big armchair. They were equally frightened. But guilt shone from Oom's aggression. He lectured her about being out in the night, in her nightdress, that she had no shame. The sweet soapy sweaty smell of the black woman swirled around him, moving in and out of her nostrils as her uncle moved back and forth. She laughed. Aloud. He put his hand around her mouth to stop her, really hard, and told her to keep her mouth shut. To go to bed. He would try and forget her impertinence, her forwardness. She looked at him and felt the pillars of her world crumbling in a slow landslide into numbness. They had nothing more to say to each other. She went inside, not to go to bed, but to change.

And then she slipped out of the house, took the keys to the truck, rolled it a little way down the drive, started it and roared off.

The light was just beginning to make itself felt over the horizon, the softest shimmering to indicate the day, a light that made telephone poles look like trees and shrubs look like animals. When she turned the truck around, she miscalculated the ground on the side of the road. Instead of scrub grass it was long grass in a ditch. The front wheels fell into it and she was pitched into the windscreen. The engine stopped.

Jeremy Carter and Teddy Brumfield were driving back from the Kimberley Country Club when they saw the old blue truck with its nose in the ditch. Jeremy, who was very slightly less drunk than Teddy, also saw the figure in the front seat. He slowed the car.

'There's a person in that truck. Could be a bloody corpse,' he whispered frantically to Teddy. They stopped the car and, giggling in stage whispers, pushed each other towards the driver's seat. 'Bloody hell, Carter, it's a girl!' Jeremy pushed him aside. She was slumped across the steering wheel, with a lot of blood on the front of her dress. It looked like she might have broken her nose on the wheel. Feeling sheepish, the two men argued in loud stage whispers as to the best way forward. They were arguing about moving her versus going for an ambulance, the nearest hospital being some seventy miles away, when Melanie came round.

'It's all right,' she managed. 'I'm all right.'

They stared. She remembered thinking how funny they looked in their black suits and bow ties. They had to be English. Her chest was hurting, her face hurt and her head where she had hit the windscreen. She eased her way out of the driving seat, feebly waving them away as they tried to help her down. 'Don't touch me. It hurts too much. Don't touch me!' They flapped around her like a pair of puppies, getting in her way and making the simple task of climbing into the front of their car more difficult than seemed possible. So funny in their concern, so gentle.

Jeremy drove her home, trying his best to protect her against the rather springy suspension. She had no means of knowing that their chivalry was not directed at her own prettiness until they left her in the hands of Tannie Esther and Bessie, both in nightgowns and hair rags, both unnerved by the two young men. Then she was seated in front of a mirror and left to contemplate the blood that had dried all over the lower half of her face and throat.

Jeremy came back to visit her. She liked to listen to his voice, with its soft vowels. She liked his manners, the way everyone else seemed clumsy around him, the way he could make you laugh at your own silliness, without feeling at all embarrassed about it, but leave you with a sense that you wouldn't want to be that silly again. And Oom hated him. It was his Englishness, first and foremost. Then it was also his confidence, his social grace. 'He thinks he's better than us. Certainly better than her,' Oom muttered to Tannie Esther in bed at night. 'They all do. He'll never get really angry with a Boer because it's beneath him. She doesn't know what she's letting herself in for.'

He was right in that respect. Much of Jeremy's attraction lay in what he didn't represent, as she had no real knowledge of what he did represent. But he was kind and he was English and he had only been sent out to Kimberley for three months by the British bank that he called 'the firm'. She vaguely expected him to disappear at the end of the next month, but in the interim she was charmed by his stories of a life and a land so diametrically opposed to her own experience. And there was some sense that possibly she might belong to this tribe of the English, because she was no longer able to pretend membership of the tribe with whom she lived.

He called her the 'Refugee', made up stories as to why she had been abandoned in a strange land to be rescued by a young man from home and, as he said one day, looking long and hard at her, how he would like to take her back to that country, take her to his home, in fact make her his wife, if she would have such a silly fellow? She hadn't expected it, but once said, she knew it was inevitable. A chapter closed for her.

The wedding was a traditional affair, a bit scaled down because she was, after all, marrying a Rooinek. Oom received a lot of commiseration from the community, which Jeremy of course couldn't understand. Men shook his hand and insulted him in their own language and he smiled and thanked them and they laughed a lot and went away very pleased with themselves, which seemed to add to the general sense of merriment. They were careful in front of Melanie, however, and the women restricted themselves to tactfully worded doubts about her future happiness, just because you know Melly hasn't got any real family and we are all concerned for her.

Oom watched Melanie dancing with Jeremy and later took the young man off into a corner to tell him, now he was properly wed, of the strange heritage Melanie brought with her. He put his arm around the young man and made the story as alarming as he could and then shook his head and said he was glad Melanie had someone like Jeremy to rely upon.

Jeremy looked expressionlessly at him and the uncle felt the glint of something rather unpleasant in those blue eyes and wondered if he had, after all, misjudged the strength of the young man.

The farm-workers sat in a circle around the fire behind the

prefabricated block of rooms where the house-servants lived. The talk, as always, was of the coming republic. But tonight they had a visitor from the city. The young man looked so clean in his suit, with his shoes so polished and new, Sophie felt he brought an air of possibility with him. He, like all the others, was against this republic. She couldn't understand what difference it would make. The men said that it would mean the Boer would be independent of the rest of the world, independent from Britain, that there would be less influence upon him to change his ways. That the people would be even more oppressed. But what had the British or anyone else done to help anyway? Now eighteen, she had long begun her journey into passive resistance. Endurance. She did not see any other way forward. She would live and die on this farm and hope that some days were better than the rest, do what she could for her two children.

Her mother had named her after Sophiatown, that urban centre of music and poetry and crime, a place where the people talked all night and where ideas were valued and people listened to each other and argued. The cramped living caused fights and drunkenness was a problem but it was still a place where people owned property and where talk, talk could flourish through the night. And then the Boers bulldozed it in 1954 when Sophie was thirteen and the sounds and words of Sophiatown, which radiated out to the whole country from Johannesburg, were heard no more. They moved the sixty thousand people of Sophiatown to the south-western township which the people called Soweto, a long way out of Johannesburg, because black people could not live so close to white people, it was the law now; and they built a white suburb that they called Triomf (Triumph) on the land that was Sophiatown. And with Sophiatown went the hope and the courage in Sophie. From childhood it had beckoned like the luminous eye of an owl in the dark. At sixteen she had her first child and married thereafter, as was the custom.

Now not only did the former residents of Sophiatown (and everyone else for that matter) have to travel a long way to work, they also had to carry papers to say they were entitled to be where they were. So no one black was allowed to travel freely in the country any more. Permission had to be requested to move from one district to another. And if stopped by the police and found with no pass, then you would be arrested and sent to prison.

It was ridiculous. So, as the young man explained, all over the country, the people who were living somewhere for which they had no papers presented themselves for arrest. To demonstrate how ridiculous it was. But in Sharpeville they had over twenty thousand people present themselves for arrest. And the young man told how he was standing outside the police station with the others when the crowd of which he was part had suddenly moved, like a living wave, struggling to flee its own confines. The knowledge of the shooting in the front spread more slowly than the movement itself. How he turned to run with the others, and saw the people lying on the ground near the fence. How, even as the people were fleeing, he saw the shooting continue and the people who were trying to run falling, stumbling and lying in the blood that was pooling in the dust of the road outside the police station in Sharpeville. How the people were still in shock.

What the young man didn't see was the sweat on the hands of the young policeman who trained his machine gun on the crowd, or the shaking of his legs that he was finding hard to control as he saw the ever growing crowd pushing against the fence. It stood as the flimsiest of barriers around the police station where the handful of young Afrikaner policemen stood at their posts and remembered Blood River and every massacre that had ever happened, especially the killing of the policeman by the angry black mob the previous January in Cato Manor. The young man had relived that episode in his mind a hundred times already. The commanding officer smoked a cigarette and tried to calm the young men. They would not do anything until the perimeter fence was breached. That space of time, he privately hoped, would also allow reinforcements to arrive. The young Afrikaner policeman looked at the peeling paint on the bars of the window open to the sight and sound of the crowd, the chanting and the singing, clenching his guts. He tried to focus on the cigarette stubs that were lying on this forgotten windowsill that was now etched in perfect detail in his mind. But then the crowd pushed forward and the perimeter fence bulged. He opened fire and raked bullets backwards and forwards. When the people began to scatter, he was exultant and with the joy of a terrified child that has escaped danger he kept shooting until his commanding officer dragged him from his post.

The small group around the fire digested the story in silence. Not one stone had been thrown, the protest had been peaceful, but sixty-seven men and women were dead. The pass laws meant that Sophie or any of the others could not leave this area where they had been born unless they had a six-month or one-year permit. To get a permit they had to have a job. Only after ten years' continuous employment with the same employer could they expect to be allowed to change their place of residence to that of their employer. The fear was that the white madams would realise this and know they could demand anything they liked from their maids and get it too. Sophie smiled at this. That was nothing new either. Her madams, Madam Esther and Nonnie Bessie (who now wanted to be called Madam), had no restraint anyway. And she had no choice but to comply. She had never had a choice. She looked under her eyelashes enviously at the young man from the city. Last year, Sophie's own husband had disappeared. Just vanished. She did not understand how a man having fathered two children could vanish and not leave any trace. Not a good man like Matthew Makela. In her heart she did not expect him to return but she could not accept that this meant she knew he was dead. Thank God her mother was still alive and able to help with the children. She realised she had inherited her mother's life.

Their two families, Bessie was moved to tell Sophie before special occasions, like the Day of the Covenant or the anniversary of the Great Trek, had a history that went back many, many years. She would open up the old family Bible, a leather-bound battered book that she kept in a glass case specially made for the purpose in Kimberley. On the inside cover in different handwritings were written the birth and death dates of every member of her family since their ancestor Jan Freek. That this Good Book had been on the Great Trek, even went back to before the Great Trek, making Bessie part of the sixth generation of South African Freeks, was a matter of some wonder to her. Sophie looked at the Bible as she did every time, smiling and nodding as always, and saw that Melanie's name was nowhere to be found. Then Bessie would take out the family tree which she had worked on at school and explain how it was constructed.

And how the English had, during the Boer War, destroyed the land and the farms to the north of the Karoo. How the families had to sell the land to finance the one farm. How it was sold to an Englishman who died rather suddenly, leaving a widow, Ida. A thin, bony woman with a quiet demeanour. And how Oom Karel, that wily Boer, had married this Ida, and so tried to regain the land for the family. But the devious Englishman had left the land to some nephew in England, who arrived with his wife to farm it. The Wilmots. Melanie's parents. And Karel was left with an English wife now with no dowry to speak of! But still, Bessie would say, Ida died and we have Melanie and she brought us the land.

And then the photographs would come out of the old leather-bound album and Bessie would show Sophie how her great-great-grandmother Hester had escaped being a prisoner in the British concentration camps. How her maid Katy had gone with her and Hester's daughters and granddaughters and how they had survived the war years because Katy knew how to find food on the land. They had lived in caves that Katy knew in the mountains, because Katy was of Bushman blood. But how the burning of the farmhouse (another picture) had broken the heart of Ou Hester and she had died soon after.

Sophie would look at the photograph of Katy, whom she supposed in some way was her ancestor, a tiny figure next to the Boer matriarch. She does not look happy, Sophie thought. I wonder why she saved them. She should have run away. But then she too did not run away. We are like prisoners, she thought. Released, would we know what to do for ourselves? We have no confidence, no belief. Without these whites we are not sure we will survive.

Bessie would enquire after Sophie's own history. Surely they kept an oral record of the generations? Sophie would smile, look away and shake her head, her hands knotted under the apron of her uniform. Well, Bessie would say, you should keep a record, Sophie. For your children. Then the books would be put away again and Sophie would go back to the kitchen.

She took the battered enamel mug (this too had been her

mother's) and plate from the part of the cupboard that was designated hers (next to the cleaning materials) and made herself tea and some slices of bread and jam which she would eat outside the back door. It amused her and it didn't amuse her that there was this apartheid of crockery. It amused her because her hands prepared the family's food every night and if she wanted, and sometimes she did, she could spit in the soup or any of the dishes. Where it didn't amuse her was in that place in her mind where sometimes she feared she would lose control and go mad. Bessie considered her a sullen girl. A lovely smile, Sophie had, but a sullen temperament at heart.

5

England, 1970–1991

It would be another two hours before Jeremy walked up the hill to the terraced house in Croydon. He would catch the 5.22 from Waterloo and be at the front door between 5.55 and 6.05. It depended on the trains. But he liked the brisk walk from the station after spending most of the day at his desk in the bank. Melanie understood that he liked the routine. She was astounded at first, felt terribly sorry for him, but then realised he liked it. It was one of the foundations of his life.

Routine was everything in this world. For the past ten years her next-door neighbour, Shirley Williamson, had done her laundry on a Tuesday, rain or shine. When Melanie first arrived, they had called each other Mrs Williamson and Mrs Carter, both newly wed, both relishing their new status. In their infrequent exchanges they referred often to their husbands' likes and dislikes. It was a common bond; they belonged to the same club. Shirley had produced three children over the ten years, but then she was older than Melanie, as Melanie frequently reminded herself. She and Jeremy had no children. There was plenty of time, Jeremy had been fond of saying, but now no one mentioned it any more.

Jeremy belonged to the London club that his father had belonged to before him. He had recently been invited to join another one and he was very, very pleased about it. Melanie, always watching him carefully, learned that a certain buoyancy in his mood, a small gift for her, could generally be traced back to something he mentioned in a rather offhand manner. She learned the language of the place and her husband at the same time.

But at first not fast enough. Things changed, as they were bound to, between Melanie and Jeremy after the wedding. They were happy together as they wandered around the Cape before flying back to England. Somehow they were equal in the winelands and on the beaches. They found the same things funny, they relaxed into a friendly banter, a gentle physicality made them happy. But England made a difference. Suddenly she was thrown into stark relief against the backdrop of his life. And she knew in her deepest heart that even though Jeremy would never admit it, he was sometimes embarrassed by her ignorance, by her accent, by her lack of subtlety and restraint. She had stilled herself as she watched this old world and tried to understand how it functioned.

From the shelter of her front room she watched Shirley Williamson with her children, locking the front door, setting off into the rain, pushchair cover zipped up against the weather, little James barely visible through the opaque plastic. The rain here wasn't a celebration like the rain in the Karoo. There you would go out into the rain, run through it, hope that it would continue, that the raindrops would get harder and more dense, turn your face up to it. Even, if you were a child, run around in it with no clothes on. Stupid that you couldn't do that when you got older. No, this rain was fine and endless and people fought against it. Melanie herself waged a long battle against the damp it created. It was a damp that entered into her soul as much as into the nooks and crannies of her windows and doors.

Jeremy's family had been a challenge. She had a heightened sensitivity to their subtle assessment of her failings. Early on she became aware that there was a girl called Veronica, whom they were all terribly keen on, but who'd had to bow out of the picture now you're here, Melanie dear. She knew her table manners were different from theirs, that she suddenly became very clumsy, that she blushed when spoken to, that she behaved like the caricature they had in their minds. And Jeremy hadn't helped her. He'd been all right until they were really in the middle of it. Then he became oblivious, switched himself off from the tussle between the old and new parts of his life, assuming the protagonists would sort it out eventually between them.

His sister Julia had been the worst. She was constantly bursting into braying little giggles, often in response to some terribly ordinary comment of Melanie's, forced out of her by his parents' determined efforts to include her in the conversation. They had been in England for three months, visiting his parents every Sunday, before Julia addressed her directly. And then it was to ask her to say things so that she, Julia, could get a better handle on her accent, because she 'did' it for the girls at the office and they all thought it was such a scream, so could she say 'of course I did' and 'I really like', because 'reely' was really terribly quaint.

Jeremy, eventually concerned by Melanie's silent reluctance to attend the weekly ritual, had chosen his side and taken Julia off into the front room. She left shortly after that, in tears. His mother, drying as Melanie washed, said, 'It needed doing, dear. Things will change now. I'm glad he's finally put his foot down. They're terribly close, really.' A weight was lifted. It wasn't her imagination or her hypersensitivity. Everyone knew and now everyone would do something about it. Perhaps they could even be friends, she had thought. It had not happened that way. Julia took her war underground. Time and Melanie's inability to produce children, never mentioned but ever present, wore away her defences. She laboured under the knowledge that everyone felt sorry for her and even more sorry for Jeremy, especially Julia. But not today, she thought. Not today.

Shirley and the children paused in front of the window and waved. Shirley mouthed, 'Do you need anything?' Melanie shook her head and smiled, waved back. Blessed Shirley. Not even Shirley knew. But this morning, this morning the doctor knew. The practice nurse knew. And today, Jeremy would know. Then she could tell Shirley. But not the family. Not until later. Funny, she thought, whom we will allow into our vulnerabilities.

She took off her apron and went upstairs to her dressing-room. In the top drawer was a small package wrapped in newspaper and string. It had a little beaded tassle on the string. Written on the faded newspaper was the message, *To Melly. Come back one day. Sophie.*

Ten long years ago, opening their wedding presents, Jeremy had been enchanted. 'Who's this, darling?'

'We were friends when we were children. Very close friends. But we grew apart. It wasn't encouraged.' Melanie hadn't wanted to open the gift. It was too painful. Even the tassle hurt her. It was home, it was everything about home that she didn't allow herself to miss. The traditional bride's beaded headband that came out of the wrapping, with all the blessings inside the intricate work that must have taken months to make and so had been hurriedly adapted for her, had pressed down on her like a dark weight of loss, a crying and a craving that she couldn't acknowledge.

Not today, she thought. Today she wanted to hold the

beads against her tummy and let the child feel the energy of Africa that came with them, the bright colours that looked so gaudy in this sitting-room but that would flash proudly on a woman's head under the vast blueness of the Karoo sky. I can give you this, she thought. I can give you a land that will cradle you. Out of habit she brought the beads to her nose to see if there would be some hint of the smell of the hands of the women who had done the work.

She was six months pregnant when they went to the South Downs for the day. It was spring, miraculously the sky was blue. Clouds floated quite low above them as they drove down in Jeremy's father's car. They parked at Ditchling Beacon and then joined the throng walking on either side along the ridge that crossed the Sussex Weald. They walked slowly, stopping every now and then to admire a kite or to watch the shadows the clouds cast fleetingly over the land. Jeremy was carrying their lunch and they found a quiet spot on the slope of the down to eat it. Melanie lay back on the grass. It was beautiful, carefully laid out, the English countryside. She knew that it was this sense of structure, the routines, the carefully laid out hedgerows that had been there for generations, the oak trees that were hundreds of years old, that gave Jeremy and his family, even if they didn't realise it, the sense they had of always being right, knowing very clearly what was the right way for things to be and the wrong way. Anything that wasn't the way that they were used to was the wrong way. Anybody who did things the wrong way wasn't one of them. Never would be. She would always be foreign. Somehow she didn't mind now. Her baby wouldn't be foreign. He could be like them if he wanted.

She was reluctant to leave that afternoon, pressing Jeremy to stay just a little longer. In her entreaties and promises he rediscovered the contrast between her past life and her present life. He rarely thought about the claustrophobia bound to beset her, had assumed she would eventually find urban English life as normal and reassuring as he did. But now it came tumbling out. How she wouldn't complain even to herself if she had to walk along nothing but streets again for another three months if they could just stay here a little longer, please Jeremy, the sky is so beautiful and the horizon is so wide, please . . .

They stayed into the evening, until the stars were out and she could lie back and look at the sky, a different sky from the one she was used to, but a black dome above her head nevertheless. Wrapped in the picnic rug, staring upwards, she was in another world. Jeremy felt the difference. Suddenly she was the slightly wild, humorous girl he'd found ten years ago in that dour household, with the gentle smile and the giggle that started quite low in her throat. She was changed, quieter, he thought. Almost English now in her appearance. She looked fragile, heavily pregnant, with a distant longing on her face that he knew she normally kept from him. He took her hand.

'I'm sorry, Melly,' he managed.

'It's all right, I'm all right,' she said.

'The last time you said that you had blood all over your face,' he said. 'We'll move. We'll find somewhere where you can sit in the garden and watch the sky. We'll move as soon as the baby's old enough for you to cope.' She gripped his hand tightly. He was undone by the weight of her gratitude.

Michael Carter was born by Caesarean section at 4 o' clock in the morning. Melanie Carter, exhausted by a difficult labour and groggy from the anaesthetic, stared into the baby's coal-black eyes. They were misty, as though he wasn't yet quite of this world. Perhaps, she thought, he isn't altogether with us yet. He is still drifting in the realm of the miraculous. But when he does fully come to belong with us, then he will be warm and held and loved. This world will not frighten him until he is old enough to stare it down. The nurses laid the child in the cot next to her bed and encouraged her to rest. Through the day, tended by the nurses around them, the mother and child watched each other, drifting back and forth through differing planes of consciousness, but with the eyes of each always resting upon the eyes of the other.

Jeremy brought noise, excitement, flowers, conversation. He cradled his son, talked to him, kissed him on his nose. Stroked his wife's hair. Grinned a lot. She smiled at him. It was nice to see him, to feel his happiness. It would be good for her child to have a happy father, one who loved him and who taught him the ways of the world.

She and the child reverted to their silent communion once he had gone.

The small band of !Kung watched in silence as the military trucks kicked up clouds of dust from the newly created dirt road towards Tsumkwe. Their land was invaded. To the north the land was being filled with mines, evil tins buried in the sand that could blow a man or a child to bits. Such indiscriminate killing and maiming was a deliberate horror. Evil planted into the fabric of the earth. No one would admit to fear, but watching the bodies of the men the whites called terrorists dragged by the feet behind the army trucks through the villages and settlements of northern South-West Africa, the !Kung knew they would not escape. And the black men, the Tswana, the Herero, the Ovambo and all the others who were joined together in this war, were adamant they would spare no !Kung or Hai//om or Nharo or any other Bushman tribe that aided the white oppressors.

They would not be left outside this horror. !Katchu and his family discussed their options at length. The whites wanted them to be trackers. They would not have to fight as such, just track. But whoever heard of a soldier who was not expected to fight? If they wore a uniform then they would be part of this war and they would have to fight to defend themselves. Against people with whom they had no quarrel. Alongside people they feared and hated. And no !Kung could respect a man who told others what to do, who put himself above his fellows. How could they manage this army experience then? But what choice did they have? The South Africans were in their lands, war was spreading its evil. And it seemed impossible that SWAPO could win this war.

The South Africans were too fierce, too well equipped. The young men that came in their hundreds and thousands to the border posts were well fed, strong and armed with guns, tanks, bigger guns that could shoot rockets. They had helicopters too, great machines that could stand almost still in the sky and relay to those below a bird's view of the battlefield. But it was in the dense bush that they could be defeated by ambush, by even the simple wire strung from one tree to another that removed a head like a knife the tip of a thumb. It was here they wanted the !Kung. To find the men and women who were crossing the line they had drawn across the land.

The South African army would provide food, shelter, training. SWAPO could not protect the !Kung. If they stayed, they would have to help the South Africans. The only alternative was to leave. !Katchu sighed. Again. They would move down, away from the border, into the centre again. They would share the hunting lands of the G/wi. But he resented it with a deep bitterness. This land was the land of his birth. It held his life story. Realistically he could not fight for it. But he would not fight for the South Africans. No man was going to tell him what to do. He and his family would leave. Many others waited, hoping the uniform of war would not be inevitable.

When Michael was two years old, Jeremy inherited his uncle's estate and he moved his family into the large house he had visited as a child in the lee of the Sussex downs. The house in Croydon was replaced by a small flat in the City, where Jeremy stayed for a couple of nights a week, taking the train from Lewes on Mondays and Wednesdays.

Coming home on a summer's evening he would find Melanie and the boy under a tree in the garden, tea things and toys spread around, and he would stand watching her reading and his heart would fill with something enormous and slightly painful. Then he would descend upon them, kissing his wife and scooping up his son and wonder at his good fortune.

All was well then, and yet . . . Melanie. She was at home, safe with his son. She was kind, gentle, loving. But frequently he would wonder if she was really engaged with the world. She was restrained, quiet. These were not things a reasonable man could complain about. The job of building a career was consuming and it was natural and normal that he should take his family a little for granted. There was the pressing business of providing for his son's education. He tried to dismiss the little nagging worry about his wife, she was everything a man could want. He totally ignored any loneliness he felt.

Melanie and Michael routinely climbed to a small clearing at the top of a hill overlooking a wide valley with a stream at the bottom. There she would lift him out of his buggy and leave him free to run around and poke at things in the undergrowth, let him get used to the scratchiness of the world, so unlike the baby-powder softness of the nursery. He fell over frequently, and on one particular day, they both encountered the aggressive sting of nettles. Melanie, not knowing what it was, was unable to soothe Michael, who began to scream. As his tears poured down his face and his screams tore at her nerves, she wrapped him in his clothes, put him in the buggy and began to go as quickly as she could down the hill. She was at the bottom, wondering whether to go first to the surgery or to drive to the nearest house, when she realised a large black woman was bearing down on her and that her own stinging had stopped. Michael continued hysterical.

'What is it?' the woman was standing solicitously over the child in the pushchair. 'What's worrying such a fine young man?'

Melanie tried to explain, pointed to the red rashes on their skins. The woman laughed a great shaking laugh, swung an instantly quietened Michael up into her arms and led Melanie off in search of dock leaves. It was too late, she explained, to do much good, but this was the local solution to the problem of the nettle and Melanie wasn't to feel bad about it, because she, Jasmine, had made a similar mistake when she first arrived in the English countryside. So, where was Melanie from?

She didn't want to say. She was suddenly ashamed and she didn't want to say. 'Africa,' she managed at last. Jasmine showed no surprise. Little thing had been very frightened by the nettles. That was the problem with England, in her opinion. It lulled you into a false sense of security, with everything so beautiful and orderly. Then out of nowhere a plant could bite you like that. You couldn't trust appearances in England. And yet you so wanted to. You so wanted to believe that no harm could come to you in this beautiful ordered myth of a country. That was it, you wanted to believe in the myth and disbelieve that it was filled with human beings who weren't necessarily a part of that myth at all. Until you turned a corner and saw a hate slogan painted on a wall.

Melanie was anxious to get away from the woman. She

didn't want to answer questions. So she thanked her, made her excuses and walked off quickly. Feeling guilty, cross. She had left it all behind. It had no right to pop up in Sussex. What was the woman doing here anyway?

When she picked Michael out of the buggy and held him close she could smell the woman on his clothing. A sweet soapy smell of rich skin and firm hands. Hands that had pink palms with deep brown lines in them and melted chocolate outsides. Hands that could soothe a child in milliseconds. She carefully changed him and put the clothes into a drawer. She wanted to hoard the smell. Then she unwrapped the beaded headband she had received from Sophie. She scraped her hair back in front of the mirror and placed the band firmly on her head. She dropped her shirt and slipped her bra off her shoulders, fetched a bright red towel from the bathroom and wound it around her chest. She took off her pedal-pushers and her shoes and walked barefoot around the house, swaying her hips and singing long soft notes. Then she hung the beads on her dressing-table mirror. And then removed them before Jeremy came home. They looked incongruous and accusing, on the dressing-table mirror.

Africa is not easily dismissed by its children. Sometimes at night Melanie would wake from a dream in a panic and lie, smothered by the damp closeness of the world around her, longing for the sweet smell of the land after rain, for the damp, strong breeze that heralds the storm and for the clean freshness of the early morning. And most of all she would long for open space and big horizons, for a place where she could turn three hundred and sixty degrees and not see another person or even a house in all her field of vision, just the land.

It seemed to her that she would never return. To go back was impossible now. But she had little in England that was hers. She liked the people she knew, but she didn't understand them very well. Occasionally she longed for the familiarity which came from not being polite, from sometimes saying what you thought and to hell with the consequences. She didn't really have that with Jeremy. In some way she believed herself to be here on his suffrance and that her duty was to keep him happy. And she was grateful to him. Which didn't equate somehow with being able to complain. And how could she complain about civilised behaviour? And why should it be Jeremy's problem that there was no one around her who could share her history? Who understood her second language and who would know what it was like to come down the kopjie in the dark with a lantern and see the sudden huge shadows, black patches in the blue-black of the night, bats swooping overhead? Know what it was like to sit inside and see in the pool of light that came from the dining-room window the flying ants that would come after the rain and crawl all over the ground, leaving their wings behind them? It wasn't something you could explain.

There was a rhythm to her days with the child. She was careful to meet with other young mothers, to provide him with a social group. She reflected on how easy it was to be busy and not engaged, to be present and yet not participate. For months after the encounter with Jasmine, she found herself looking for her. She wanted to talk to her, even, if truth be told, find some way whereby she, Melanie, could be held by the woman and weep, just weep for everything that she couldn't express. But of course that was outrageous.

The people around her began to accept that she was quiet, and liked her the more for it. She listened well and asked kind questions and rarely offended. But sometimes she could be caught unawares staring into the distance in the queue at the bank, and there were strangers who wondered where the young woman with the toddler holding her hand had disappeared to, because she was a very long way away indeed.

The images in her mind hadn't lost their clarity over time. No, she could use her memory like a library. She would draw upon a colour seen in a catalogue or on a child's jumper. Crimson became the soft, four-sided tulip boxes of the bougainvillaea that flowered on the white wall of the farmhouse. Charcoal grey in the ashes of the fire would become the steaming, shimmering border of the mountains under the white haze of heat that rose up against them. There was no memory attached to deep green grass, nor to the thick carpet of leaves that filled the forest paths in autumn. The translucent, light-reflecting yellow of the leaves was new and carried no memory, like the red-edged leaves that glistened in a carpet pattern on the tans, yellows and rich greens at her feet.

The child was the bridge for her to the old world and slowly she tried to cross it. They would walk in the woods with books tucked into the back of the buggy. She would try and identify a leaf, a tree, every day. Then she would mark it, intending to review it when the seasons changed. She would, for her son's sake, and later for her own, learn to love the evolution of the silver birch from spring to spring. They could identify the nettle now and shout at it the two of them, 'Horrid, horrid thing!' and there was no one to consider them strange. They watched squirrels together, and birds – she wanted to show the ones to her son that would go back to Africa for the winter. And then together they would welcome them when they came for the summer. Perhaps the birds would bring with them a little of the land, and surely, if they could be so happy here, sing so sweetly in the spring, then she too could learn to be in two places at once?

She set out to adopt Jeremy's customs, traditions and

values. They were more comfortable, and needed no questions. They were right. She stepped on to the bridge for reasons of love. It was all a question of balance.

When Michael was four, Jeremy Carter sat at his desk in his study and watched his wife and son playing with the newly acquired dog on the lawn outside his window. The scene made him uncomfortable. They didn't speak much, the two of them. They communicated, but they certainly didn't speak very much. When something happens quite slowly, you don't always immediately register what it is that worries you. But now as he watched them throwing the ball for the dog and heard only the dog barking and the odd laugh from Michael, he finally decided that something was wrong. This wasn't normal. Melanie had become quieter and quieter over the past six years, but that was a different issue. The boy shouldn't be this quiet. Boys were meant to be noisy and dirty and full of cheek. Not quiet and observant like his son.

He completed the application form to the school he and his father had attended and put it into an envelope to be mailed. He'd walk down to the village with it in the evening. No need to worry Melanie about it until it was arranged.

When he did break the news to her she seemed to cope fairly well. Of course, it was an alien concept to her. But when Michael was eight he took her and the boy to the school so that they could see the cosy, small dormitories with the brightly coloured bedcovers and the warm housemistress and the excellent recreational facilities. Every generation gets it easier, he thought. My father thought I was positively mollycoddled. He smiled at what his father might have thought about the Beatrix Potter motifs on the bedroom walls.

Melanie was, if it was possible, even quieter that evening. He tried to explain about it.

'We need to do the very best for him, don't we?' A nod in agreement.

'And giving him the skills he needs to succeed in a competitive environment is part of that. There's no point in bringing him up to be privileged and completely out of touch with reality, is there?' A dark shadow in her eyes as she tried to assess if this was a criticism.

'My dear, there is such a thing as too much love.'

The dark eyes went quite cold. 'Not for a child there isn't. And he is a child, Jeremy. Not a little man. A child. Let him go when he's eleven or twelve.'

'It's much easier the earlier they go. Believe me. It can't hurt him, Melly. If he is desperately unhappy he can come home. Does that make it easier?' She didn't reply, just looked at him in the way he had come to know meant acceptance. He took a great deal of their silent communication for granted.

Michael learned a lot in his first terms at school. The core lesson was privacy. Keeping things to yourself. You didn't give people ammunition to use against you. If you let them know that something mattered to you terribly, then you were at risk. And mockery was everything. It kept you in your place, stopped you from taking your homesickness too seriously, stopped you from feeling too sorry for yourself, gave you a means of hitting back in revenge at anyone else, it toughened you up and made you self-sufficient, mockery.

And overcoming, that was another lesson. Overcoming your fear of the dark and the agony of bedwetting and the violence of the rugby field, that toughened you up too. You were part of a club, a club that could overcome and do it with good humour. You were better because you could endure more and feel less. You wanted to belong to the club because it was the only one available to you. And if you didn't belong adequately enough, then you might have to go home and find another, lesser club that would accept you as a lesser, failed human being.

When Melanie drove up to fetch Michael for his first holiday, she watched him carefully through the goodbyes to his new friends, his reserved hello and his new, even more self-contained demeanour. He was solicitous of her and yet distant, a different child from the one she had brought to this place a few weeks ago. She didn't say much, just let the silence work its way over them both. There was a new tightness, though. A sense of enclosure in the child. He was held together inside himself by a form of will. Restraint. He was absorbing restraint. She turned the car towards the coast.

'Where are we going?'

'To the sea.'

'Why?'

'You'll see.'

The windscreen-wipers slip-slapped. It was misty grey outside, the sort of grey that enclosed you inside a car and made the progress of raindrops down the side windows something important, though it was impossible to say why.

It had stopped raining when they finally reached a long stretch of wet, dark-grey sand. She parked and locked the car and told Michael to take off his shoes and his socks, his blazer and his tie, everything except his shorts and pullover. He stood in front of her, questioning. 'But it's my uniform. I'm not allowed . . . '

'You are if your mother insists. And anyway, without the blazer and tie you'll be a boy in a pair of grey shorts.'

He did as she said and then stood shivering a little as the breeze was fresh and the greyness still surrounded them, merging with the steel-grey of the sea. 'Now what?'

'Now run to the edge of the water and splash your feet and then run on some more and do it again. And yell.'

'Yell what?'

'Anything. I'll come with you. We can yell together.'

She took off her shoes, her stockings and the jacket of her suit and they ran to the edge of the water and she threw water at him and tried to swing him into the sea and he shrieked and raced away, and she left him to run with the dog, across the sand with the wide expanse of the sea next to him and nothing on his skin except his grey shorts, and yes, he did, he yelled, meaningless threats at seagulls that he and the dog chased off the beach. He jumped up and down, looking at the small waves of the quiet sea, and wanted to fling himself about.

Finally she joined him and they stood for a while skimming stones across the water, throwing a stick for the dog to retrieve, the boy taking long runs to show his new bowling technique. They held hands as they walked back to the car, restored. She knew. She understood. She hadn't embarrassed him at the school. She'd dressed up, which was good, and she looked pretty. That was also good. And even better, she'd been a little formal with him. She'd brought the dog to meet him. And now everything was OK.

That evening when she went to tell him a bedtime story she held out her arms to him for a hug, and as she felt the small body nestled up against her and smelt the childhood of her son, she knew it was unlikely that she would be able to reach him like this again. The school would absorb him and turn him into his own private person. It was how he would survive. Her bridge was down. It wasn't the child's fault.

In the years that followed, both Melanie and Jeremy wished that they could create a bridge between themselves. But somehow the distance between them couldn't be spanned. They managed extreme politeness to each other, a comforting, gentle courtesy that they accepted as the most they could achieve. Jeremy found stimulation in his work. He continued to advance quickly and surely. His circle of friends grew, he was often delayed in town. And Melanie's horizons narrowed. Sometimes she felt as though she was bearing a weight that would crush her, but she never let Jeremy know. She missed her son.

She practised deception remarkably easily. It was important that Jeremy believed she was all right. Why this was so was not something she questioned or even thought about. It just was important. And so she would get up in the mornings with him and make him breakfast and chat gently, bringing in the milk and unfolding the newspaper. As soon as he left, she would drag herself upstairs, quite spent, and go back to bed. She would sleep until midday at least, lying cocooned inside the bed, ignoring the telephone, the occasional visitor.

In the afternoon, after encouraging herself for at least an hour, she would get up, run a bath and begin to plan how she would clear the breakfast dishes and organise Jeremy's dinner in the remaining time available. He was her deadline. Some nights she cut it a little fine and would have to invent some social afternoon thing, and he would always be pleased then, to see her busy.

It was a slow process, this losing touch with each other. For Jeremy it was not a conscious process. He had married her and she had borne him a son. He loved her, there was no question about it. Now he would provide for her and his son to the best of his ability. That was his job and he was going to do it damned well. The office was the office and home was his escape from it. Melanie and his home were the places where he had never yet been a failure, where there was no trace of the occasional dressing down, no lingering mild humiliations. And as Jeremy moved up the ladder he had chosen for himself, the achievements became more frequent and the fear much less. Then he looked at his wife and wished that in some way she could better appreciate his success, that he could find a way, without being ridiculously egocentric, to communicate it to her. He bought her jewellery, increased her allowances, told her to buy clothes, smiled happily when she asked whether they could afford it.

It dawned on him, one evening as they were sitting listening to a radio play, that they hadn't had a real conversation, something that excluded Michael, in months. Maybe even years. He waited until the play was over and they were getting ready for bed.

'Melly . . . Do you think we talk enough?'

She'd been surprised, turned with that gentle slowness of hers (when had that started?), said, 'Is there something we need to talk about?'

'Not need to talk about, no, certainly not need to talk about . . . I just wondered, this evening, well, if you're all right, really . . . I mean if you're all right within yourself . . . '

'I'm fine . . . Jeremy . . . is there something the matter?'

Now she looked a little frightened. Dammit.

'Nothing, really. It's just that we've both been so busy, you with the charity shop and me, well I'm always busy and tired . . . I just needed to check, that's all.'

Melanie opened her wardrobe, turned her back to him. She had given up the charity shop a year ago, never told him.

They made love that night, the first time in what seemed like ages, and it cut Melanie's heart and she cried, quietly in the darkness.

Jeremy was England and humanity, unexpected and completely innocent random acts of kindness. His lovemaking had often done it to her. His inside was so clean, somehow, that it was more than she could bear. If he had asked her then, when they were curled together, when he had opened her up and caressed the bruised heart of her, then she would have told him. It would have all come spewing out, the exhaustion and depression, the sense she had of carrying the heaviest of weights around with her, the need and the impossibility of making things right. Jeremy had no experience of real corruption. He was clean. And she wanted to keep him like that. And wanted him to approve of her, wanted to be for him everything that he deserved.

It lasted, this unexceptional subterfuge, throughout Michael's schooldays. In the holidays they took as a family there were enough 'recovery periods', when the two men went off together, for Melanie to lie in a dark room and black out the world. She would give herself a whole day on occasion, running out for the last two hours to do some shopping that she had quietly pinpointed the day before to justify her hours. Her weakness made her efficient. She imagined that this was how an addict would behave, carefully planning life around the next fix.

The deception exhausted her too. She was on a treadmill that she didn't understand. Jeremy, referring to Melanie's quietness in public, would occasionally wonder if it was true that she had always been quiet. By the time Michael was finishing his A levels and thinking about his year off, it was a real effort for Melanie to speak. He was a stranger to her now, a strong young man whom she loved but who had grown up away from her; he was a person, an other, a part of the deception. And perhaps, deep in her heart, she resented that he could no longer be her bridge to the world. He was of it, she was not.

She gave up the day after Michael's twenty-first-birthday party. They had done it all at home, and she had drawn on every reserve she had to make it a success. Once the marquee was gone and order restored, she lay down on her bed and found she couldn't get up. The deadline she set for herself was missed. Jeremy arrived home and called the doctor in a panic. She couldn't speak. She just lay with her eyes shut and wished that everyone would go away.

The doctor checked her into hospital and they ran endless tests. She still didn't speak. Eventually they moved her to Tranquillity, a rest-home for the well-insured mentally ill. She saw Jeremy's suffering, heard his repeated entreaties that she speak to him, but did not have any sensation at all. No guilt, no pain, no answering pangs. She was quite unaffected. No longer having to make the effort to function, ending the constant deception, was a matter of peace. It was a numbness of the brain, a soupiness, a softer world where all the edges were slightly blurred. And if she felt so inclined, and she very much did feel so inclined, she could let the blurring eclipse the entire picture. She could sink into herself like a marsh-mallow and squat, cushioned, with no pressure to come out and no real reason to attempt it either.

6

England, 1999

The letter accused him. Michael didn't want to open it. It would mean a visit to his mother and he would feel obliged to go and he didn't want to. The cream envelopes from Tranquillity were easy to recognise. They used to be brown and when they changed to cream he'd opened one without the necessary preparation. He had two responses to the envelopes. On good days, he'd open it right away, get the moment over and make the necessary arrangements. Usually he would want to hide it, leave it to wait malevolent on the kitchen counter for a stronger moment. Which never came. Then another envelope would arrive a few weeks later and this would be a little more urgent, referring to the previous, still unopened, envelope. And if he didn't open that one then there would be a telephone call. And he would despise the feeble lies he would create to avoid responsibility for the damned missives.

He opened it. It informed him that his mother had a new therapist, Dr Cunningham, who would like to interview him. Perhaps he could combine the interview with a visit? And then the standard paragraph about how it was always helpful for patients to be reminded of their homes and the love of their families. And what about the family, he thought. Is it helpful to us? They arrived like cream assassins, invading his London flat, the damned things.

He hated seeing his mother. Hated, hated, hated it. The first time had been the worst. He'd come home from university and gone with his father. Jeremy had done his best to explain the inexplicable. They'd driven mostly in silence, unable to communicate, joined together in their helplessness. At first he'd been convinced that he could do something, that he, Michael, would find the necessary stimulus, the necessary response to bring her back to life. But when he'd looked into the emptiness of her eyes he'd recoiled, felt sick. There was no one there to stimulate, no one to bring back. He'd held the thought tightly inside himself that she was actually dead.

Afterwards he and his father had gone for a drink. They hadn't been able to say much – had taken refuge in practical arrangements. His father had aged. Michael didn't want to be around his father's new-found fragility, evidenced in a bizarre tentativeness. He couldn't bear it. They were his parents, for God's sake.

The impact of the letter was less like a black cloud descending than like a dull weight that he'd temporarily been able to lay aside reappearing, bearing down on his private universe. It was a feeling not unlike suffocation. It had occurred to him to see a therapist himself, or some sort of counsellor, but it went against the grain somehow. Letting a complete stranger into the labyrinth of his anger felt obscene. It wasn't something to share.

He went down to Sussex the following weekend. The house was hibernating. The trees around it stood bare and frightening, stick monsters that had haunted Michael on winter's nights as a child. He had telephoned Benjamin the day before and expected that the basics would be done, the heating turned up, the fireplace laid, milk and bread in the kitchen.

The portico light was on. Michael let himself into the hallway. The house was an odd mixture of colonial style and English chintz. The only part of the house that seemed to change at all was the kitchen, where Benjamin's wife Sally seemed to move things around all the time. Benjamin and Sally had lived in a cottage in the grounds ever since Michael could remember. Benjamin looked after the house and grounds and Sally was a potter. Michael's father had installed a kiln for her in one of the sheds and her wares were all over the kitchen and in gift shops across Sussex. Sally was a large, matronly woman. The sort who should have had five children. Sally too had become quiet over the years. Michael could remember her when he was eight or nine and she was always laughing.

Sally had left a note for Michael.

Dear boy, I have some things for your mother. Please come by the cottage before you go. Casserole in the oven.

Yours, Sal

Michael slept in one of the guest bedrooms now. His childhood bedroom remained untouched, with its books and toy aeroplanes, fishing tackle and model ships. The guest bedroom he chose looked out on to the fields that his father leased to a local farmer. He opened the window, felt the sharp shock of the raw country air in his lungs. Shut it again. The house had a stillness that Michael both sought and avoided. His sensibilities were tuned now to constant background noise. Here in the shadow of the South Downs there was no sound at all. He remembered being startled by the faint scratching of his eyelashes against the pillow.

He went down to the kitchen and took the casserole out of the bottom of the Aga. It smelt gamey. He set a place at the kitchen table and went into the cellar for a bottle. He would have a decent one, a tribute to the casserole. The stillness, food, wine and pure sounds of the King's College choristers should have sent him early to bed. Instead he found himself wandering the house.

His parents' room remained as it had always been. He knew that his father never used it. He too chose to use a guest bedroom. He sat on the double bed and looked at his mother's dressing-table. It was an evocative and dangerous piece of furniture. He sat at it to conquer its potency. Opened the top drawer. It was tidy. Bits of make-up and a hairbrush with fine brown hairs still lodged within its bristles which made him feel slightly nauseous. There was a small package, wrapped in tissue paper. He opened it idly. It contained an old beaded African band with a red, yellow and blue pattern, similar to things he'd seen in Camden market, and a couple of stones. The stones were still rough, one with a streak of amethyst, the other a dull red colour. Since they held none of the power of the past for him, he found them appealing and pocketed them. They neutralised things, somehow.

He woke at first light, with little of the combative struggle against waking that characterised weekdays. It was cold when he left the house and he thrust his hands into his jacket pockets, zipped its green oiliness up to his throat. The sun was ahead of him, a blood redness across the sky as it tried to penetrate the lines of cloud that hovered near the horizon. A white track across the dark-blue sky above, the trail of a plane that had left from Gatwick, was the only reminder of man.

Michael had a deep relationship with the English countryside. He loved it like this – quiet and just awakening. He had fancied, as a child, that, like the children in Kipling's story, he too had his own Puck and could summon up from the land the sense of its ancient history. For all that it had been thoroughly tamed, it was still possible to discern ancient England, feel the wilderness that underlay the cultivated fields.

The valley that was his destination was a wild place, parts of it overgrown with brambles and in spring its clearings covered in bluebells. A stream ran through the middle of it. Michael reached the brow of the hill from where he had intended to view the frost in his valley. It was covered in mist. The mist reached to the brow of the hill, making a cauldron of the hollow below. The bare tops of the beech trees were visible, looking like water trees peeping out of a lake. The red sun was tinting the sky, but down here there was only blue light. Michael climbed on to the stile and sat, watching.

He heard a rustling behind him, was startled to see a fox staring at him. He sat perfectly still, admiring its huge brush of a tail, its chiselled face. The fox continued to stare at him. Michael didn't move. It looked away, looked back at Michael. He looked into its eyes. Then it turned and flashed into the undergrowth next to the field.

The mist was slowly dissolving below him as the sun gradually changed from scarlet to golden. There were deep shadows still in the valley but he could make out the familiar trees. They were bleak skeletons with a white frost carpet beneath them. Michael sat and waited for the sun to expose the full picture. He was not thinking about anything, an ability that was perhaps the most valuable of gifts.

His appointment was at eleven o'clock. He arrived on time, turned in between manicured lawns. The place itself wasn't threatening. Everything was orderly, there were no obtrusive bars on windows or anything like that. No overly excitable cases. Tranquillity afforded its occupants and their relatives a private measure of comfort. But his heart still raced a little and a mild nausea, present since breakfast, made his movements a bit uncertain.

Elizabeth Cunningham had a pleasant face. A pleasant voice. She poured the tea and sat across from Michael. He wondered if he was sitting in the chair his mother sat in when she came for sessions. Once a week, as Elizabeth had explained. He hadn't seen her yet.

They had covered the introductions, the niceties, and now sat in silence.

'Michael,' she began gently, 'how does your mother's condition make you feel?'

He felt disinclined to answer. 'I don't think how I feel has anything to do with it.'

'You sound angry. Are you?'

He was closer to tears than rage and the knowledge appalled him. 'I'm not sure I want to talk about it.'

'Do you talk to anyone about it?'

'No.'

'Are you ashamed?'

Oh, for fuck's sake. He took a deep breath. 'Look. I . . . Well, I feel the way any right-minded person would feel about it. Bloody awful. OK?' It had come out aggressive, defensive. He took another deep breath. Stirred his tea. Slopped it.

'It is a very hard thing to endure. For you and your father.'

He wanted to leave and he wanted to howl. He said nothing.

'Michael . . . Tell me about your mother. How would you describe her? Before she was ill.'

He sat looking at the view of the fields outside.

'She was . . . She was perfect.' He hadn't meant to say that. 'She . . . she just knew things. You didn't have to tell her. She just knew. If things were bloody, she knew. And she knew what to do about it.'

'What sort of things?'

'School, things like that. She knew when to leave me alone. She knew when to . . . When to be there. Her knowing things made a difference.'

'She sounds remarkable.'

'She was.' He paused, breathed out. 'And now she's dead.'

She let the sentence float about the room a while. Something in his chest relaxed.

'And you can't grieve because her body is still alive.'

'Yes.' He wanted to stop the tears from falling and so he stared at the fields outside, focusing hard on a tree. She gave him space to recover.

He hated asking. 'Will she get better? Ever?'

'I don't know. It's been a long time. I don't want to give you false hope. But, Michael . . . you are entitled to mourn the loss you have experienced. It doesn't mean you've given up on her. It just means that you've suffered the loss of her. You are entitled to grieve.'

He wanted to say that he didn't know how. That he couldn't, alone, open that Pandora's box of pain. He hated this, feeling like a child. And yet he wanted to stay here, with this woman, and get rid of it.

She began to ask the traditional questions. He'd been through the process before.

When he left he felt bereft. She'd held his hand, not shaken it. Suggested he might like to seek bereavement counselling. He knew that his mother was her patient, not him. Stupidly he wished it were the other way round. She directed him to where his mother was sitting in the conservatory, but he escaped to the men's room first.

Sitting in a stall, he held his head in his hands and tried to calm himself. Shit, shit, shit. This was the worst visit so far and he hadn't seen her yet. He felt indescribably tired.

His mother was sitting in a wicker chair. From a distance she looked absolutely normal. She even had lipstick on. He went to sit next to her, kissed her cheek, murmured greetings. As ever there was no response. He stared at her. It made no bloody difference if he was there or not. But he always felt obliged to try. He took her hand. She didn't return any pressure. Then he took the stones and the beads out of his pocket. He wasn't expecting any response, it was more to have something to do. He reckoned the minimum time he could decently stay was thirty minutes.

He wrapped her hand around one of the stones. She closed her eyes and he saw the hand tighten on the stone. Or had he imagined it? He put the other stone in the other hand to see what would happen. Yes, she had definitely tightened her grip on it. There was no reason to feel excitement, but he did. He took one of the stones away and replaced it with a tea-cup. Deflated, he watched her hand tightening around it. He wanted to abuse her, in that moment. Mummy's little party trick. Holding things. He took the cup and the stone away from her, leaving her hands open in her lap. Then he put the beads across them. She closed her hands around them and then stiffened. Her eyes opened and she looked at them. Dropped them, suddenly. He was watching her intently. Then she picked them up and brought them to her nose. She was smelling them. Jesus. He felt sick. He had to get out, get some air.

The rear gardens of Tranquillity sloped downwards into a valley that was an impenetrable density of brambles, nettles, shrubs and creepers, disguising the fencing and hiding the trunks of the trees which waved stark, bare branches above the greenery. Melanie Carter stared down into the foliage from her chair on the lawn. Something about the greenery, its matted wildness, was prompting her memory, while her hand in her pocket held tightly on to a beaded headband.

The little red-headed nurse was sitting on the bench at the

top of the lawn, keeping an eye on her charges. The sunshine had been unexpected and they had all been willing to brave the cold for an hour outdoors. Most of them were drugged into docility but occasionally one would begin to wander about aimlessly. Like Mrs Carter had started to do. Unusual for her, Sheena thought as she went to steer her gently back to her seat. They were all intrigued by Mrs Carter. She seldom demonstrated any of the more unpleasant behaviours associated with mental illness. Her withdrawal was complete, as was her silence. But on the surface she managed her necessary daily functions with decorum, submitting docilely to the hairdressing, the manicures and pedicures. Unlike some, she never tried to undo their handiwork.

Sheena took Mrs Carter's arm and tried to turn her around, speaking gently. 'Come on, Mrs C, you could get lost wandering about. How about a nice cup of tea, hmmm?' Melanie Carter became aware of the distracting clucking at her side, the pressure on her arm. She looked down at the little freckled red head with the wide smile and then she growled. At least that's what it sounded like to Sheena, a deep, vibrating sound that froze the nurse for the seconds that Melanie needed to step up her pace and head for the valley.

Sheena watched her, stunned. Mrs C hadn't said anything, but she had made a sound. That had to be communication. Of a sort. Melanie Carter was twenty yards away, standing looking at a bramble with deep concentration. Sheena decided to edge closer to her but to stay within rescuing distance from the main house. She hadn't felt afraid, just stunned. There must be a rational explanation for it. Dr Cunningham would know. She would ask her. It might even be important to Mrs Carter's progress. Sheena kept a respectful, watchful distance alongside an oblivious Melanie Carter.

There was a residue of dew glistening softly in the folds of the nettles and dock leaves that grew around the base of the bramble. She distilled the panorama from the big valley down to the bramble, to the dock leaf, to the smallest drop of dew she could find. She stared and stared at it. And the background began to change, to harden, dry, become tan, brown, chalk-white dust. And the dew was a sparkling drop hanging at her mother's throat, but what was it doing here where she was lost?

Melanie could feel the heat, pushing down on her, the dryness in her throat that rasped. Her tongue, swollen, thickly searching for moisture in her mouth. The constant swallowing that hurt now, that was no longer worth the effort. And here was the dew drop, on the pale yellow stick of grass, so pure, so perfect, it couldn't be real. She stared at it and stared at it until it disappeared. It just got smaller and imperceptibly smaller and then, quite quickly, it was gone. And then? What then? The fragment slid past and the dew was still there, lying perfect in its English greenery. She turned to face the nurse. It took Sheena a minute to realise that the incomprehensible story she had been watching on Mrs Carter's features was now over, that she was needed. She took her arm and gently steered her towards the garden chair.

Sheena clucked and fussed reassuring sounds as Melanie Carter sank into the white wicker chair on the green, green lawn, submitted to being tucked into a rug, exhausted. She stared at the countryside that, had her memories remained intact, would have brought back the toy farmyard she was given as a child, one which bore no resemblance to the arid landscape and dirty grey sheep outside her front door.

Dr Cunningham was bent over her papers in her wood-panelled, carefully contrived office. Sheena tried to explain the sound. Elizabeth Cunningham listened carefully. Perhaps there was some link between it and the son's visit or the reduced medication. It was hard to tell which may have stirred her patient, even if momentarily, out of passivity into activity. To a self-determined action. She was pleased. She would ask the son to come again, soon.

The taxi-driver took Michael home over the pink-birthday-cake Albert Bridge. Lost in separate thoughts, the two men didn't see how the Thames was swollen by the primeval pull of the moon out of sight above London's mantle of cloud. They drove past the window behind which lived the Indian woman who was polishing everything to please the mother-in-law who was in love with her son, past the window behind which lived the family where the father had made good and the daughters went to private schools and spent their summers in the country, past the windows that were an endless and, to Michael, a reassuring guarantee of anonymity.

'It's economic slavery, eco . . . nom . . . ic slavery.' Basher's head drooped over the ice bucket. He steadied himself, carefully picked up his glass and emptied the contents down his throat. Then his head dropped forward again. Michael could see a fine line of grey in his parting. He was peering at Michael from under a fringe which sat like a small mat on his bulbous forehead. Basher's face was a mass of contradictions. A delicate nose and a fleshy mouth, a stubborn, dimpled jaw and delicate cheek-bones. As though two faces had been forced to compromise.

Michael considered how drunk he was himself. Anybody who could derive some meaning from Basher's face had had too much. 'Y'see,' Basher persevered, 'haven't got time. Time to do things, make things. No time. Just spend it making money. And drinking. A lot.' He giggled.

Michael moved the ice bucket away from Basher's flapping elbow. 'I'm off,' he said.

'Pissawfthen, you boring bastard,' Basher managed. 'Where's Roop?'

'Chatting up Malvern's secretary. At the bar. Why don't you join them?'

'He'd kill me. He'd fucking kill me!' Basher's laughter was like an inverted suction pipe, hissing as it went in and emitting a high-pitched sound as it was released.

It was a damp evening. Not wet, just early November grey damp with the acrid taste of London air. He thought he'd walk a bit, clear his head. Basher had yelled after him, 'You're apeckular chap, Carter, bloodyoddbod,' followed by giggles and mutterings that he hadn't waited to hear. The City was quiet, a few dark-suited drunks finding each other hilarious on the pavements.

It was inevitable that Michael had followed his father into the City. But it wasn't the City that he or his father remembered from his childhood. It was a more brutal place, one that seemed to foster the worst aspects of character. What do you expect, he thought to himself as he walked past the bank, from something that's built on power and greed. It was probably always like this, just covered itself more modestly before.

Not for the first time Michael wondered why he did what he did. Everyone seemed to think that it was exactly the right thing for him. And he was quite good at it, he admitted to himself. He had done well and still had an excellent future ahead of him, according to the bank. But it didn't feed that nagging part of him that he had been trained from youth to consider slightly shameful, possibly even unstable. He took the Thames path towards the Embankment. He'd walk until his head cleared and then he'd take a cab.

He loved London. Loved knowing his way around it and feeling utterly confident about his place within it. He had always been fascinated by the Thames and now he stood facing it, with his back to an illuminated St Paul's, distorted somehow by the perspective to seem closer and lower than it really was from the top of a flight of stairs leading down to the river. He watched the water flow. It was high tide and the water looked slick and oily black, the rolling waves more solid, slug-like and more viscous in the night than in the clarity of day.

He turned around to stare at the dome. People had probably thought Wren was a bit unstable, he thought. And then admitted it to himself. The real issue is having the guts to do the things you might not succeed at. Being able to take risks, do the unexpected and the unapplauded. Because you want to. It's guts. Having the guts to find out what matters to you and then pursuing it. I don't have that kind of strength, he thought. Everything has been too easy for me. And there's no reason why it shouldn't continue to be easy. And if I want excitement why don't I go and do what chaps do, hang-gliding or hunting or something physical? Because that's easy too. Damn, damn. Too much wine and all this introspection is very unhealthy.

Michael didn't particularly want to go home alone to his flat but right now there was nowhere else. He'd ended things with Janet a few weeks back. It wasn't, as he'd tried to explain, her fault. He could have chugged along with her for another couple of years. She was undemanding, good company, sexy. But he wasn't going to marry her and it was bad form to go on, using up these years of her life. She'd been upset, so had he. But relieved too. He let himself in, picked up his mail from the mat and went through it as he stripped off. He'd have a long hot bath.

The large mirror in the bathroom steamed up and the extractor fan began to hyperventilate. He liked it really hot, and full of herbal bathsalts, the hell with the machismo factor. He tried not to think about the following workday. It would arrive soon enough. Great, he sighed, there goes ninety per cent of your waking time. The mail had been good, even a letter from his friend Alec in Hong Kong.

Michael slid into the water and shut his eyes. He'd switched the bathroom light off, but street lighting still came into the functional modern room through the frosted glass in the window. He had placed the two stones on the side of the bath by the taps. They changed colour when they were wet and pleased him, somehow. He surfaced, opened his eyes.

In the steam patterns that swirled across the window, a face appeared, an ancient face, terribly lined, with peppercorn hair and a smile so broad it could have been a caricature. As the steam drifted over the glass the face crystalised for a second and the merry, ancient eyes winked at Michael. Then it was gone. Michael blinked. It was the Bushman. He hadn't seen the Bushman since he was a child, when he used to see him all the time. His father hadn't believed him. His mother had told him to keep it a secret. 'It's your own little bit of magic, Michael,' she'd said. 'Keep it close to yourself, don't give it away to other people. They won't understand and you'll lose it.' His mother . . . He got out of the bath. He had been careful, not told anyone about him, but the little Bushman had stopped coming as Michael grew older.

The Cunningham woman ambushed him with a message on the answerphone.

His mother was sitting alone in the conservatory. He wondered if it was because of Elizabeth's careful attempts not to raise his hopes that he tried not to think she might be a little more alert than usual. He sat down beside her, making small talk about the weather, how well she was looking, how his father sent his love, would be visiting the following week. He was self-conscious now there was an outside chance she might be absorbing what he had to say. He'd paused, uncomfortable, when she turned and looked at him. It was shocking. There was a person behind the normal blank of her eyes. A person that came and went, but a definite presence. She held his gaze for long seconds, then took his hand and held it in both of hers.

All the longing and missing of his mother that had lain stagnant and fermenting in Michael shot through him. She lifted her hand, stroked his face and with the most gentle of movements closed his stinging eyes. The caress was dazzling, disarming and painful. He opened his eyes. She sat perfectly still. Then she repeated her movement to close his eyes. Then he sat, every nerve-ending alert to the presence of her. She stroked his hand rhythmically.

Unbelievably it was calming. He felt himself relaxing into an experience he remembered from his childhood. He had been an occasionally anxious child, and his mother had used this calm stroking of his hands to soothe him. It created a deep relaxation that permeated the cordoned-off areas of his psyche, lulled him into a state not dissimilar to sleep. He fought the sensation, trying to reopen his eyes, but eventually succumbed to the half-world of waking dreams. Perhaps he even slept.

There was a bright light, a light that hurt his eyes and heat that seemed to dry the inside of his lungs. He was standing under a bowl of sky on a completely flat saucer of earth. In front of him stretched scrubland until it touched the edge of the bowl that was the relentless blue sky. Behind him were mountains that seemed to shimmer in the haze. He could feel the sun burning his scalp. To the left was a whitewashed farmhouse in the Cape Dutch tradition, with a thatched roof and a gable on the front. Some small outbuildings and a couple of paddocks were next to it. There were no animals.

He walked towards the house. There was a mewling sound coming from the interior, it sounded like a child crying. Michael walked faster, began to run. The front door was open. He stopped in the doorway and saw the blood on the walls. There were sticky pools of blood at his feet. He could hear his heart beating, feel his legs begin to tremble. The mewling sound had stopped. Inside the vaulted front room he registered a familiar rattan bench and his grandfather's sketches of herds of antelope on the walls. The mewling started again. He moved into the room, trying to avoid the blood on the floor, and saw the bodies lying in a heap. A white woman and a white man, both in their twenties, a black young woman dressed as a maid. Their throats had been cut and already the flies were settling on the black-red gashes that had almost severed the heads. The woman's eyes were open. She looked familiar – the blank eyes were those his mother had inherited. The mewling started again. It was coming from behind one of the curtains in a corner of the room.

The child was buried in the curtain, muffling hysterical cries. In his dream state he was powerless. He ached to pick her up, take her out of this grisly room. Such terror in a child should split that perfect bowl of sky. He heard a clicking sound, turned around. The Bushman was standing, his Bushman, holding out his hand to the little girl. The clicking was musical, like a lullaby. Michael knew that the child would respond. She let go of the curtain and, still sobbing, stared at the wizened little man. He was small, about five foot high, incredibly wrinkled, a strange dark apricot-yellow colour and completely naked, except for a bow, a sheath of arrows and the long sharp stick he held in his hand. He continued the little clicking sounds, moving closer to her.

The next thing Michael was aware of was a gentle shaking.

'Come on, it's home time.' The red-headed nurse was grinning at him. 'Time to go . . . '

His mother's chair was empty.

'She's been gone a good few minutes,' the nurse smiled at him.

Now he stood at his favourite spot on the river again. The gulls were bobbing on the tide beneath him. A young girl went by, humming and lugging a violin case. The South Bank, he thought. Music. He wondered how a young person grew up knowing they wanted to be a musician, or a writer, or a juggler, or a restorer of old paintings. People chose these professions, assuming they would never be rich. His father had instilled in him a clear sense of the need to get on, to make sure that he was ahead of or at least keeping up with his class. An occupation that did not ensure the eventual house in the country and a lifestyle that delivered security of place amongst his peers was unthinkable. He'd never even contemplated one. He watched the girl trotting along in her neat black clothes. He had never stamped his own identity on his life. He had followed a traditional rut that centuries had deepened and narrowed and whose entrance was closely guarded by 'people like us'. Anyway, what would he have done?

Suddenly he needed the unemotional logic of work to anaesthetise himself against the creeping instability he could feel looming around him. He hurried back up towards King William Street. Work. Prices, movements, trends, opportunities. These things would ward off the dread that seemed to be sapping his energy, pulling him downwards. Work. That was what he would do, work, work, work. He wouldn't ask why.

It was still raining when Michael set off on his run from

Chelsea towards the river. He had met his father for a drink earlier.

'You're looking tired m'boy.' His father peered carefully at him. 'How long is it since you've had a holiday?'

'I took Janet to Venice a couple of months back.'

'I don't mean a long weekend. I mean a holiday. You've got to pace yourself, Michael. Take a holiday. A long one.'

'I've been thinking about going to Africa, actually. To the Northern Cape.'

'Excellent! But go to Kenya, do it in style. There isn't anything in the Northern Cape.'

'I want to see Grandfather Wilmot's old farmhouse.'

His father folded his arms. 'There isn't anything there, Michael. It was abandoned years ago. Your mother's guardian held the land in trust for her and then bought it from her when she was twenty-one. Then he sold it to someone else.'

'What about my cousins? I've never met them.'

'I don't know anything about them.' His father's face was set, a look that Michael knew well. The conversation was supposedly over. Rebellion flickered in him. 'What happened to Grandfather Wilmot?'

'He had his throat cut. So did your grandmother. I believe they killed the maid too. It's all best forgotten, Michael.'

'Look . . . I need to know. What happened to mother?'

'She disappeared for four years. They thought she'd been kidnapped. And then one day she appeared again. No one knew what had happened. She couldn't remember. She was only six and a bit. She had to learn to speak again.'

'Did she click?' Michael felt something cold filling his stomach. He could hear echoes of the melodious clicking somewhere in his mind.

'Click? God knows. She'd been with the natives, obviously. They must have returned her. Look, Michael, she never speaks about it. I wouldn't have known if her ghastly uncle hadn't told me at the wedding. I thought it was a yarn. They're given to exaggeration over there. But it upset her enormously when I mentioned it. It's better forgotten. Best left alone.'

Michael breathed in the icy, misty air and felt the sweat cooling on his body as he ran. He would go to Africa. He would go to that old Cape Dutch farmhouse. His father had made him even more determined. Michael had seen the veins on his father's hands, the light-brown age marks, as he steadied himself for a second on the arm of the old leather chair. His father was suddenly an elderly man who needed to think about getting up out of his chair. He ran faster, harder, although he was having difficulty breathing. He would have to stop soon.

He stopped just after the Albert Bridge, lit up like a Christmas tree. A couple were snogging under an umbrella in the darkness after the bridge. Michael went a decent distance past them and then stopped to stare at the river again. The tide had turned and the banks were exposed underneath him. The river looked docile now it was reduced to half its strength. The Buddhist pagoda in Battersea Park was visible through the rain. Michael could see a couple jogging along the path underneath the little white fairy lights that ran the length of the park's river front. Janet. He wanted to call her. He headed for the phone box at the bridge. He had no change. He'd reverse the call. And say what? 'Hello Janet, I'm lonely.' Hardly. Did he really want to see her? Or did he want to be distracted from himself? He walked back towards the King's Road, the short route home.

He took a bottle of beer into the bath, lay stewing and sipping the cold bitterness. He didn't want to see the Bushman. He didn't want to think. He wanted to go backwards in time to before he had ended things with Janet, before his visits to Tranquillity, before he had broken one of the unwritten rules that governed his relationship with his father.

As the bottle emptied Michael felt the tension in his neck that had prompted the run easing away. He felt a degree or two lighter. The weights seemed to have lifted a fraction. Perhaps he could forget it, compartmentalise it, get on with life. Enjoy himself a bit. He'd become dull, that's what had happened. He needed to get out, have some fun. Maybe he'd rope Basher into something. He'd stop thinking about going to Africa. But it was moving, that particular thought, solidifying into a when rather than an if.

The lights never went out completely in Tranquillity. Michael's mother stood at her window and tried to ignore the gentle glow that came from the building she inhabited. Outside it was dark. The clouds that in London seem to form a blanket were revealed as huge patches across the sky in Sussex. Occasionally she could see stars in the spaces between. She stared upwards, completely still, waiting for the stars to come out. It was in the dark, looking up at the pinpoints of light, that she felt the pieces of her mind drift down into a layer of calm that made her feel whole.

She was trying to remember another moon, another night, a completely different landscape. It was there, somewhere in the shattered fragments that wouldn't hold together. She let the fragments play past her, a kaleidoscope of images, waiting. It would come. It must come. She had to tell the young man who had come to see her, the young man with the eyes she remembered out of the time that she didn't remember any more. It would come. Every night now she waited at her window for these moments. She did not know what she was doing. She simply did as her instinct drove her to do. A triad of stars appeared and she felt a warm glow. She relaxed into it. The sky clouded over again. She left the window and climbed back into her bed with its pretty, patchwork quilt.

Six thousand miles away the Karoo sheep huddled together in the paddock, a woolly brown mass under the swollen orange moon that hung miles and miles above them in the massive dome of sky.

7

The Karoo, 1999

Bessie lay absolutely still, ears strained to the darkness. She could hear breathing, it seemed quite close. She looked for a shadow to cross her window, waiting to hear the footsteps that must accompany the breathing. Nothing. Her reason began to assert itself. Would they stand so and wait? The breathing again. Her heart drummed. Her eyes scanned the dark bedroom. No strange shapes, everything could be identified. In the tiniest of movements she slid her hand under the pillow next to her head, wrapped it around the gun that pointed at the door. She removed the safety catch (how many times had she practised this?) and waited. The breathing again. It was outside her window. But no movement. Then a scratching sound.

Oh for God's sake! Jan had forgotten to let the old dog in. Again. She relaxed in anger and relief, felt the arthritis return to her fingers.

She replaced the safety catch and mentally ran through their fortifications. There was the electric fence with the alarm. There were the four pit bull terriers that ran free in between the two fences. The blacks feared those dogs. There was the CCTV, cameras so high up that it was impossible to spray or cover them over. There was Jan in the next room with his repeater shotgun. There was Karel in his cottage with the same. She had her own handgun. There was little chance that anyone would scale the electric fence and the second, razor-wired fence, face the pit bull terriers and then the farmers themselves. But if . . . if one of their own workers were to sabotage the system . . . if they were to poison the dogs . . . if the gates were to be opened for them . . . if they were to catch the house unawares . . . then they would be quiet. Stand and wait. Listen until they could stand over your bed with a knife or a hammer and kill you before you could reach for the blessed gun. Every night she tried not to run through the scenarios and often she managed it, but she was sensitive to the lightest of noises. So many farms had been attacked. And for no reason that she could fathom. Just meaningless hatred. A sport, an initiation, a dare. Who knew? And nobody seemed able to stop it, to protect them. She felt adrift in anarchy.

When the farm attacks had started, Jan had asked her if she wanted to move into his room again. She had been grateful, aware of the size of the sacrifice. Over the years they had both learned to value their privacy, it was one of the reasons why their marriage was successful. No, she would rather face her fears than inhabit his personal space. The romantic love in their marriage had nearly been extinguished by the too familiar. The daily personal details of coughing and throat clearing and toenail clipping and hair trimming were too much for her. They repulsed her. A man must be allowed to fart and belch and scratch in his own space. But she did not want to share those private moments. Jan had resisted at first, then learned to woo her when he wanted her, to shower and wash his hair and prepare for sex. Eventually it pleased them both.

The clock said three a.m. She may or may not sleep again before morning. And in the morning Michael would be arriving. Karel would be getting up soon to fetch him from the airport. The plane got in at ten. Karel would have to leave the farm by five. He was a good boy, Karel. Like a son. She shifted her thoughts away from that pain. She had learned how to out-manoeuvre herself over the years. Melly's boy. Well. It had taken them long enough. She hadn't heard from Melly in over twenty years. Hadn't seen her for close on forty years. Forty years. The very thought! And it had been Jeremy who rang, spoke to Jan. Men! There was so much she needed to know and of course Jan hadn't asked anything important. Just the time of arrival, that sort of thing. Michael, that was the boy's name. Not that he was a boy. He must be in his late twenties already. Men had no curiosity. 'He'll tell us himself when he gets here,' Jan had said. But she felt unprepared, she needed more information. She'd been ready to phone Melly herself but Jan had said that Melly was unwell. Even that he couldn't tell her any more about. Sometimes Bessie despaired of the simplicity of men.

She longed for daybreak. To think that for so many years she had slept secure in her bed, and now she was nervous about going to the kitchen and getting herself a drink. She didn't drink anything before bedtime now, not wanting to make the journey to the bathroom. The alarm system scanned the entire house except for the corridor, the bathrooms and bedrooms. The infra-red rays comforted her. As soon as the sky lightened she would get up. She needed less sleep now anyway. Melly. Well, well. How the time had gone. A life slipped by so quickly. Melly was lucky to be in England. To have settled there so long ago.

There's no escape for us, she thought. We're here for better or worse. And we'll die here. Like our ancestors. But the future for the children is less clear. Karel will have the farm. But he hasn't married yet. And it's hard to see the country going to the dogs. We knew it would once they were in charge, but it's been so quick. Where will Karel send his children to school? Private schools cost too much. They'll have to bring back governesses, she thought. Club together. Boer schools. Like we had before. We won before. We'll win again. The Boer isn't defeated so easily. Things will change. And we're not going anywhere. The shameful Aids thought came into her mind again. If twenty per cent were infected, then you could expect an equilibrium in the races in ten years. Maybe even a white government. They had seen the statistics. God forgive me, she thought. God forgive me. But I am insincere. I want the old ways back. I want to go shopping in town and not have to fight my way through all the market traders and a sea of blacks. I want law and order. I want a white society. I never realised there were so many of them. The squatter camp that had grown out of nowhere on the northern boundary of the farm scared her. They'd had the blacks there moved somewhere else nearly forty years ago. And now they were back, cutting the fences, making themselves right at home.

We paid for that land. We worked hard for it. What did they ever do? The squatter camp haunted her. It seemed destined to grow. Karel had established communications with their representative. He said there was nothing to be done without causing even more problems. That he was prepared to give up the land, create new borders. That there was no choice. This government wouldn't move the people. You could forget about the police. And you wouldn't dare do today what you would have done even twenty years ago. Then you knew that if you shot a black you just had to make sure they were on your land. Then there would be no problem. Drag them on to the land if necessary, the policeman had said.

The television screen was tracking a tiny aeroplane moving its way across the Mediterranean and now inching slowly across the Sahara Desert. This excruciating mirror of his journey was irritating Michael intensely.

He was flying South African Airways, having taken the first available flight to Cape Town after it happened. Michael tried to block it out. It was humiliating, embarrassing, best forgotten. But fragments haunted him in this enforced stillness. He closed his eyes and pulled the blanket he'd been given over his body. If only he could sleep and wipe out the mocking accusations running through his brain. He desperately wanted oblivion, but not through drink. Not again.

He wouldn't think about it. He would think about flying, about crossing continents, the now. The little screen showed that they were flying at thirty-five thousand feet. A long way up, Michael thought. The solid seat suddenly seemed too heavy for the thin flooring. No comfort in thinking about flying.

It had all happened terribly fast. He had joined the others for a drink in the pub after work. Nothing unusual about that. Except the speed with which Michael drank. After an hour he'd actually had enough. But he didn't care. The devil in the bottle had reeled him in with his first glass. Basher and the others had left him silent, staring into his glass. He'd moved from beer on to brandy, slinging at least three down his throat in the fifteen minutes before closing time. The devil was spinning in glee, pulling clumsy marionette strings as Michael weaved his way out into the cold. Frost had already begun to settle on the paving stones. The outdoor ice rink at Broadgate was deserted. Left-over Christmas lights were strung around the carefully positioned bare trees. The cold air closed down the conscious part of Michael's brain. He remembered the lights, and setting off towards his office. He remembered falling down the stairs next to the bookshop. He still had the bruises. He didn't remember, other than in fragments, anything else. He remembered . . .

He opened his eyes. He picked up his guide to Southern Africa. He leafed through, mainly looking at the pictures. He couldn't settle. He wanted a sleeping pill. When you're drunk I suppose your true self comes out of hiding, he thought. Well, that's comforting. Face it, Michael, he thought. Face it and then perhaps you can sleep. Apparently he had managed to slip past the security guards, gained access to the floor. The dozen or so all-night lads, trading with the Far East, were at their desks. Michael had gone to his desk and begun to make paper aeroplanes, sending them flying into the pit. One of the traders had apparently come over to him.

The trader, a Chinese chap that Michael had never really noticed before, wasn't torn between his corporate duty and the plight of a colleague. He called security. There had been an embarrassing game of tag, with Michael running across the tops of the desks to evade his would-be captors. Eventually they caught him in the pit, dragged him off the desks and helped him down to reception.

He remembered sitting with one of the guards, a chap he recognised, having coffee thrust at him. 'You flash bastards think you've got it all sorted, don't you. Well, look at you, sunshine. Just look at you. You're bleeding pathetic, you are. Who're we going to call then to take lover boy home? Come on, you're not passing out in my office, sunshine, give us a name and a number.' He'd slapped Michael's face gently, repeatedly, after that, thrown a cup of freezing water into his face. All Michael wanted was to slide into oblivion. Oh yes, now the devil was ready with his anaesthetic. He must have given Janet's name and number. He didn't remember going home with her. She had put him into bed and his mouth had developed a life of its own. He couldn't remember what he had told her. But he knew it would have been a hideous dumping of paranoias, pettiness and grotesque self-aggrandisement. Of ghastly, unvarnished truths. Jesus. It hadn't stopped there. In the early morning she'd woken up, shaking him, angry. He'd wet the bed. Oh yes, Michael, you're a real hero.

He'd rung the office the following morning to say he wouldn't be in. Malvern had asked to speak to him. 'Michael. Bit of a do last night, old man.'

'Yes. I'm sorry. I lost it. Unforgivable.'

'Well. Pretty unprofessional. And unpleasant for the chaps trying to do some business. Busy night for the Asian team, you know.'

'No, no I didn't know.'

'Well, you're not going to be fit for anything today. Tomorrow morning, my office, seven-thirty, OK?'

'Seven-thirty. I'll see you then.' He'd wanted to add 'sir', like he was still at fucking school. The effort of the phone call had taken all his strength. Janet was getting ready for work. He was incapable of moving. Waves of nausea were flooding over him. He wanted her to leave so that he could hurl himself into the bathroom and purge. He was hot and cold. Janet had thrown him out of the bed and made him sleep on the floor in the fouled linen. She'd made herself a bed on the sofa in the living-room.

He could smell his own stale urine. The smell was adding to the turbulence in his stomach. Oh, God. Oh, God – go, Janet! Please go out the front door. He couldn't move, had begun to breathe through his mouth to contain the fumes. It was a race. Which he didn't win. A tidal wave had risen in him. He'd had to stumble to the bathroom, where Janet was putting the final touches to her make-up, and throw up. He couldn't look at her. He hugged the white porcelain and gagged relentlessly. She waited for him to finish. Then said that she was going. He could let himself out. She sounded concerned, gentle even. He still couldn't look at her. Jesus. She'd left some Alka-Seltzer and a glass of water next to him on the floor. The sound of the door closing was sweet.

It had taken about five hours for him to surface. Even then he'd been shaky, his head a seething cauldron. He managed to put the linen into the washing machine, hang it out to dry. He had ordered a new mattress and a new set of linen from Peter Jones, who delivered everything to the flat and took away the soiled mattress. Thank God for the account he'd opened last Christmas. The flat was now restored; it was five in the afternoon when the cab dropped him at home. He'd ditched his suit and his underwear, which was chafing his skin. He'd eaten an instant meal and gone to bed, disconnecting the telephone.

Malvern had been decent enough. 'It won't do, Michael. What the hell was going on?'

It was the moment for Michael to eat humble pie and receive forgiveness. He couldn't do it. He just couldn't play. It was alarming. The rules required a display of penitence, some boyish charm, an apology, something to make Malvern feel that he had taken whatever steps were necessary. Michael couldn't do it. He said, 'It's personal, David. I don't want to discuss it.' Malvern looked at him. 'You don't want to discuss it.' Then he went ballistic. 'Come off it, Carter. You come in here, blind drunk, chase about the bloody room, try and hit the security guards, we won't even mention the verbal abuse, and you have the bloody cheek to say that you don't want to discuss it?'

Michael considered Malvern. He was a decent enough chap. He didn't want to have to discipline Michael. 'Look, I'm sorry, David. It was unbelievably stupid and humiliating. Can we leave it at that?' Now Malvern's ego couldn't accept it. 'No, we can't leave it at that. Have you any idea what might have happened? How bloody irresponsible it was? For Christ's sake, Carter!'

For Michael it was a moment of clarity. Let the organ-grinders find a new monkey. He offered his resignation.

It pricked Malvern's anger like a balloon. They'd talked back and forth, but Michael was adamant. Eventually they'd agreed on a leave of absence. A year. Michael hadn't bothered to go back to his desk, had simply handed over his security card and walked out of the building.

And now he was here. A small smile happened somewhere inside him, the first since it had happened, a week ago. Here he was. Anything could lie ahead. The video in his brain ran out. He managed to get some sleep.

The air hostess opened the little plastic flap that covered his window and offered him breakfast. Michael settled the plastic tray on the precarious table in front of him and looked out of the window. They were flying over barren land, a golden dust plain. The sun had just risen on the other side of the aircraft. He'd slept reasonably well. The landscape below him was changing, becoming greener. After breakfast they flew over some mountains. Soon Table Mountain lay beneath them. Then they were circling the bottom of the peninsula.

'You should see it from the sea, like the settlers,' the businessman next to him said.

Stepping off the plane was like stepping into a dry sauna. Michael could feel the sun frying his whiteness as he walked across the tarmac to the terminal building. The Europeans were a gaggle of ghosts in the crowd awaiting their luggage.

A tall, thickset blond man with a moustache, wearing long navy-blue shorts, sandals and a khaki short-sleeved shirt was holding a piece of cardboard with Michael's name on it. Michael guessed he was in his thirties. He went up to him. 'Hello, I'm Michael Carter.'

'Karel van Heerden. Pleased to meet you. I'm your cousin! Well, in a way. Through marriage.' Karel shook Michael's hand. 'Come now, I've got the bakkie parked outside. You got everything?'

'Yes, thank you . . . where are we going?'

They were striding out of the terminal towards a white truck with a double cab, darkened windows and a steel sliding cover on the back. Karel slung the luggage in and locked it shut. He gestured to Michael to get in. 'We're going to the farm. Tannie Bessie has made me promise to bring you straight there. She said, Karel, you bring him straight home. He can see the sights another day. And I don't argue with Tannie Bessie. Hell, no one argues with her!' He shook his head, smiling.

Karel took a handgun out of a holster that fitted under his shirt and put it on the tray between them. Fortunately it was pointing at the windscreen. 'Pass us a beer, hey?' he pointed to the cooler bag at Michael's feet. Michael opened it and took out an ice-cold can of beer. Karel cracked it open and drove with one hand holding the beer and the steering wheel, the other resting on the windowsill. 'Go on man, have one!'

'Is it safe if we have an accident?' he pointed at the gun.

'Oh, ja. Safety's on.'

He wanted to ask if it was strictly necessary but thought better of it.

The air passing through the open windows of the cab was hot and Michael was thirsty. Just as he was beginning to relax, Karel shut his window, told Michael to do the same. He put the air-conditioning on.

'We've got to go through a bad bit. Pal of mine had a nasty time going through here. Bloody kids throwing rocks off the bridges, stones at the cars.' Looking out of the window Michael could see the beginnings of rows of shacks, mostly just their roofs. 'It stretches for miles. And the gangs rule the place. One of my men went to a shebeen there and didn't come home for three months. He can tell you stories that make you shit scared.'

'Why didn't he come home?'

'The totsies stole his money and then said he hadn't paid

for his drink. So they beat the shit out of him and told him he had to earn money for them. He had to go up north and hijack cars, all sorts, before he could get away. He's a good one, too. But what can you do?'

'I suppose, where people have no other hope, robbery has a different meaning,' Michael ventured.

'No other hope! Hell man, this is the land of opportunity. They've got more hope here than anywhere else in Africa. And they run the place now. If you can call it that. No, they're just bone idle, that's all. Bone bloody idle and corrupt. I can count on one hand the number of men who can do what I would call a decent day's work on the farm with me. Count them on my hands.'

Michael decided to avoid further conversation along this line.

'Tell me about the family,' he said. Well, there was himself, the nephew of Tannie Bessie and Oom Jan, and they had the farm. Karel's father and mother had a little shop in the town, 'like a Sparshop, you know'. His younger brother ran the store and he, Karel, had finished college about five years ago and now managed his uncle's farm, 'but not without his personal supervision, I can tell you!'

Tannie Bessie was his mother's stepsister, by marriage only. The daughter of the aunt and uncle who had bought his grandparents' farm. Karel's father was Tannie Bessie's brother, Piet. 'How come Tannie Bessie ended up with the farm?' Michael asked. Surely it should have gone to Karel's father? 'It just didn't work out like that,' Karel said. 'Tannie Bessie holds the farm in trust for me.' Michael decided in favour of discretion.

They had been travelling towards Table Mountain, but were now moving away from it. 'How long will it take to get there?'

'Ag, not long. About four hours. But it's not a bad drive.' As they cleared the outskirts of Cape Town and headed into the hinterland, Michael could only agree with him. He kept looking backwards to see Table Mountain, but did not want to miss the snatches of sea that he could glimpse through the foliage on the side of the Highway. Karel drove fast, he was on his third can of Castle by the time they entered the wine country. He turned to Michael to ask him for another one and found him asleep. The heat, the beer and the long flight had undone him.

Karel stole long glances at him. He was very pale, but then all poms looked like they'd risen from the grave. And he was dark. Fine features, slim body. He wasn't short but he looked underfed. Well, Tannie Bessie would sort that out. Put some flesh on his bones. So this was Melanie's boy. Melanie who'd married an Englishman. Melanie, the one they always said was 'otherwise'. She'd been something of an enigma to Karel and his brother. Tannie Bessie had apparently been like an older sister to Melanie. And Melanie had not stayed in touch. Melanie had disappeared into England after her marriage and they hadn't heard any more from her since she wrote to thank Tannie Bessie's father for the wedding. Her husband had written when Michael was born. Then nothing but Christmas cards. And they stopped years ago. Oom Jan said that she'd got ideas above her station, that she was embarrassed to be a plaas meisie (farm girl) with all the smart people in London. Tannie disagreed. She said that Melanie was just otherwise. That she couldn't handle too much of anything, that she probably had to let go altogether of the Karoo in order to manage to live in England. She used to repeat what Melanie had said when she was leaving, 'Bessie, if it doesn't work, can I come back?'

'Ag, don't be silly, Melly, why shouldn't it work? You love him, don't you?'

'Ja, I love him. But I didn't know it would be so hard to leave.' She'd begun to cry. 'Bessie, how am I going to take my feet off the land and get into the aeroplane? I can't do it!'

'Of course you can. Because you know you can always get into another aeroplane and come home. Come now, Melly, you can't settle down with one of the farming lads around here. You know it and I know it. You scare them. And he's a good man, your Jeremy. A bit stuffy maybe, but a good man. It'll be all right.' Tannie always said that when Melanie left, she, Tannie, had cried and cried. 'She loved the land, Karel. If she'd been a man, she could have stayed, you know. Kept the old farm. But she was too strange to be really happy around here. People still talk.'

He'd never worked out what they talked about. There was something that one of his school mates had said about his family being 'Kaffir boeties' but that was a long time ago. They'd been fighting and the little Marais boy had kept yelling, 'You come from Kaffirs, your auntie lived with Kaffirs, we know your type.' But it hadn't seemed possible then and looking at Melanie's pallid son it didn't seem any more likely now. Maybe he'd ask Michael one of these days. It was strange that the father had been in touch, not Melanie. But Tannie Bessie would find out all she needed from Michael. You could rely on women for things like that. He hoped Michael had brought pictures. He'd like to see Melanie. They'd crossed the mountains, were heading into the open land. Karel visibly relaxed. He didn't like the towns much, found the order of the valleys too enclosing. He needed the vastness, the nothingness of his own barren territory.

He woke Michael once they'd entered van Heerden land. Michael started, took a minute to work out where he was. The bakkie was racing along a dirt road, scrubland stretching uninterrupted for miles on either side. 'Where are we?'

'You're on van Heerden land now, cousin!' Karel had

donned a pair of sunglasses. Blinking in the impossibly bright light, Michael wished he'd retrieved his from his luggage. 'How big is the farm?'

'Ag, it's about ten square kilometres. You need a lot of land out here. There's bugger all grazing for the sheep.'

It was a flat landscape, completely different from the coastal Cape.

Michael looked at his watch. He'd slept for nearly four hours. 'I'm afraid I haven't been very good company.'

'It's the flight. Takes it out of you. It's unnatural to move so quickly. This jet lag, they talk about it being the time zones. I think it's just the body saying, "Hey man, this is unnatural, put me down!" ' Karel laughed. He was jubilant now, so close to home. Michael passed him another lager. The cold blocks in the ice bag had softened but the beer was still cool. 'You English like warm beer, don't you?'

'Not in a hundred degrees of heat,' Michael responded. 'Look,' he said, 'it's very good of you, you know . . . to fetch me like this.'

'It's nothing,' said Karel. 'Hey, you're family.'

Not that you look or sound like any of us, he thought. I wonder if this Englishman will handle the heat. Michael was wondering the same thing. This heat was different from the heat of the Mediterranean. It was relentless, like being under a grill inside a convection oven.

He put his hand outside the bakkie and his fingers touched the roof. 'Bloody hell!' Karel laughed. He enjoyed the extremes of his country, wanted Michael to be awed by them. He'd been nervous that he would try being superior. But the country always managed to put people in their place. Tannie Bessie said she'd seen it many times. 'They come out here, Karel, and they think they know everything because they've travelled the world and they've read more books than you and I. Well, their weather doesn't give them much chance to do anything else, I can tell you. But out here there's only nature. You need strength of the body out here and strength of character just to get by. No fancy education's going to get you through a drought.'

They were approaching the house. First came a tiny settlement of terracotta-coloured mud huts with reed-type roofs, painted in bright designs, and a long, low building that looked like a stableblock. 'Who lives there?'

'That's the kraal. Black farm-workers live there with their families.' A battered Land-Rover was parked next to one of the huts. 'Oh shit. Oom's going to be mad as hell.'

'Why?'

'Timothy is here. There's always trouble when he's here.'

'What kind of trouble?'

'Just trouble.'

Michael caught a glimpse of a tall, immaculately suited young black man talking to an older, bearded black man wearing khaki shorts and a blue-denim shirt. They both turned to watch the bakkie go by. About half a mile farther down the dirt track was the main house. Around it were two fences, each at least three metres tall. An armed black man in an army camouflage outfit stood guard at the massive gates. Karel stopped the car a little way back from the gate.

'Just checking that it's Paul and all is in order.' The black man gave a salute of sorts and went to open the gates. Karel drove up to him and opened the window.

'Alles reg, Paul?' (Is everything OK, Paul?)

'Ja. Ja.' The man grinned at them. Michael stared at the fences. The first one was electrified and the second was entirely made out of razor wire. The house wasn't the gabled white Cape Dutch homestead of his dream. It was a sturdy, green-tin-roofed house with a deep veranda running around it. There was no front lawn; a few hardy looking shrubs and a paved area seemed to demarcate what would, in other places, be the garden. Karel drove around the side of the house.

Tannie Bessie was tall, elegant, and not what Michael had expected. Her blonde grey hair was cut in a bob and she wore a soft, unstructured dark-blue trouser suit. She came out of the side door that led into the kitchen and opened Michael's cab door. 'Welcome to Rooisand, Michael! I'm your Aunt Bessie.' Michael wasn't sure whether he should kiss her or shake her hand. Before he could get past hello and implement his resolve to kiss her on the cheek, she'd moved towards the house, ushering him to follow.

'Well, I can't believe it! Melly's boy! Now, let me look at you properly!' She searched his face intently. 'Yes. You're Melly's boy. Come, let me take you to your room. Now this room used to be your mother's, a long time ago. I'm going to put the kettle on while you use the bathroom which is down the passage on your left. Come through to the veranda when you're ready.' They had travelled down a long corridor and she was in and out of the room before Michael had finished his thank you.

The windows in his room looked out on to the scrubland that seemed to go on forever. Not that far away a heat haze was shimmering, creating a false horizon. The room itself was cool, with a single bed under a white counterpane and a huge, old-fashioned wardrobe. There was a small table with a chair in front of it, an old-fashioned dressing-table with mirrors that had begun to lose their shine around the edges and white doilies under glass on each of its three surfaces. The walls were white, the floor parquet. There were a couple of wildlife prints on the wall. On the table there was a small Bible. This was his mother's room. But apart from the view which she must have gazed out on, there was nothing of hers here. He missed her, suddenly, with a vehemence that took him by surprise. He went to the bathroom, a room that contrasted with the rest of the house. It was a modern confection of maroon bathtub with matching basin and loo and a deep-grey linoleum floor. He washed his hands, splashed water on his face and went outside.

The veranda was cool, with a table and comfortable old flaking leather armchairs. Aunt Bessie had laid out tea. 'This is melktert and these are koeksisters. Do you take sugar?'

The koeksisters were fried dough soaked in syrup and twisted into the shape of a short, stubby plait. Karel was sitting on the veranda wall, wiping syrup from a koeksister off his chin. Michael opted for the melktert. This tasted like cheesecake without the cheese. Still, it looked less challenging than the plaited thing. There was a silence.

'This is awfully good of you,' Michael began.

'Nonsense. How long can you stay? Of course, you can stay as long as you want, I just wondered how long you had . . . '

'I honestly don't know,' said Michael.

'So what made you come over then?' Karel emptied his tea-cup.

'It was an impulse . . . I just wanted to see the country.' It sounded pathetic. They were waiting, expecting something from him. He didn't know what to say.

'Well,' said Karel. 'I'd better get going. See you at dinner.' He left Michael to Tannie Bessie's gaze.

'It's all right, you know,' she said. 'Sometimes you don't need a reason for doing something. It's good that you came.' Michael smiled at her. 'How is Melanie?' She didn't know. Or did she know? Should she know?

'She's fine,' he said. 'She seems fine.'

'I wondered what happened to her. I never hear from her.' Oh, bugger.

'Aunt Bessie, look, I must apologise . . . I didn't really expect to be here, you see. I didn't know that you were expecting me immediately. I haven't brought you anything and I haven't really thought this thing through. I – well, I just really wanted to see where my mother had lived. She . . . she isn't well. She hasn't been for years, actually. She's in a nursing home. No, no, she's physically fine. She just stopped talking. About eight years ago. She just stopped. I'm not very good at talking about it.'

Bessie considered the young man. He was leaning forward in the wicker basket chair, the tips of his fingers tightly pressed together. Melly was very ill, that much was obvious. And her son was in some sort of crisis. There was a tautness about him, a sense of controlled tension, a jaggedness. Well, there would be time to find out what was going on. Melly ill! Well. And they hadn't told her. Still, it wasn't Michael's fault. Children tread so carefully in their disclosure of family matters. He really didn't look too well himself.

'Michael, we're family. So you don't have to behave like a guest. And I'm very glad you're here. I didn't know about Melly, but we'll talk about it another time. Now I think you should go and get some sleep. It's been a long journey for you.'

Michael crawled under the cool white counterpane and fell immediately into a deep sleep. Bessie sat a while on the veranda, drinking another cup of tea. Melly hadn't spoken for eight years! Good God. And here was her son, a boy with no real life in his eyes, a cardboard cut-out. It would take a long time to know this young man, Bessie thought. Not just because he was detached, like all the English, but because he hadn't any knowledge of himself. He looks as though he's been broiled in a pressure-cooker for too long, she thought. He needs rest. And tomfoolery. Well, Karel can supply the entertainment. We can rest him and feed him. Ag, Melly! What has happened, Melly, that your son is like this and you aren't speaking? What kind of a home are you in my girl? She couldn't quite take it all in. Melly, in a home! It wasn't right. Something would have to be done.

It was still unbearably hot. Michael held the cold bottle of beer against his cheek, looked into the darkness that stretched beyond the couple of feet of light that edged the veranda. The others had gone to bed, Tannie Bessie, Karel and Oom Jan. Jan van Heerden was a quiet man who seemed to accept the presence of this young English relative with the same equanimity with which he said grace, the first Afrikaans that Michael had heard in the house. Having told Michael that he was welcome, that he hoped all his family was well and that he should make himself at home, Jan applied himself to his food. He was darker and smaller than Karel, but still a sturdy and obviously strong man.

'So, Michael, what do you do in London?' Karel had pushed back his plate and was watching Michael over the rim of his glass of red wine.

'I work in the City,' he said. Karel looked blank. 'I mean, I work for an investment bank.'

'We're not going to pick up the papers tomorrow and find out that you've wrecked Barclays Bank, are we?' It was mostly a joke. Michael didn't smile.

'What else do you think I'm doing here?'

Karel wasn't sure until Michael laughed.

The gang had left the white woman blindfolded and blood soaked in a sewage ditch on the edge of the township. Already dogs were yapping at her. It wouldn't be long before someone found her. Hardekop didn't care. They'd never trace it back to him, and even if they did, they'd have to catch him first. It had been Redrage's initiation. For every new member of the gang they had a white female sacrifice. Everybody chose a different type. Hardekop knew that the woman chosen generally reminded the picker of something that had cut and rankled and would now be excised. That's the way it is, he thought. We are cleaning our spirits using these white women. Most of them lost their minds. You could tell when they cracked, when the fear became mindless and the obedience perfect. He liked watching for that moment. He found it interesting. This one had been almost too easy. The stories of their rituals were everywhere, she knew what to expect. And before they had even cut a slice off her, she had cracked completely. They never killed them. That would be too easy for everybody. No, this way the husband and the family had to deal with it too.

No, the woman wouldn't be a problem. She would never be able to identify them and all the gang members had had their turn, with the knife too. It was the robbery that was worrying him. Pigs were making enquiries. Everyone told him as soon as they heard anything. But the pattern of these enquiries was very clear to Hardekop. He sighed. Damn fool security guard. What sort of self-respecting black had a job like that anyway? He hadn't meant to kill him but the fool had kept coming. These things happened. It wasn't anyone's fault. It looked as though he would have to disappear for a while. And he was happy down here in the Cape. He had a community that respected him. Who else could give loans and supply money for doctors and food when things were bad? No, no one here would give him away. The ones who might want to were too frightened. But somehow they had real evidence this time. CCTV most likely. He couldn't go home or follow his usual routines. He'd clear out for a while. Get a car and head for Namibia, why not. He'd never been there. It was quite possible to get across the border without going through a border post. He'd sent enough cars through.

He threw a stone into the ocean. Shit. He hated being controlled. Hated anyone or anything having the power to tell him what to do. He'd been his own man since he was a kid on the streets of Johannesburg, long before the city belonged to the people. When his mother disappeared and his father never came back from the mines he had been left alone. There was a mix-up – he was supposed to go to relatives in Soweto, but he never made it. Hardeklip had found him wandering around Hillbrow, looking for Soweto. Which was, as Hardeklip had told him, a long way away and a much harder place to make a living. At twelve years old, Hardeklip had a wealth of experience. Pickpocketing, running messages for Umkhonto we Sizwe, burglary. He was a professional. As soon as he started ordering Hardekop around (his name for him), Hardekop felt better. Patronage meant provision, protection. Belonging. Each gang was a brotherhood. Outside of politics, outside of everything, outlaws, true freedom fighters. He kicked at a pile of seaweed and litter. An empty Coke can clattered away. But now they wanted them to stop.

We ran messages. We took risks. They didn't mind us being ungovernable when it suited them. But now we have to do as we're told. There isn't any work for us. And even if there was, who would look after the community like we do? He wouldn't give up his prestige. Forget it. Only last week Mama Letyana had said she didn't know what she would do without him. He'd had to give her kid a talking to. A smack as well. Little bastard. If he was going to run for anyone, he ran for them. But he'd promised Mama Letyana that the boy would go to school. And so he would. The kids hero-worshipped him. Any attention from the gang was good. Something to brag about. No, he wasn't going to give all that up. Just a short trip until things had blown over. That's what he'd do. The boys would cover for him.

Michael stood at his bedroom window staring into the night, listening to the sounds. The silence of a Sussex night was deeply quiet, not a rustling, chirping, active silence like this African variety. The sky was just a vast blackness filled with points of light. The stars were in a different place and there were thousands more than he was used to. Looking up, Michael could almost see the infinitely receding universe. It was alarming. In Sussex the sky had boundaries. It didn't suck you into itself without warning. The farm's night-time security ritual had been an education. He felt nervous, locked up like this.

8

In the pre-dawn Michael sat on the veranda at the back of the house. Ahead of him there was a vast scrub plain, with a few hills in the distance. Much, much farther off there were, he thought, mountains, a black smudge on the horizon, thrown into relief by the light that was beginning to show itself behind them. He sipped his coffee and breathed in the air. It was clean. He felt extraordinarily awake, as though this huge land mass had energy, transmitted it to him.

He could just make out sheep a long way away. They were dotted over the landscape with wide expanses between them.

The sky was lightening rapidly, in layers, with the layer above the farmhouse still a dark grey and the layer above the mountains a bright yellow. The rim of the sun appeared slowly and then, as though lifted by a puppeteer, it rose more quickly than seemed appropriate to the grandeur of its surroundings. It was a golden ball, but it had no clouds to tint with ochre, just the different bands of colour of the sky as it pushed back the barriers of night across the huge dome. Michael felt his skin, his muscles relax. The fences looked like a transparent veil.

It was an hour's drive to the church which sat by a broad dirt road a short distance from the Sparshop, the post office and a liquor store. A small settlement of red-brick houses with tin roofs, a township, he supposed, had announced the beginning of the village. There was no air-conditioning in the huge old Mercedes and the windows were kept almost completely rolled up to keep out the dust. Michael's one good shirt was soaked by the time they arrived. The only suit he had with him was a lightweight dark woollen one. It was tailored for him, had cost a small fortune. He would have traded it willingly for Karel's beige cotton. Finally they were inside. It wasn't air-conditioned but the walls were thick and the air seemed cooler. He wished he could take his jacket off. But this was a formal, bleak church. The crucifix was a huge bare wooden cross. The standing up and sitting down were similar to his experience, but he was unprepared for the rigid attention given to the pastor. Not a head turned around, not a bottom shifted position. The congregation was sitting at attention. The service was in Afrikaans, meaningless to him. He was having difficulty maintaining the required stillness. The pastor was speaking with some emotion. The women all wore hats. Tannie Bessie's was an elegant blue that dipped across her face. In front of him was a large black hat with a satin bow at the back. He tried to look at the people without moving his head. His field of vision was quite small. Two young girls sat next to the large black hat. They had identical long blonde plaits falling down their backs and were wearing pale-blue dresses with tiny white polka dots and straw boaters, with pale-blue ribbons around the brims and trailing part way down the plaits.

Michael felt his eyelids drooping. He tried staring at a mole on the black hat's neck, then tried to count the white dots on the blue dresses. The heat and the enforced stillness were bearing down on his eyelids. His left foot had pins and needles. He tried to flex it unobtrusively and it was seized with cramp. He lifted it slightly, wide awake now, and tried to bend back his toes within his shoe. The solid English leather didn't give very much. He desperately wanted to take his foot out of the damned shoe and bend it with his hands, but that was unthinkable. How long did cramp last if you couldn't do anything about it? His entire being was focused on his left foot. Slowly the pain eased. Now he didn't dare move the foot in case it came back. Finally the dominee signalled a shift and the congregation stood.

They filed out of the church and milled around on the lawn. He was introduced by Tannie Bessie to what felt like every member of the congregation, including the dominee as 'Melanie's boy, out from England to pay us a visit'. They were, without exception, friendly. He received at least a dozen invitations 'to visit'. It came to him, as he was talking to the owner of the formidable black hat, a Mrs Connie Viljoen, that he was being treated as though he belonged to the community. These people knew more about his mother and his mother's family than he did. Every single one had mentioned her.

Lunch was in the garden. Michael was relieved to change into shorts. Karel was cooking meat over a fire in a brick barbecue in the backyard. Tannie Bessie was sitting in a fold-up chair under a tree. He went to offer what assistance he could.

'This,' said Karel, 'this is the best braai marinade in the province, not so, Tannie?'

'It's true, they ask him for the recipe all the time.'

Karel thrust a beer at Michael from an ice-box at his side. 'Man, it's hot. So . . . what do you want to do this afternoon?'

'I thought I might take a walk, look around the farm.'

'I'll take you around in the bakkie if you like . . . '

'Thanks . . . but I'd like to walk, get some exercise . . . '

'You'd better take a gun with you then. Can you shoot?'

'Well, I've done a bit with a rifle.' Thank God for the school corps.

'I'll lend you one.'

'Is it really . . . ?'

'You don't want to take any chances.'

'Karel, you'd better find him a hat too,' Tannie Bessie added.

After lunch, Michael collected a battered felt hat and a functional, clean and loaded rifle. It was a good weapon, Karel told him, but he should have a go or two with it to check the sights. He was given additional ammunition despite his laughing protestation that if that many people were going to attack him he'd be done for in any event. Then he set off east, towards the vista he had seen that morning. He would be able to watch the sunset on the way back. Tannie Bessie had slipped some biltong, water and a couple of beers into an old haversack that he had slung over his shoulder.

Tannie Bessie settled in her chair on the veranda. Karel brought tea for her and another beer for himself. They sat a while in silence. The sound of the dominee on the radio, drifting over from where Oom Jan was listening to the afternoon service, was muffled. It was hot. Even the flies seemed too drugged by the still Sunday afternoon to make much of an effort. They watched Michael's figure receding.

'I hope he knows how to use that thing,' Karel said.

'He knew how to check it over. He's more likely to get sunstroke than hurt himself with that.' Tannie Bessie sighed. 'Melly's boy. It's hard to believe.'

'Does he look like her?'

'Oh ja. He looks like Melly all right. He's got her eyes. But he's so thin. And pale.'

'He'll relax,' Karel said, sensing that Tannie needed some reassurance. 'He seems all right.'

'Of course.'

Karel was consumed with curiosity. Something must have happened for the man to leave his job like that and come out here at such short notice. But what? He was a closed book, didn't say much. Hell, he hadn't volunteered anything about himself at all. He answered questions OK and asked quite a lot of questions too, but they were polite ones, ones he knew you wanted him to ask. Nothing that could embarrass anybody. It was bloody irritating, really. How were you supposed to get to know a man if he was so controlled? It came across as a form of superiority. He didn't dislike Michael. But he didn't warm to him either. Early days, he thought as he sipped the lager. Early days.

Tannie Bessie sat watching the figure of Michael get smaller and smaller. He was such an English boy, she thought to herself. Melly's boy. She must ask him about Melly. Perhaps she could write to her. It was a disgrace, really it was, that the husband hadn't let her know. All this time she'd thought it was Melly. Michael had said that Melly didn't speak. Did that mean she'd been struck dumb by the Lord? Or that she chose not to speak? Or that she was completely mad? How much did Michael know about Melly, anyway? Probably as much as any of them. Melly had never spoken about it, even when pressed. Claimed she couldn't remember. She'd been very young. Bessie could remember when Melly came home.

She'd been wearing skins, shaped like a pair of broekies. She was a deep red colour that they at first thought was sunburn and then found washed off to reveal the brown little body underneath. And her hair was a tangled bush that sat like a hat on her head. It must have been a way of protecting her. She was thin but not in bad health. But she couldn't speak. She mimed and clicked in the way of the Bushmen. Heaven knows why they took her or what had happened to her or how they knew where to bring her. The doctor said she was all right, had been well looked after.

She had been a strange child. Standing in the early morning or the evening to stare at the land, just stare, perfectly still, for a long time. Little girls didn't do that. It was as though she was listening for something, looking for something she could only find if she stayed absolutely still. People called her strange, said some unkind things about her. She had been strange. Before they taught her differently, she would try and play with all the black kids on the farm, follow some of the women about. Bessie's mother had made her untie the shawl that she tied around herself to carry her dolls. They'd given her a little pram from England for her birthday. Bessie had outgrown dolls but even she could see that it was a fine present for a little girl. Melly had put her dolls away and never used the pram. She'd been a different little thing.

It would have been easier for her if she hadn't been so different, Bessie thought. Then the women would have made her one of themselves. In some communities you have to be very strong, very hard, to be 'other'. Melly had been neither of these. And she had been otherwise. She had made people nervous by being so different. But she shouldn't be stuck in that damp, grey island away from her people. It was wrong. She should be in the sunshine; let the land make her well.

The ground was hard, covered in random scrub. It was a tan-red colour, dust puffed around Michael's ankles, he could feel the heat in the earth through his walking shoes as he headed towards the horizon. It was also deceptive. What seemed from a distance to be completely flat was uneven, with trenches appearing occasionally, small rises, but still it was like setting out like an ant across a barren backyard in the afternoon sun, seemingly infinite distance ahead of him. It was still hot but the intensity of midday had passed. He was sweating with the heat and the exertion. He wanted to put a reasonable distance between himself and the farmhouse. His sudden discovery of his family had been unexpected, he had yet to absorb it. England and winter were hard to imagine.

He quickly covered a couple of miles. He could just see the farmhouse. He had no intention of losing sight of it, he would certainly be lost. He found a small outcrop of rock, sat down to open one of Tannie's beers. The sun was soporific. He lay on his back, the hat shading his face, and tried to discover why he was here, how had this come about?

He tried to picture Janet on Sunday. What would she be doing? She would be having lunch with friends, possibly a picnic in one of the parks. Nonsense. It was winter, for heaven's sake. She'd be curled up with a video this afternoon, or going to see some obscure film that she'd read about in *Time Out*. Did he miss her? Yes. What did he miss? A friend, he supposed. Someone with whom he could share the strangeness of it all, who would discover this new landscape from the same starting point. Who would have found the church service funny, whom he could have told about his bloody foot. Who would have found Karel and Tannie Bessie as impenetrable as he did. But do you really want company, Michael? No. It was a form of homesickness, his missing Janet like this. What was he going to do here? He would stay a few more days, learn what he could about his mother. Then he'd take his father's advice and go on safari. Send gifts. He'd hated arriving empty handed. It put him at a disadvantage. He dozed in the sunlight.

Melanie Carter sat in a wicker basket chair on the veranda, staring out at the grey day. The sky looked lower than normal, enclosing the countryside in a damp blanket. The perennially green grass was studded with the skeletons of trees. The one advantage of winter was that it cleared the foliage from the horizons, created a sense of space. She had been unsettled, lately. It was hot, wrapped as she was in a thick woollen shawl with a heavy tartan rug around her legs. But it was not a warmth she wanted to throw off. She relaxed into it, felt it radiating through her. It was soothing, this warmth. She nestled, snuggled into it.

Sheena watched the peacefulness taking hold of Mrs Carter's being. The conservatory was warm, but surely not warm enough to give that sense of luxurious basking Mrs Carter seemed to be experiencing. Sheena picked up her novel.

Melanie heard a sound, a faint sound, a barely distinguishable groaning of dry grasses, the sound of a stealthy foot. She stood up and said in an intense whisper, 'Michael! Wake up! Someone's coming! Michael!' Sheena shot out of her chair, went to her. She was speaking! 'Mrs Carter? Are you all right, Mrs Carter?' Melanie shooed her away with her hand. And then she started to move, crouched down, dancing lightly sideways on her feet, making unintelligible sounds. The strange purity of the movements impressed Sheena, but she had a patient on her hands, a middle-aged woman darting left and right and making unintelligible noises. What did she expect? This was a madhouse, after all. She bleeped for support. An orderly arrived. 'All right, flower?'

'I'm all right. She's just being so weird. I thought we might need to calm her down.'

'Daft as a brush,' said the orderly.

'Come on, Mrs Carter,' he said as loudly as possible. 'Time to settle down and stop playing Red Indians, love,' moving slowly towards her.

She stopped, stared at him and the nurse. Then sat down in her chair again, wrapping her shawl and rug about her. Tears started to roll down her cheeks.

Something hard landed on Michael's stomach. He sat up, looked at it. It was a bullet. A young black man wearing khaki shorts stood over him, pointing the rifle at him.

'Bloody hell,' Michael said. 'Don't point the thing at me.'

'It's empty,' said the young man. 'A gun is a responsibility in this country. I'm not sure you should be allowed to have one, Englishman. Anyway, white men with guns are to be avoided.' He laughed as he handed the rifle back to Michael.

'I'm Michael Carter,' he extended his hand.

'I know. Timothy Makela.' They shook hands and Timothy sat down. 'How're you finding the heat? Man, you need more Factor 15,' he said pointing at Michael's red legs.

Timothy Makela didn't look much like the ominous threat that Karel had inferred. In fact, Michael could visualise him quite easily on the tube, in Notting Hill, or anywhere else in London.

'So, Englishman, what are you doing here?'

'Visiting . . . I wanted to see the country.'

'There isn't much to see here.'

Michael disagreed with him. He was struck by the spaciousness, the sense of the earth that surrounded them. 'I don't know. It's pretty extraordinary out here.'

'Well . . . England's so small and tidy. Such neat little farms and everything so contained. You know, I used to have to go to the sea all the time when I was there, just to believe that there was something that wasn't bordered and edged and gardened. Even the wilderness you have is enclosed somehow. It's a great place, you know, a generous and kind place, England. But I couldn't breathe there.'

'When were you there?'

'I left here twenty-five years ago. The ANC got me out. Sent me to university . . . Durham.' He laughed. 'I had to leave and go and do my A and O Levels, the whole thing took seven years. My education was a sad affair. There was a white nun who taught me before I left. She was a good woman. But it wasn't enough. Anyway, how're things in the white man's house?'

'I've only just arrived . . .' Michael felt on tricky territory. 'Do you know them well?' he asked. Damn. What a stupid question.

'Well? Well enough. They aren't bad people, I finally realise that. They're just stupid people.'

Michael didn't know how to reply.

Timothy looked at him. 'Anyway, they're your family.'

Michael nodded. 'My mother . . . '

'Melanie Wilmot. I was too young to meet her. But my mother remembers.'

'Did they know each other well?'

'You'll have to ask my mother. She was sorry to see her go.'

'I'd like to meet your mother.'

Timothy laughed softly. Pulled at his ear. 'You already have. She's the maid in the house.'

Michael struggled for words. 'Yes, yes, of course I have. I'm sorry . . . ' Timothy smiled. 'It's OK, Englishman. You couldn't know. Anyway, you'd better not try and talk to her in the house. She'd find it difficult. Come by and see us. I'm here for a couple of weeks.'

'I'd like to.' He liked Timothy Makela. Instantly. They sat for a while in the sun. Timothy must have grown up here.

'Do you come and visit your mother often?'

'As often as I can. But I'm not very welcome. Still, there's nothing the Boer can do about it now. Not legally, anyway. They don't trust me.' He laughed again. 'They have reason not to.'

'Why?'

'My job is a difficult one, Englishman. I have to establish the original tribal boundaries for my people. You see, we never owned the land on paper, so the only way to find out is to talk to the old people who remember from their fathers and their fathers' fathers what land was ours. Then we can apply for it to be given back to us. It's part of the reconstruction and development programme. We won't get it all, but we'll get some of it back. Then we can farm our own sheep. And the Boer will have us as neighbours.' He laughed softly again. 'No, Englishman, they have good reason not to like me.' Timothy was pleased at the thought. 'It's going to happen. It's just when. Everything takes so long. You know, they think we lie and cheat. They should sit with the elders of my people and listen to them argue about where exactly the boundary ends. It takes a long time, all of this. And the young are impatient.'

'You're not exactly an old man,' Michael smiled.

'I'm fortunate . . . I got out, I got an education, I got a chance. There are millions who didn't . . . they sold their youth for freedom. But that's easy when you're young. Now they know they gave their whole lives.'

'But surely,' Michael started carefully, 'surely there will be opportunities for them now? They must see some benefit?'

Timothy threw stones at a large stone farther away. 'We cannot give them enough in a short enough time. We cannot borrow from the rest of the world like the rest of Africa and then scrape a living paying back interest for the rest of our days. We will not bankrupt our children's future. The only miracle in the short term will come from some sort of redistribution of wealth. But the white man won't give much. And without the white man the rest of the world will lose interest in us.'

'Surely not . . . '

'Come, Englishman . . . ' Timothy was getting impatient. 'We don't want to be like the rest of Africa. Too poor to advance our industrialisation, made more poor by low commodity prices, crippled by debt, no, that's not for South Africa. And the white man is ahead of us. He knows it, we know it. Until we can do what he does and until the rest of the world believes that we can do what he does on our own, then we cannot be independently successful. The Boer made this problem for us. Now he should help us solve it, but he doesn't want to. He's too busy getting money out of the country and working out how he can get his children British passports, American, Australian passports, anything but South African passports.'

'But people like . . . ' he stopped himself. They were his family, dammit. 'Some people will surely never leave. Especially the farmers. They must want to help make it work.'

'Ask them, Englishman. I can tell you what they'll say. They want us to behave, to be good Kaffirs and not frighten them or threaten their lives. But other than that, they don't want to have anything to do with us. Hell, they haven't had to in their lifetimes, why should they start now? When I ask your uncle for thirty per cent of his land, what's he going to say? "Of course, Makela. In the interests of the new South Africa, I will willingly give you back thirty per cent of what my father's father took from your father's father. I will give it to you, Timothy, because for over forty years I supported a government that deprived your people of education, that prevented them from earning a decent living by excluding them from jobs, that denied them good medical care, prevented them from owning property." No. He's going to say that this land has been in his family for generations, that his people died for this land, that it is their land and their country and that what we are doing is theft. He will be outraged.' Timothy smiled at Michael. 'So you see what a difficult job I have, Englishman!'

Michael laughed. 'I think you're up to it,' he said.

It had grown a bit cooler while they talked. Michael turned around. The sun was a huge red ball above the horizon.

'You'd better get back. They'll be sending out a search party.'

They stood up, shook hands. Timothy set off north-west, Michael walked west towards the setting sun. A few stray clouds were near the horizon, glinting fierce red, purple and orange. By the time he reached the house the sun had set altogether, leaving a royal-blue sky with pale stars beginning to shine through.

Melanie Carter looked at the blackness of the early English winter evening. It was cold. She traced a figure over and over on the windowsill with her finger. She looked into the blackness of the night. The white-painted window frame came into focus as itself and remained that way. She watched her finger tracing the strange shape over and over. She was disassociated from this. This she did not recognise. She waited for the panic to overtake her. Not this time. Somehow she was able to accept that her hand had knowledge that this momentarily lucid part of her could not comprehend. The hand slowed, stopped. She was calm.

Karel wanted to know if Michael had found the gun to his liking. They were having dinner. 'I didn't use it, actually,' he said.
'But it's empty.'
Damn. Timothy still had the bullets.
'Oh . . . well I did some target shooting. It's a good weapon.' The lie wasn't a good one. Karel didn't believe him, he could tell. Sophie was serving them. Timothy's mother. She never looked at him, not at any of them. Just got on with it. She was a small woman, very neat in her crisp green uniform, her hair covered with a green scarf tied tightly around her head, the ends of the scarf invisible.
'Have things changed a great deal for you, in the new South Africa?' he asked his uncle.
Karel snorted. 'It's a bloody joke, the New South Africa. It's just a gravy train for black politicians, man. They're going to destroy the country.'
Michael waited.
'What's happened since the ANC came into power? I'll tell

you. Hospital services, education, everything's gone to hell and they want to take our land away. And the rand! It's a bloody joke, a joke, I tell you.' Karel was aggressive, angry.

'But . . . it seems that the transition has been peaceful enough . . . '

'Peace? What peace? Before they could kill you in the name of politics. Now they just kill you in the name of crime. And the police around here are nearly all black now. They're inefficient – you can't trust them – you have to type your own statements because they can't . . . The new South Africa's going to be just another African disaster, that's what the new South Africa's going to be. They're not all educated like Mandela, you know.'

Michael didn't know how to respond. Where did one begin?

'You don't think,' he began slowly, 'that this is a fairer society? More just?'

'Fair? Fair? How fair is it that they want to take our land? They've not done a bloody thing for the land and now they just want to take it from us. They'll ruin it. It won't take a year. Fair? It's a scandal. Jislaaik . . . '

'Karel!' The word had offended his uncle.

'Ekskuus, Oom, maar ek word so bleddy vies(I'm sorry, uncle, but I get so angry) . . . Hell, it's a total bloody disaster.'

'What do you think should be done?' Michael was repelled and intrigued.

'We should be a federation of states. Give us some autonomous rule. The only place that's still functioning properly is the Cape. And why? Because we still govern it. We can't be governed by these idiots. They haven't got the first idea! It's a joke, man, a joke.' Karel was shaking his head.

'And Mandela?' Michael ventured.

'Well. OK, but he's old, isn't he? And there's always Winnie waiting in the wings. What'll she do, what'll Mbeki do when

Nelson goes? Do you know we've got cabinet ministers that have got less education than a child of seven! You tell me how they're going to run things.'

'I can't. But is it really their fault that they don't have an education?'

'Look,' Karel said, 'I don't want to give offence. But you don't live here. You don't know anything about us. Take it from me, the ANC are bloody poison.'

'You're right,' Michael said, 'I don't live here. I'm just trying to understand.'

Karel relaxed a bit. 'The problem with everyone overseas is that they think the African black is just like your English black or like the American black. They aren't. They're not sophisticated, they're not civilised. The only thing they understand is a firm hand. You meet some of them. Then you'll see what I mean. The rest of the world doesn't understand. They think that the African black is a person just like you and me. But they're not. Hell, most of them can't even write. And now they're running the show. It's jobs for the boys all the way.'

Michael nodded in what he hoped was a noncommittal way.

Michael lay on his back, listening to the night. What was he doing in this room, this house, this country, what had happened to his life? He felt as if he had walked blindly into a time and space where he was a detached and slightly alarmed observer.

Somehow his new-found family, Timothy, even the landscape, seemed unreal, hard to fit into his life as experiences relevant to him. He was engaged because he was undergoing the experience, yet he was completely detached. What had happened to his job, to his relationships, his friends, his life? He'd slunk off like a fugitive, arrived empty handed (that still rankled), and to what purpose? The enormity of the changes he had set in motion arranged themselves in his consciousness, dark shapes of anxiety speeding his pulse.

Sod it. What was done was done. He'd send postcards to his friends, he'd get out of this Fort Knox, he'd have an adventure to make it worthwhile. Michael did not want to wound his credibility fatally by being seen to go under, however briefly. He would window dress this escapade into an anecdote that would fit into the meetings he would have with his clients and colleagues when he returned. An African adventure. Surely somewhere in this harsh landscape he could find exploits that would make him more interesting, more amusing, better value? Perhaps that was it. He'd become deathly dull, morbid, he'd lost his sense of humour. Just as well he'd taken leave before he'd made a mistake that cost him more than a little embarrassment.

Nobody knew what happened after he'd been carted off by security. Only Janet, and she was on his side anyway. He must remember to send her a postcard. The thing to do was brazen it out. One of the boys. Too much by way of high spirits. Blessed mockery. Turn the thing round. His thoughts were sending adrenalin coursing through his body. He would see Timothy's mother and then he'd get out of here.

Michael opted to spend the following morning with Tannie Bessie. She was elbow deep in flour, the week's bread was being processed on the kitchen table. Karel had not insisted on his company. Michael was going to use this time productively. All the gaps in their own personal history that his parents couldn't or wouldn't fill he was going to charm out of this elegant woman. Like every child, he assumed his right to their secrets and their experience.

'How did they meet?'

'Well . . . First Melly crashed the truck and your father

brought her home.' Tannie Bessie was kneading dough with a movement that seemed to use the force of her entire upper body. 'Then he came to visit her. And there was this dance in Kimberley . . . I remember Melly never said much about it, but you know how people talk in small places. I found out about this young Englishman, he was something to do with one of the banks, something to do with loans to the mining houses, I think. Well, you can imagine, the family wasn't very happy about it.'

'Why not?'

'Well, the English had a reputation. Especially after the war, you know. They would flatter a girl and promise her everything – and then one day they'd be gone, no letter, no word, just gone. Leaving the poor girls to face everyone. And the local boys would laugh at them, of course they would. So I wasn't pleased. But Melly said he was all right. It went on from there.'

Mindful of her audience, Bessie did not elaborate on the fears that had beset her at the time. Bessie distrusted the English. When they were friendly, you were charmed, and then you wondered if they were being patronising. And if they weren't, you wouldn't know either, because they all came with the same impenetrable façade. They all stuck together, too, shared the same jokes, talked about things that meant nothing to Bessie. Her instinct told her these people found in her some novelty value, as though the world's great diversity had been created for the entertainment of the English with their firm faith that only they knew how things could and should be done. The confidence, hidden behind that charming put down of the self, was in their genes. She had thought it would be good for Melly to get away, but would she be happy? And what about Bessie? Could she manage without Melly around? And what did they know of this Englishman anyway? Bessie pummelled the dough with a concentrated frown deepening between her eyes. Well, she'd been right to worry. Melly was sick now. Remembering Jeremy Carter, she looked at his son. He was like his father. A closed book, a pretty cover. But he had Melly's eyes. Definitely.

Michael wanted to know about his mother's time with the Bushmen. His grandparents' farm was much farther north, closer to the Kalahari, Bessie told him. They got out a map and she showed him where the fertile banks of the Orange River bordered an expanse of rusty brown. They apparently had had access to the river. And because of that access and their endeavours to keep people off their land they had been killed.

'It was a tragedy. A farmer must protect his land. You can't have everyone coming on to the land. Your animals will disappear! And what happened to Melly, we don't know. She was well cared for. I often wonder why they didn't kill her too. Nowadays they'll kill anyone. There was this story in the paper the other day about this woman in Johannesburg who drove her car into her drive and totsies drove in behind her. They held a gun to her head and the husband came out and told them they could have the car, they could take anything they wanted, but they must please leave his wife alone. They shot him. And the little three-year-old daughter came running out calling for her mommy and they shot her. In front of the mother. Shot her dead. I don't know what happened to the woman. It's terrible, the crime. They've got everything now, you know. Why do they have to go round killing the people as well? In the towns you see white women begging on the pavements.' Tannie Bessie shook her head. She was lost for a while in the horror of it all.

Michael was patient. She held the stories that went back to before his beginning, stories that would broaden his life, stretch the continuum back beyond his own experience.

'Tell me about you, Michael.' Damn. He wasn't keen to

trade. 'Well, there isn't very much. Nothing as exciting, I'm afraid, as everything around here.'

'Have you got a girlfriend?'

'No. I just broke up with a girl called Janet. She's a solicitor.'

'Shame. Still, there's plenty of girls around. And now what are you going to do with yourself, Michael?'

'I think I've earned a break, actually. I thought I might go on a tour, travel around Africa a bit.'

Tannie Bessie nodded slowly. 'You'll have to be careful, you hear? Speak to Karel. We can lend you an old Land-Rover or something, help you put together what you need. Where will you go?'

'I really don't know – I thought I might go and look at Grandfather Wilmot's old farm . . . then a safari . . . '

'There isn't any farm any more. It's part of a big farming co-operative. Why don't you go to Botswana? Go see the Okavango, go to the game farms, see the Drakensberg, you know you haven't even seen a wine farm or the Cape yet . . . ' She headed into the pantry.

Michael realised that Sophie had been standing quietly listening to their conversation. So quiet and unobtrusive was she that she seemed capable of being invisible. Now she walked past Michael and said in a hushed whisper, 'Timothy says you should come tonight. After eating.' And then she was out the back door. The practised quiet and the keen, discreet observation were unnerving. Was this how revolutions were won?

As the morning went on he tried to explain his mother's illness but it was hard. Bessie looked more and more severe as he stumbled on.

That night they sat outside Sophie's rooms. Timothy had built a small fire and passed around a bottle of brandy. It was heady, the combination of the vast dome above them and the huge blackness outside their patch of light. Sophie sat on an old kitchen chair, Timothy and Michael on upturned, empty orange beer crates. Sophie cleared her throat, looked directly at Michael.

'Your mother was my friend when we were children.' It was a strangely formal approach. 'I am sorry to hear she is not well.'

'Thank you,' Michael said. 'She is not ill in her body but ill in her mind,' he added.

Sophie nodded. 'Melly was a good person, and the little people, those Bushmen, they can make her well. Melly is not well in spirit. Melly has a good mind, a very good mind. Melly's mind was never sick, not like some people. She must see a Bushman healer. You are her son, you can go for her.'

Michael looked at Timothy, who laughed. Michael didn't laugh. Sophie was looking at him intently. 'Can I go for her? She's so far away.'

Sophie smiled. 'You're her son. You come from her body. You can go for her. Sure.'

'Where would I find a healer?'

A rapid exchange between Timothy and his mother followed. Timothy got up and went to the edge of their circle of light. He turned around and continued the dialogue with his mother. Michael saw the frustration in his face. She was convincing him to do something.

'Englishman . . . we will go together.' He was resigned.

'I really don't want to put you out . . . '

Timothy sat down again. 'We don't have any choice. This is a matter that my mother has decided because of the relationship between my mother and your mother. We don't have any say in it. Apparently the relationship is stronger than I thought. They are sisters.' He laughed at the look on Michael's face. 'Not blood sisters, Englishman! You don't have to be a blood relative to have a sibling connection, it's the nature of the relationship that determines what it is. They were sisters.' He shrugged, but looked at Michael more closely. Why had his mother never mentioned any of this?

Michael was sure that he could manage with a map, but Timothy and Sophie were adamant.

'What about your work? You can't just drop everything, can you?'

'In Africa we haven't yet become complete slaves to your empty work ethic, Englishman. There are things more important than work. And anyway my mother will speed my work while I am gone.'

'What'll you do, Sophie?'

'I will speak with the people. They must decide. I will speak to the other women. We will help them to decide.'

It was getting late. Timothy walked part of the way back to the double fences with Michael.

'Do you really believe in this stuff?' Michael asked.

Timothy shrugged. 'There are things we don't understand. If my mother believes that this will make a difference, then it may make a difference. Are your doctors helping your mother?'

Michael shook his head.

'Then you have nothing to lose.'

They said good-night and as he left, Timothy pointed at the fences. 'These . . . ' he said, 'these are an insult.'

Michael sat a while on the darkened veranda staring at the insult. Here was his adventure. It probably wouldn't help. But the thought that he might be able to do something to help his mother was comforting. A weight that he hadn't realised was always there felt a little easier. He had nothing to lose. Why hadn't he thought about doing anything to help her before? He would have to explain his plans to Tannie Bessie and Karel.

The two little girls had shared the loss of front milk teeth. They had wobbled the loose teeth at each other in perfect reciprocity. If Melanie's was the first to come out, Sophie had stared with fascination at her friend's pink gum and now dark pink, nearly black cavity. That was when they weren't playing extended, impossible-to-remember games with extremely arbitrary rules. They were often early Boer pioneers, trekking in a makeshift wagon, attacked by marauding impi. Neither child could raise much enthusiasm for a sustained attack upon the other, so they would take it in turns, more often than not forging some grand alliance between the brave impi and the equally brave settler. Often they would fight together against an unknown third enemy, possibly another tribe of impi or even the British, although here they were again a little tentative. So the other tribe was always easiest. They quarelled over who would be the impi. It was by far the more interesting role. The settler was destined to build a laager and wait, passive, while the impi could crouch around, occasionally throwing a few stones on the ground or raising a makeshift spear behind a bush to heighten the tension before her charge.

The whole farm was their playground, but the area around the cement reservoir was their favourite spot. There was more vegetation, for starters, and they could build forts in the almost dense patch of undergrowth. And then there was the water. They weren't allowed to swim in it, but they could dangle their feet in it in the afternoon heat and feel the delicious coolness.

Their friendship had been banned the following summer. Oom Karel sat Melanie down after her bath one evening and explained to her that she was different from Sophie, that one day Sophie would have to do as she, Melanie, wished. That this was the way of the world, it was set out like that in the Bible and Melanie must learn to obey. The little girl had studied her uncle gravely. It was outside her comprehension. He had reported her stillness to his wife. The child had looked and looked at him. He had taken her silence for consent, kissed her forehead and sent her to bed.

The following day Melanie reported the conversation to Sophie. The two little girls sat in a puzzled silence for a while. Then Sophie turned on her friend. In her stilted Afrikaans she had yelled at her. 'Go away then! Go and be the big fat Boer woman! I don't want to be your friend anyway!'

Sophie smiled. Sitting in the quiet after Michael's leaving, remembering.

Melanie had been utterly still. Tears had started to roll down her face. Sophie remembered the heaving of her own chest, the tightness, the wanting to hit something.

'Please, Sophie . . . Please don't . . . I didn't say I would . . . '

She hadn't been able to stop herself. It had all come out, all the things they'd been able to put aside between them. Melanie's clothes. How Melanie was clean and good and she, Sophie, was dirty and bad and it wasn't her fault, it wasn't, wasn't! How she, Sophie, had a mother who had to wash, by hand, the underwear of the people in the house and her mother found it disgusting, did Melanie know that? She found it disgusting. It wasn't fair. Then her Afrikaans had deserted her and she'd reverted to her own language.

That was how Oom had found them, Melanie shaking and crying and Sophie screaming. He'd grabbed her, Sophie could remember it now, taken off his belt and whipped her. Melanie had flung herself at him, pleading for him not to. He'd thrust her aside and continued to beat the little girl, Melanie becoming increasingly hysterical. Finally he'd had to put Sophie to one side in order to smack his niece hard in the face. All three had stared at each other. I should have run away then, Sophie thought to herself. But she hadn't. And he hadn't finished with her. He'd strapped her wrist to the piping on the side of the reservoir with his belt. The piping had been baking all morning in the heat and she'd screamed and screamed while he went to fetch a branch from one of the trees. He'd beat her with that branch while her mother, who had come running, stood pleading with him, crying, asking him to beat her instead.

She had forgotten Melanie, standing rigid with horror. They had met once after that. She'd come to visit her, which was allowed, this once. She'd sat on Sophie's bed, with nothing to say. Sophie had found herself saying that it was all right. She was strong, it was all right. She could still remember the little girl's face. Melanie had kissed her, left a gift and never returned.

Now Sophie held the little jewellery box in her hand.

Opening it that afternoon so long ago she had found her friend's most precious possession, a carefully constructed necklace of tiny ostrich beads, the beads she had come home with. Melanie had shown them to her in the first flush of their friendship, allowed Sophie to wear them for a few precious minutes. It was, as she had explained, the only thing that was truly hers.

The fire was dying down. Sophie pulled a blanket around her shoulders. Ah, Melanie. She'd followed her life, through the gossip and the talk around the fire of the goings on in the white man's house. Inevitably she'd become one of them. Sophie had been bitter. But she was a child, she'd had no choice. Neither of them had been able to exercise any real choice. And from the safety of England, Melanie had written to thank Sophie for her wedding present. In the end Sophie had been glad for her, to see her go.

And now here was the son. With her son. She felt proud to see her son talking with the young Englishman like an equal. She had encouraged Timothy's rebellion. And she had been proud when he went to England, even if he might never return. But here he was. Untouched. The future. Talking about things with Melanie's son. She smiled then, laughed. Timothy came out of the shadows to tease her.

'What are you laughing at out here in the dark on your own? People will say my mother is a mad woman.' He kissed her head.

'I'm laughing at Baas Karel.'

He chuckled. It was an old joke. Bessie's father, Baas Karel, had died in the sheep dip, struck down by a heart attack. And the farm-workers with him had watched his struggles intently, eventually sending one of their number on a leisurely mission for help. And then Sophie's father had started to laugh. Oh, the rage in the man as he lay dying amidst their laughter. It made him flop like a fish. He died from a second attack, no doubt brought about by his sudden surge of anger. It had heartened the whole community, that laughter.

9

'Well, we're here.'

Timothy turned left into a long driveway. Driving on the highway it looked as though the land was completely flat, the horizon ahead of them curving round like the edge of the earth, but you could never see what was at the end of these long driveways.

The houses they approached were small and round, made of brick with red concrete verandas and green pitched roofs of corrugated iron. Two small girls were sitting on one of the verandas sewing tiny stitches into white squares of material. Timothy asked them if Sister was home. They giggled and nodded and nudged each other, stealing long looks at Michael. Then a nun came out on to the veranda, a lined, small creature with skinny white legs sticking out the bottom of a habit that was both too big for her and looked like it had shrunk and was now too short. Timothy introduced Michael first, who shook the bony hand, and then he disclosed his own identity. The long fingers with the plain silver band clapped over her mouth.

'Oh oh oh! Not Timothy Makele! But look at you! Look how wonderful! How well you look! And you are here! Today! Oh, Timothy, it is so very good to see you!' The accent was soft West of Ireland and each exclamation a caress. Oh, but they must come and have some tea. She would make tea immediately. Timothy must put a table under the jacaranda tree in the yard, had he ever seen it looking so beautiful? Every day it reminded her of how wonderful the world is that God provides for us. Then there was a bustling with tea things inside the sparse round room, with its sideboard that served as a pantry, and the small gas cooker was enlisted to boil the water and Michael to carry a tray, then chairs were taken outside and finally they were seated and Sister Ignatius could ask after Sophie and insist upon the entire story of Timothy's life from when he had left her care to today.

They both pointed out to Michael the small room in the row of what looked like stables where Timothy had lived for the three years before he went to England. They interrupted each other with anecdotes about his learning and his frequent running away and his most inventive excuses for not learning his Latin verbs.

'It was the first time I heard that God could intervene in the matter of verbs,' the little nun said. 'He didn't want Timothy to spend time on them because it wouldn't help Timothy's comrades nor contribute to His wonderful creation in any way that was relevant.'

'But you can't argue with a Catholic nun about God,' Timothy laughed, ' . . . she just goes straight back to Him and gets Him to overrule things. She has a direct line, you see.'

'Oh, get away . . . '

Timothy told her more and more about what he was doing; at length, satisfied, she turned her attention to Michael.

He had no difficulty talking to her about his mother. The little nun seemed a creature outside the world, as though she already inhabited a spiritual ether which hung about her like a second veil. 'I will pray for her,' the nun said. 'She has a special place with God, your mother. He has kept her close to

Him for a reason. God is most clearly heard in silence. It is there that we find Him.'

That evening Timothy and Michael sat alone over a small fire, feeding it sticks and watching the moon rise in the turquoise blue of the sky that reflected the crimson sunset on the other side of the world. It was cooler now, the warm earth hanging suspended between day and night. They listened to the high-pitched cadence from the bush around them. The constant twitter and swooping of the birds in and out of the violet-wistaria-laden trees subsided as the darkness grew deeper. Michael breathed in the smell of clean air, dust, woodsmoke and evening chill. Timothy opened another beer.

'I didn't know you were Catholic.'
Timothy looked at him. 'Catholic? No no. And you?'
'Church of England. Same as everyone.'
'Everyone?'
They laughed.
'Does it matter to you?' Timothy asked.
'Not really. It's just there. A bit like cricket. What are you?'
Timothy shrugged. 'African.'
They sipped their beers slowly. When the fire was hot enough they would wrap potatoes and onions in foil and shove them into the embers, cooking the boerewors they had brought with them on the banked-down flames. Sister Ignatius had supplied a green salad which they were both raiding with their fingers as they waited for the fire to build.

'Sister fought a losing battle with us,' Timothy laughed. 'And she knew it. But it didn't stop her.' He shook his head. 'She would give us things like the Ten Commandments and we would learn them and when we all had them perfect then we'd ask her why the settlers didn't know them.'

'And she said?'
'That we shouldn't make our own decisions based on the

evil of others. That we should trust God to see hypocrisy. That we must beware of the devil that was tempting us with violence.' He laughed. 'She did her best. But we saw religion had been a way of keeping us oppressed. Which it was. Is.'

'How long has she been here?'

'Oh . . . I don't know. A long time.'

'Does she ever go home?'

'Once every ten years. And there was this other American nun who came around every six months in a van and exchanged books and things. She went all through the war zones – still does, I think – taking books to the schools.'

'Bloody hell.'

'Oh, no one would hurt her. Land-mines though . . . She was always dirty and you know what nuns are like about being clean. Well this one's habit was always covered in dust, and she wouldn't have had a bath for days before she got here. We told terrible jokes about her and her van.'

'They sound remarkable.'

'Well . . . they didn't just want us all to be good Kaffirs, white Kaffirs, really . . . they saw us as people.'

He looked at Michael. 'So who took care of your spiritual well-being?'

'School, mostly. Church on Sunday. Spiritual well-being didn't feature very much. It sort of took care of itself.'

'Do you believe in the existence of God?'

'It seems unlikely . . . '

'Don't you get lonely then?'

'Lonely?' Michael laughed. 'Good God no. Sorry. Freudian slip.'

'I would . . . '

'So you believe in Him?'

Timothy nodded. Pointed at the stars above them. 'He's everywhere. I don't believe in the grinding of bones in hell or eternal fires for the damned. I don't believe in the punishment ethos of Western religion . . . but I've absorbed enough to lose whatever beliefs I might have had without it. Which may or may not be a good thing.' Despondency had begun to tag itself on to Timothy's words.

'Is this hard? Being here?'

Timothy nodded, stretched. 'It brings it all back. Oh, we were going to change everything. And now, even though I know we have changed a great deal, sometimes . . . We underestimated, continue to underestimate, what we are fighting. We absorbed so much of the enemy that now we sometimes cannot see the difference between our behaviours and the behaviours we hated so much. Because we envied them, you see. And if I am horribly honest I have to say that we admired them. They seemed to know so much.' He shook his head. 'They still do. And in some ways, even with all the violence, the struggle felt clean. We had one issue, one result. But now we are left with no clear way forward. The whites are still our paymasters. That hasn't changed . . . They haven't changed.'

He flung a stone into the darkness.

Michael felt the bitterness.

'How will it end then?'

Timothy shrugged, picked up a handful of sand and let it stream through his fingers. 'We are too different. This is us. Just grains of sand that make up the land. We know we're not important as individuals. Go and ask a black factory-worker if he wants to be paid more than his fellow workers for the work he has done, even if he's done more. He'll tell you no. He exists as part of the group, part of the community. Alone he doesn't exist at all. The group is always more important than the individual. It is what we call *ubuntu*. Even the leader of a group is only important because of the group. His responsibilities are great.'

Michael considered. 'Communism?'

'In a way. But purer. It was the fabric of all African society. Apartheid gave us a common enemy which also helped. But now . . . ' He shook his head. 'Now, we too have Western appetites and hate and an apartheid of money. And government is hard. Sometimes it doesn't work at all.'

Michael looked a question.

'Oh, I know it sounds disloyal. They haven't the faintest idea how to do the job, many of them, but because they don't know – shit, they don't even know what they don't know – they think everything is OK. They've finally emulated the settler who has money for nothing and doesn't have to work, which is what they saw, what they thought. And the machinery around and underneath them is slowly breaking down. And the whites. Well. The racists try and lead them down every dead end there is.

'And the liberal whites? They think that now we have a democracy and a constitution, the debt's paid. It's all squared off. A level playing field. Now they can reveal what they've always thought underneath . . . ' He shook his head. 'Have you heard the white opposition attacking us? All they want is power. We need help, consensus politics, and they want to beat us. They want power and they don't want to share it and they think that we will elect them one day but they are out of their minds if they think that. And then you hear the whisper that the Aids epidemic will solve the country's problems, there will be a white government here again in fifteen years because we can't make the people listen to us about this disease and it's true, Aids is quietly killing off Africa; they test the drugs here but we can't afford to buy them . . . Oh yes, to be an African is to be . . . Well . . . ' He stopped. Laughed. Shook his head. Michael opened another couple of beers.

'You won though. In the end you won.'

Timothy looked at him. 'Of all people, Englishman, you should know that winning is a temporary thing.'

They laughed. 'Imagine,' said Timothy, 'imagine if Germany had invaded Britain way back, and then after three hundred and fifty years of oppression the British finally got the upper hand, but the Germans still held on to all the fancy cars and houses and jobs and you British were uneducated, starving, out of work, living in shacks, listening to the Germans say what rubbish, what savages you were – I wonder what you would do?'

'It's hard to tell.'

'Isn't it.' They grinned as the concept played itself out around them.

The following day they took their leave of Sister Ignatius. Michael began to realise that he and Timothy had different inner clocks. There was little hurry about Timothy. Being with Sister Ignatius and taking Michael around the school buildings were important to him. Michael felt impatience itching in his nervous system and yet, he thought, to what purpose? It's a habit. I have no appointments, but still I must rush. The children sang for them and Michael was asked by Sister Ignatius to explain to the children where he lived and how he had come to Africa by aeroplane. By the time they left he had become attached to the place, had been glad of the delay.

As the morning advanced they pressed on along the exceptionally high-quality tarmac (to make it easier for the defence force to move across the country, Karel had explained), with fenced, barely arable lands stretching on either side. It was getting progressively hotter, the road ahead dissolving into white wavy lines of heat, when Timothy pulled over into a service area. The petrol station doubled as a general store. They parked in the only available shade next to the building and ate from the cooler bag Tannie Bessie had provided.

Timothy suggested they rest awhile in the Land-Rover. 'That way if it goes missing at least we go with it!' They would not drive in the extreme midday heat. Even the petrol-station owner was shutting his doors. There was an almost complete absence of traffic. South Africans didn't readily venture north in the summer heat. Michael found he dozed off quite easily.

They travelled farther in the late afternoon. As the sun began to set, a red ball that would soon be level with the left-hand side of the vehicle, Timothy turned left. They drove for a few miles and stopped near some trees, a rare sight in the flat emptiness around them. Timothy set about gathering wood for a fire. Michael dragged the sleeping-bags out of the Land-Rover. As the sun slid below the horizon, now bordered by a low range of hills, Timothy lit the fire. Michael played barman and chef, opening beers and lighting the little gas cooker. They agreed on an impromptu stew of baked beans and bully beef, with rolls. The sludge in the pot on the fire thickened. Michael poured some beer in to dilute it.

Their final destination was the outskirts of the Kalahari Gemsbok Park, the nature reserve that now took in most of the Kalahari Desert. On its perimeter was land allocated for the housing of Bushmen, given to them once they were forced out of the reserve. 'For their own good, you understand,' Timothy grinned. It was impossible for them to live their traditional hunter-gatherer lives without the land. So most were reduced to begging from tourists, selling knick-knacks. There was a liquor store just outside the park that did a brisk trade with Bushmen. They had no tolerance for alcohol and no interest in or aptitude for the cash economy.

As Karel had said, shaking his head, 'Sure, you'll find Bushmen there. But they're not the real thing. They're off their heads with drink or dagga most of the time. No, the real Bushman is gone.' He was quite sorrowful. He had suggested a visit to Schmitsdrift, a town near Kimberley created for Bushmen disbanded from the South African Defence Force, but Timothy objected. He had been one of the people those

Bushmen were paid to track. And anyway, he had heard that the social problems in Schmitsdrift were bad. They would be more likely to find a genuine healer in the desert itself, but first they had to find someone who would take them there.

Michael went to fetch his camera.

'Do you mind?' he asked, pointing the camera at Timothy by the fire. Timothy shook his head.

Not knowing each other that well and keen to oil their growing friendship they steadily worked their way through the cooler bag of beers that Karel had provided.

Timothy fished inside his vehicle for pictures of his future bride and his little girl, Zinzi. He was saving up to pay the lobola that his fiancée's parents expected. She was expensive because she was qualified – a nurse, he told Michael. Timothy was looking forward to more children. Michael didn't say anything about Janet.

'What does your father do?' Michael asked.

'He is dead.' Timothy poked at the embers of the fire, added more wood.

'I'm sorry . . . has he been dead long?'

'Since I was a small child. We did not bury him. My mother does not know where his body is. We know he is dead because he never came home. He may have been in trouble with his employer, who said he just disappeared. He would never have left his family. He was killed. My mother knows he was killed. There was talk that the farmer killed him. Murdered him.' Timothy stabbed the fire viciously. 'We registered it with the Commission. I have tried to have an investigation opened. It is on the list, the very long list of things that my people need to find out. We need to see justice. I need justice. When I was a young boy I went to see the farmer. I asked him if he knew what had happened to my father. He laughed at me. I swore I would kill him one day.'

'Will you?'

'He is dead now. I didn't kill him!' They laughed. 'But I must work within the law. There has been too much blood already. It is all red, the blood, but most of it comes from black bodies.' Timothy brooded into the fire.

As the fire died down Timothy amused himself by giving Michael a lecture on the bush, how to shake out your shoes to check for scorpions, how to be on your guard against snakes. What creatures could arrive in the night.

After an uneasy but mercifully uneventful night, Michael woke with the very first light. It was a blue grey but you could just determine where the sun was going to appear on the eastern horizon. A few late stars and the moon were just visible. The air was wonderfully cool, a relief after the relentless heat of the previous day. Timothy was curled asleep on the other side of the cold fire. Michael slipped carefully out of his sleeping-bag. He picked up his camera, checked his shoes for scorpions and quietly left the camp. No need to wake Timothy. He wanted to capture the sunrise on film. There was a definite triumph in gaining the dawn. He headed towards a small outcrop of rock, about half a mile away. Even in this barren terrain there were subtle noises as insects and birds took advantage of the cool and light. He settled himself at the far end of the rocky outcrop, found a good place to balance his camera.

The sun was still hiding below the horizon. He had a sense of the outline of the earth's curvature as he watched the massive flatness. It struck him that the sun would not appear above the horizon but the earth would slowly turn to face it. It seemed entirely possible that he was watching the earth turn in space. The sky was lightening quickly. Michael wanted to capture the first glimmer of the sun on the eastern horizon, the daybreak. He would also take a picture of the western sky, try and get the contrast.

As he pressed the shutter for the first time he heard the

shots. Two of them. Well, how else would Timothy let him know that he was up, that they should leave? Michael turned and took the picture behind him. Then he climbed down the rocks and headed for the camp. There were puffs of dust behind the trees, the sound of an engine. Timothy must be impatient to go. He started to run. As he got closer he could see the vehicle in the distance. In the clearing Timothy lay much as Michael had left him, except for the pool of blood that seeped out from under his head. There was nothing else. Just Timothy, blood, empty Castle cans and the blackened ashes of the fire. They had taken Timothy's sleeping-bag, his boots, left his legs lying strangely. Oh God. Michael felt for a pulse, for a breath. But Timothy was dead. He could sense he was dead. There was no life in that body. Michael was shaking. It couldn't have happened. It was a dream. Jesus Christ. Not Timothy. Not like this. It was too casual, too quick. People didn't just die like this. It couldn't have happened. How had it happened? Oh shit. No, his mind whimpered, no, please no.

Timothy must have been asleep when the bullets went into his head. The unknown 'they' had taken everything, even stopping to pick up the cooler bag. Michael felt fear, bowel-dissolving, stomach-churning fear. He was exposed, there was nowhere to hide. What if they came back? His gun was in the Land-Rover. Everything was in the Land-Rover. Sophie. Oh, God. Sophie. He had been careless. He should never have left him. Then you'd both be dead, said the voice in his head. He shut down the surge of relief. Jesus. Timothy is dead. Thank God, his eyes were shut. The sun had appeared. Michael didn't know what to do. He sat shaking and watched the body. His mind was empty. He simply sat.

As the sun began its climb the flies arrived. He shooed them off Timothy. What was he going to do with him? He couldn't leave him here. He would have to get to the road. He would carry Timothy to the road. Wait for a car. Someone must pass. He had no water, no hat. He would get sunstroke if he sat in the heat by the side of the road all day. Perhaps he should make a shelter. He should move. He should start.

There were birds that looked like hideous, black-winged, red-cropped turkeys. They had been circling over Michael and Timothy for the past fifteen minutes. Now they landed twenty yards away. They were massive. Michael ran at them, yelling. They moved off. But waited patiently near by. He couldn't delay any longer. He took pictures of the crime scene. Felt ridiculous. Then he went to pick up Timothy. As he lifted him there was a movement, a sound. To his shame he flung the body away from him. Then checked him over again. He was definitely dead. Television had taught him that bodies release air and may make sounds. He lifted him again. How does one carry a body? Not in one's arms. Too heavy. A fireman's lift was the only method Michael could sustain. He started to walk back towards the road.

The vultures were circling above them. Good God. Timothy's arms were slapping against the back of Michael's legs. He felt the stickiness of the already congealed blood against his neck and arms. One arm seemed permanently occupied in waving off flies. He headed east, following the tyre tracks they had made the previous day. The second set headed north. Timothy's body was heavy, but Michael was reluctant to put him down. He would have to pick him up again. After an hour of one foot in front of the other he could feel the top of his head overheating. My brains are going to simmer, he thought. But he carried on. The road would appear, must appear, soon. A vulture flew at the part of the carcass dangling behind him. Michael felt the extra weight as it landed on Timothy's back. He swung around, nearly overturned. The bird flew off with an ugly squawking sound. He was an unwilling Pied Piper. He stopped for a rest, threw stones, hard, up at the vultures. Another hour and he reached the road. The vultures took up residence on the telegraph wire opposite him.

He laid Timothy down, took his handkerchief out of his pocket and, tying a knot in each corner, put it on his head. There was no cover. The road extended on either side into the wavery heat haze. He would wait. There was nothing else he could do.

It had been harder than Hardekop had anticipated to find a four-wheel-drive vehicle that would get him off-road and across the border into Namibia. The anti-theft devices were getting better and better. And most of the four-by-four drivers had anti-hi-jack devices or were armed themselves. He had seen Timothy and Michael asleep in the Land-Rover as he pretended to fill up the BMW he had taken out of the car park in the centre of Cape Town. He knew they would fill the Land-Rover's tank for him. He drove past the petrol station and parked on the side of the road, waiting for them to pass him. The rest was easy. He had been surprised to find the brother alone, but glad he was asleep. No fuss. He had abandoned the BMW a few miles back.

After an hour of driving he pulled over and checked the contents of the vehicle. Karel's gun, the maps, the compasses, the sleeping-bags, everything in Michael's luggage, all these would be useful. And everything would ease his way. A little gift here, a little gift there, and people could be persuaded to look away. Nobody would ever convince the people that stealing from whites was really wrong.

He tuned the radio. He'd open a beer, light a spliff and be in Namibia by nightfall. He looked at himself in the side mirror, adjusted his mirror shades and smoothed his hair. The two scars, one stretching from his left eyebrow to his forehead and the other across his left cheek and the corner of his mouth pleased him as always. They were the proof. Anyone who knew anything would know he won his battles. Only the living carry scars.

Michael sat throwing stones at the vultures. They were less and less intimidated by him. Tannie Bessie's voice went round and round in his brain. She'd been very anxious about his plans.

'So Michael. You will be careful on this trip? I don't want to be the one who has to tell Melly and your father that anything's happened to you. How long are you going for?'

'It's really hard to say. Timothy says the journey will take three or four days. He'll spend a day or so with me getting me settled and then he'll come back. He's coming back here, so you can see him or Sophie can let you know how it went. And then I'll carry on from there. I thought I might have a look at the Namibian desert, Botswana, Zimbabwe, see where the adventure takes me.'

Tannie Bessie had searched for the right words. How was she to convey her experience of this land to her young nephew, who seemed to think he was setting out on a scout trip? She would sound old, frightened, paranoid. Perhaps his very naïvety would keep him safe.

'Michael . . . I know you are British and so you see the people differently from us. But it would be very easy for you to disappear out there and for us never to find you. A Land-Rover is worth a lot to some people. A gun, petrol, hell they wouldn't think twice about killing you for your watch. Even your body parts have value.' He looked incredulous. 'The witch-doctors. Sometimes they need a human body part. Sometimes they need a specifically white body part. It happens, Michael. Just be careful. Remember you are carrying more on you than some of these people will own in a lifetime. This is Africa, Michael, not a Buddhist or Hindu country.

Africa. And you don't know your way around here.'

Michael had been irritated. Of course he'd never been here before. But he wasn't a child, he was a grown man. What did these people take him for, for heaven's sake? He had reassured Tannie Bessie as best he could. She could see he was angry although he tried hard to cover it. Her resigned smile had said, 'Ag well.' She had done her best.

Michael threw a large stone as hard as he could at the biggest vulture and had the satisfaction of a direct hit. Damn. Damn. Damn.

When the minibus appeared out of the powerful midday haze he found himself hoping for a white male driver. Stop it, he thought. You have no idea what colour monster killed Timothy. The driver was black. All twelve of the occupants were black. They stopped. He felt his watch shining and burning on his wrist. He explained. His tongue felt thick and coarse. There was no room for Timothy in the van. Strictly speaking there was no room for Michael either, but he could sandwich himself in next to a large lady and her smaller son would sit on his lap. He wouldn't leave Timothy. He pointed to the vultures. They unpacked the luggage on the roof and strapped Timothy down with the boxes and bags. A Coke was produced. The redness of his arms and the 'too too badness' of his experience was discussed at length. He tried to force words, be polite, recognise their kindness. But it was beyond him.

The bus was unbearably hot; the insistent township jazz blaring on its cassette system jarred his nerves. They drove to the police station in Upington.

The policeman, white, young and clean-looking, took notes.

'Well, that's it, Mr Carter, you can go now.' Michael had signed his statement.

'What happens now?'

'We tell his family. The body goes to the morgue. They arrange to fetch it.'

'Will you find them? The murderers?'

'They're long gone. Probably crossing the border as we speak. We'll do our best, but . . . '

'Can't you radio to the borders?'

'We'll do what we can, Mr Carter.' He'd been doing this job for long enough, thank you. He didn't need some uitlander (foreigner) telling him what should be done.

'I'm sorry,' Michael said, 'but I can't believe that there's nothing you can do. A man's been killed, murdered . . . he was sleeping, for God's sake!'

The young man looked at him. 'Go home, Mr Carter. There are more people killed in Africa every day than you want to know about. But I'm sorry you had this experience. Would you like to use the telephone?'

He had Tannie Bessie's number in his wallet. She answered. 'Michael? It's wonderful to hear from you! How's it going?'

'Aunt Bessie . . . ' He crumpled. 'They killed Timothy. They just came and killed him.' His voice was going.

'Michael! Michael where are you?'

'In Upington . . . in the police station.' He recovered himself. 'Aunt . . . Sophie . . . we'll have to tell her.'

'Michael, we're coming. Karel and me. We'll bring Sophie. We'll drive straight through. Have you got a pen? Write this down – 67 Brandt Street, David Pretorius. He is the dominee in Upington. Go there. I will tell him that you're coming. Michael . . . are you all right?'

'I'm fine, fine . . . '

'Well thank the Lord for that.'

'Aunt . . . tell Sophie . . . tell her he was sleeping. They shot him while he was asleep.' And where were you, Michael?

Taking pictures, Sophie, using my nice camera that I bought at duty free.

The young policeman drove him to the dominee's house. It was cool and dark inside. The policeman and the dominee's wife, Annelise, had a conversation on the veranda. Michael couldn't understand a word. He didn't care. Didn't even care that he must seem like an English schoolboy whose adventure had gone horribly wrong. Like those people who end up at the consulate needing to be taken care of, sent home. All he could think about was Sophie. What would he say? He would like to offer to pay, to replace the stolen items, pay for the funeral, but how to offer without looking like he was trying to pay his way out of this? He would have to go back for the funeral. He would have to tell his mother, whether or not she was able to take it on board. He remembered her emptiness and the strange experience they had shared together. Would he have to tell his father? This trip was not working out. How on earth was he going to find a Bushman, the right Bushman, and even when he did find one what good would it do? Michael, he thought, you're an ass. A mumbo-jumbo idiot.

The craft room at Tranquillity was bright. If you were looking through the window from the wet darkness of the winter afternoon you would see Sheena handing out paper and crayons to the patients. She liked this duty. It made the patients seem more real when they were doing something. Mrs Carter never did anything but Sheena always put the tools in front of her anyway, removing them untouched at the end of the session.

Today Melanie picked up and put down each of the crayons. She was aware of their nature and what they did. She had no idea what she was going to do but she knew that there was a need to do something. Her mind was unfocused, it seemed her hand was going to draw without her. She was detached from the process. Not curious.

She selected an olive-green crayon. A criss-cross of lines began to appear. Then a brown crayon. From Sheena's position it looked like a green smudge on a brown background. Oh well.

Dr Cunningham approached. Melanie was sitting still, her hand poised over the paper. The drawing was of a hut, it looked like a grass hut on brown sand. A rounded shape, no door, just a small dome with a front opening. Melanie put the crayon down and folded the paper into a small square. She put it and a black crayon into her pinafore pocket. Then sat as she normally did with her hands in her lap.

'Melanie?' There was no response. 'I'm very glad you did that,' Elizabeth said. There was no recognition of her words. But it was a leap forward. Or was it? There would have to be more, Elizabeth reminded herself firmly. Don't get over-excited about this. She looked past her own reflection into the deepening dark. Perhaps it will snow, she thought.

Melanie slipped back into the craft room in the quiet of the evening. Now she sat, perfectly still, holding the black crayon in her hand. Scraps of images began to form. A tiny foot, covered in red stain, flexed its toes in soft red sand. The little foot nestled into the sand and then, clutching sand in its toes, felt the sand run through the spaces between as it was lifted out of its cool nest. Closer there was an equally small hand clutching a pointed stick. The stick was scratching lines in the sand. Her hand firmed around the crayon, mimicking its movements on the craft-table top. Then it went away. She felt sorrow. She sat, passive, waiting.

The man looked down at the concentrating figure of his family's adopted child. She would sit for hours with him, scratching with her stick, trying to copy his own work. Then, coming to stand against him, holding herself as tall as possible with her arms around his leg, she would look at his work. Disappointed at her own result, she would slowly rub it out, create a new blank work-space. She was improving all the time. She was, of course, much too young to work with the paints he prepared from earth, water and plant dyes. But often when he had finished he would take the belt of ostrich-egg paint-pots from his waist and they would play with the remains of the paint. She would dip her fingers into the bowls, a colour on each finger, and then dab them on to a little rock just inside the cave entrance which they had selected for the purpose. She made colourful little swirls, tried to paint the hut they may have constructed that day. He couldn't understand her need to draw and paint the domestic, things that were so transient.

He, as his father had taught him, chronicled the events of his large, extended family, particularly the great hunts. His work was a celebration, a thanksgiving for the spirits of the creatures who fed them, a recognition of the role of the modest hunters who were unable to boast about their achievements.

Today he was chronicling the excellence of his nephew's first eland kill. The boy was now a man. The kill had been, those who accompanied him assured him, a masterly performance. To come close enough to the eland to shoot with the arrow was a matter of extreme skill. For hours the boy had lain in the long grass, moving excruciatingly slowly towards his target. With his hand in front of his eyes, inches from the ground, he would constantly test the direction of the wind by dropping the tiniest amount of sand and seeing which way it would blow. When he was sure that the wind could not betray him, he would move. To find the eland had taken two weeks. Each minute invested in getting closer to it made the next minute more important. The boy had shown great patience. When finally, from deep in the grass, he had sent the arrow curving into the neck of the great eland, the animal had still not seen him. It was an impressive first kill. They had followed the track of the wounded animal as it steadily weakened. The boy had offered apologies and thanks before the quick killing. This too, all had agreed, had been done with great humbleness and grace. The killing was clean. There had been marvellous feasting and dancing. The young man, of course, denied that he had done any of these things, which was the proper way.

Now the artist looked at his work and tried not to be too pleased with it. His father's work from the years before when they had come to this place following the game was also on the walls. It was early work, but served to remind the young man of his own lack of experience. His father had been killed by the large white men on his way to another place of telling some years ago. His own apprenticeship with his father had not been finished. He could make most of the colours and he trusted that the spirit of his father would guide him away from mistakes. Perhaps today he had let his affection for his nephew carry him away a little. Was the scene a touch too boastful? But he had had to create the grey without guidance and he may have lacked confidence in using it. Perhaps his father would have given greater glory to the eland. He must be on his guard against error next time.

He signalled to the little girl. They would now investigate the water supply hidden in the depth of the cave. It had been a good season for rain, welcome after many dry seasons. At the back of the cave there was a hollow which filled with the water that seeped through the roof of the cave when it rained. The young man's father's father had deepened this hollow many years ago. The rain had helped to make it into a very shallow well. This cave would house their paintings until the white man found them. Then it would be abandoned, disowned even. The white man must not know what was important or magical. No one would ever tell everything. Just enough for the immediate purpose and then often with a twist, for fun.

The man began to fill the large ostrich shells he had brought with him with water. The little girl had recently acquired the skill of sucking water into a long reed and then transferring the water from the reed into the ostrich shell. They worked slowly, but methodically. This water, which would be buried in the floor of the cave under the paintings but clearly marked for those who could read the runes, might be the only source in this area in the dry season. Throughout the family's large territory there were known water-storage points, there for the use of the people. The two worked carefully and quickly; the little girl's dark hair was matted but long, much longer than the hair of any of his people, which tended to grow close to the head. The gods were good to the people. There was a lot of water.

Melanie sat as fragments of ochre red, sienna brown and thick, dull, yellow entered and left her consciousness. No pictures, just a sense of colour that carried with it a pungent smell and an abiding coolness disturbed from time to time by a waft of warm, dry air, barely a breeze.

Then he was there, with his kind, honey-coloured face, lined more than seemed possible for his age. His lips were rounded on a long reed and his prominent cheekbones were clearly outlined by the vacuum he was creating in his mouth. Melanie knew she knew him. That his mother was her mother, that his brother was her brother, they were one. She raised her hands to try and touch his face, her mouth made the clicking noises that would say in the polite greeting, '!Katchu, my brother, who is so tall that I see him from a great distance, !Katchu I greet you.'

Sheena stood at the door of the craft room. Mrs Carter

was making a soft click-clicking sound, her hands raised as though she were stroking something in front of her. Then she stopped. The clicking sound became urgent, as though she were losing something, trying to get it back. Then her hands dropped and tears were running down her face. Her expression was desolate. Sheena went to her, tried to comfort her. Mrs Carter pushed her away. The tears stopped. She looked exhausted. On the table top was a black crayon drawing of what looked like a cow.

10

Timothy's sister Celia and Michael drove back from the undertaker's together. They had exchanged barely a word. He didn't want to leave it at that. There were no cars at the four-way stop on the edge of town. He didn't move forward.

'You hold me responsible.'

She turned her impassive face towards him, looked at him. 'For what?'

'For Timothy's death.'

She shrugged, losing interest. 'If that is what you want to believe.'

'It isn't what I want to believe. I want to know what you think.'

'Why?'

'Because you're Timothy's sister . . . Sophie's daughter . . . Because Sophie said we're related.'

She laughed, an involuntary, ugly sound, but the amusement was real enough.

'My mother,' she said, and she shook her head. 'What you really want, Michael, is for me to make things better for you. I have lost my brother. You had known him for only a few weeks, but you still think I have something to spare to give you. It is the old riddle of Africa.'

'I'm sorry. I didn't mean to burden you. Truly. I am.' He started the engine again.

She turned to look out of the window again, so he would not see her anger.

Last night she had tried again to dream her way back. Back to the fear of the first journey, the hunger and the dust and the joy of finally arriving, safe, with her comrades in the clearing in the bush, the training camp at last. She was fourteen and cared nothing for the life prescribed for her. That first night they had been drunk on dreams of liberation, drunk with the freedom of not being in their own country, drunk on their communality of courage and the possibility of change. They sat around the fire and drank weak coffee and remembered the courage of their heroes. It was her most precious memory. The beginning of anything, she thought, is always most precious and yet at the beginning you cannot wait for the beginning to be over.

That night she left Sophie asleep and went outside. Michael had built a fire and was sitting staring into its depths. She vaguely regretted her earlier treatment of him. He was just a child, a grown child. She went to sit with him.

He had no idea what to say. The girl made him feel that the second he opened his mouth he would damn himself. 'Hello,' was the most he ventured.

'Hello.'

They sat a while in silence.

'Did Timothy ever tell you about his life before he went into exile?'

'No, no he didn't. He talked mostly about the future. And about his time in England. We did meet Sister Ignatius, though.'

She smiled. 'Sister Gateway. I always wondered if she knew she was being used as a way station for the journey out. I always suspected she did.'

They sat a while and then she listened to the heart of her brother, much kinder than her own, even with more reason to hate, and she said, 'Michael . . . Timothy considered you his friend. I don't hold you responsible for his death.'

'I was clumsy and self-centred. I'm sorry.'

'It's OK.' She offered him her hand to shake.

'I didn't know him well,' Michael began, 'but I did like him enormously.'

'Good. Good.'

They sat a while in silence.

'I would like,' Michael began, 'I would like to get to know you too.'

She looked at him with that look that seemed to see into the crevices of his inadequacies and said quite gently, 'What would we have in common?'

'Well, that's what getting to know you would be about.'

The desperateness welled up inside her again. She shook her head and smiled. 'We have nothing in common. Nothing.'

'But how do you know? You don't know me at all.'

She sat looking into the fire, not answering. White boy from England, have you ever killed anyone? Have you fought in a war? Have you suffered seeing the ones you love betrayed by the ones you love? Have you ever hated so you can taste it, so that it rises like nausea in your bones? Have you ever wanted to kill someone, to make them suffer the most horrible pain and fear first because it is just, and done it and been glad, glad, glad? Have you ever known a battle where the victors had to let the enemy take everything? Have you ever been so afraid that your brain has become empty?

She got up. 'We have nothing in common, Michael. Nothing at all. Good-night.' Then she walked away, her arms folded in front of her, her head bowed.

Michael watched the girl's back disappear. She was right, of course. He was an alien in this land. She left him feeling insubstantial, clumsy. His quest, his mother, it must all seem childish to her. Tonight the stars were less a source of wonder than an ineffable canopy, awesome, disturbing him with his irrelevance.

Proper sleep evaded Celia. Thoughts and images raced around her brain. She envied her mother's pure grief. Her own was locked away behind the sorrowful look on her brother's face, there where she could not look. But I was right, Timothy. I was right! She was an impizimpi, a police informer, she betrayed you, she betrayed me, she – the friend of our childhood! They had been at a soccer match, she with messages for others, snatching handshakes in the crowd, the intensely important arm around the shoulders under the guise of celebration.

She was permanently changed, she knew that. Some damage was irreversible. The white men had stripped her naked and been obscene with her. She had detached from it, from the horror, from the knowledge that she could die here and no one could help her. She had moved her being away from the pain of the blows and the shocks and the obscene fingers, from the revolting pinkness thrust into her face, and she had slumped down, overtly submissive, in reality far away in the bush, leaning on the example of the dead, no longer concerned with courage or cowardice. As Biko taught us, fear of death is irrational. It is only a matter of when. Better to die with honour.

A doctor had come and examined her, she had been aware but not present. Eventually she was released, numbed and alive. Then, surrounded by her comrades, she had seen her. Theresa Nkopi, the only one who could have told them. The look of surprise on Theresa's face had been enough to release her rage, start her running towards her, start her shouting the words of condemnation and accusation. Oh, how pleased she had been at the look of fear on the girl's face as she tried to lose herself in the crowd. And then they had taken the tyre and she, Celia, had spat in her face and poured the diesel over it and set the match and left her to her twenty minutes of agony. That was for David, for Isaiah, for Pele, for all my brothers . . .

And when she and Timothy finally saw each other in England and she had told him what had happened in that tiny bedsit in Brixton and he had looked at her and cried for her, held her and cried for her, she had felt the slow emergence of herself again. And then, many days later, he had held her hand and told her that what she had done was wrong, unacceptable. That by mirroring the brutality of the oppressor she had damaged herself. She must show restraint, she must be better than them. And she had argued, hysterically, that if she had had a gun and could have killed her cleanly she wasn't even sure that she would have done because there was evil, terrible evil in betrayal of the people. And Timothy had stroked her, calmed her, forgiven her, left her with the seeds of doubt. She had subtly avoided him after that. And now he was gone and she was left with that look, that look of sorrow for her and for what she had done. And when something is done. It is done. She couldn't yet believe that in that madness of fear and rage she had betrayed herself, betrayed the movement. But something was growing in her. She turned again in her bed. She would take one of the pills she had been given for sleeping. She seemed to take them more and more often now there was peace.

Lying on her bed pretending sleep, Sophie watched Celia get up to smoke a last cigarette in the doorway of their rondavel. She had no words for this daughter of hers. After 1976, when Timothy left and then Celia followed – too young, much, much too young – she had seen herself through her daughter's eyes. A subservient being, a frightened servant, weak, ineffectual, cowardly. Afraid. Above all afraid. For them, now. More afraid for them than for herself. And through the fear the pride. That her children should be so brave. That they should refuse Baasskap, refuse to accept what she had endured, refuse to be anything but people of dignity. Power shifted then. And the child never spoke to her about anything thereafter. Not where she was, whom she was seeing, not about anything. It was understandable. Timothy had explained it. The need-to-know principle. The rule of never telling anybody anything about yourself which could place them or you in danger. But with peace it hadn't stopped. She was still shut and locked. And there was pain there. Not just the pain of Timothy's death, which God knew lay waiting, lurking and ready to claim them, but an older pain.

With cigarettes, drink, marijuana and sex, Celia hurt herself. The aunt with whom she stayed in Soweto had told Sophie. The girl seemed to love only her niece, Timothy's daughter. On the day little Zinzi had first gone to school, neat as a pin in her white shirt and school tie, with her shoes lovingly cleaned, even though they were new, by her aunt Celia, Celia had stared at the child with tears in her eyes. 'Go to school, little Zinzi. Build the future.' And then she had spent that night in the shebeen and who knows whereafter.

Sophie looked at the strong back. She knew Celia found her work hard. She was supposed to be learning clerical duties in some government agency. She found the routine and the occasional raised looks to the skies of her white colleagues unbearable. She couldn't learn unless they taught her. They despised her for her lack of education, considered her backward. She was. But whose fault was that? Sophie understood that work could be difficult. But there was something else. Timothy had said so. Oh, Timothy. The two of you were so close. She worshipped you. And then it stopped. Somewhere in all this you lost each other. How do I reach her? How?

The girl put out the cigarette and hugged her knees. In the drooping of her head and spine, Sophie saw a wounded animal. And out of nowhere came the honey bird, with a broken wing and full of fury. And the honey bird is precious to us, she thought. And in her drowsy state she saw how the children would go and sit near the wounded honey bird and be very quiet, and leave food for it. And water. And then go away again. And how they always let the honey bird know they were coming so as not to frighten it any further, but sang a soft, soft song with a little whistle at the end until it responded to the whistle and then, healed, finally flew away. How do I know this, she wondered. My daughter is a honey bird.

In the morning when Celia snapped at her for something that was nothing, over the long journey back to the farm and through the ordeal of the funeral, Sophie remembered the honey bird. Through her tears Sophie felt her son close by her side. He was willing her to help his sister. The girl's pain was formidable, as was the steel door of will with which she blocked it out. Sophie's own pain made her hypersensitive to her daughter's. She told the girl she needed her and asked her to stay a while.

'But, mama, there is nothing for me to do here.'

'Please, Celia . . . I need you to be here. I need my daughter with me for a while.'

The girl had shrugged and Sophie knew that she would stay.

Mother and daughter spent quiet days together. Sophie did not work and no one in the house objected. Instead she took up her embroidery and began to teach her daughter. They sat quietly together, stitching brilliant colours on to the white tablecloths. In the late afternoon they would take walks together. Sophie was very careful to be quiet. Celia would point out places on the farm where she and Timothy had played, or made mischief, or seen something wonderful. They shared stories of Timothy.

And gossiped about Michael. Sophie considered him quite good looking, Celia was less convinced. They tried to imagine if he would be more attractive if he were black and not so very white. He lacked strength, they finally agreed. He did not seem as virile as one would wish a man to be.

'But he carried Timothy a long way,' Sophie said.

'Mmmm.' Celia was reluctant to concede anything to Michael. 'Why was Timothy helping him so much?'

'I asked him to.' Sophie was stripping the leaves off a twig.

'But why?'

'His mother . . . was my friend. My first friend. She was a good person. He is her son.' She shrugged.

'This is the Melanie who left the farm just after Timothy was born.'

Sophie nodded. 'She was a quiet child. Very quiet and very shy. When she came to the farm she could only speak the !Kung language. None of us could understand her. She would sit all alone for hours under that tree . . . ' Sophie pointed to a camel thorn tree a long way away near the reservoir, ' . . . and dig with a little stick she had made with a stone tied to it. Just sit and dig the earth around her. I had never seen anyone so sad. One day I went to sit near her. I had made my own digging stick. That first day we just sat there for a long time. The next day we did the same. On the third day she gave me a new stick. We saw each other every day after that for two years, until it was stopped. She had no bad in her, that girl. No bad. But now she is sick. And when the mother is sick, the son will suffer too.'

'Do you think he will be able to help her?'

'Maybe. Maybe not. But in trying he will help himself. He is not yet a man, for all his years.'

She needed to touch her daughter, to let her hands do something to heal, and so she dressed Celia's hair in a complicated braiding and twisting that took hours, feeling her daughter relax. She sat now in the firelight like a warrior princess with her hair close to her head and her skin so smooth and perfect. Every now and then she would storm off. One night she came home very drunk, aggressive. Celia remembered the frightened pecking of the honey bird and helped her out of her clothes and was careful to let her sleep in the morning, putting flowers and water beside her bed for when she awoke.

That afternoon Sophie sat on a blanket in the shade of the buffalo thorn trees with her embroidery. The ground around her was littered with their small reddish fruits. Flies feasted, the heat slowing even their movements. Celia came out in her sunglasses with her own work.

'I am sorry, mama.'

'There is no need to apologise, my daughter.' Sophie took a deep breath. 'If there is any apology, it should be from me to you.'

'Mama?'

'You have been so brave, my daughter. I have been so very proud of you. You and all your comrades, you have given us this dignity. But sometimes we, the elders, we are ashamed in the face of your bravery. Why did we not give you freedom? Why could we not secure for you the chances you have secured for your children? Why were we less brave? Sometimes in the face of you, my daughter, I feel ashamed. A coward.'

'No!'

'The truth cannot hurt us, Celia. Only lies and hidden things.'

'I am the one to be ashamed. But I cannot talk about it. I cannot think about it. I cannot, mama.'

Sophie nodded. 'Now you cannot. But you will be able to. And then you will be free. One day you will tell me your story and I will feel that I am your true mother, that I can do you this service, to hear your story and to love you for it that you may know that I too am brave. For you. As you have been for me. For us.'

'It doesn't feel like we did something special, mama. When I am at the office with those cold white women and they raise their eyebrows at each other with a look that I am supposed to be too stupid to understand, then it is hard to remember that we are in charge, that we have won back the land. It is hard to remember how we felt that day when Madiba walked free and the world was ours, we knew we had won and the joy, the joy was everywhere. When I see you in your maid's uniform doing what you have always done and the bastards getting richer because they own the land and you have nothing, never will have anything, and I do not know how to change things for you, then I wonder what we really did. And I cannot blame the ones who grab everything there is to grab, although I know they are wrong.'

Sophie sat in silence for a while. Then anger rose up in her. 'Celia! You have freed a nation. A whole nation of people, think of it! You did that. You and your comrades. It is going to be hard to find the way forward, it is an untangling of things, a slow process, and we know the whites do not change until they have to, but why care about them? They are answerable to God as we are. They cannot stop us any more. Or beat us or kill us for no reason. You did that. I am only fierce because of my pride in you.'

After a while Celia kissed her mother and walked off. Sophie sat trying to calm her frightened heart. The forward thrust of the girl's chin and shoulders had always slightly worried her. Such strength turned against itself. She asked her son if she was doing the right thing and felt a little calmer. He was with her, alongside her, she could almost touch his spirit.

That evening Celia cooked a special meal and Sophie knew that she was getting ready to leave. She stayed quiet, waiting, waiting for the honey bird.

'Do you remember Theresa Nkopi, mama?'

'Little Theresa. Oh, yes. Always giggling, you two. How is she?'

'Dead. I killed her.'

Sophie took a deep breath. 'Tell me,' she managed as gently as she could.

'Do you remember Pele Pointy Head?'

'Oh, yes. How you bad children would tease him!'

'I killed him as well. And Agnes Mpayu. And another person whom you do not know but who was my closest friend in the whole of the struggle. David.'

'Tell me.' The food was gently moved aside.

The girl squared her shoulders, stared at the table. 'I was a cell leader. Four people were in my cell – David, Isaiah, Pele and Agnes. We trusted each other, we were very careful. I think we were effective. My higher-level contact was Theresa. Things went wrong. Theresa arranged for us to get hand-grenades which we were to use against the Caspars in the township. I gave out the grenades, but on the day of the conflict I was arrested. While I was in custody, the others went ahead as planned. But the hand-grenades were booby-trapped and exploded as soon as the pins were drawn. They were all in different places and one after another each of them died with a grenade exploding in their hands. There was so little left of them, they were scattered everywhere, that the coffins were light at the funeral and children could carry them. But I was in detention and there it was ... disgusting ... disgusting.' She shook her head. 'And when I came out the people thought it seemed a bit too convenient that I had been arrested and did not die and after all I had given out the hand-grenades. But I had the grenades from Theresa, and while those pig men were beating me they would say, "And how did we know to arrest you? And who do you think arranged for those grenades to be booby-trapped?" and so I was convinced that it was Theresa and I . . . we . . . She was killed.'

'How did she die?' Sophie's hands were clasped tight together under the table.

'I necklaced her.'

The silence grew thick. Sophie's hands, even held tightly, would not stop trembling. But she could not fail now. 'And now you wonder if they did not arrest you to get Theresa.'

Celia nodded. 'But who got the grenades, mama? Who betrayed us? I do not know. Maybe it was Theresa. Maybe it was not. But they are all gone now.'

Sophie nodded. Sat still, absorbing the story. Timothy was nowhere to be found. There was just the pain and horror of her daughter's life that was now her own.

'Perhaps we will never know.'

'Perhaps.' Celia picked at the tablecloth. 'It makes me tired, mama. Very tired.'

They sat again in silence.

'I remember, when you and Theresa would walk to school together. You always met at the place that was exactly half way. Such a long walk it was too!'

'Please, mama!'

Sophie took her daughter's hands. She spoke firmly. 'Celia. It was war. Theresa was your friend. If she betrayed you, then that was another person, a frightened person who maybe did not have your courage. You cannot know her reality. And if she did not betray you, then it was a terrible mistake. A terrible thing. Either way, you have to make your peace. Or your life will be wasted too.'

'Maybe that is justice, mama.'

'I do not believe that. I believe it is your duty to make amends. Which is maybe harder than drifting your life away.'

Celia shrugged. 'How can you make amends for that? How? The Commission?' Her voice rose, high pitched.

'She has a family. A mother. A grandmother. You must look after them. Did she have children?'

Celia shook her head.

'Then it is her relatives that you must care for. The duty you give to me you must give to her mother and her grandmother also. You must go and see them and see what their needs are. Then you must arrange as best you can for those needs to be met. For the rest of their lives you must look after those relatives. There is no other way.'

'It does not seem much.'

'It will when you have to face them.'

'Must I tell them? They may want to kill me too.'

'Maybe so. But you must explain yourself well. Honestly. But not in the beginning. Only when they have learned to trust you, when they can see that you are reliable and dutiful and sincere. Then the choice will be theirs. But you must do what you can. Only her relatives can release you. If you are not released, then the enemy has won something else again.'

The strong jaw set itself. Tears filled the girl's eyes. She stared them out until her mother came to stand behind her, gently held her head against her, kissed the braided hair.

Celia left and Sophie resumed her duties in the house. It kept her busy, the routine. At night she sat and let the pain of her losses overwhelm her. It was better like this, alone in the quiet and the dark, to face the pain and let it take over, let the tears fall. First her husband. Now all of this. And with each new pain it seemed she experienced the old ones afresh. That is why we old ones are so cautious. We know that it all adds up. She sat on the edge of her bed and rocked, holding her stomach. She remembered the words of a lullaby, Toolah, Toolah, and sang them softly to herself. Sometimes Melanie slipped in and out of the landscape of her memories. She was glad she had made Michael promise to continue with his journey. It had been kind of him to pay for everything.

Karel offered to accompany Michael on the next leg. The offer was sincere, but impossible to accept. Michael had joined them for breakfast in the linoleum-floored hotel.

'Why don't you just go to the Falls and the National Parks? You're not seeing anything beautiful, Michael, it's a shame,' Tannie Bessie tried.

Michael inspected his cup of coffee in the thick white china cup with hairline cracks stained brown on the inside.

'I've started now . . . I might as well go on.'

'I don't understand, Michael. It isn't safe.' Bessie was getting annoyed.

'I can't really explain it,' he said. 'But I will be careful.'

Bessie and Karel looked at each other and at their plates. Karel shook his head.

'I tell you what. There's an old pal of mine at the army base north of Upington. Why don't you head there. He can maybe help. Anyway, he's got Bushmen in the camp. You can meet them and then go on to have a holiday.'

It was agreed. Michael would go and meet up with David Serfontein. Karel would ring beforehand. A new vehicle would be hired, new supplies purchased. Tannie Bessie was tight-lipped with disapproval. Michael wanted to pacify her, stop her worrying. Still, he resented her knowledge of his failure, her lack of faith in his ability. They parted politely.

Finally they had all said their goodbyes. Sophie looked

immensely tired. She managed a wan farewell. Just as she was about to leave, Michael took her to one side.

'Sophie . . . are you sure you don't want me to come?' She nodded. 'I had these developed.' He handed her the photographs in their wallet.

She put them silently into her handbag and took out a small, square box, a flattened, battered jewel case. 'Melanie gave me this. It may help you.'

They left in a subdued flurry of waves – a manly handshake from Karel, a recap of directions to the army base, and the bakkie was disappearing down the road. The dominee had offered Michael the use of his car to organise his trip. He would stay in the rest camp one more night and leave the following morning.

Sorting his purchases into the hired vehicle in the late afternoon, he opened the little blue box. Ivory-coloured shell beads on a fine leather string, a primitive necklace. It looked like an artefact from a museum. Some of the shells had been chipped in the box, minute fragments of shell lay on the soft padded interior, which was stamped 'Le Roux Jewellers, Kimberley'. Otherwise it was strangely robust. He showed it to the dominee, who was sure that it was some means of warding off evil spirits, probably prescribed by a witch-doctor. Michael thought it too pretty to ward off anything.

He felt his spirits lift a bit as he drove out of Upington. The shepherding time was over. He managed to tune the van's radio to an early-morning business programme. It was mostly local information, the movements of the international markets on the previous day. It seemed that everything was still holding up. Listening to the programme, he felt the thumping gut-squeeze of the addict, the need to play, be on the line, one of the boys. A sense of panic, too, at being out of the game, not even on the sidelines, but out of the game. It didn't wait for you. What the fuck was he doing? Why didn't he just turn around, get back to Cape Town, go home? He pulled the van over, left the engine idling.

OK. If I go back, I go back to the same stuff. If I carry on here I might find something. And what about Timothy and Sophie? And Her? Do you really think this is going to make a blind bit of difference? No. I don't. So why are you doing it then? Because I'd like to believe that it might make a bit of difference? Possibly. But not enough. OK, then, because I need to do this and I don't know why. Jesus! Someone got killed because of your don't know why! You can't say it was my fault. It just happened. I don't want to admit to being afraid.

'You're questing, my son, that's what you're doing.' How had Basher's voice got into his head? Questing? 'Too right. Holy Grail stuff. Ancient programme in your genes, old man.' Sod off, Basher. He smiled as he drove back on to the road.

The childish drawings were a disappointment to Jeremy Carter.

'Can you tell us anything about these images? They are quite unusual, you see, and it is Melanie's first attempt at communication.' Elizabeth sensed Jeremy's disappointment.

'Are you suggesting that Melanie has . . . well, regressed, forgotten how to communicate?'

'No, no, not forgotten, become unable to communicate as she has done in the past. This is something new, not a replacement.' The pictures had shocked him. She had tried to play it down. 'They are not meant to be skilful . . . I wondered if perhaps they mean anything to you.'

There were a few grass-hut-type drawings, a few stick people and a drawing of what looked like a cow. 'The style of the drawings suggests a very young age, probably before ten years old . . . can you tell us anything about Melanie's early years?'

'I should imagine they have something to do with her experiences in Africa. Melanie never spoke about it herself, it seemed to be a cause of some pain – her uncle told me something about it on our wedding day.' He outlined the little that he knew.

'And no one has any idea what happened to her while she was in the care of these people?' Why hadn't anyone told her about this before?

'No. But it seems she was well cared for. I'm afraid that's all I know about it. It wasn't something we discussed. Could you tell me what these drawings mean to you?'

'I can't be sure, but it seems that Melanie is reliving that experience. Whether she intends us to be part of it or not, I don't know. But I do think that it's positive. She has somehow moved forward from the near catatonic state that she entered at the beginning.'

'Will . . . will she get better?'

'I can't say. I'm sorry.'

'No, of course. Thank you.'

He left, refusing to allow himself the temptation of hope. He had seen Melanie earlier, serene and distant as always. She was not ageing rapidly, nor did she look completely barking, for which he was grateful. He had told her about his coming retirement, the same way he told her about everything. He'd hoped . . . damn, he had hoped. There wasn't much to look forward to . . . Less work. More time to think. He shouldn't have hoped.

Elizabeth looked again at the drawings. The African influence was now quite clear. She would need expert advice. She put a call through to the Department of African Studies at her Alma Mater. There must be a cultural explanation. She would go and see them, find it.

'And that is all you know?' Dr Ephraim Motlane could anticipate what was coming next.

'Yes. But there can only be so many possibilities... I hoped you could give me an insight.'

'You don't know which people took her? You don't have her clothing or any other identifiers?'

'No.'

'Then how can I help you?'

'There must be something generic possibly?'

Here it was. Perhaps it was time to go home. He was more than usually irritated.

'Is there a generic white thing, Dr Cunningham? Would you say that you can give me a breakdown of the history of a child who has been living with any white person in any area of Europe on a generic basis? White culture is not homogenous and neither is black culture. Rites, traditions, roles, beliefs, these all differ quite dramatically. I can only help you if you can give me an idea of the geography and the time period, which will allow us to select a defined number of peoples. You will then have to wade through the sociological patterns of all those peoples to find something that matches her actions.'

Elizabeth winced. Damn. 'Dr Motlane, I do apologise. This is the first opportunity I have to support this patient and in my excitement I have over-simplified the task and exposed my appalling ignorance. I do apologise, most sincerely. I can understand how irritating it must be for you.'

His stomach was playing up. He shouldn't have had the spicy chicken at lunch. It was playing havoc with his ulcer. The woman was very attractive, he thought. Too polished, too angular for his personal taste, but immaculately presented.

Clever too. It would be very ungracious to refuse to help her now.

Elizabeth took the drawings from her briefcase. 'She is drawing these. It seems that they relate to the period from 1940 to 1945 in the north-western territory of Southern Africa.'

The huts were recognisable. Only one people would have erected these makeshift grass structures. The drawings were extremely crude, but Motlane was almost convinced that they were those of a Bushman tribe. It made sense too. The Bushman, with his gentle ways, may well have taken on a young orphan.

'I cannot be sure, you understand, the drawings are very rough. But my first impression is that your patient has spent time with one or other of the Bushman tribes. If I am correct, then she is a most fortunate woman. I would be very interested to meet her.'

'I am afraid that part of her condition is complete silence.'

'What are her other symptoms?'

'Complete withdrawal. An occasional manifestation of extreme pain, indications of enormous sorrow. And now the drawings. There are no other abnormalities. Recently she has become more animated.'

'Has anything happened recently?'

'Her son is currently in Africa, but I don't see a connection there. Her medication has been stopped, which is a more likely reason.'

'Dr Cunningham . . . I am not a psychologist. I am an anthropologist. In the African experience there are many ills that are not 'nervous' in the traditional Western understanding of the word. They are illnesses of the spirit. The spirit does not respect material boundaries. You should enlist the help of a sangoma, a witch-doctor. Your patient is suffering.'

'Do you have any documented cases of these illnesses of the spirit?'

He was feeling irritated again. Science, science! There was more to the world than this obsession with science.

'Not to hand. But, Dr Cunningham, please make full use of the library. I will ask one of my research assistants to prepare a list of readings for you that may be helpful. Now, if you will excuse me . . .'

The list was quite short. There was some quasi-fiction, field trips by academics. Elizabeth sat for a number of hours with the reference books. They contradicted each other in more than one way. All agreed that the South African Bushman, mainly the !Xam people, had been hunted to the point of near extinction, some maintained total extinction. Other tribes were pushed ever farther into harsher environments. Their story was one of decline, of peoples caught between worlds. They seemed capable of charming their visitors without effort, giving an impression of a fluid, egalitarian community. Pictures of their temporary grass huts were very similar to Melanie's scribblings. It was hard to imagine Melanie as part of the communities that were documented before her.

Dr Motlane sighed. No sooner had he handed the woman over to someone else than here she was on the telephone.

Years ago the young lecturer Ephraim Motlane had been delighted when his opinion was sought by others. He had felt passionately about the need to reconcile Africa with the West, to educate the European in the ways of Africa, hoping that in this way there would evolve a mutual respect, a resolution of cultural differences, perhaps even, he admitted to himself in quiet moments of reverie, perhaps even a better way forward for the world as a whole. In his innocence he had frequently mistaken curiosity for genuine interest, charity for neighbourliness, cultural plagiarism for appreciation.

It had taken years for him to see through the myth of European superiority. When sophisticated cultures are convinced of their own superiority it is difficult not to be seduced by the strength of their own belief. But after the seduction came the knowledge of misplaced intimacy. And he saw the weakness in his own vision of himself, that which had allowed him to be seduced. It was a bitter awakening. If he, one of the most successful of his own people, could look at himself and his culture with some deep-rooted sense of inferiority, then he had been colonised in a more seditious manner than through territory. This was a colonisation of his soul, his value system, his gods and his love for his community. But there was no going back. Daily he toyed with returning. But he knew that the colonisation had gone too deep for him to reverse. He was Westernised, a quasi-European. Once you have spoiled the child in you, you cannot revive its purity. It will wear the scars of the life you have lived. He was a spearhead for his people and he was sunk comfortably deep in the flesh of the enemy. It didn't help to know it so well.

Elizabeth sensed his reluctance to meet with her again. Damn. 'You mentioned witch-doctors,' she said. 'Perhaps it would be useful if I consulted one. Could you tell me how I go about it?'

'I can give you the name of a woman who came over from Swaziland. I don't know of any others from Southern Africa. She lives in Brixton, looks after a community there.'

The witch-doctor was younger than Elizabeth expected. They met in her room – ceilings, walls, floor, all painted a royal blue. A sparse arrangement of bed and red and orange floor mats. A chest of drawers was bulging with roots and dried plant matter. The woman was wearing a blue tunic and a sort of turban, bright oranges and blues in an African print.

'What shall I call you?' Elizabeth asked.

The woman hadn't spoken a word since Elizabeth arrived. Now she spoke, ignoring the question.

'You have a sick woman patient. Ephraim, he tell me. He say she has sick spirit.'

'Well, I don't know about that, but she is ill, yes . . . '

'She not speak?'

'No, she doesn't speak. You see . . . '

'She cry?'

'Occasionally, yes, but not excessively. Well . . . '

'But she cry?'

'Yes, yes, she cries.'

'She eat?'

'Yes, she eats . . . '

'You show me pictures.'

Elizabeth produced the drawings again. The woman looked at them, shaking her head and muttering. She put the drawings down on the mat between them and took a small blue bag from her waist. She took bones out of the bag and held them in her hands, chanting quietly and rocking back and forth. Suddenly the woman let out a breath and a shout and threw the bones on to the drawings. They landed in a random fashion. In spite of herself, Elizabeth found herself staring at them as though she could read something in them. The woman looked a while, picked a couple up and threw them again. Then she looked at Elizabeth.

'What you want do with this woman?'

'I want to help her, make her better.'

'You can't.' It was said with complete authority.

'Why not?'

'She not sick. She travel. She not in same place, same time as you. But she not sick. Cannot make better if not sick.'

'Are you saying I should just leave her alone?'
'What she ask you?'
'Well, she asked to be cared for.'
'She ask you to make better?'
'I don't know. She doesn't speak.'
'Then you not make better. She OK. She on big journey inside.' The witch-doctor pressed her chest. 'You do nothing.'
'But she isn't well . . . '
'She not sick!'
'How do you know?' Elizabeth was becoming annoyed.
'I know. I know. She has boy, yes?'
'Yes.'
'He will journey with mother. You no journey. You no make better. You watch.' She put her hand on Elizabeth's. 'You be good doctor. You no make sick. You OK, do big thing by not doing. OK?'
'Can you tell me more about this journey?'
She shook her head. 'Some people must travel to a place to be there. This woman she can go anywhere. She is free inside.' She pointed to her head. 'Not like other peoples, like so . . . ' She put her hands around her head as if to hold her thoughts inside. 'This woman, she . . . ' And she spread her hands, floated them upwards.
'Can you tell me more about the importance of the son?'
She shook her head. 'He is far away, but they will be together. It is a good thing.'
It was over. The witch-doctor was very pleased with the session. Elizabeth paid her and left. She had seemed delighted, thought Elizabeth would be delighted too that her patient was 'not sick'. Well. Now what? Do nothing. But how had she known about the son? That's the problem with all this stuff, Elizabeth thought, it makes you doubt yourself. There is no rational basis for following her advice. None at all. But she knew she wouldn't show Melanie any of the

pictures she'd copied from the reference books just yet. She'd try and find out about Michael's movements first. After all, a week or two wouldn't be material in this case.

Michael couldn't find any shade. The road was the same shimmering track behind and in front, it seemed pointless to stop. But he was hungry, needed a break. He pulled off the road and took out the sandwiches the dominee's wife had prepared for him. Scrub alternated with stretches of semi-desert all around him. He opened a beer, got out of the van to stretch his legs, relieve himself, curse his nervousness at leaving the safety of his wheels. He didn't go far from the vehicle. He was making good time, would easily reach the army camp by nightfall.

He stretched out on the front seat, leaving the windows open a few inches. He didn't think he would be able to sleep, but he needed to rest his eyes. The road had become hypnotic, seemed to be rising up to meet him. The plastic seat-covering stuck to his clothes and his flesh. It was like lying in a sauna. But he daren't leave the windows wide open, not that the air was cool. If he did fall asleep and . . . but it was the middle of the day, for God's sake. So? Timothy was killed in the early morning. Daylight isn't sacred, you fool.

Timothy is dead. Even though he had carried the corpse, it didn't seem possible. It was too casual, sudden. Game over. It didn't seem real. A creeping sense of panic filled Michael. His heart was racing, his breathing shallow. He sat up. This was ridiculous. Timothy was dead. He, Michael, was alive. But the panic didn't recede. Jesus. He hated it when this happened. Hated the feeling he had of hanging desperately on to something stable when all around him was threatening to dissolve, flow, go in forbidden directions. He would not think about it. He would not! He started the van, found the action pleasing. To act is better than to contemplate. Less frightening, anyway.

11

The weighted digging stick struck stone, gouging the little girl's hand. She showed it to the pregnant woman alongside her. The woman removed the splinter, put her mouth to the small wound, sucked the blood and spat it out. Together they searched among the trees for the leaves she needed to clean the wound.

This was part of the child's training. All the girl children were expected to begin gathering food at a very early age. They worked with their mothers and aunts, learning the differences between the plants, which leaves signalled a tuber hidden in the earth, which berries, leaves, roots and bark should be kept for medicine. The women provided most of their families' food.

Now they would find a dressing, not because it was really necessary, but to teach. The child was tasting her own blood now, smiling up at the woman who had become her mother. The learning was simple, nothing was by rote, everything in the context of a story that related to the shape or characteristics of the plants. The oldest members of the family were the best storytellers, it was something you got to do when you got older, something to look forward to. There was no pressure to remember the stories or the plants. Melanie had difficulty with the leaves, with recognising and remembering them. Still, she worked carefully with her digging stick and her diligence made her endearing. Her adoptive mother felt sorry for her, she was obviously born lacking many basic skills. Her mind was not adapted to absorb the oblique metaphors of the people. Her white skin burned in the sun, forcing them to cover the child in a thick paste of protective mud, the fine hair tangled so badly and seemed to grow endlessly, the eyesight was so poor.

The women had debated as to whether the child's hair should be cut, but being unsure as to how it would affect her health, they had taken to including it in the mud treatment, making a hat out of the hair itself. Cleaning the child was out of the question. It would take too much water. Still, she was a good child, grateful for her care, quiet and utterly devoted to !Katchu.

The woman was a little jealous at first, but how could one mind when the child had so little? And !Katchu was her cousin, a fine artist, strong in healing. The woman and her husband had no sons of their own, for some terrible reason she was not yet able to deliver good babies. This child she now carried was the third of her pregnancies.

The other two she left in the bush after birth. The spirits attacked her at some stage of the pregnancies and the children were deformed. She could not return with such children. She and her mother buried each child. She knew she should not feel sentimental about a creature taken over by the bad spirits, should not feel any affection for it at all, but this was hard.

The women, of course, knew what had happened. They welcomed her back with traditional cries of triumph, she had survived the ordeal placed before her, she had shown courage against the spirits, she had been compassionate. She felt recognised for her sorrow and her courage. It made it easier.

It was shortly after the second time that her uncle returned with the little girl. The group had debated who should care for the child. She was honoured when one of the older women, indeed not of her immediate family, said that she, who had shown much courage, who had the wisdom of sorrow, although childless, she was the one who would face this difficult task with the most skill. There was unanimous agreement. She had accepted. Now she was pregnant again. She felt hopeful. The care of the little girl stopped her from dwelling too much on the past. Perhaps it would give protection from the spirits.

They had found the leaves. Now they crushed them between two stones to make a paste which she smeared over the little girl's hand. Melanie felt the stinging sensation of the antiseptic leaves. Felt the warmth and strength of the hands that smeared it on. Tried to remember the leaves, the look of the tree. Then the woman began to sing. From the camp came singing too. They had sung this song a few times in the past weeks. Melanie knew what it meant. The men had killed a wildebeest. It was the season for it, they had come here specifically for this game. They hurried back to the camp. The women would start to prepare for the carcass while the men carried it the ten or twenty miles back to camp. How the women knew, all together, the same knowledge, Melanie hadn't been able to work out. She thought it was something to do with being older. But now, as they reached the camp, she saw that one of her friends was singing the same song with the women. Perhaps it wasn't an age thing. Perhaps it was for the same reason that she couldn't remember the plant names like the other girls. She had tried to ignore her difference. But if her friend could hear whatever they heard, then it was too much. She couldn't pretend any more. She hated to cry when everyone was happy. So she slipped into !Katchu's hut to smell his smell and let the tears forge the tell-tale tracks through the red paste smeared on her face.

Melanie Carter put aside a long thin stick tugged free from the pile of wood and kindling collected from the grounds of Tranquillity. She pulled a splinter from her palm, held the wound to her mouth, tasting warm blood, her back to the nurse. Tears mixed with the light drizzle that started to fall. Sheena went inside to fetch an umbrella. Mrs Carter never did seem to notice the weather.

One of the young soldiers at the entrance to the army camp escorted Michael from the car park to the Portacabin that served as Colonel David Serfontein's office. He was of an age with Karel, but shorter, clean-shaven, dark-haired. They shook hands, drinks were poured, pleasantries exchanged.

'So. Karel tells me you're looking for Bushmen.'

'Well . . . Yes . . . I am.'

Serfontein picked up his telephone. 'Tell Goodwill I want to see him in my office. No, he's on duty. Yes. 'Bye.' He turned to Michael. 'We've got them here. Best trackers in the world. What do you want with them?'

'I'm doing research into traditional healing.'

'Karel says you work in the stock market. In London.'

'Yes. This is a private interest of mine. How do you know Karel?'

'We went on officers' course together. Did a stint or two on the border together. He's a good man.'

There was a knock on the door.

'Kom binne!' (Come in!)

A small, slender man entered the room, saluted. He was wearing camouflage and a beige-coloured beret with a rhinocerous badge.

'Goodwill, this is Michael Carter. He is looking for your

people. He comes from England. Do you know where England is, Goodwill?'

'Yes, colonel.' The small man was standing to attention.

'At ease, Goodwill. You can ask him what you want. His English isn't bad.'

'How do you do. Look, this is a bit awkward . . . there isn't a way we could do this more informally?'

'Goodwill, hy wil met jou alleen praat. Is dit all right?' (He wants to speak to you alone. Is that all right?)

The dark eyes looked carefully at Michael. Goodwill nodded. Serfontein got up, indicated a chair for Goodwill. 'I'll leave you to it. Goodwill, bring him to the officers' mess for supper when you've finished.' Then he was gone. Goodwill sat silent. He didn't look like the Bushman of Michael's childhood. His skin was more a dark copper than the yellow brown Michael had expected. He looked, Michael thought, like a Bushman crossed with Timothy. Goodwill was waiting for Michael to begin, not looking at him.

'This is very good of you . . . ' Damn. This wasn't easy. 'What I wanted to find out was where I could find a Bushman healer, someone who could tell me about medicines and illnesses.'

Goodwill nodded.

'Do you know of such a person?'

Goodwill nodded again.

Right. Forget the yes/no questions. 'Where can I find this person?'

'Up north. Not here. Here is army doctor.'

'Do you know of anyone who might be able to help me find the healer?'

'Why do you want healer?'

'I need to ask advice. I need some help.'

'What help?'

Michael took the small jewellery box out of his pocket,

showed Goodwill the beads. 'These belonged to my mother. She was given them by your people when she was a child. Now she is ill. One of her friends said that your medicines might be able to help her.' Goodwill looked at the beads for a while. He did not move to touch them.

'I know not of medicines. I know not these people. You must go in the desert. Now you will come to officers' mess.' He led Michael out of the room.

Serfontein offered Michael a billet for the night, a junior officer's room. 'We're hardly busy up here now. There's lots of room.' Over dinner they discussed the changes in the armed forces. Serfontein was experiencing great difficulty in integrating the armed forces under his command. The troops of Umkhonto we Sizwe found normal military life boring, pointless after the excitement of the struggle. They were unused to the discipline, resented it fiercely, resented taking orders from white oppressors.

'Terrible things were done over the years. Terrible things. But not everyone did them. You didn't have to. You could say no . . . But we didn't blow the whistle. We didn't do anything to stop it. They can't forgive us for that. Or maybe I can't.' Serfontein was looking at the table, dragged back into some place deep in his own psyche. He slowly shook his head, roused himself, regained his New World enthusiasm. Still, he was trying to inspire his command with an understanding that the enemies of South Africa existed outside South Africa, that the nation had a duty to be strong, to protect itself. He was stumped when they asked him who those enemies might be. But we can't predict the future.

The small room allocated to Michael had a single bed on a linoleum floor. A small bathroom and a desk with an orange plastic chair completed its facilities. Michael opened the louvre windows, showered and went to bed. Goodwill had been a disappointment, but then the circumstances were difficult. He'd asked Serfontein about the Bushmen. Apparently the South African army had offered the serving Bushmen purpose-built camps to protect them during the bush wars. It seemed the Bushmen ranked very low in the inter-tribal pecking order. But Serfontein had enormous respect for their tracking skills. 'We'd put one in front of the vehicle and he'd read the tracks of the terrorists. He'd just indicate left or right with his hands. They never got it wrong.'

'Of course,' he added, 'they ended up on the wrong side of things. Can't go home, can't live in the urban world. Most of them stuck in Schmidtsdrift. They are not naturally aggressive. They're peace-loving, really.' He shook his head. 'Poor bastards. We didn't do them any favours.'

If Goodwill was right, Michael would have to go to Namibia or Botswana to seek his healer. But whether he would find him or not was another matter. Perhaps they were like most things, you found them when you were looking for something else. Serfontein said that the Okavango was one of the most beautiful places in Africa. But Michael should take a guide. He should ask the tourist office in Johannesburg for details. Or ask in Gaberone. But probably easier to set it up from here.

Michael fell asleep quickly, to be awakened almost immediately by a hand across his mouth and a shaking of his shoulder. Goodwill was standing over him, motioning to him to keep quiet. Michael nodded frantically. Goodwill removed his hand. 'You come with me now,' he whispered. 'My grandfather, he is here. But the colonel must not know. You not tell.' He waited for Michael to put on some clothes. He had come into the room through the open louvre window. Where there had been strips of glass there was now a large black hole, the strips neatly laid on the desk in front of the window. It was two o'clock in the morning.

They walked in the dark past the long rows of huts to a small fire behind a screen of saplings. The grandfather was sitting with his feet drawn up in front of him on the ground, wearing a torn T-shirt that was probably once white, brown trousers with very ragged hems and trainers that were gaping at the sides. This wasn't Michael's Bushman, but by the light of the fire he could tell he might be a close relative. Goodwill introduced them. Michael knew he would have difficulty in pronouncing the elderly man's name, it sounded like a shout with a guttural G. He resorted to 'sir', hoping Goodwill would interpret it as a sign of respect. 'My grandfather welcomes you. He wants to hear your story.' The old man nodded.

'Well,' Michael began, 'it isn't so much my story as my mother's story . . .'

Goodwill interpreted with much enthusiasm in the clicking that Michael remembered from the strange experience with his mother. The old man responded with interest, many sage shakes of the head, some tut-tutting. Finally Michael produced the beads. The old man looked at them carefully. A discussion with Goodwill ensued. Eventually, Goodwill said, 'My grandfather does not know who made these beads. He says it is another family. But he says he is sorry, very sorry your mother is sick. He says perhaps her family can help. You must find her family. They can make her better.'

'Does he know my mother is thousands of miles away?' Goodwill asked the question. The old man laughed.

'He says she is still of this world.'

After some further discussion between Goodwill and his grandfather, Goodwill and Michael started back.

'Where does your grandfather live?' Michael asked.

'In the north-west.'

'How will he get home?'

'He will walk.'

Michael had included a bottle of cognac in his overnight bag. He invited Goodwill to join him for a drink in his room. They climbed in through the window and Michael found a couple of indestructible glasses.

'How often do you see your grandfather?' Goodwill shrugged. 'Two times in one year maybe.' Michael had been fortunate to see him. As the brandy relaxed them Michael was able to piece together Goodwill's story. His mother had been of the Bushmen. His father of the Tswana. When he was very young his mother had taken him to see her family. That was when he had first met his grandfather. The old man had thereafter visited Goodwill twice a year every year for a couple of days at a time. Goodwill didn't visit his grandfather. First, there was the problem of finding him anew each time. Goodwill had been raised outside his Bushman family and did not know, as his mother did, where they were likely to be at any one point in time. Secondly, he felt like an outsider. When a small community spends all of its time together over years and years then you are going to be a guest no matter what your blood ties may be.

His mother had eventually left her husband and gone back to her family group, leaving Goodwill with his father. The father had gone to work at the mines and Goodwill had joined the army. He had learned something about tracking and hunting from his grandfather. The aptitude he thought had come with his birth. He just knew how to do it. He had been initially suspicious of Michael because of the other people who had come in the past to study his people.

Goodwill's grandfather spent much of his time with Goodwill trying to understand things about the modern world. While Goodwill agreed with his grandfather on many counts, he was reluctant to adopt his passivity. He was determined to get an education, to learn how the world worked in order to make it work to his advantage. 'I am not Boesman,' he said, sombre. 'I am not that victim.'

His time in the army had taught him that, all else being equal, the man with the best technology will win in the end. There had been no prisoner-of-war camps in the dirty border wars. Each side had done its best to extract information from its prisoners, at best beating the innocent and sending them on their way as bait, sometimes carelessly executing them when they proved stubborn or the information was too easily obtained, at worst indulging in the act of murder as sport. 'You do not want to dig up the ground behind the toilets in these camps. Too many people lying there.'

Goodwill remembered one particular platoon that chased a man up a tree. When he tried to climb down the tree they shot at his feet. Then they shot higher and higher into the tree, forcing him to climb on his damaged feet. Then they shot near his head, forcing him down again. They spent the best part of half a day in this sport before riddling the tree with bullets.

Rather than carry the injured enemy, they would administer fatal medical treatment. On one occasion he saw them pour undiluted methylated spirits on the stump of a man's leg. The land-mine hadn't killed him but the coronary did. What disturbed Goodwill most was that the people laughed while they did these things. He considered it barbaric, but conceded that both sides were capable of equal barbarism. He had seen the end result of all their handiwork.

Michael wondered why he had joined the army. It was one of the few places were Goodwill could get an education, he explained. He would learn languages, both English and Afrikaans, to add to the Tswana that was his native tongue and his grandfather's !Kung language. The army had a library, provided regular meals. It was understood that as a tracker he would not be heavily involved in combat. He and his colleagues were left much to their own devices. It had not been a bad life. The alternatives were to work in the mines in Johannesburg or find some form of manual labour here in the Northern Cape. Neither appealed to him. Those of his colleagues who had gone down the mines had many terrible stories to tell. But he, Goodwill, was not going into the bowels of the earth. He was too separate from his Bushman family to go to them. The army had become his people. He seemed unmoved by the momentous political changes. He would wait to see what happened to him on a personal level before he judged them for better or worse.

The sky was beginning to lighten when Goodwill left. Michael carefully replaced the louvres in the window before sleeping. He was overtired though, his mind racing. Well, he had found a Bushman. And a half-Bushman. It wasn't quite how he'd planned it. He supposed he was guilty of theme-park romanticism. He'd particularly liked the grandfather. He was self-contained, he didn't need anything, least of all approval.

In a filthy shed, no bigger than a chicken pen, two hundred miles north of Michael and Goodwill, an old man lay curled up on a pile of rags. Stacked in a corner were a dozen empty brandy bottles. He could make a few cents on each bottle. The man was incredibly thin, his arms and legs like sticks, his abdomen puffed out. Flies settled on the corners of his eyes. He reeked of alcohol. No one warned him when he was young and proud that this liquid would destroy in him any power he had to escape from it. In the stink of the shed, !Katchu was waiting, hoping, for the eventual dignity of death.

The following day Michael set off for the Botswana border. He would make his arrangements in Gaberone instead of hanging around the army camp, although he sensed that Serfontein in his state of enforced isolation would have welcomed his company.

He had been driving for about an hour and a half when he saw a figure up ahead at the side of the road. Where did these people suddenly come from on these bleak stretches of road? He drove past, but then, recognising Goodwill's grandfather, pulled over and reversed up to the old man. He had been holding his arm out as though he wanted Michael to stop.

Conversation was impossible. But it was clear that the old man was coming with him. With many smiles, nods, gestures and unintelligible remarks on both sides he was finally ensconced in the passenger seat. All he seemed to have with him was a half-empty gym bag, a pack of cigarettes and a lighter. The old man's skin was wrinkled and papery, the colour of golden-red sand. Michael opened a window. It wasn't an unpleasant smell, but a strong one, the same smell that came from a wild animal, distinctive, mixed with old tobacco. In the daylight he was far more wrinkled than Michael had realised, much smaller and his smile much younger.

After repeating each other's names again and again, they drove in silence for a while, the old man watching all Michael's actions, occasionally shaking his head and saying something. It was frustrating, not having even a smattering of language in common.

They carried on in this way for a few hours, the old man pointing directions. They seemed to be heading for the Kalahari Gemsbok National Park. The landscape around them was utterly flat, covered with scrub, seemingly uninhabited. Still, there were always fences on either side of the road. After a few hours the landscape changed. Where there had been tired dried scrub and flat muddy terracotta earth, now the road seemed to go up and down in regular waves and the earth on either side became an unmistakable red. Shrubs of a surprising bottle green were dotted across the red-orange sand, with no ground cover in between. Occasional clumps of grasses, a luminous light green, fanned out over the sand and shivered with reflected light in the slightest of breezes. Petrified grey bushes seemed reduced to charcoal by the sun.

Michael was reassured to see a vehicle or two pass by. He felt adrift, the endless road his only point of reference in a landscape that remained unchanged as each rise was crested, each valley reached. There were no turnings to the left or right, just the black tarmac running up and down through the ocean of red sand.

In the early afternoon they turned at last into the road leading to the park. The surface was challenging. The van alternated between a bone-crunching juddering on occasional stretches of gravel and a surfing motion as it temporarily lost traction on powdery sand. The old man signalled for Michael to stop as they approached the first desert sand-dune on their right, incongruous next to the thorn trees that lined the dirt road. The old man let some air out of all four tyres. The improvement was noticeable. After half an hour they came across a trading store set back from the road. The old man talked animatedly as he guided Michael towards it. Inside, still talking, he filled up a basket with three T-shirts, a carton of cigarettes, four packets of sugar and three bottles of brandy. He gave the basket to Michael and waited for him to pay. The man behind the counter was indifferent, slowed by the heat. Michael added a few bottles of water. They loaded the van and the old man indicated that Michael should wait. He took Melanie's beads from the dashboard and a bottle of brandy. Then disappeared behind the store towards a small shed.

!Katchu shielded his eyes from the light of the open door. He recognised the silhouette of his cousin //Ga, turned his face away. //Ga opened the bottle of brandy and poured a capful which he handed to !Katchu. His hand trembling, !Katchu swallowed it and gave it back for a refill. After three capfuls he was able to sit up. //Ga crouched next to him.

'!Katchu, my cousin. Perhaps you are . . . not well.'

!Katchu shook his head, rubbed his face with his hands.

'You have a visitor, come from far. It is the son of your white niece.'

!Katchu tried to comprehend. 'White niece?'

'You have told me of this child from many years ago.' He handed him the beads.

!Katchu fingered them. He wanted to remember, but his thinking was not straight these days.

'You told me the story of the child that lived with you. Her son is here. He is looking for you. For the family.'

!Katchu shook his head. Shrugged. //Ga nodded. Indeed, he was not strong. There was little left within him. But the young white man's identity must be verified.

'Can you look into his eyes and see if the mother is there?'

!Katchu shrugged again. //Ga poured another capful. Then he closed the bottle. 'Will you come with us to your family?'

!Katchu eyed the bottle, looked a question.

//Ga indicated three with his fingers. !Katchu looked at his own hand. The trembling had eased a little. He could feel some life back in his body. //Ga helped him out of the hut. His vest and trousers were filthy, stained with stale urine and brandy. They each lit a cigarette, !Katchu constantly rubbing his face. He put on a pair of battered black shoes. Then he grinned at //Ga. 'I remember. I will look at the son.'

Michael sat with the van door open, wondering if he would see the old man again that day. But then he appeared, with another, older, man. Stick thin, reeking of alcohol and stale tobacco, the second man had a protruding stomach although his skin hung in folds on his arms. The hair that formed nodules on his head was peppered with grey. His face was grey too, under the copper colour of his skin. He looked carefully at Michael and then came very close and stared deep into his eyes. Michael held steady, breathed through his mouth. Then !Katchu moved away and held a consultation with the old man.

'It was a long time ago.' He shook his head. 'Maybe . . . But I would need to watch him, see his character, his walk . . . his feet . . . '

//Ga nodded. This was perfectly reasonable. !Katchu should come with them. Then he could study the son at close quarters. And anyway, there was a van. They could go most of the way by van. !Katchu would never be able to walk it, not now. This, of course, he didn't say. But he did say how good it could be for a man to see his family once more. To be in the land, to follow the natural order. !Katchu understood. He could die in the traditional way. He nodded. It would be good. They both climbed into the front of the van.

A woman came out of the back of the store. She was slender, with front teeth missing, a scarf tied around her head, a blue apron over her dress and slippers on her feet, their backs flattened under her heels.

'Hai, Boesman!' she yelled. The sound was harsh. //Ga and !Katchu ignored her. 'Boesman! Jy gaan dan kom jy nie terug nie, hoor jy, Boesman?' (Bushman! If you go you don't come back, do you hear, Bushman?)

Michael looked at his two passengers studiously ignoring the woman. As she moved to come closer he started the van. As they drove off she yelled a few half-hearted comments after them, her hands folded under the apron. //Ga and !Katchu shared what sounded like a laugh.

They spent the rest of the day travelling slowly along a dirt road that seemed to run parallel to a boundary fence. The road alternated between hard, rutted and pot-holed dirt and the soft red sand that seemed to clutch at the tyres. !Katchu, snug in the corner of the passenger side, feel asleep almost immediately. //Ga smoked, played with the air-conditioning and chatted to Michael, occasionally pointing out an animal or two just visible on the other side of the fence.

On one particularly pot-holed stretch of the deteriorating road, //Ga indicated for Michael to stop and be quiet. A number of tiny squirrel-like creatures were standing on their back legs watching the van from their burrows. A few dashed back to safety, leaving just a couple to watch the occupants of the van watching them. Michael turned off the engine. //Ga and !Katchu slid quietly from the van and went into the bush on the opposite side of the road. Michael sweated in the car, watching the surricates. After half an hour or so they grew used to him and resumed their foraging. There were about twenty of the little creatures arguing, squabbling and playing with each other. Suddenly they were alarmed, raced for their burrows, the two sentries staying on watch as before. Then even they disappeared down their holes. !Katchu and //Ga each took up position at a burrow, but not, Michael noticed, the burrows of the sentries. Each had a stick they must have fashioned on the other side of the road, a long sharp stick looking, at its point, like a harpoon.

They stood and waited as still as marble. Ten minutes passed. Fifteen. Then simultaneously they thrust their sticks into the burrows, very hard, and kept pushing. After a minute of this each pulled out a bloody and limp surricate. Carrying them by the legs, they swung the heads against the trunk of a thorn tree before climbing back into the van.

They drove off, the two small old men, Michael and the dead surricates in the van that bravely lurched down the rapidly deteriorating road. After a jarring half-hour, //Ga became suddenly agitated, pointing to the left, shouting, pulling the wheel to indicate that they should urgently pull over. A capful of brandy was poured for !Katchu, while //Ga and Michael sipped from a bottle of water. Hot air pressed like a thick blanket around the car. Michael poured some water on to his handkerchief and rubbed his face and arms. //Ga disapproved, pointing at the water and shaking his finger. The words were unintelligible, the meaning clear.

When !Katchu had finished sipping the brandy the two men went through Michael's possessions, discarding some, including others, weighing his bag until they were satisfied. He replaced the discarded insect repellent and sunscreen. They put the T-shirts, sugar, cigarettes, brandy and extra water into //Ga's gym bag. He took out of it a pair of wire clippers with which he cut a neat hole in the fence on the right-hand side of the road. !Katchu shepherded Michael across the road, holding his arm, making him step into //Ga's footprints. They went through the fence and the two men quickly repaired the hole. Then, still walking in single file and all stepping in //Ga's footprints, they set off to the east.

When Michael tried to break out of the crocodile he was firmly moved back into place. Suddenly he stopped. The glare of the sun and the hours of driving with the wavery heat haze constantly shimmering on the horizon made him edgy. What was going on here? He needed to know – where were they going, and why did he have to walk close on //Ga's heels? //Ga shrugged, picked up a few heavy stones and started throwing them over the high fence back on to the road ahead of the van. He put a heavy rock in Michael's hand and indicated that he should do the same. He bowled it over the fence and watched the road explode into a fountain of sand and rock. The force of the explosion passed through what felt like every molecule in his body. His legs shook. They were walking him through a minefield and he had no choice but to do as they said. //Ga was pointing and explaining and shaking his head. Michael could pick out the odd swear word. Then the old man set off as though nothing had happened, advancing at a steady pace, Michael close on his heels.

They must have covered four or five miles in the late afternoon before they made camp. I don't even know which country I'm in, Michael thought. The soft red sand of the desert rose and fell like a solid sea, relentless peak after trough after peak. The sand was compacted and there were patches of stony gravel at the bottom of some of the troughs. It was impossible to see very far from any of the peaks. He had been reassured to think that the footprints would remain clear for days. They could easily have crossed a border. He began to retrace the route with a stick on the ground, trying to match it to the map. He was confident that he could remember the path they had taken. Left, right, these things were easy enough. But in the red sands of the afternoon he lost his orientation. The sun set in the west, and from that he knew their general direction was north-east. At a guess he would say they were still in the Kalahari Gemsbok Park, but which side? South Africa or Botswana?

Where else but in the game park would there be the ostriches that so excited the two men? They had spent some time setting a trap, a round leather thong held in place by twigs planted in a small circle in the ground. The bait was a few white stones. The thong was attached to a sapling bent down towards the ground. 'Hy's dom,' they'd tried to explain to Michael, laughing. 'Hy's dom, dom dom.' Something was stupid. He hoped it wasn't him.

The two surricates had been skinned and skewered with astonishing efficiency and were now being turned occasionally over the small fire. Michael had taken a tin of baked beans from his small store and made to put it in the fire. The two men had stopped him. //Ga had firmly taken charge of the tin and of the water supply. Michael was aware of being thirsty. The two men didn't seem to sweat like he did. But he didn't want to ask for more than his share. God knew how long it would have to last. The thought chilled him, then excited him. He was here. It was heady, like walking into the pages of a book or a filmset. The night sky, the desert – it was more perfect than any set designer could make it or any writer describe.

!Katchu sipped the brandy slowly from the bottle cap, one sip at a time, felt the tremors in his body easing. One sip at a time, that was the extent of his world, the limit of his horizon. He looked over at Michael. There was something in the way he paid attention, in the way he focused on a person that was vaguely familiar. Now Michael was scratching a pattern in the sand with a stick and the little girl came back to him. It was shocking. With her came his younger self, tall, proud, free and strong. With a future as wide and unknown as the desert itself. He wanted to bolt the brandy, but sipped again. For a familiar fleeting second he considered throwing the alcohol away, but knew he couldn't any more. Without it he lost his centre. He needed this steady sipping. This last journey was important. He would sip enough to stay whole, to see and feel the land around him.

12

At first light the men checked the ostrich trap. It lay untouched. //Ga shook his head, picked up one of the stones. The thong snatched his fingers, the sapling pulled back. He laughed, untied the leather thongs. They built a small fire and now //Ga released the tin of baked beans. The three passed the tin amiably between them, scooping the beans out with their hands. !Katchu sipped his capfuls of brandy, each had a few mouthfuls of water.

The dawn was fragile, powder-blue, with tentative lilac and pastel-pink tints in the east. The air was soft, cool, the terracotta sand pleasant to rub through fingers, clean hands. There were shadows in the hollows, the tops of the dunes glowed orange. //Ga poured sand on the fire and they set off north-east again. The temperature rose steadily with the sun. First a gentle benediction, then an unwelcome fire. The three men walked fast. By midday the land had perceptibly changed. The dunes were replaced by barren soil, stony, with only the odd clump of thorny trees. Now they headed for one of these clumps and the modest shade it offered. Water, brandy and rest. //Ga and !Katchu collected the dried pods lying under the camel thorn trees, split them open and poured the small black seeds on to a large flat stone. Then the three took turns at grinding them. Another of Michael's tins, corned beef this time, was shared between them. It tasted extraordinarily good. //Ga put the ground seeds into the tin and roasted them. Then poured water over them and heated the mixture. It made a bitter, charcoal coffee, but Michael considered it good.

They lay down to rest. Michael found himself breathing as lightly as possible, inhaling uncomfortably hot air. Flies appeared out of nowhere, remorselessly seeking water in the openings of eyes, ears, nose, mouth, behind the knees, they whined and crawled their delicate way towards the deepest possible irritation. Michael swished his handkerchief. Finally he covered his nose and mouth and lay back, eyes shut. He would learn to accept.

//Ga smoked, planning the rest of their journey. There was no possibility of moving on until the late afternoon. But even then, we will only manage an hour or two, he thought. !Katchu is not strong. He will not complain, but I know that he is at the limit of what he can manage. And the white boy has problems with his feet. Michael had taken off his shoes and socks and //Ga had seen the beginnings of red swellings. They were the feet of a child. No wonder the white man needed all these things if he had feet that couldn't carry him anywhere!

There would be no leaves to soothe the blisters for a few days yet. It was a matter of some importance that they maintained their pace, as each day's journey was determined by proximity to water. The white boy's water would not be enough. Still, with the van they had travelled farther than he would have done on his own. The old man was glad that no son of his was like this boy. Fully grown and yet helpless like a child. Still, he would take him to his people. The beads had spoken to him. They were particularly beautiful. As a gift they showed the recipient greatly loved. Many hours would have made those beads. He would help this boy because of the ones who had made the beads. Anyway, travelling with this white man-child was amusing. He would have many stories to tell his own family when he got home. And !Katchu. He made sure that the gym bag with its supply of brandy was safely under his own head before he allowed himself to sleep. He knew its strength.

A drop of water formed on the rim of the tap. It gathered weight, elongated, then fell into the cream plastic washing-up bowl. Melanie was in the staff kitchenette. Sheena sat on a stool reading. Mrs Carter was developing a profound interest in water. Dr Cunningham had suggested that Sheena take her to the outdoor fountain. They were on their way there when Mrs Carter had noticed the dripping tap. Sheena was beginning to doubt Dr Cunningham. Mrs C was just plain cracked. All this writing down what she did during the day was a complete waste of time. Nothing had changed, nothing was likely to change. Sheena was bored.

She would have been more interested had she known that Melanie's current obsession with water had to do with the fact that Melanie had stopped drinking. She didn't know she had stopped, she just had. Now the drops of water assumed enormous significance. The thirstier Melanie became, the larger the drops seemed. She was waiting for something.

Elizabeth came into the kitchenette to Sheena's smile and shrug and the sight of Melanie's intense concentration. She picked up a green mug, went to wash it, shook it. Melanie watched the droplets of water running down the side of the mug, put out her hand for it. Elizabeth ceded the mug. The hairline cracks on the mug became the light veins of a leaf tilted to release a drop of water. Melanie let the drop fall into her mouth, held the mug against her cheek. Elizabeth watched carefully. Sheena watched Elizabeth.

'She's off now,' Sheena said. 'I can tell when it happens. She'll stay like that for ages now.'

The girl was right. Melanie had gone somewhere else. She was oblivious to them, the green mug had somehow provided a stimulus for the experience. Perhaps it would be possible to create artificial stimuli. Elizabeth had already tried using pictures. The hands-off strategy recommended by the witch-doctor had not lasted long in the everyday routine of the clinic. But Melanie had ignored the pictures as she would any other printed material. Perhaps a real artefact, Elizabeth thought. There must be something, somewhere. She'd try the museums.

The little girl and !Katchu had been walking for days. She had said goodbye to her family quite calmly, it was not yet clear to her that she would also have to say goodbye to !Katchu. They were on a barren stretch of their journey, surviving on the water sucked up from underneath the dry river-beds and the leaves they spread for dew in the morning. The thirstier you were, the more you tasted the water, the more thankful you were for the leaves. They carried nothing with them except !Katchu's bow and arrows and hunting stick. The little girl had her cloak and the beads the women had made for her. They were very fine, the perfectly smoothed white ostrich beads with the patterns carefully pricked into them. Horns and bones hammered the basic round shape, but it was with the teeth they achieved perfection.

It was while they were crossing a salt pan that it happened. The pan was white with the light reflecting off its crystals. This light was known to play tricks with you, most frequently pretending to be water to tempt you off your path. !Katchu did not greet the people approaching them. Two old men and a strange young man all wearing odd things appeared out of the light. As they passed each other the young man looked at Melanie and she knew that she knew him. He made as if to speak to her, but they were both tied to the pace of their guides.

They looked back at each other until the light swallowed them up. !Katchu said he did not see them. It was the light.

Michael could feel the heat of the vast platter of salt and sand through the soles of his shoes. His already stricken feet were burning up. It was the fourth day. Each day they had travelled farther. Seeing the salt pan and knowing they must cross it without water, the reality of his plight struck home. He was utterly lost. Without the old men he would die. His feet made every step painful, yet the steps had to be taken. He might die. He could easily die. It was only the implacable calm of the old men that kept Michael from panic. It was obvious they knew where they were going. He had not seen roads or people since they left the van behind. Now they were travelling in an unpopulated universe of white light. Michael looked up at the blue of the sky for reassurance and then down at the brown legs of //Ga.

Out of the watery light ahead came a child and a younger Bushman, perhaps of an age with Michael. The young Bushman was looking straight ahead, as if he did not see them. //Ga and !Katchu were doing the same. Only the child looked at him. They looked at each other with the same eyes and Michael tried to talk but his mouth was dry and with the silence of the past four days had lost its elasticity. The child looked back at him as they passed and he turned to watch it go.

It was the child of his dream. His mother as child. Here, in this terrifying place. It was her, he was utterly convinced. The recognition between them was instant. It was impossible, of course. The couple disappeared into the light and the pain returned to his feet. But now he had something to distract his thoughts. He would come out at the other side of this white salt plain. He just had to keep moving.

The mug fell to the floor, startling Melanie and her nurse.

Melanie looked at the nurse, at the kitchenette. She knew who she was. 'Michael,' she said. 'Michael is in Africa.' Sheena stared at her.

Melanie slid down the kitchen cabinets and sat on the floor. Sheena could almost see her mind closing over.

'Oh don't, Mrs C! Stay with it, Mrs C, come on, you can do it . . . ' But there was no response. The total impassivity had returned.

There was no river on the other side of the salt pan. Just an endless expanse of more scrub, red sand instead of white. Michael had hoped for some sort of oasis. //Ga saw his disappointment, indicated that Michael should take a pebble and suck it. His tongue felt too thick to bear anything but it gave some small relief.

They didn't stop. Michael wondered at the old men's stamina. They didn't seem to feel the heat or the lack of water. They were at home, fearless, as though it was normal to spend your days on a survival course. And laugh. They laughed at everything, squabbled a lot. Now //Ga was pulling a long stick of dried reed from a straggly, almost white clump. They were standing in a wide, barely recognisable river-bed. The old man began to dig with his hands. He dug down until the earth seemed slightly moist. Then he carefully drilled downwards with a stick. His eyes were shut. He went a long way down, slowly. Then he inserted the reed. Michael and !Katchu sat and watched him. When about six inches of the reed remained above the ground, the old man knelt over it and began to suck. After a few minutes of effort he spat a brown liquid on to the river-bed. Then another mouthful was spat out. And then he drank.

Michael pulled on the reed with all the energy he had left. He felt as though he was creating a vacuum that extended from the earth to the bottom of his torso, as though he might stand up and with his lips shift the world on its axis. But it didn't work. He couldn't make the water rise up the reed. The old man took over again, sucking the water up to the top, putting his thumb over it and encouraging Michael to quickly take the straw and suck up the water already inside it, as he had already done for !Katchu. They did this a few times. The water tasted of the earth. Then they carried on.

Now the two old men were providing all their food. But this night there was no food. In the afternoon they had come close to a small group of gemsbok. The animals had watched them carefully. Michael was awed by the perfectly straight, long spiral horns and the delicate black markings. Their markings and their horns looked as thought they had been crafted out of dark Belgian chocolate. That afternoon //Ga had begun to make a bow and arrows. But now they built a fire and sat staring at the flames and into the night. Conversation was always difficult, but //Ga always made the effort. It seemed important to him. Politeness demanded that Michael appear to be engaged, although he couldn't understand a thing. He tuned out the man's voice and sat watching his facial expressions, his miming. It was much clearer then, as though the sound provided static. Michael realised he was following the story quite easily. It was one he knew, one his mother had told him when he was a child. Her hand motions had been more subdued and were far fewer in number, but he remembered how she had punctuated the story with clicks of her fingers and sudden smackings of her fist into her hand. It had been one of his favourites. He couldn't remember whether she had stopped telling the story or if he had stopped asking for it.

'A long, long time ago when we were an earlier race we were given special gifts that made us different from other creatures. In addition to all our other gifts, we were given the ability to remember. We could make things, too, and so shape our world. We were given these gifts with a warning from the gods that one gift could destroy all the other gifts in the world.'

His mother was sitting beside him on his bed, the two of them wrapped up in the circle of light from the bedside lamp. Living the story for him, with him, not like a grown-up at all, she made it seem that she and he shared some special place where she became a child again.

'Each child, to this day, is told the same story so that we will always remember.'

Not every child. Not one other child at Sunday school. Mothers can lie.

'It has always been understood that water is there for all. It is where the elephant will drink with the wildebeest, where the zebra goes and the hyena. Water is the first gift of the gods to all creatures. Now there was one year when the rivers did not run. No water fell from the sky, the river-beds were empty. The water-holes were smaller than they had ever been and some were dry. The animals travelled in search of water and we travelled too.

'It is a very sad thing to reach a water-hole and find it empty. Many animals died in this terrible way. The hyena and the vulture feasted and drank blood. It was then we decided that we must find places and ways to save water. We could remember where the water had been and we would always have a supply. That is why when you travel the bush you are taught where the water is hidden. It was also agreed that you would always try and leave some behind for the next person. And, of course, whenever possible, you would fill the ostrich shells with water. This system worked very well.

'But the next year was even drier. There was a man amongst one of the families who said that each family should look to its own waters, that the water of one family belonged to that family and that family was responsible for filling its own shells. You were not to take the water from another family.

'This did not work very well. Some men supported this idea, mostly those who had deep water-holes in their territory. The women did not like the idea. There were too many of them who shared relatives across the families. They had always shared water and did not see how they were going to say no to someone they knew.

'It did not take long before there were two sides arguing across the families, but eventually it was decided again that each family would look to its own water. That year the families did not travel as much as they normally did. No one could afford to be too far away from their own water. Hunting was restricted to their own area of water, visiting became difficult, the world became much smaller.'

'For one family it became a very bad time. The wife of the head of the family decided that they must go to her sister, for they had water. Surely she would not refuse to share, not when the children, her own nieces and nephews, were drying up like the animals that littered the veldt? But her sister was the wife of a man who had been most strident in his support of the new way. He would not give access to their water, for fear that there would not be enough for his own family. The man's wife could not bear to turn away her sister's family – they were weak and had walked many miles. So her husband said they could fill their shells just once from the water-hole and then they must go. With time, that family died from lack of water.

'The woman who had seen her sister walk away to her death ran away from her husband. She travelled across the world telling the story of the injustice done to her sister and her family. She drank when she needed to from the supplies she knew existed and she gave thanks for the gift of water which, she said, was given by the gods to all. The women became very angry when they heard her story and much grumbling was heard at the fires at night. Food was not prepared with care and the women grew sullen and quiet. The men gathered together, each bringing his own water, to discuss the matter. The women were happier then.

'Discussion began quietly, there was much reluctance to speak. People had died although there was enough water in the world and no one needed to die. The man who had turned away his wife's sister spoke of his experience, of how he had done a terrible thing, how he had lost his wife and members of her family. He felt he must be sent away from people, he was not fit to live with them. The women, who were listening in a ring behind the men, nodded to each other at this. Then the man who had suggested the idea in the first place told how he found this way lonely, how he did not like the world being so small for him, tied as he had been to his own water. Many of the people nodded at this. It was a very long night. The men who had supported the idea now blamed themselves for their foolishness. Those who had not supported the idea blamed themselves for not fighting harder against it, for not resisting with more strength. Eventually the man who had wronged his wife and her family turned to her and said, "Wife and mother. We have wronged you. We have concluded that we are all guilty, some more and some less, but we are all touched with the death of your family. We wish to ask you how we may find a solution. I myself will leave you and go to the driest land and never return if that is your wish. We must ask you now for a way forward." The woman sat for a long time. The women around her were nodding their heads. This was as it should be. Eventually the woman turned to the men and said that she must consult with the women. They would give them an answer at daybreak.

'The night was long with the murmurings around the fires. The women listened to the thoughts of the wronged woman and said their piece. Eventually all were agreed. As the sun warned of its arrival the women approached the men. The wronged wife said, "We have decided on many things. We do not want more death in our families. The journey of one cannot be easier if it makes the journey of another harder. We must agree to this. What the gods have given freely to the earth, belongs to all on the earth. No one shall ever take more than he needs from the earth. It is how we have always lived."

'The men nodded. They had thought this too. The woman continued, "There is also the question of this thing that has come amongst us. We do not understand it, but we know that it can grow if you feed it with more of itself. It was a different person in my husband that turned my sister away. We must find a way of cleaning ourselves from this thing. We must ask our ancestors to guide us. We must be cleansed of this and never let it back into our lives." Then the woman walked to her husband, who could not look at her, and she said, "Husband, once you are free of this thing you must come home with me and we must make our peace with the spirits of our family." The husband nodded gravely, still looking at the ground.'

The story had always stopped there. But //Ga was continuing. Michael lost the thread as his familiarity with the narrative ended. //Ga relaxed his efforts. The two smiled at each other. It seemed natural that his mother and this old man should share this story. This, the mirage in the salt pan, his presence here, were becoming less strange. His mother had been here before him, his childhood was tinted with her experiences. The sky seemed less threatening, his scanning of it less a desperate attempt to remember bits of navigational astronomy and more an appreciation, a delight in recognition. His mother was with him. He just knew.

//Ga was pleased with their communication. Every evening he tried to keep the young man distracted, tried to stop his thoughts wandering to his lack of food and water. He saw how the young man's face would tighten and his jaw would set as he fought against hunger and thirst. He may have the knowledge of a child, thought the old man, but he is brave in his own way. He wanted to tell him that he was sure they would find the tracks of the people in the next two days, but he didn't know how. !Katchu had said he was now sure the boy was the son of the mother who was his own beloved niece.

!Katchu had listened to the story with pleasure. //Ga told it well. He had stopped before the moon dance, and that was fitting. This boy may be the son of his niece, but he was not of the people. The daily walking was hard. //Ga had estimated the rationing of brandy well. They were agreed that it would be two days before they reached the people. There would still be brandy left. Thereafter it was up to him. He stared unseeing into the stars.

!Katchu was still awake when Michael fell asleep. Every night he watched Michael sleep. It was a way of telling if something was wrong. Michael normally curled himself into a state that excluded the world. He tucked his head down and retreated in sleep, a tense curling that for the old man betokened an anxious, unsettled mind. The regularity of the pose told him it was his normal state of being. He did not relax into the earth and into sleep. Rather he hid inside the sleep and carried his troubles with him. But tonight he was a little looser, a little more elongated. The arms did not cover his chest and one was even flung out towards the world. It was a good sign, !Katchu felt. He did not sleep easily himself.

It was late morning. The odd tree and hill made the world more familiar, less surreal. Michael felt emptied, light headed. He had woken cool and still felt cold. He walked mechanically now, his mind blank.

Memories of his childhood kept surfacing, as if rising from some cellar in his brain where his real self slept. His real self. The enforced lack of conversation was allowing him to rediscover the lengthy silences of his childhood. Where did the later noise come from? And what did he value, remember even, of the noise that he had learned to contend with? So many years and what? Not much that was meaningful. Wasted time. Money, of course. The pursuit of money. Modern man's purpose.

He'd been hopeless about the brown bush rabbit in its burrow. Couldn't strike it hard enough to kill it. The old man had taken over roughly, killed it cleanly. The blinding sun was erasing all nuance from the landscape, flattening it into a sheet of white heat.

Michael thought about how he would represent this experience once home. His old life felt so far away from him that it might never have existed, much like his sense of the sea had faded once he'd left it behind him. Michael had a vision of his colleagues as in a goldfish bowl, masses of frenetic activity in one small place. We cover our globe, he thought, but somehow it is tiny. It would be swallowed up by the space out here. He had spent years of his life dedicated to being a big fish in that cramped environment. It seemed ridiculous now, in this huge emptiness.

They stopped. //Ga was pointing to a footprint in the sand. It was small, narrow. He made a print himself, then showed the two prints side by side to Michael. This was a different print, but similar. Perhaps they were near their destination. Michael wanted to cry. His fear had been kept at bay by his will not to recognise it. Now that he could see that there was an end to this journey, he felt his interior crumble. The old man saw his shaking. He set off at a cracking pace, much faster than usual. All Michael's energies were directed towards keeping up. As he examined his reaction, it dawned on him how carefully he was being shepherded along the way.

They had a shorter rest at midday. The bush around them had changed, there were white-yellow grasses to knee height, top-heavy, spindly trees appeared frequently. It seemed they were on the bottom of a vast valley, with trees scattered about them. Suddenly the men stopped, motioned to Michael to stay still. Melting into the background colours of stone and terracotta was a small herd of buck, daintily nibbling their way through the grasses around them. The closest had its head up, was sniffing the air around it. Michael and the men stood motionless.

It was the first sign of wildlife not equipped for near desert conditions. Michael's heart was beating loudly. //Ga slowly took up his recently created bow and an arrow. He motioned for Michael to stay where he was. Then he sank into the grasses and on his stomach approached the herd. He stayed downwind, his approach so silent that Michael, if his eyes had not been fixed on the old man's bobbing head, would have lost him almost immediately.

Then the little band started, began to run. They flew past Michael in a ballet of dust and earth smells, one so close that he could see the shock in its enormous liquid eye. This was the one that had //Ga's arrow lodged in its neck. The old man was calling to Michael to follow him, follow the herd. They trotted after the herd until //Ga realised that Michael and !Katchu could run no farther. They slowed to a walk, the two old men excitedly marking out the injured buck's tracks from the others. To Michael they all looked the same. Towards dusk they found the buck lying panting on its side, the arrow still sticking from its neck. Michael watched the old man say what seemed to be a quick prayer before he slit the animal's throat. !Katchu's hands were cupped to receive the blood. Saliva flowed into Michael's mouth at the sight of the red stream. He quickly drank his turn. It was warm, like soup.

Shadows stretched far ahead as the old man followed the footprints of his people. Michael's shoulders ached with the weight of the small buck. They had stopped at a small water-hole, only two feet in diameter. //Ga had with him the ostrich shells he had uncovered earlier in the day. Now he carefully filled them and set off back to the place where he found them. Michael and !Katchu sat in silent guard over the buck. He felt dazed and exhausted but thoughts of predatory animals kept him alert. Near the dry river-bed they had found lion spoor; the two old men had been excited at first, but reckoned the tracks were at least two days old. What he would do if one chanced upon him, Michael didn't know. Look for help to the old man sipping his capful of brandy? Instead another creature appeared on the horizon. An old Land-Rover puffed up clouds of dust half a mile or so away. He leapt to his feet to wave, yell, and then stopped. He stood watching it drive across his field of vision.

What if these people, friendly or malevolent, did stop? Would he go back? Go home? It wasn't a real temptation. Somewhere in his journey he had accepted that it might kill him. The thought no longer frightened him. He was locked into a process that was more important than his own safety. What it was, he didn't know. He had long abandoned any naïve thought of helping his mother. This was his journey. It didn't make any rational sense but he could no more abandon it than he could not drink heavily from the water-hole. He watched the Land-Rover disappear with a sense of calm. !Katchu said something Michael couldn't understand. It sounded soothing.

The two old men were increasingly excited by the tracks

they occasionally crossed. They pointed them out regularly, smiling, eager. Michael struggled under the weight of the buck. He was close to dropping when they came upon the settlement.

Six shacks, some with more than one entrance, were scattered in a clearing, taking advantage of the shade of the few sparse trees. A washing-line holding a khaki shirt was strung between two trunks. The place seemed deserted. An old woman came out of her door. She smiled a greeting, seemed to express concern at the buck on Michael's shoulders. As instructed he deposited it inside. The shack was made out of grass, cardboard, bits of corrugated iron. It held only a blanket folded on the floor, a cardboard box that served as a table, a candle, a box of matches, a tin mug, a spoon. Some pieces of bone and stone. There was nothing else. People began to appear, casually greeting the two old men, giving sidelong glances at Michael.

Two children came from nowhere, ran into one of the huts and emerged wearing beads and brandishing two small bows and arrows. They began to dance in front of Michael, smiling engagingly until a few short words from //Ga stopped them in their tracks. They wandered off, but not before he caught a few muttered swear words.

Soon there was a growing circle of people sitting under the trees. The apathetic atmosphere of the settlement lightened as preparations were made to cook the buck and //Ga removed the sugar and cigarettes from his gym bag. Then the old man, a small child hanging on to his hand, pointed at Michael and the group grew silent. He stood submitting to their assessment. There was no sense of welcome.

He felt filthy in his clothes. His hair was matted and his beard a straggly, unpleasant growth on his face. He must stink, he thought. The children stared at him and the women cracked jokes amongst themselves. The looks they gave him were appraising, not particularly friendly. The men were gathered around the two old men. //Ga sat down, indicated that Michael should sit a little to one side. Then he began to explain their story. On demand, Michael took the small jewel box out of his pocket and handed it over. The contents was passed from hand to hand; the women, seeing the beads, joined the men and began to exclaim over them. Now !Katchu was verifying the story, //Ga explaining the connection.

There was a great deal of talking. Michael began to feel dissociated from it all. He watched with detached interest the beads of sweat dripping from his beard on to his chest. Extraordinary considering he was so thirsty. Felt himself keel over, the side of his head pitching into the earth. He wanted to sleep forever.

One of the women drew the attention of the old man to Michael's inert form. They felt him for fever. After some discussion four of the small men lifted him into one of the shacks. A bucket of water was brought. His clothes were removed, the men's T-shirts were stripped off and soaked, placed on top of him. His feet were raised on stones. The old woman came to inspect him. Michael registered the lined old face hovering above him, thought he saw the universe in the eyes that mesmerised him, felt surprisingly strong fingers prodding, kneading his body, testing the elasticity of his skin. Then he was given water to drink. It tasted salty. He sank into blackness.

Elizabeth banged on the door of the sangoma's apartment. The woman eventually opened the door and went with awful slowness about dressing herself, packing the tools of her trade, locking her flat. Elizabeth paced impatiently, drove dangerously through the blancmange of evening traffic between London and Sussex. On the M25, when she had changed lanes at least a dozen times in an unsuccessful attempt to make headway, the woman intervened.

'Doctor, you will not help your patient like this.'

'You're right. I'm sorry. I just don't know what to do.'

'We will know when we get there.'

'I hope so, I really hope so.'

Sheena had raised the alarm. Melanie had barricaded herself under the desks in the craft room and was sitting wrapped in a blanket and chanting to herself. Elizabeth could not get any response from her. She was chanting something they couldn't understand; she was in a different place. Melanie had taken a bowl and a pestle from the shelves and was crumbling bits of paper into the bowl, mashing them over and over with the pestle. First she tore them into strips, then she chewed them until they were a soft crumbly mass, then she placed them in the bowl and mashed them. She had the strips all laid out in front of her and seemed to be listening to instructions as to what to do next. Professional training suggested medication but Elizabeth couldn't do it. She wouldn't medicate what might be progress. Melanie wasn't harming anyone.

She went to fetch the witch-doctor. Now she was praying to a God she didn't believe in that she had done the right thing. But with the syringe ready she had looked into Melanie's eyes and seen as if through the wrong end of a telescope that her patient was beyond the confines of time. Melanie calmly continued mashing her papers.

Was it her instinct that she was following or her professional curiosity? Elizabeth didn't know, didn't care to ask herself. The witch-doctor wouldn't give anything away, said she had to see the patient first.

Melanie was in the same position, sitting with her legs drawn up, one on either side of the bowl. For the first time she looks truly mad, Elizabeth thought. The witch-doctor set up camp a few feet away from Melanie. She didn't look at her, simply spread out a mat and a strange variety of objects, a flat wooden platter, a selection of bones and stones. She sat leaning to one side, supporting her weight with her arm. Then she shut her eyes. Elizabeth slipped out to fetch a video camera.

When she tried to set up the equipment in a far corner of the room, the witch-doctor left her place and demanded that she take the equipment and herself away.

'I can't leave my patient.'

'The spirits know you mock them. You dangerous to us.'

'You can't expect me to leave my patient. I must observe her.'

'You must go. You must. I will tell you. Not now. Later.'

She had brought the woman here. She couldn't now disobey. And there was something about the woman in the weird cape of skin with the dead animals stitched to it that inspired obedience. She looked like a voodoo queen.

So she kept vigil outside the door, petulant as she had been when denied access to the company of her parents' friends as a child. She wondered what had happened to her calm rationality. Staff passing in the corridors looked at her strangely. She ignored them. A colleague tried to discover what all the fuss was about. She took refuge in her acclaimed previous research. It was an important experiment. Very important. Her agitation was betraying her. Experiments were conducted coldly, scientifically. Findings were recorded. Still, she wouldn't leave her post. The hell with it.

Inside the room the sangoma painted her face with blue lines and white markings. She needed strong protection in this room where there was so much power, where she could feel ancestors unknown to her. She had not admitted it to the white woman but she was worried that she hadn't the skills to deal with the situation. She had left Africa too young to finish her training properly. Much of her art was the same as that of the clairvoyant on the beachfront. The placebo she gave acted as much on the spirit of those who came to her as any medicine would, but there had been enough truth in her limited training and in the gifts passed down to her for her to be aware of the power around her. She threw the bones once, twice. There was illness. The son. There was death. Close by. But not in the centre, on the edge. She began to study the woman carefully. She was making a medicine. It must be for the son. Where was he? How did this white woman know how to make a medicine, to chew the leaves and bark and mash them together?

The sangoma shut her eyes, began to recite an incantation, asking the spirits for guidance. But these spirits were not centred on her, they were focusing on the woman. She felt on the outside. She would close her eyes and listen inside. She was protected, but the faint stirrings of her own ancestors were shadows compared with the palpable presences in the room. She heard an old woman in a tongue she did not understand. The old woman was talking to herself, but the mother was listening. The mother was doing as the old woman did. But this old woman was alive! Not here, but definitely alive. She felt a coldness in her blood. This was her gift working more powerfully than ever before. She heard other voices, then the old woman gently singing, syllables that did not make sense to her. She began to sing along, softly, then more strongly. Melanie began to sing with her. The words came from another place and the witch-doctor had no idea what they meant, but their meaning was somehow clear. It was a lullaby, a soothing song for the young and the sick. A song about being in the dark, about the knowledge of a mother as to the safety of her children, about the ancestors who gave help to those in need, about being cradled in the lap of the world.

Elizabeth heard the singing and went to fetch a tape recorder. It was midnight when the sangoma came out of the room and found Elizabeth slumped in the chair outside. She shook her head over the tape recorder. She was tired. She stroked Elizabeth's face to wake her. Elizabeth smelled the hand as much as she felt it. A pungent, rich, earth smell that she couldn't place. They went to the kitchens to prepare food.

The old woman stood outside Michael's hut and looked into the night. He was in the hands of the spirits now. She held the beads the young man had brought with him in her hands. So this man was somehow related to the child that !Katchu had spoken of. !Katchu. How old he looked. How ill. Shame made him smaller. They had exchanged formal greetings. He had not met her gaze. Her heart still sorrowed for him. Her first husband. After the divorce she had, of course, taken another husband. But the loss of !Katchu to the white man's poison was a pain that had never quite healed. He had begun to disappear for long stretches. His own children were neglected. She had not had news of him for most of her life.

Ah, !Katchu! We didn't know about the poison then, but now we do. Without the beads she would not have tended her patient. Why should she? In three lifetimes the white man had taken the animals off the land, stopped the flow of water, pushed the people farther and farther into the desert. And he had brought weapons that he put under the earth that you had to learn to detect, because these weapons would rip a body apart. And diseases she did not know how to treat.

But this young man . . . she felt she was not alone as she had mixed the medicines. The people who were with her could hear her but not speak to her. It was unusual that they should hear her. She would sleep next to her patient tonight, make him drink the salt water through the night. Perhaps they would see an improvement in the morning. She would get up with the light and fetch the tsama melon she knew was growing to the east. It would be ready for picking and good for him.

Michael was in another world. It was dark, mostly, in this place. But his mother was with him. He could feel her hand in his. He ignored the creatures that came out of the darkness, distorted people, some strange and some familiar. His mother was singing to him. He clung to her hand. Michael lay on his back in the shack under the wet T-shirts and a rough blanket, his one hand holding the other.

13

The young man still lay in the other world when morning came. The group exchanged opinions. The women and children were going that day to a grove of maroela trees. If they didn't get the fruit, the monkeys would. They didn't know what to do with the sick young man. He was white. That meant trouble would follow. //Ga felt a hint of resentment against him for burdening the group with this trouble. But the old woman spoke for the young man.

'I, Warda, will wait. !Katchu will wait. We will tend him until he is better or dead.'

The rest of the group set off. It was a blessing really, as they could now discuss !Katchu's return and ask //Ga all the questions they had about the young white man. One of the women knew that !Katchu had been a good artist and a great medicine man. He had undertaken many dances for his people. She herself had been cleansed by him. The little girl she did not remember. No one did. But there had been a little white girl, she knew that because her mother had told her. Her mother had cared for the little girl for some years. She herself had only been a baby. They picked over the scanty details, each trying to work out their own relationship to the young white man through the family that had tended his mother. It didn't occur to them to dispute the original relationship, it was as it had been conducted. The woman who had been cleansed by !Katchu concluded that this young man must be her nephew. The younger children began to make extravagant claims of kinship, dissolving into fits of giggles when they thought about the strangeness of the young man. The funny things he had been wearing. And the terrible sores on his feet!

Michael drifted into consciousness and saw the day shining through a thick lattice wall of grasses. An old woman was sitting next to him. Seeing he was awake she forced some vile-smelling stuff into his mouth. He was terribly thirsty and it was liquid. She gave him some water to wash it down. Then he was back in the darkness.

In the early hours of the morning the sangoma, Elizabeth and the orderlies were able to lift a sleeping Melanie and put her to bed. The craft room was restored to order, a room was made ready for the sangoma. Melanie and the sangoma slept for most of the day. The medical doctor Elizabeth called in to check on Melanie gave her a clean bill of health. 'Maybe a touch of dehydration. But otherwise, more your department than mine!'

The greetings between !Katchu and what remained of his family had been restrained. It was over ten years. His memory was playing tricks with him now, but he knew there had been a great deal of unpleasantness before he left. He had wronged many people, but he could not remember now who or why. He recognised most of the faces, but none of the children. Warda, his ex-wife had greeted him politely. His lack of remembering and the tentative greetings made him hesitant. He borrowed a panga to build a hut for himself and Michael.

    Warda tapped at the edges of the round ostrich shell discs

and surreptitiously watched !Katchu strapping the saplings he had cut down into a dome shape. He stopped frequently to rest, under the pretext of untying a piece of string or sorting through the grasses. He was an old man now, frail. She focused on the beads, relaxed. She had been frightened when she first saw him. She would never forget the blow that smashed her nose. It was then, looking at her own blood and his twisted features that she knew she had lost him. He may as well have died. This was a stranger pretending to be her husband, an evil spirit had taken her husband away. She was divorced now, he was frail, he could not harm her, but the fear had lingered. I could fight back now, she thought. I am stronger than him. I could knock him off his feet and bloody his nose. She smiled to herself. As the hours passed and she saw how he struggled, always pretending that there was some problem that needed slow and careful examination, her heart was moved to pity. I remember, she thought, I remember how we used to play as children and laugh, we would always laugh. And when we were first married, the jokes we played on each other.

She took him water. They didn't say much, but during the morning they came to understand each other. By the time the others returned, !Katchu was feeling a lot brighter.

The illegal buck had been eaten the night before, but sufficient meat remained for another meal. //Ga consulted with !Katchu. The mood amongst the people was for the trance dance. !Katchu's n/om (spiritual power) was legendary. It might help the white boy. !Katchu accepted the compliment and the task. The day was unfolding well.

!Katchu lay in the shade of the late afternoon. His mind felt very light, very open to the slight breeze, very close to the white blue of the sky he could see through the small leaves of the tree above him. His stomach was distended, his trunk and limbs dressed in outsize sacks of wrinkled skin. And yet he felt at peace. When he was the healer of his people, before he became as a dog at the foot of the brandy bottle, he had fought against the negative, destroying influences that threatened to attack his people. !Katchu knew it was unrecognised weakness in themselves that made the people vulnerable. He himself had been attacked through his weakness, where he was least able to resist.

!Katchu would have laughed in the face of a Faustian pact. You did not lose your soul in a direct trade off. No, bad things slowly infiltrated your life, sapping the energy you needed to resist them, until one day you realised you had given your life to the negative that had always lived inside you, and then it was generally too late. No, the bad things were too cunning to offer a weak man a straight deal. Only a strong man would have the courage to accept it and a strong man would be unlikely to take it. No, it was the weaknesses in man that were a magnet for the bad things.

But this afternoon !Katchu felt free. Sometimes after a deep trance he had felt like this in the morning, clear headed, purified, full of light. He did not fear the trance. If it was his final calling, then he was happy indeed. He had no love for his life. He would go gladly with the messenger. A smile crossed his face, momentarily lifting the drooping sides of his mouth into a glimpse of the man he used to be. He would join his father and his father's father. They would take away his self-disgust. They could stop weeping over him. Laughter would enter their souls once more.

He lay very still, trying to clear his mind even further. But there was no messenger for him. Only a message. An urging, not articulated, not understood through the brain, just an urging that pervaded his body and the tatters of his emotional self. This urging was for the dance. He could feel his hands beginning to shake. Any small deprivation or damage to any part of his psyche, no matter how gentle, provoked the need for the alcohol. His supplies had run out. He could not do the dance until much later. He would have to wait without alcohol. He would wait. He would do the dance. This one time he would not give in.

The flames were higher than !Katchu himself. They had built the fire with extreme care, and now he danced around it, singing with the rest of the group. The women clapped the rhythm of the dance and the men circled the fire. Again and again they called for the giraffe medicine song. The singing had improved over the last hour and !Katchu felt his n/om boiling up inside him. He moved back from the flames to allow himself to cool, it was too much too soon. Then around he went again, his tiredness forgotten. He inhaled the smoke from the roots smouldering under the burning coal in a small tortoise shell and approached Michael, who was lying near the fire, inside the circle. The women raised him up, //Ga held him and !Katchu placed his arms on his shoulders and drew, drew the sickness from him. He felt it leave Michael's body and then he leapt and shouted, triumphant, as he expelled the arrows of Michael's sickness from his own back. Strength came from somewhere, allowing him to stamp and shuffle rhythmically, his mind empty now, drawn from this person to that, taking out illness and sorrow. There were dozens of people around the fire. Word had spread far of a great healer.

His eyes were shut, the heat of the fire guided his steps as he trod the long round path back through the races. The women sang for him and clapped the rhythm of the dance, saving him from the flames, pushing sand between his feet and the fire, cooling his heat. The women sang through his spirit, protecting him with their sounds, the men danced with him, beating out a rhythm around the fire as he sank deeper into the trance.

He searched for the source of the sorrow that seemed to be drifting like a thick fog in the infinite landscape of his psyche. It was a female, one of his own. He didn't know who this woman was, but he knew that he was joined to her in a place where neither distance nor time could intervene. She was his child, he was her father. He couldn't touch her to release the vast pool of darkness inside her, he could only howl as he would have done if she were with him, shriek at the demons and scare them from her, take the darkness into himself and cleanse it in the fire.

Melanie Carter retched until it felt as though a stinging lump had permanently lodged itself in her throat and her stomach had turned itself inside out in its efforts to expel it. The sheer force of her vomiting caused tears, a desperate panting for breath. And a thought, crystal clear, 'I am losing all that has polluted me. I shall come out of this.' The clarity of the thought, just the fact of its existence, was as shocking as the force of the physical illness. She waited over the toilet bowl until it seemed that she could move. Then she flushed the toilet, rinsed her mouth and her face. Her stomach started to churn again. She sat on the linoleum floor and rested her head against the tiles. She was burning, sweat drizzled down her body.

Then she sank back into the place of fire, the white watery heat that wrapped itself around her and her beloved father, that stroked and soothed and eased the gashes in her spirit, took the arrows from her life. They were floating together in the watery heat, unafraid, above the land, but still of the land, cradled by it, made whole.

!Katchu had collapsed, unconscious. The women continued to sing and clap, the men to dance. They would not stop until he was back from the land of the spirits. They were his anchor to this world, as he was their medium to the other world. They would sing in the dawn, united, all bonds strengthened, all sorrows and anger dispersed. Those who could, tranced together; not all would journey, but the dance was collective, essential.

Elizabeth found her, covered her in blankets, issued instructions, put her to bed. The witch-doctor was sleeping in the recreation room. Elizabeth woke her, perhaps a little roughly.

'My patient has a fever. I have put her to bed.'

The woman rubbed her eyes, came slowly back from sleep. 'Good,' she said. 'Very good.'

'She was in danger.' Elizabeth couldn't keep the accusation from her voice. Didn't want to. The sangoma listened carefully to what was being expressed rather than what was being said. She heard the words, she also heard her own dismissal. She had been necessary when the woman was frightened, but now, for some reason, this woman was no longer so fearful for her patient and resented the witch-doctor's powers. She toyed idly with frightening the woman. Her ancestors would not have hesitated. After all, due respect ought to be shown those who braved other worlds with no spear but themselves for protection. But she was tired.

Now, too, she was mostly concerned about herself. The last day had revealed to her the extent of her gift. She had yet to absorb its reality, its implications. The way of the charlatan was only open to the charlatan. She was not displeased with these changes, but neither was she pleased. Her life had been comfortable. So she merely asked what time it was and indicated that she would speak to Elizabeth in the morning. Then she went back to sleep.

Elizabeth didn't say that the fever was in some way helping Melanie. She had said thank you as they helped her between clean sheets and handed her water to drink. All would be unravelled. So why am I irritable? Elizabeth thought. Why?

Because I will lose this puzzle? Because I will not know the answer, even when the riddle is solved? Yes and yes.

Out in the open Michael slept a rich, deep, dreamless sleep.

The group dozed through the next day. In the late afternoon, a cool breeze swept across the land. Michael woke with the cold. White light spread itself in a sheet across the purpled sky. He struggled to raise himself on his elbows, disorientated. Then he heard thunder rolling across the dome above him. The old woman came over and felt his chest, his forehead, gently put her finger inside his mouth. She smiled, indicated the approaching storm. The entire community was up now, rushing about. Michael watched them putting odd containers out into the open, the children jumping up and down with excitement. There was no fear, just the most extraordinary amount of noise, laughing and chattering. The air was becoming steadily sweeter, cooler, there was a sense of waiting. The community calmed down and sat huddled in twos and threes, still high spirited, but waiting. Michael joined //Ga and !Katchu.

The old men had brought him here. He had been ill. He had no idea how long he had lain in the hut. He had no clothes on, just his boxer shorts. He supposed they had saved his life. But they didn't seem particularly bothered about him.

There was now an expectant stillness. The pauses between the thunder and the lightning grew shorter. The storm was coming closer. The entire landscape was now bathed in flashes of white light, the trees alternating between a gentle rocking in the wind and a wild stampede of branches. When the first fat raindrops fell the children began to dance. They stood with their mouths open, trying to catch raindrops. The adults too, even the old men and the old woman, raised their faces to the sky. Then rain came down in an almost solid sheet. Everybody ran for cover. It came streaming through the slight shelter of Michael's hut. Then he stood outside and opened his dry mouth. Sweet water. The ground outside was soon one large puddle. The children splashed themselves and each other. In the half-light, a container, half a large tin can, was overturned; a mother moved the children away from it and hurriedly set it upright. It rained for no more than fifteen minutes. Michael was soaking, laughing.

Melanie Carter slept for five days and five nights, barely eating. When at last she woke, it was not the half-waking of the past week, but an unequivocal, real awakening. She tried to sink back, to return to the peace of sleep, but there was no turning back. She opened her eyes. It must be very early, she thought. It is barely light. She looked around. She knew the familiar surroundings, but not why she knew them. Jeremy. Where was Jeremy? And Michael? Michael . . . Michael was grown. A man. He had been with her before she slept, but he wasn't there now. She had seen him, with the family. I am mad, she thought. I have been mad and I am still mad. I don't know where I am. She got out of bed, felt herself to be weak. Her body felt stiff. She went looking for a bathroom.

Sheena heard a thump from the bathroom. Mrs Carter was lying slumped on the floor. The girl pressed a bell for help and tried to lift her patient into a sitting position. Melanie came round, nausea rising in her throat. A nurse was holding her up. She looked at her.

'Who are you?'

'I'm Sheena. I'm a nurse. It's OK, Mrs C. You're OK. Just had a fall.'

'I'm old.' She clutched at the nurse. 'I'm old.'

'Let's get you up. Have a sip of water.'

'Where am I? How long have I been here? Where's my husband?'

She was standing now, staring into the mirror. The orderly arrived.

'Fetch Dr Cunningham. Call her. Mrs Carter's woken up. Go on. There's nothing to stare at. Go!'

'Come on, Mrs C. Let's get you back to bed. You've had a big shock.'

'But I need to know . . . Am I mad? Have I gone mad?'

'Look – you'd better wait for the doctor. But you don't seem mad to me. Far from it.' She helped her into bed. 'How about a nice cup of tea while we wait for Dr Cunningham? I'll get it for you.'

Sheena shot off. Her hands were trembling. Bloody hell. Poor cow. Tea. Bloody hell!

The doctor looked familiar. She sat next to the bed and explained as best she could.

'But what was wrong with me?'

'We're not entirely sure. You just went away for a long time. No one could reach you. But now you're on the way back. Your husband will be overjoyed. I've called him.'

'Jeremy? Is he all right?'

'He's very well. But I should imagine he'll be even better once he's seen you.'

'But I'm so old . . .'

'He has visited you every week. And he has aged too. A good-looking man.' Elizabeth smiled. She wanted to open a bottle of champagne, but the confusion and fear of the woman restrained her. 'Rest a while, have something to eat. It is a big shock. Then get up and we'll talk some more. Your husband will be here this evening . . . do you feel ready to see him?'

Melanie nodded. 'Yes . . . of course, yes . . . have I really been here all that time?'

'Yes.'

'And Michael? Where is Michael?'

'He is in Africa . . . '

'Yes, yes of course . . . have you met him?'

Elizabeth nodded. Smiled again. 'He will be very happy too. He took it hard.'

'Oh . . . ' Melanie's eyes filled with tears, spilled over. 'Oh God.'

Elizabeth passed the tissues. 'He's all right. He's stronger than he thinks. You did a good job there . . . '

And he's brought you back, it seems, she thought. She must telephone the sangoma. She handed Melanie a gift.

'It was your birthday last month. This is from your husband. There are more . . . He brought you a present for each anniversary, Christmas, birthday – they are all safe. He asked me to give you one today.' Melanie took the present, held it to her lips. Jeremy. Michael. What have I done? What have I done to us?

Melanie was sitting in her usual chair in the conservatory, a newspaper in her lap. She was staring out at the evening light. Jeremy watched her for a minute. He hadn't been able to believe it, but the newspaper . . . a newspaper! She turned and saw him, began to get up. He rushed over, held her. They stood like that for long minutes. She was shaking and he gently held her away from him, looked into her eyes. She was crying, tears tumbling over each other down her face.

'I'm so . . . ' she gasped for air, 'I'm so sorry, so sorry . . . '

'It's all right, it's all right . . . '

Sheena saw Jeremy Carter's shoulders begin to shake and turned away.

Warda was pleased. !Katchu had been filled with n/om. And it seemed to have eased his own suffering. She included the three men in her food arrangements. Milk came from the goats belonging to the smallholder on whose land they lived. In return for the milk, she gave ostrich-shell necklaces and small bags made from animal skins. Occasionally a tortoise shell. The smallholder sold them to a man who took them to a shop in Gaberone. She had no idea how much the work was worth, she just made what she could and went for milk every week. Every morning she went into the bush and dug for roots, searched for fruits, eggs. She knew the area intimately and could assess which trees, which roots would be ready at what time. It made her foraging efficient.

The men could no longer hunt as they had hunted in the past. They didn't understand exactly what they could and couldn't hunt, but they knew that the game in the parks was out of bounds. Sometimes people went to prison for hunting. This was clear evidence of the terrible times through which they were living. White hunters took rifles and Land-Rovers and went in search of game that had already been found, then they shot it, sometimes not even leaving the Land-Rover, which could ride roughshod over plants she had been waiting on. They paid money for this. The disdain felt by the hunters when they saw these charades of manliness was indescribable. They really couldn't speak of it. It was beneath speech, beneath recognition. That they in turn were restricted to bush rabbits and kori basters was too much for many of them. Warda had seen how the men's spirits had been damaged by these restrictions. Bringing meat to the women is their part in a shared life. They made bows and arrows, as badly as was possible, for sale to the smallholder. No one would shoot those arrows straight. They stitched bags that the women decorated with beads. Looked after the cattle of other men. But it was not hunting. The excitement, the triumph of the hunt was lost forever.

With so much taken away from the men, it was not unreasonable for them to turn quarrelsome. The liquor and the drugs given to them by the army and some of the farmers hadn't helped either. For a while they could forget their reality. The forgetfulness became precious over time. And then it ruled them. They brewed more and more berry beer. The children did not learn the old ways. And they did not learn the new ways either. We have fallen to the bottom of a dry well, Warda thought. And the walls are smooth.

Michael spent his convalescence stitching bags under the supervision of !Katchu and Warda. Sometimes there was food, sometimes there wasn't. Whatever Warda had she shared with the three men. !Katchu in return brought a bush rabbit. It took him two days to find it. His hands were shaking less these last few days. He had no more alcohol. Somehow the gentle weaning that //Ga had supervised had eased the craving. There was acceptance in knowing that none was available to him anyway. He smoked instead, which soothed his anxieties.

On the third day, a new man came into the settlement. He brought with him a bag of mealie meal, some tobacco. His wife shared the mealie meal amongst the women and he shared the tobacco with the men. They kept larger portions for themselves, but no one went without. The visitor – for he was only visiting and must return to his work in a day or two – had a smattering of English. It was agreed that Michael would go back with him to the shop. Which it would take them a day to reach. At the shop there was a telephone. They would go in two days.

    Michael leant against a tree in the late afternoon. He hadn't had a bath in nearly three weeks. He had lost weight. Now he knew he would be leaving he could think about the things he missed. Beer. Ordinary food. And conversation. Hot water. Soap. Toothpaste. Shaving. Bed. During his convalescence he had remarked the extreme poverty of the group. There was no litter because there was no consumption. The women foraged for food, traded beads for milk, for odd bits of money. Each person had only the one set of clothes. Some of the children had none. There was no consumption because there was no money. The water came from the smallholder's borehole. Labour was exchanged for use of the borehole water and the land. A cigarette lighter was a considerable asset.

The group seemed puzzled by their circumstances. With the smattering of languages they could muster between them, Michael gathered that above all else they wanted land. But the amount of land they would need to live in the traditional way was quite out of their reach. Their complete experience was one of betrayal, of oppression by all societal groupings. They were at the very bottom of the social scale. People were interested in them, they had visitors, but nothing much changed.

The local smallholders wanted them to become a tourist attraction. They were unsure. Other people had done this and found it amusing for a while – and then depressing. If people were so interested in them, why didn't they help them more? There was money, international money, benevolent foundations, they knew these things existed. But somehow this group didn't see the virtues of money. They were an anachronism, lost in the world. Maybe, they said, maybe if we wore our skins all the time, then we would be recognised as worthy. But the skins were despised by the pecking order above them as uncivilised. And they were not as comfortable or as warm as even the shabbiest clothes, it had to be admitted. A woollen hat was important in the winter. Yet they knew that they were clever. They knew the land and the animals like no other peoples. But this would be lost too. If a man spends all his days tending another man's cattle and doesn't hunt to feed his family, then he will lose the knowledge of hunting.

Michael felt helpless in the face of their dilemmas.

On the walk along dusty roads and through patches of open veldt, conversation with David was limited. But as they approached the shop, a tin-roofed, one-roomed building with a veranda, next door to a single-pump petrol station, he became agitated. He asked for money, took a note from Michael and indicated that Michael should wait. Presently he returned, with more supplies of mealie meal and tobacco. Then he sent Michael off to the shop with a note of the same value. It was a rough, warehouse of a shop. It displayed candles, matches, basic cooking utensils, Sunlight soap in big bars, sacks of mealie meal, packets of sugar and rows of bottles of alcohol. He asked the prices of the shopkeeper and bought mealie meal, tobacco, candles, matches, sugar. He paid with the note and received change. Outside he and David held a hurried conference. David was livid. He had known, Michael gathered, he had known that the man was cheating them. Whatever money David gave he always got the same things. But he didn't understand how the money worked, so he couldn't argue.

Michael went back into the shop and bought some paper and a pencil. Then he wrote down the prices of everything in the shop. He and David sat outside and worked through the entire inventory. A coin was matched to an item. A series of coins made up a note. A series of items made up a note. It wasn't the same as being able to count, but it was sufficient to give David some leverage. If he had been staying longer he could have explained the money better, Michael thought. David carefully folded the pieces of paper, shook Michael's hand, accepted the tobacco and mealie meal and set off. Now he was alone. There were a few people hanging around the store and the petrol station. He went in search of a telephone.

At the petrol station the attendant spoke some English.

Michael learned that he was in Botswana. How to get back to the hired van and then back to Rooisand? He didn't want to call Bessie without having a plan. And he wanted to take supplies back to the group. He had marked the route as carefully as he could. But he could not walk at night. He asked the petrol attendant if there was somewhere to stay. She indicated that there was a farm, not far, not long, to the west. Would he be able to reach it that night? She said she thought so. He left his supplies with the shopkeeper. He would return in the morning. He took water, food for a meal *en route*, and set off.

After he had walked for an hour the sun was setting and there was no sign of the farm. He was too far to go back and yet he could see nothing ahead. In the eerie light of dusk, spirits purportedly walk the earth and strange things are seen in shadows; the wise man does not linger on his way home. Michael was glad that night came quickly.

There was a three-quarter moon and he could just see his way; the dust road glowed luminous. He was alone in the landscape. A black shape swooped in front of him. His heart racing, he finally identified it as a giant bat. The veldt around him was alive with sounds. Out here, 'not far' could be a day's walk. He would keep going.

Melanie Carter sat in her usual place opposite Elizabeth. They had spent a few days on contextual orientation, Melanie catching up on the world that had moved so far ahead without her. New technologies, new world orders. The long snaking queues of people waiting on the veldt and in the townships to cast their vote, finally to have their say. She played and replayed the video footage feeling a joyous pain that made her cry. Elizabeth was content to let the process unfold as it must. They needed to find the root, the cause, bring it out into the light and deal with it. The underlying emotion was one of pain. It permeated everything about Melanie. The thought process was quite intact. It was remarkable.

'Melanie . . . do you know why this happened to you?'

Melanie looked out of the window. She wasn't sure she could talk about these things.

'I can't tell you. I think I was in mourning. But I'm all right now. I'm quite all right now.'

'I think you are a lot better. But you can't pretend it didn't happen. If you don't work it out perhaps it will trap you again? What were you mourning for?'

Melanie struggled. She liked Elizabeth. But she didn't want to talk to her about this. 'For something I can't explain. For family. For innocence, beauty. I . . . I really don't want to talk about it. Talk might . . . cheapen it.'

'It can also remove the pain.'

'I cherished the pain. It was a connection.'

How to explain? Why not just be grateful that now the knowledge of purity can live alongside the knowledge of an imperfect, unjust, cruel world without crippling one with the pain of it all? Miracles can happen. She had seen it on the television. Now she had to convince this woman to allow her to go home. I am adult, she thought. Somehow I have been made less afraid. I am my own effect. And I have unfinished business.

The driveway to the long-awaited farmhouse came into view. Labuschagne was the man's name, Elandsrus the name of the farm. Michael sat on one of the whitewashed boulders that marked the entrance. He was about to step back into his own world. Still, he wanted to hover on the threshold. He had been in the company of extraordinary men.

He opened a beer, looked up at the sky and thought about home. His mind wandered to the plaque he had seen as a boy on a church wall. It was in memory of the son of one of the villagers who had deliberately flown his plane into a German bomber headed for London's East End. His first solo flight. It had disturbed Michael a great deal. Would he be able to give his own life so selflessly for his tribe? England was his home, the English were his tribe. And he had given nothing to it, he thought. Nothing for which he might be remembered. Not one act of exceptional kindness, not one small feat that had made any sort of a change to his own world. I take the tribe for granted, he thought. I consider it owes me something. I take, take, take. We all do. And when do its resources get replenished?

Suddenly he wanted to sit on a bus and have someone foreign do something out of the ordinary and catch the eye of the person opposite and share a moment of understanding. We care about each other, he thought. That's what queuing and stupid stuff like that is about. It's about giving everyone a fair chance. Not walking all over your own people just because you can.

But if you only protect your own, then you must accept that you will walk over others. But others, he had found, will take you in, look after you and give you what little they have, no questions asked.

He was reluctant to move. What do I have, he thought . . . what do I really have? Thoughts of Janet came then. She had been lurking on the edges of his mind for days. Shame had stopped him from thinking, really thinking about her. I have short-changed you, Janet. I have used you as a mirror of myself, and I have not been truly aware of you. I have looked inward all the time. I have not recognised you. I have lacked humanity. The bush sounds and the night air were soothing, but his face was hot. I am ashamed. Timothy would not have behaved like I have behaved towards you. Timothy was a man.

He picked up his bag and headed down the drive.

14

Sophie dragged herself out of sleep. Hair, thick black and oiled, alien hair, straight and limp, lying across her mouth, like a horse's tail. Then weight. A body lying across her body. Then smell, perfumed soap, the disguised acid of male sweat. Her hands, lying on either side of her, not wanting to touch him. And his mouth. Kissing the scar on her wrist. His smile at that. 'Wilde kleintjie.' (Wild little one.)

Breathing hard, Sophie got out of bed. Random pieces of the jigsaw puzzle of her life arrived in the early morning, invading her sleep, causing her to lose her breath. She dressed slowly and took a bucket to go to the borehole. If once, just once, she could have proved to him that there was cause and effect. The land was not made by God for their pleasure and theirs alone. There was effect, there was.

The early-morning light, the vast horizon and the coolness of dew in the air soothed her mind. She drew water and tried to avoid the inevitable next thought. There had been an effect. She had buried it in the fields. She had been repulsed by it, its mixed colour, its existence as evidence. Bessie – hah. Bessie had enquired, threatened the police, demanded to see the child. Bessie so self-righteous, staring, trying not to vomit at the pale corpse. Not daring to ask. Never saying another word. Sophie staring out across the land while her madam retched. Walking back to the house together. Preparing the vegetables for that evening. The sharpest of knives and a split-second of uncertainty in Bessie's eyes when Sophie chopped the carrots so hard.

She balanced the bucket on her head and started back. Melanie's letter was tucked safe in her dress. She had read it a thousand times. She moved to the squatter camp the day she received it. She borrowed a tractor and a trailer without permission. Old Tom helped her load her bed and her belongings. A chair, a table, a paraffin stove, a washing basin, two cups, a biscuit tin of papers, toiletries. She had taken sheets of corrugated iron from one of the barns, old cardboard boxes, helped herself to sacks of mealie meal too. And left. Nobody even noticed. Now she had a shack and was surrounded by children and noise and a community that didn't ask questions. They knew who she was, they knew about her family, they knew she had recently lost her son. No one questioned her right to be here. She shared what she had with the other women and that was proper.

Karel had come to see her. Asked questions. She said nothing. Just looked at him. He tried to persuade her to return, nobody could understand why she had left. What would she do for money? How would she live?

Free, she thought. She poured some of the water into a basin for washing. I will live free. Like the other women, she had started a vegetable plot. It was hard, irrigating her small crop, but she liked it. It was hers. Together the women were hoping to buy goats so they could have milk for all the children. Now she was waiting for Michael's return. He would help her do the right thing. She could wait.

Bessie folded the letter. Her head felt heavy on her neck. Her mind wandered around the kitchen. The stone floor, once a matter of some shame to her mother, was desirable now.

They had sat around this table every morning for breakfast, Oom Karel and Tannie Esther, she and Melanie and Piet. Eggs and toast. Porridge in the winter. We fed her, she thought. Fed her and clothed her and cared for her. This is how she repays us. Sophie's replacement came through the back door, saw Bessie's face and retreated.

I used to cut her toast into soldiers for her boiled egg. I washed her hair for her, put lemon juice in the final rinse to make it shine. We read her stories at night. Sent her to school. She cried when she left, hugged me, promised to stay in touch. And now this.

Sophie's behaviour was understandable now. And who has caused damage here, she thought. Who? Michael, that's who. He got Timothy killed. He's the one they should come after. She stared at the table, the old whitened wood, scrubbed and scrubbed. Why? Why did she have to do this? It was in the past. If it ever happened. My father. Would he do such a thing? Melanie is not a liar. If he did this thing then he must have had his reasons. But he is dead and cannot defend himself. But Piet . . . Piet is still here. Piet helped. She says Piet helped. Still she could not move.

It is possible. Quite possible. There was that baby. Sophie's coffee baby. And the farm. Not left to Piet. Not left to his son or hers. The farm was to be kept safe. And it was. Karel had nothing to do with this. But Piet. He is our brother, Melanie. How can you betray your own brother? What good can it do to tell now? What can it matter any more? What will Sophie do? Another one. Looked after all her life, her and her children. What will she do now? What trouble is she stirring up in that squatter camp?

I should get going, she thought. Call Piet. Show him the letter. He may have to leave the country for a while. They will find the body, if they haven't found it already. Why hasn't anyone come to arrest him? I must get going. But still she sat at the kitchen table. He cannot go to jail. He will be raped and beaten. He will die from Aids. He cannot go to prison. He will have to leave. Or kill himself. He could kill himself. Would he? Not if there was some escape for him. We will have to arrange an escape for him. What will Sophie do? Why hasn't she done anything yet? She lacked the energy to put the kettle on. She folded and refolded the letter.

Matthew Makela had been on his way to see Sophie when the Boer and his son drove up in the blue truck. He stopped, suddenly nervous. Karel Freek and his son Piet told him to get in the truck.

'It is my day off,' he told them. 'I work for Baas Dirk.'

Piet Freek raised his shotgun from his lap. 'We know who you are. You are on our land. Get in the back.'

He climbed into the back of the truck. He would try and jump out when there was cover to run. They didn't head for the farmhouse. They were heading for a ravine where the dry river-bed carried water only in rare moments of rain. Matthew considered his choices. They may beat him. Or they may shoot him. Or both. Beating first, shooting later. He was on their land. Anger mixed with his fear. His body was shaking. They have guns. I cannot fight a gun. I can only run. Dust clouds followed the truck.

As they turned towards the ravine he threw himself out, rolling in the sand that felt like concrete. He stumbled to his feet, then ran, his left arm feeling numbed, towards the low hills. They would follow when they realised. Which was mercifully not immediately. He reached a small hill and began to skirt it. The undergrowth was pitifully sparse. The truck stopped, turned around, came slowly back, looking for his tracks. He ran on, reaching the river-bed. His shoes left perfect prints now that the sand was softer. Rock, he needed rock. On the far side of the river-bed there were rocks. He ran a short distance along the river-bed in the direction opposite to the one they would expect and began to climb sideways, towards the spot they had destined for him. He could hear their voices as he climbed. Bent double. He reached the summit, and there was a white woman sitting facing him.

'Please,' he said, 'please don't shout.' The girl said nothing, just nodded as he went past.

Melanie watched Piet and her uncle in the river-bed. They had guns. She stood silent. They separated, climbing the rocks in different directions. Piet came upon her. 'Melly! Wat maak jy hier?' (What are you doing here?) 'Have you seen him? Where did he go?'

'Who?'

'The Kaffir.'

'No.' She looked at the ground.

Piet signalled to his father. 'Pa! Die kant. Kom!' Her uncle turned towards them. Melanie felt her legs shake. She sat down.

'What has he done?'

'Nothing for you to worry about. Go to the truck now. Go to the truck. Move!'

She stood again and, her legs shaking, began to make her way down the rocks. At the bottom she waited. She heard shots and ran to the truck.

Oom and Piet came down a while later. There was blood on Oom's khaki shorts. They took a spade out of the back of the truck. She sat in the shade of the truck and listened to the crickets, pulled a reed of grass, chewed the end. Her legs still felt shaky. The two men returned, sweaty, covered in dust, strangely elated. They took beers out of the truck and offered Melanie one. She refused.

'What did he do?' she asked

'Nothing for you to worry about. Let's go home.'

There is no proof it was him, Bessie thought. It could have been anyone. A thief, a vagrant. But when he was missing, when Sophie tried to find him, there was no reason for his disappearance. We thought . . . I thought . . . he had just run off, the way blacks did. They had no sense of responsibility. There was no crime unsolved at that time. If it was him, then there was no reason. Except Sophie. The baby. The dead coffee-coloured thing with that straight black hair. Whose baby? Karel, my father? Piet? No. It's disgusting. Neither of them would have . . . Not because of a black woman. No. Surely not. Melanie says it was my father. It isn't possible. She is lying, they are all lying. Sophie killed the baby. She is the murderer.

She put her head on her folded arms on the kitchen table. Why now? What good could it possibly do?

Sophie's replacement slipped into the darkening kitchen and began to peel potatoes. Bessie looked at her.

'I have a bad headache. Make me a cup of tea, Agnes. And bring it to my room. I am going to lie down.'

'What must I prepare for supper?'

'Just do sausages and mash and gravy with some peas and carrots. Don't forget the onions. I will have mine on a tray in my room.'

She drew her bedroom curtains, lay on her bed under the patchwork quilt she had made herself. The letter she locked in the drawer of her bedside table. Habit, tradition, these said she should take it to Jan or Karel, at least Piet. But she was reluctant. It was still in the realm of women. If she gave it to them they would act. Hard to say how, but they would act upon it. It was the nature of men. She would let it rest for the night.

Agnes brought her supper. She sat up, took the letter out of the drawer. What had Melanie said at the end? That Matthew's life was as important in God's eyes as her own, or that of Bessie, or Piet, or Karel. If Bessie could accept that as true, if she could put herself in the place of Sophie, of Matthew himself, then she would know what to do. Anger surged through Bessie again. How dare you, Melanie? You leave us, you have nothing to do with us, you disappear into some strange place and then all these years later you think you can interfere in our lives. We've lived it, you know. We've been here for all of it. We're still here.

The following day Bessie drove into town. The church was locked but, as arranged, the dominee was waiting for her in his office. They exchanged the usual pleasantries, coffee was poured, the health of wives and husbands and children accounted for.

'Mrs van Heerden . . . Why don't you tell me what is bothering you?'

'God, Dominee. God is bothering me.'

He waited.

'God said . . . God said that the blacks were the children of Ham, destined to be hewers of wood and drawers of water, and we have always believed that. Why does God persecute us for following his word?'

The dominee waited a considered minute before replying. 'Did God say this or did we choose to interpret His word that way? God is a God of love as well as a God of power and might. Does he not love all his creation? Does he not tell us to love our neighbour as ourselves, to do as we would be done by?'

Bessie van Heerden frowned. 'Is the black man our neighbour or our servant?'

'God lives in all human beings. All humans are our neighbours. There is no distinction in God's eyes between the races.'

'The black man is equal to us in the eyes of God?'

The dominee nodded.

'What, Dominee, what have we been doing all these years then? How could you let us?'

'We were wrong. We believed the wrong thing. It was wrong.'

'How can it be right one day and wrong the next? How?'

The dominee shook his head. 'Some of us knew it was wrong and often we tried to tell the people but the people would not believe us or hear us. It is our sin that we allowed this wrong to continue. It is my sin. We, the Afrikaners, we used God to persecute another people.'

'We used God?'

'I think we did.'

'So He is angry then.' Bessie nodded at her own words. It made sense.

'He is just. Christ said, "Forgive them, Father, for they know not what they do." But when we know what we do is wrong, and we throw our wrongdoing in the face of God, then we must accept His anger. But always, always there is His love to guide us back. It is in your heart that God resides. Follow Him, no matter how hard the path He shows you, and it will be the path of righteousness.'

Bessie had slumped a little in her chair. The dominee poured them each another cup of coffee. 'Dominee . . . I have been praying to God for the return of the old ways.' She laughed, a harsh sound. 'He must think I am mad.'

The dominee watched her get in the bakkie and waved her off. He envied the slender blonde woman. You have no doubt about the existence of a benign God, he thought. It is merely the terms of the relationship that you need to clarify.

Bessie decided to drive a while, mull over the words of the dominee. Perhaps God had guided her there, to the church. Well, she would let Him lead things for a while and see where they went. But she wasn't going to church any more. No, she would read the Bible herself and she would talk to God herself but she was not going to listen to anyone else telling her what she could or should believe. Ever.

At the last turn-off before the entrance to Rooisand she swung left and headed up the western border of the farm. When she could see the shacks clearly outlined in the distance, she slowed the engine. Her heart was pounding. I don't want to go in there, she thought. It would be a form of madness. But I must. And if God says I must, then it is God's duty to protect me. She parked the bakkie, took her handbag and began to walk across the veldt.

The children saw the blonde woman first. She was wearing a beige linen trouser suit. White skin, blonde hair and rich clean clothing – they came to stare. There must have been a dozen of them, of varying ages, the littlest hiding behind the painfully thin legs and ragged skirt of the oldest, who couldn't have been more than twelve. Why weren't these children at school? She stopped and smiled at the little group. The littlest one giggled and pointed. She smiled back. Shy smiles all round, more giggling. She spoke slowly to the oldest girl. 'I am looking for Sophie. Do you know Sophie?' The child smiled and shook her head, scuffing her foot in the sand.

Sophie stood inside the dark of her shack and watched Bessie talking to the children. What was she doing here? Curiosity moved her into the light. She stood watching the children see her and pretend they hadn't. Bessie turned around and came towards her.

'Sophie.' Sophie nodded and went into her shack. Bessie followed.

It was a small room, hot, stuffy and dark after the relentless glare of the late-morning sun. Bessie took off her sunglasses, let her eyes adjust to the dark. Against the far wall there was a single bed propped up on bricks. It was neatly made, the dark-green cover unwrinkled. An old kitchen chair (that she recognised as once her own) was next to the door opening; there was no door as such. A formica-topped, steel-edged table (it has a number of pot burns on it, a pattern of semi-circles in the green-marble effect, we threw it away, what, fifteen years ago?), a series of hooks holding clothes on wire hangers, two sturdy cardboard boxes, a small paraffin stove on the table, a steel bucket of water underneath. The floor was earth, but carefully swept, free of stones.

Sophie indicated the bed, sat herself on the chair. Bessie half sat, half leant against the raised bed-head.

'Well,' she said, smiled.

Sophie waited.

'Sophie . . . I thought we should talk. I have had a letter from Melanie.'

Sophie looked hard at her. And waited some more.

'Sophie . . . I don't know what the truth is. But I'm sorry. I'm sorry and I want to make things right.'

Sophie stared at her hands folded in her lap. Before the washing machine came, she thought, I washed your underclothes with these hands. From when I was thirteen you hit me every time I did something wrong – when you hadn't bothered to explain properly what was right. All the years of my life you have been there to shout and make me frightened, and God help me, I am frightened still. I don't know what to say.

'Can we talk? Sophie?' The silence was unnerving her.

The children were playing around the entrance to the shack, peeping in at Bessie, giggling. Sophie turned in her chair, said something quietly and the children ran off. Sophie raised her eyes to the bed, to Bessie's hands. Bessie tugged nervously at a small frayed piece of leather. Her left hand was shaking. Suddenly aware, she slid the hand under her thigh. Sophie felt a small rush of courage.

'It is not a bad thing that you have come here,' she managed.

Bessie smiled. 'I . . . I don't know where to begin. I really don't know what to say.' The silence began again.

Then Sophie cleared her throat and said, 'This is also not a bad thing. If two people do not know what to say, then they have a chance of a conversation.'

Bessie smiled, tugged at the piece of leather. Where do I go now, God? Come on. Help me. 'The children . . . Is there no school for the children?'

Sophie shook her head. 'When the people were moved off their land the school was bulldozed down. You remember.'

Bessie looked at the floor. Oh, I remember. We were pleased to be rid of them. We had plans for the land. It was all right because we paid for it. Where did the people go?

'Where did the people go?'

'They were moved to a place two hundred miles north where they had never been before and where there was one borehole and nothing else. They had no transport, no map, no idea how far away they were from anything or anyone else. The police moved them in the dark of the early morning and then you bulldozed the houses. All the old people from that time died early.' Sophie raised her head and steeled her gaze. I accuse you, she thought. I do, I accuse you.

The entrance to the shack framed a thorn tree in the distance. Bessie stared at the tree, at the whiteness of the light behind it. She felt empty. 'It was wrong. I see that. I am sorry.'

Sophie stared at her hands. She felt like a boxer whose punch has missed its target but who is still carried by the momentum of the blow. She breathed to calm herself. 'So now there is no school. And there are no homes. And we begin again.'

The children ran giggling past the doorway, unable to resist.

'Karel is arranging to give back the land.'

Sophie nodded. 'But only part of the land. We need more land to keep goats. For milk. For the children.'

Those thin legs and arms, Bessie thought. Even Sophie has lost weight. 'I will speak to him.'

Sophie looked up quickly, then back down again. Her heart was leaping about in her chest.

'I would like to do something to help. The children . . . a school.'

'These children will not go to school in Afrikaans. These children will go to school in English.'

Bessie nodded slowly. That hurt. That really hurt. I cannot do much more of this, she thought. Sweat was beading on both their foreheads. She stood up.

'May I come again?'

Sophie nodded.

'Tomorrow?'

Sophie nodded again.

Bessie walked through the frame of the opening and headed back across the veldt towards the bakkie.

Late that afternoon Sophie walked slowly through the heat across the van Heerden land, gathering small sticks and twigs along the way. In amongst the rocks above the old ravine she pulled screening branches away from the entrance to the cave. With her twigs she lit a small fire to smoke out any snakes or small animals that might disturb her peace. When she was sure the cave was empty and she had swept the floor with a branch of leaves, she sat in the doorway facing the setting sun.

This was where we came the first time, she thought. When we were little more than children. She shut her eyes to bring Matthew Makela to life. She always saw him first in sunlight. He had a smile that lit her heart. He had been tall, her

Matthew. Tall with beautiful, strong rounded shoulders, flesh firm under perfect skin, warm and solid. He was perfect in her eyes and before they had come to this place whenever they had seen each other her mouth had dried of words and she had run from him and his beauty, fearful of herself. And Matthew had watched her confusion and in his youth he thought she did not care for him. They had both grown bolder. The first time they had spent real time together they did not want that time to end. They had dawdled and talked and she could not remember one thing that they had talked about. Except Matthew, standing under a tree and leaning his arms along its branches and looking down at her, serious for once, saying that he would not live like this. He wanted more from life. This life was not acceptable. He wanted more.

Sophie's mother had shown her the cave years ago and she had kept it for herself. It was far away enough from the farm that the smoke of a small fire would be invisible. They had sat by such a small fire and her heart had beat faster and faster and her mouth was drier and drier, till she put a small stone in it. He knew then, or so he said later, that she thought he would kiss her and she wanted her mouth to be ready. He had asked to borrow her stone. She had laughed and pointed at the thousands around them, but he insisted it must be hers. So gently did he put his hand to her face, his fingers brushing against her lips, his palm cupped against her chin for the stone to fall from her tongue. And then he put it in his own mouth, and although she could not look at him, she knew he was watching her as he covered the stone with his tongue. She took his hand, and unable to meet his eyes, she replaced her stone with his finger, tasting the saltiness of his skin and the charcoal from the fire. She rolled her mouth around that finger until she felt it should always be hers, she would never be able to free herself.

The slowest, gentlest of kisses Matthew demanded. He forced her to hold back her appetite. Desire built with his restraint. He sat behind her and she leant into his arms. He kissed the back of her neck, her ears, softly, slowly, each warm breath, each grazing of his lips calling for passion, removing restraint, demanding more. She could not move. The slow, soft caresses under, around, over her breasts teased the nerve-endings, she craved relief, her mind emptied. He restrained himself, restrained them both, until she would have done anything, without question. She was liquid in her limbs when he finally turned her in his arms. He leaned back against the wall of the cave, his arms around, under her, lifted her on to his lap, but not yet, not yet. He kissed her then, tender, slow and endless, she was wrapped inside the smell, the strength, the universe that was Matthew Makela. And then they rocked, slowly, his eyes, his mouth, his self, around, inside, borderless. Endless pleasure. And Timothy too. Sophie smiled. Such a beautiful son. And no wonder.

The sky was beginning to tinge itself with red. Sophie stared unseeing at the horizon. That deep river of tenderness made us gods. We had that. Death did not take it from us. The boring drudgery of life didn't take it either. But now it is different. What do I do, Matthew? Evil must be punished or it will think it is our master. Justice, justice is important. Not revenge. I have not the heart for revenge. The thought of more evil, more suffering, that sickens me. We must look to the future. Timothy is gone. Timothy who aged past you, who let me see what you would have been like as a child, as a man. I miss him, Matthew, I miss him so. The pain came again, aching in her throat, pressing in her chest, filling her nose and eyes. I must do the right thing. You must guide me. I will sit and wait. The right thing will come to me. You will guide me. Melanie and Michael will act for me. Melanie is coming home.

Michael lay shaved, bathed and well fed between clean cotton sheets. The farmer and his family had provided hospitality of a quality that no longer surprised him. Bessie, Karel, the car-hire firm, everyone was contacted, everything arranged. The adventure was over. He could go home now. He turned in the bed, felt a jumpiness in his legs. First he had to go back to the settlement, take gifts. Then he would leave – and return to what? To a life that didn't make sense before I left and makes even less sense now. Perhaps that's the challenge. To make it make sense, to make your own part of it make sense. To see what sort of footprint you can leave behind.

Bessie had told him about his mother. He couldn't quite believe it. She was coming out to see them. Bessie had sounded different too. But it all seemed far away. Everything did. He was resisting the normal business of his life. But this too is the normal business of your life, he thought. This is what you have chosen to include in the normal business of your life. Expand your life to include everything you want inside it. You do not have to leave forever. There is no 'either or' here. You can leave footprints in a number of places. Just be proud of the way you leave them. Make sure you will be welcomed back.

His legs calmed, he stared into the night sky. I wonder how everyone is, he thought, and felt the depth and calm of the universe above him. The crickets and the night owls called him to sleep.

Warda sat in calm communion with her ancestors. It brought great comfort to her to look at the stars and relate to herself the long line that stretched behind her, knowing that each of the women whose knowledge she carried inside her were shining in the heavens, watching over her and her daughters.

A star arched across the purple-black of the sky, the infallible sign of a Bushman's death. The star's coming towards the earth to connect with the soul of the dead person indicated a good death. !Katchu, lying in the hut he had made, came to her mind. So that was who it was. And such a bright star! She was intensely grateful for the quiet and the privacy that surrounded the moment of goodbye.

How she wished him well! He too would sit above her now, looking down on her and guiding her way. And one day they would sit together at a fire and talk over the adventure of their earthly life. The star was proof that he had redeemed himself. A weight lifted from her. The possibility that !Katchu may never join their ancestors had sat under her consciousness like a grain of sand against the skin. She never doubted the picture that had come into her mind. !Katchu was joining his father and his father's father. All would be well. The old woman smiled to herself. There had been rain this year. The young women would start to bear children again after a couple of barren years. She herself would soon go to her ancestors. She had demonstrated courage in her life. She would be welcomed. She was comforted by the thought of it.

Bessie made the trip to the airport on her own. Melly! She'd dressed with care. Then looked at herself dispassionately. Forty years and the unforgiving sun did a lot of damage to the face. But Melly would have changed too. I'm getting old, really old, she thought. But I don't feel it. I feel the same way I've always done. Just my body, that's what's old. Would Melly recognise her? Would she recognise Melly? Melly was coming home.

At the airport Bessie pushed her way to the front of the small crowd waiting for the London flight. She scanned the trolley-pushing passengers anxiously. Then she saw her. Hair streaked with grey, her face a little dead, but she recognised Melly immediately. She came out of the cordoned-off tunnel and then they were facing each other. In the first seconds they read the changes in each other's faces, then looked for the person underneath. Bessie was crying. Then Melly was hugging her, stroking her, 'It's all right Bessie, it's all right.'

'Ag, Melly girl, Melly . . .' she struggled to compose herself. I've been lonely ever since she left, she thought. And I never knew it until this minute. 'Look at me,' she managed. 'A silly old fool! Ag, Melly, it's good to have you home.'

They went out to the heat and the car. There was too much to ask, too much to say, to exchange many words on the drive back. They talked about the flight, Bessie went on about how things had changed, about the farm, about the idea of the co-operative, 'because we have to share, you know, it's how it should always have been', how Jan was looking forward to seeing her, but someone had to be on the farm, and that Michael was fine, he was off with Karel on that holiday he'd never had, but they would be back in a day or so. Melly was quiet and when they were out of the town and climbing the pass there was a moment of silence. Melly leant across the broad front seat, stroked the side of Bessie's face. 'I'm sorry, Bessie. Sorry I never wrote to you.'

'Well, you're here now. That's what counts,' Bessie managed. They smiled at each other. I don't get tenderness, Bessie thought. It's been years and years since I felt tenderness. Since someone touched me like that. She too was quiet then.

Melanie got out of the car to open the gates to Rooisand.

'Bessie . . . I'd like to walk up to the house. On my own.'

'You'd better have a hat then. And take a bottle of water.'

Melanie watched the old Mercedes drive up the dusty road that was the driveway of Rooisand. Soon the dust clouded it from view. She waited for the sound of it to die away. Then she crossed the road and walked a little way back. Four trees stood in a small group just outside the fence of their neighbour's land. Melanie went to stand under the trees, her eyes closed. She braced herself to look back consciously.

The young Bushman was decidedly uncomfortable in all this obviously settled land. He had no access to water or food, was aware that his position was vulnerable. Since they had been in the land of roads, they had travelled at night, shrinking from any contact with people. The little girl knew then what the animals must feel like when the lion is circling them. She was frightened, because !Katchu was nervous. She wanted to go home.

I never knew, Melanie thought, how he knew that these were my people. But then we have always been settled on the land, not of the land. Their world watched ours more intently than we realised. She opened her eyes and looked around the tiny clearing. It was under that tree, she thought. It was much smaller then.

In the darkness before the dawn !Katchu had tried to explain to her that she had other family, people like her, with whom she must go and live. That this was something that she must do on her own. A brave thing, a very difficult thing. But something that would make him very proud.

The little girl stared at the spot where his voice was. Surely he wasn't going to leave her? Not in this dangerous place? And if she did this brave thing, then when would he come and fetch her? He tried to explain that he would not come and fetch her. That he would be with her in spirit always, but that the family had decided that she must be with her own kind. Like the animals – they are always together with their own.

The thought of others like her didn't help. If she couldn't be with her own family because she was like some other people, then why would she want to be with these other people, who like her, weren't wanted? But !Katchu, for whom she would have cut herself in two had the need arisen, was asking her to do this. She must go to that gate and climb over it. Then she must walk, without looking back, all the way to where she would find a big house. She must go into the house. There she would find her family. The enormity of the task and the shock of parting numbed her. As first light threatened to expose their little camp, !Katchu steeled himself against the rigid set of the child's features. She was trying so hard to be brave but the tears still ran in those familiar little rivers in the red paste on her face. He knew that he too would weep and he could not add that to the child's burden. He sent her off.

Pain doesn't get less if you shut it away. This pain was fresh. Unexposed, preserved, it sprang to attention. Melanie walked slowly back across the road, to the gate.

The little girl's stomach churned over and over as she climbed the bars of the gate. How she wanted to look back! But !Katchu had said she must not and if she must do this brave thing, then she would do it as he said. The dusty road stretched ahead of her and she began to walk it, her legs watery and uncertain. It was slow going. Each step was an effort, each step a going against herself.

!Katchu watched from the clearing. He had told her not to look back and there the tiny figure went, soldier straight and achingly slow. His face was wet with tears, his chest tight with sobs that he must subdue. He would go to this house under cover of night and see that all was well. For now he would will her forwards, witness her courage, record it for his people. They would be proud of their tiny warrior.

Melanie Carter opened the gate and slowly started to walk the length of the drive. She had no idea how long it had taken, back then. It had seemed to be without end. But eventually the little girl came upon the huts that housed the farm labourers. Walk into the house, !Katchu had said, and you will find your family. She stood on the steps of the first hut and peered in. It was dark inside, too dark to enter. So she sat on the steps and waited for someone to come. The young mind was blank. She would submit to whatever came. Submit and survive. She would be brave.

Then the children came. They looked different from her brothers and sisters at home. They were darker, longer, they looked at her. Then, in the way of children, they giggled amongst themselves and began to talk at her in words she couldn't understand. She stood her ground, feeling vulnerable. With the hut behind her and the children in front she couldn't move. One of the boys came up to her and flicked her hair. Something in the child stirred. He did it again and she tensed but stood silent. Then he came and pinched her arms, with a taunting shaking of his hands in front of her eyes. And she launched herself at him with all the pain in her and threw him to the ground. Something in her wanted to kill him. The children were screaming but she didn't hear them. She had the boy's throat in her hands and she wanted to squeeze it until he stopped his laughing. Hands took her off the child. White hands. Belonging to a girl who must have been about twelve, with tight blonde plaits down her back.

'Wat maak jy? Haai, gedra jou, kleintjie!' (What are you doing? Behave yourself!) Bessie had pulled the little feral scrap off the boy. In the hands of something much stronger than herself, she subsided. She remembered Bessie looking at her, rubbing some of the mud off her cheek. She took her by the hand and started to walk on past the huts. The child could bear it no more and looked back. Behind her stood the dozen children. She couldn't see behind them. Then her resolve crumbled and she pulled away from the girl, tried to push her way through the children, screaming her father's name. !Katchu! !Katchu! Come for me, !Katchu! That was when

Bessie picked her cousin up and carried her screaming and kicking into the house.

There was no doubt about who she was. The timing, her appearance, everything made perfect sense and the people said it was a miracle. That first night in the strange house, where the walls felt threatening and malevolent, she lay on her back with her arms stiff beside her in the bed that was too soft and stared at the ceiling, at where the stars should have been.

!Katchu, looking in through the window, saw the white, clean little face immobile, with the eyes looking straight up. It was done now. It was for the best. Everyone had agreed. Now he must go home.

Melanie stopped a little distance from the small room where Sophie had lived. All the way along the road she had looked at the ground, seeing the soft dust and the hard stones as she had done that time before. Now she looked around her. It was still there, the space. It expanded inside her, freeing her, letting her breathe. It didn't feel like a homecoming. It felt more like an escape. She had an irrational urge to lie spread-eagled on the ground, dead still, feel the heart of the land move through her, to roll in the reddish dust of it. Instead she bent down and picked up a handful of earth, rubbed it between her hands. Then she went towards Sophie's home. The door was padlocked. Of course. On a day like this Sophie would be up at the house.

She increased her pace. Bessie was walking towards her, a little girl in a ragged pink dress at her side, holding on to her hem. 'Shall I walk with you?' she asked. Melanie smiled. The interruption was probably for the best. There was only so much she could take at one time. The two women linked arms and walked towards the house.

'Bessie . . .' Melanie stopped, turned towards her cousin.

'No. It's all right. You did the right thing. These children had no school and those mothers had no food. On my own doorstep.' Bessie shook her head. 'I am ashamed. They said to us when we had our first community meeting . . . They said, "Things will never truly change while you believe that you are better than us. We do not want to be on the edge of your lives, kept by you. We must be a community together. Only then will we all be strong." And they are right. We had to be introduced properly. Now even Jan will go and sit with the men and drink and they will talk about the farm together. That is a miracle in itself. We have thirty-three children and twenty adults on the farm at the moment. But the community is growing every day. Thank God we have no Aids yet. We are all trying to teach the children about it.'

The marked-out foundations for a criss-cross of buildings surrounded the farmhouse. Bessie explained the design. 'Everyone helps to build everyone else's house. Like the old building society. We all share now in the profit of the farm. The men know a lot about the land. But come, there's someone who is very eager to see you.'

They walked to the one finished rondavel, raw in its new paint and with dug earth around it. A plank led across the red mud to the door and there stood Sophie. Melanie walked across the boards. The two women held each other's hands and searched deep to find the person they always knew. Then they embraced. Bessie took the little girl by the hand. 'Come on, let's go and see what the other children are doing.'

Hardekop left his car a half mile or so from the entrance to the farm. The board had always said 'Rooisand'. Now he was welcomed to 'Ubuntu: The Matthew and Timothy Makela Memorial Community Co-operative'. He was only able to travel at night now. There had been a few unfortunate 'necessities' over the past year in Namibia. He was apparently now a 'most wanted' criminal. He wondered if it was harder to hide yourself in the countryside than in a big city. But anyway, he'd had enough of the rondtrappery, the endless moving around. He'd run out of money a day or so ago. This looked like the right sort of place.

There was a central farmhouse and around it, spread out perhaps a half-acre away from each other, a number of rondavels. It looked something like a rural kraal might look if it had access to bricks and thatch and brick paving for neat paths between the huts. There was a pen of goats and around each of the huts there were rows of what looked like vegetables. A sprinkler system turned on behind him, making his heart leap. What sort of people could live here? There were many huts and new ones were being built at the edges. As he tried to circle the settlement he encountered the sheep pen. It sat the size of a rugby pitch, filled with sheep. There were thousands of sheep! How many men and women would it take to look after these vegetable plots, these sheep, these goats! The sheep alone needed more grazing than the land could give them surely? This was a wealthy settlement. But there was no barbed wire, no fences, no alarms. Hardekop smiled.

The farmhouse lay unprotected in the moonlight. Hardekop stood in the moon-thrown shadow of a camel thorn tree. He plotted his steps to the veranda. Then merging shadow with shadow he slowly zigzagged his way across. There was little if any security. French doors! Practically an invitation. The lock was easy. No burglar alarm, no dogs – what were these people thinking of? He felt his way to a door, eased it open. One person, clearly a woman, asleep in the moonlight. Jewellery was easy to carry, easy to sell. And there would be a handbag as well. The woman's purse and jewellery and any other wallets he could find and he would be on his way. With so little security, they wouldn't have a safe.

He approached the bed, stood silent, looking down on the sleeping woman, carefully taking the hammer out of his pocket. If she woke, she could rouse the house. Better to knock her out before she had a chance. The woman's eyes opened as he lifted the hammer. The pillow beside her exploded in a burst of feathers. Hardekop was slammed backwards by the shot. Bessie sat up, aimed this time for the centre of the man's forehead.